Praise for BROCK'S AGENT

"... a propulsive historical novel ... this ripping yarn."
— *The Globe and Mail*

"Taylor spins a well-rounded and riveting tale of war,
love of country, and friendship ..."
— *Historical Novel Review*

"... breathtaking intensity."
— *The Ottawa Citizen*

" ... Taylor writes with a passion, power, and pace that will leave you
breathless and thirsty for more. A born storyteller, Taylor weaves
a gripping yarn with the very strands of our own history."
— Terry Fallis, winner of Canada Reads and the Stephen Leacock Award
for his book *The Best Laid Plans* and author of *The High Road*

TOM TAYLOR is a Canadian writer who graduated from York University with a B.A. majoring in history. He once served in the militia with the Toronto 7th Artillery. He resides in the Greater Toronto Area.

BROCK'S RAILROAD

BROCK'S RAILROAD

TOM TAYLOR

Hancock and Dean

HANCOCK AND DEAN
6 – 80 Citizen Court
Markham, Ontario
Canada L6G 1A7

Published by Hancock and Dean

A Division of GIFTFORCE INC.

Brock's Railroad is distributed by Auralim Gift. For information about
special discounts for wholesale purchases, call 1-800-265-9898.

Cover and text designed by Tania Craan
Cover photography of soldiers by Elizabeth Woodley-Hall

Manufactured in Canada

ISBN: 978-0-9868961-1-8

For my friend Bill Barnes.
Nothing succeeds like persistence.

ACKNOWLEDGMENTS

I would like to offer sincere thanks to a team of individuals who assisted me in bringing *Brock's Railroad* to fruition: my writing circle friends, Cryssa Bassos, Fred Ford, Sharon Overend, Suzanne Robinson, Andrew Varga, Ray Williams; fellow writers Lory Kaufman and Sally Moore; Brady Polka; Geri Das Gupta; Brian Henry; Debbie Kellogg; Tom Fournier for his military historical advice; Sarah Maloney of the Niagara Historical Museum; Major John R. Grodzinski of the Royal Military College for his historical advice; Val Bunbury for her invaluable support; Shelly Macbeth, Blue Heron Books; the Humber School for Writers; Tania Craan for her striking book covers; Elizabeth Woodley-Hall for her award-winning photos; Dr. J.J. Rosenberg; Bernard Cornwell for showing the way; the gang at Open Mic in Newmarket; Bill Hanna; my editors, Peter Lavery and Heather Sangster; and Debbie Taylor, who allows me to escape household duties so that I may take the time to write.

Ontario, Canada
May 2012

Heaven was the [code] word for Canada
and the Negro sang of the hope that his escape
on the underground railroad would carry him there.
— Dr. Martin Luther King Jr.

Taken from the November 1967 Massey Lecture titled
"Conscience for Change" and broadcast on the CBC.

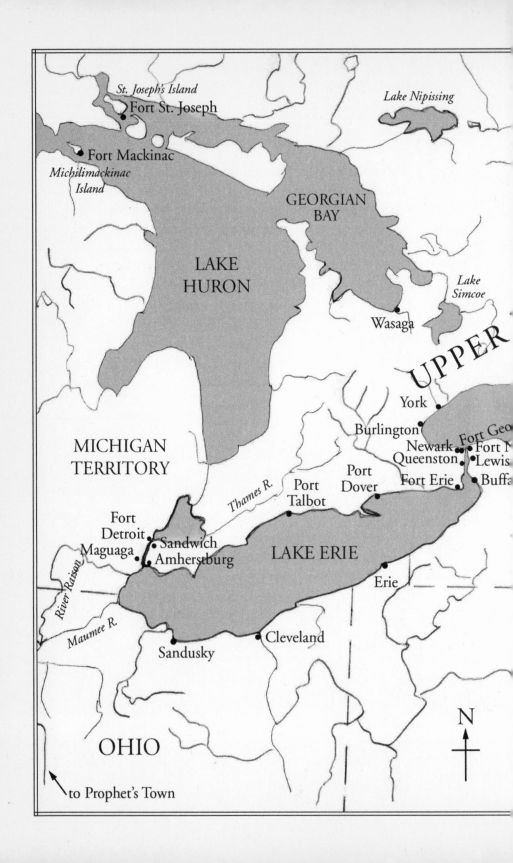

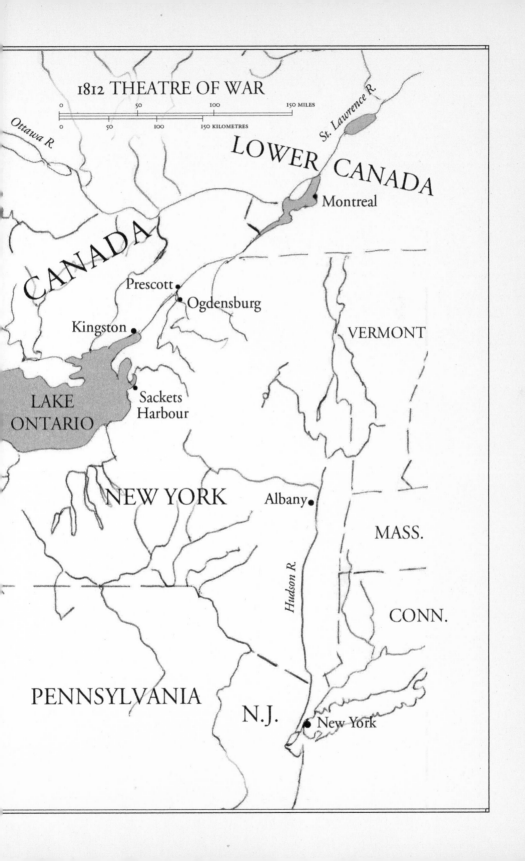

1812 THEATRE OF WAR

0   50   100   150 MILES

0   50   100   150 KILOMETRES

Ottawa R.

St. Lawrence R.

LOWER CANADA

Montreal

CANADA

Prescott

Ogdensburg

Kingston

VERMONT

LAKE ONTARIO

Sackets Harbour

NEW YORK

Albany

MASS.

Hudson R.

CONN.

PENNSYLVANIA

N.J.

New York

PROLOGUE

HENRY, LORD BATHURST, slipped down the wet steps leading to the back lawn of 10 Downing Street. He straightened his waistcoat with a tug before glancing about to make sure no one had seen him stumble. A long garden, well kept, stretched in front of his tired eyes. The new secretary of state for war and the colonies had worked himself to near exhaustion, and while waiting for the prime minister, he had determined to smell the roses.

Under a blue sky and soft sun, he bent over and inhaled deeply, letting the flowers' calming scent linger in his nostrils. *Ah, peace at last.* A raucous parliament had finally submitted to his recent demands, so now all he desired was a single minute of quiet.

"Well, Lord Bathurst, what do you think?" Lord Liverpool called out from the steps.

"Lovely, Prime Minister. They have a wonderful fragrance." He cradled a stem between his long fingers and breathed in. "Nothing quite like a rose garden. Almost a religious experience."

"The roses?" The prime minister frowned, his mouth curling down to one side. "I don't give a damn what you think of the roses." He raised his voice slightly. "The repeal of the Orders in Council! Will it have any effect on the Americans' decision for war?"

Bathurst winced, jerking upright. "Damn!" He glanced down at the blood oozing from one finger. "Quite, sir. The repeal will have no effect on their decision. So *what* if we're allowing them to trade again with France? The colony's war hawks crave a land grab of our territories and control of the fur trade, and they are the ones now driving Washington's agenda. If they can kick us out of the Canadas,

they'll do so in a heartbeat, no matter what olive branch we extend."
He took a white handkerchief from his breast pocket and wrapped it
around the bleeding finger. "You've got nasty roses, sir. Look at my
bloody hand."

The prime minister peered skyward, shielding his eyes. "And with
the blasted French stirring things up in Washington, doing everything to *stop* American grain … " He nodded as if talking to himself.
"While you've been busy smelling flowers, I'm sure you've figured how
to conduct war with America and still get Wellington's men their million bushels of grain and beef? They can't fight Bonaparte on empty
stomachs."

Bathurst squeezed his hand, the stinging relentless. "Do nothing." He glanced at the prime minister, who was staring back at him.
"That's right, do nothing."

"Nothing!"

Bathurst shrugged. "New England needs to sell its grain, war or
no war. A willing buyer and a willing seller are all that's needed for
a transaction." He said it as if the entire discussion was obvious. He
watched the newly appointed prime minister pacing on the grass as
a breeze blew up. The rose bushes swayed toward him and Bathurst
spun away.

Lord Liverpool brushed his thinning hair back into place. His stub-
born face opened in a smile and he gave his long sideburns a scratch.
"And if there's war, we order our man in Quebec … what's his name?"

"Governor-in-Chief Prevost, sir."

"… Prevost. We tell Prevost to take defensive measures only …
otherwise, do nothing to offend the Americans."

"Correct, sir."

A servant arrived with a tray, offering each man a glass of port.
Bathurst raised his glass in a toast to their decision, and the prime
minister followed. "To doing nothing." Liverpool laughed. "A fine
foreign policy."

Bathurst took a sip and then another, quenching his thirst in the
late-day sun. "Count on it, Prime Minister, war is coming and we

can't help Prevost with men and material over there until Bonaparte is crushed over here. It may mean abandoning Upper Canada just for us to hold fast at Quebec."

"Then do it, but get the grain ... or Wellington starves out there in Portugal. Remember our first priority. Those damn frogs know what they're up to."

Bathurst flicked the handkerchief off his bloodied finger, then thrust out his hand to show a tiny red hole where the thorn had pierced the skin. "No wonder it's stinging like the blazes ... and it's bleeding again!"

"I say, Henry, don't let the servants see you carry on like this. One would think you'd been shot! Phew... a bit of blood." The prime minister looked up from Bathurst's hand and chuckled. "After all, Lord Bathurst, you *are* the secretary of war."

1

· · · · · ·

TIPPECANOE, 1811

WESTLAKE WANTED TO WIN. Actually, if honest with himself, he was desperate to win the race. The prize — a hunting knife with a foot-long blade, the finest he had ever seen — would be presented personally by a warrior chief in front of the entire tribe. But it wasn't only the exquisite weapon that drove him on.

The Indians of Prophet's Town had the strange notion that Jonathan Westlake competed for the honour of all white people everywhere. *Crazy*. To him, winning was simply personal. He competed for respect — respect from himself, his peers, and, especially, from his Shawnee friend, Paxinos. He sensed that his friend felt the same way: the hunting knife mattered little, and the winning was all.

Yes, there was something about victory itself that distinguished the champion as superior, a master in his own right, a grown-up. Expulsion from school, fights with parents — winning washed all that away. Winning brought Westlake the respect that elevated him to the status of a young man ready to assume adult responsibilities.

His problem was with the damn horse, with any horse really other than Warman, the colt given to him on his tenth birthday. Now, six years later, he was riding bareback on an Indian pony as he competed for respect and a hunting knife. He could run faster and throw a knife better than most, but riding a horse well enough to win a race was an altogether different matter.

Defeating all other comers, he and Paxinos now vied with each other for the ultimate prize. The rules of the competition were few:

from the start line, race one hundred yards on foot, mount a horse, turn, and gallop back down the same one hundred yards — without crossing the start line — to throw your knife at a white target painted on a tree twenty paces away. Then turn and gallop over the one hundred yards again, to pass the tree stump that marked the finish.

Simple, Westlake thought, *except for the bloody horse.*

The natives had worked with him relentlessly, teaching him all the tricks of riding bareback. Two weeks of hard practice and still he couldn't execute the precise knee movement to turn a horse around. To compete against Paxinos, he needed to do everything perfectly, every time.

"Are you ready, Jonathan?" Paxinos grinned as he approached Westlake at the start line.

A lanky young man, the same build as Westlake and dressed in similar buckskins, Paxinos had become the brother Westlake never had. As their relationship grew, so too did their rivalry, most of the time friendly.

Westlake smiled back at his friend, nodded, and took a last look over his shoulder at the white circle on the tree. The knife, tied to the middle of his back, rested just below his neck. He imagined the race ahead of him step by step, reminding himself to throw the knife before his horse crossed the start line in order to turn and charge on past the finish. He brushed back his blond hair, put both hands on one knee, and then dug in his right foot. Waiting for the starting shot, he stared down the narrow racecourse.

Among the fallen leaves of late October, the natives of Prophet's Town crowded along both sides of the path the contestants would run and ride. The leaves swirled at their feet, tumbling down the course with every blast of cool autumn air. Westlake heard the click of a musket's hammer. He inhaled deeply, catching a whiff of smoke from the fires beside scattered wigwams.

Bang!

He was off. At twenty strides, Paxinos was no longer beside him. At sixty yards, Westlake glanced over his shoulder to see his friend trailing him by a good five paces. By the time he vaulted on to the brown pony from behind, he had a ten-step lead. His heart pounded with the first thoughts of victory. *Winning, I'm already winning.*

He swung the horse around with a tug on its mane and a gentle knee to the belly. The animal dance-stepped sideways and then turned just as Paxinos mounted his own pony in a leap. Westlake was off at a gallop, down the raceway with Paxinos well behind. The wind brushed against his face as the animal surged forward under him. The villagers jumped up and down, shouting, "Paxinos, Paxinos" as the ponies flew by them.

Westlake's little brown horse covered the hundred yards in a cannon's flash. Just before reaching the start line, he drew his knife from behind his back and let it fly all in one motion. He hit the target, as he had done all day, exactly to the centre right. He turned his animal even as he heard the thud from the rival knife.

Paxinos had turned a step later, only his pony had made a sharper move, while Westlake's horse veered wide. Westlake dug in his heels, but too late. Paxinos and his mount stepped ahead at the end of the turn, and all Westlake could do was gallop behind while his friend charged to victory and the crowd's cries of "Paxinos, Paxinos" grew louder.

The natives reached out to stop the horses, and Westlake slumped forward, feeling sick to his stomach. His eyes narrowed and he tilted his head back, so no one could see the disappointment on his face. *I've lost.* He closed his eyes. Beating the other competitors meant nothing without this final victory. Westlake gritted his teeth, swung one leg over, and slid off his mount. There was something he had to do. Now.

He patted the horse's nose, then walked over to Paxinos, where friends were busy slapping him on the back and reliving the ride at the turn. They knew exactly where he had won the race, and now waited to see if this young white man would be gracious in losing. To Westlake, every pair of eyes in the world watched him, waiting for him to concede defeat — to admit he was a loser.

"Congratulations." Westlake held out his hand and Paxinos shook it. "You're a better horseman."

The crowd gave a cheer and picked up its chant of "Paxinos." The victory was complete, yet Westlake's opponent resisted a smile.

"But you are faster on foot and throw a knife better." Paxinos gestured toward the target. The two men strolled down to inspect the painted tree where Westlake's knife stuck at least three inches closer to the centre than his competitor's. He pulled both knives from the bark and handed one to his friend.

"I was just lucky." Westlake shrugged as they sheathed their weapons and headed back toward the finish line.

"Only two weeks you practise on this horse, but you beat all my damn friends well."

"But I could not beat you, and I think what you meant to say was 'you damn well beat all my friends.'"

"Did you understand my meaning?" Paxinos asked.

Westlake nodded yes.

"Then you must make allowance for me. They are just words. I will teach you how to ride better, and in return you can teach me English."

"Deal." Westlake shook hands again and smiled.

"But still, you won't ever beat me." Paxinos didn't let go of his hand. He grinned and punched Westlake in the shoulder with his free hand.

Westlake yanked his friend's arm forward, to wrestle him to the ground. The crowd circled around them to cheer on yet another contest. The noise grew louder until suddenly the villagers all went silent. A man with a smooth copper complexion, piercing brown eyes, and a brilliant smile parted the circle and stood over Westlake. He gripped a white-handled knife in one hand while Westlake stared up at him.

"Only one man can be the victor," the warrior chief said. "It is unfortunate there are not two knives. Rise now as brothers, for you warm my heart on this cold day." He extended the prize toward Paxinos, who jumped up and took it carefully in both hands, as if it was breakable.

The wind blowing down the Tippecanoe River carried a damp

odour and pushed the bare tree branches to and fro. Westlake peered up at the steel-grey heaven, wishing he'd turned his horse a little sharper. Perhaps if he had, he'd be the one holding the prize and enjoying the respect that goes to the victor. He got to his feet beside Paxinos.

"As the victor, I accept this knife from you, Chief Tecumseh, thank you," Paxinos said with a mischievous grin. "But there *are* two knives today."

More than a head taller than either young competitor, Tecumseh now gave them a puzzled stare.

"There is the one for the victor" — Paxinos waved the knife high, and the villagers hooted and cheered — "and there is this same knife that I now give as a gift to my brother, Jonathan Westlake."

Westlake's blue eyes opened wide. He could scarcely believe the generosity of his friend. At first he hesitated. The loser walking away with the victory prize didn't make sense, but then not to accept such an offering would count as an insult. His hands reached out to receive the knife.

"I accept such a gracious gift from the victor, and for your hospitality I say thank you to yourself and to all who dwell in Prophet's Town." He waved the weapon in the air to the cheers of the crowd. "Some day perhaps I can return such a favour to Paxinos and the Shawnee."

Chief Tecumseh stepped forward and patted Paxinos on the back. "You ride a horse with great skill, but more important, you are also a good man and have learned your lessons well. I am proud that you are Shawnee."

Then he put a hand on Westlake's shoulder. The villagers leaned forward to listen as the wind stilled around them. The great chief was face to face with the young man, peering down. "You, my young prince, move your feet with the speed of the quickest deer." He smiled only for a moment before his expression turned grave. "We confront uncertain times, when grand armies will make war. Many will suffer and die. May this gift protect your life."

Westlake sensed then that, although he'd lost the race, here he had won friendship and respect. "I'll do my best, sir." He grinned, raised the knife in the air, and with one arm hugged his friend. "Paxinos," he shouted.

The villagers hooted and cheered again, and although it was nothing like the one he imagined, Westlake had achieved his victory.

2
. . . . . .

NIAGARA FALLS, 1812

LUTHER JOHNSON ran for his life. He tilted his head to listen as the sound of dogs merged with the strange rumble of constant thunder. He urged on his feet, with his older brother beside him, pounding the trail to freedom — or at least that was their plan. From Virginia to the edge of the Niagara River, with help at stops along the road, they had outsmarted the slave catchers, but he knew that the catchers' two dogs, once unleashed, could quickly close the gap.

Puzzled as to how rain could be falling from a blue sky, Luther turned one palm up while he ran. A wet wind gusted out of the west, soaking his blue shirt and torn grey pants so that they clung to his skin. The trees all around him bent and dripped, heavy with moisture. He bolted past his brother, shot out of the forest, and hauled himself up stiffly to attention, exactly three paces from a rocky precipice.

The young man gazed at a spectacle his eyes told him was real but his mind couldn't believe. He swallowed hard, gasping for air, and jerked out an arm to stop Hector from charging onward. No high waves or big splashes beat against the shore. In fact to Luther it didn't look like real water, just a rumble of foam and sheer power, white and yellow, gushing over and down the cliff before him.

"Can you fly? 'Cause I ain't jumping," Hector shouted to him, jabbing his finger at the great falls.

"We took a wrong turn, or we didn't turn when we was supposed to — I don't know which." Luther huffed and shook his head. It didn't matter why they were pressed right up against the falls; his only concern now was what to do next. To travel downstream meant confronting yet more cliffs. He kneeled to the ground, hands on hips,

10

retching with fear. His nostrils flared, taking in the scent of fresh water. He rocked backward and licked his lips, tasting the spray.

"If the catchers are close and those dogs latch on to us, we'll have no choice," Hector yelled, lungs heaving. "We got to keep running, upstream, straight along them rocks."

He stood four feet away, but Luther could barely hear his brother's words above the roar of the water. Almost out of his teens and only a year senior, Hector would usually decide what to do for the both of them. At six foot tall, he was somewhat bigger and stronger than Luther, but the younger man suspected that when it came to making decisions, his own judgment surpassed his older brother's.

"No choice to what — jump?" Luther hollered.

"We got one mighty whipping coming if the catchers grab us. Then it's back to slavin'. So start running." Hector pointed to his left, toward rocks bathed in spray.

Luther leapt from rock to rock; his bare toes only inches from a precipice that dropped more than a hundred feet. Soon he was heading upstream, around a bend, the surging water right beside him. For a time, both the catchers and their dogs were forgotten.

From his saddle, George Castor stared at Niagara Falls, wondering where all this water came from. "Isn't that something!" He pressed his black hat firmly to his head, the spray dripping from its wide brim. Uncomfortable with the noise, his horse pranced sideways a few steps, bumping Fred Bennett's grey mare.

"There's no way they jumped in there, and if they did, they're both dead," Bennett yelled with both hands cupped around his mouth. His face ran with trickles of water and sweat. His bowler hat with its narrow brim afforded little protection from the spray raining down on them. He peered into the treetops and gaped around at the mist. "No wonder the dogs stopped. They can't track through this."

Castor surveyed the drenched ground and inhaled the moist air. In a puddle underneath his horse, the dull reflection of his face and hat reminded him that he'd not shaved for three days. He scratched the side of his neck while the dogs barked in protest at the spray, chasing each other's tails in ever-widening circles. They paused, sniffed the air and the ground, and then resumed their play. Castor stared back at the falls as the current boiled past.

"Ain't you the least impressed by what you're looking at? What's wrong with you?" But Castor knew the answer to his own question, even as it came out of his mouth: Bennett's every action was contrived for his miserable self-interest, regardless of the Commandments. He didn't fear God, or the law. If they were at sea, Bennett would have easily been a pirate.

"I'll be more impressed when we have those two slaves in our hands, and not until," Bennett said. "I don't get paid for standing about gawking at yellow water. Where the hell do we go from here — that's the question."

Castor grimaced at the little man with the muscular sailor's arms atop the big grey mare. He looked ridiculous with his handlebar moustache and bowler hat, but not a man on Earth could ever say that to his face and expect to live long. Strange, Castor thought, that Bennett would choose a God-fearing man like himself as his partner.

"If those falls don't impress you, nothing will. They went upriver, of course, where it's easier to cross," Castor declared and nudged his horse to the left. "Dogs got us this far, and once we get out of this drizzle, they'll be back in business."

He urged his horse closer to the edge and peered over at the falling gush of water. "D'you get a feeling like you're being drawn over?"

"Are you crazy?" Bennett spit. "Let's go."

Castor pulled his horse back from the riverbank and sidled around. He threw down some scraps to each dog and they lunged at the food. Then he gestured upstream, and spurred his horse. Bennett followed him, with the dogs trailing. Those slaves had to be ahead; there was no way they'd jump into that churning river.

For five hundred yards Hector and Luther scrambled like rabbits, hopping over the wet rocks directly beside the precipice. Once the water curved away from them, they darted inland, hoping to gain precious distance. Luther heard the barking first and immediately his innards began to quake.

"Dogs are onto us again. Sniffed our scent where we leapt off the rocks, I bet." He pointed toward the river and sprinted, his legs straining underneath him.

He gained the water's edge, with Hector close behind. Although the current was a force, at least here it looked like flowing water and not something unnatural. He ran along the snaking riverbank, his heart bursting in fear and exertion. Over his shoulder he glimpsed the dogs swing on to the trail, barking as they pounded forward.

"You know it ... if we try to run past them catchers, they'll shoot us this time," Hector yelled in panic as they ran. "Across the water, that's heaven. That's where we got to get. We got one chance and that's with this here river."

"Then we's dead already 'cause no one can live through those falls."

"I can't stand another whipping." Hector glared at him, pointing a thumb to the slashes on his back. "Ain't gonna be a slave ever again."

The terror in Hector's eyes swept Luther along in reluctant agreement. The river surged past in front of him. The idea was crazy but other than back to slaving held the only way out.

"Maybe ..." Hector puffed and slowed his pace. "Maybe with the dogs' help we can make it. They's all big dogs, powerful swimmers."

Luther glanced behind him, the barking louder every second.

"Stand right on the edge of the riverbank and when the dog jumps up, grab him by the collar and fall back into the water," Hector continued. "Don't lose grip of that collar, and let the dog do the swimming for you."

"We'll still drown. That's the dumbest idea you ever had!" Luther nodded to the opposite riverbank. "For sure, that's heaven over there?" He smiled, but it was more a grimace of fear.

"You wanna be free or not?" Hector challenged.

"'Course I do."

"Then stop running and save your strength."

Luther felt his brother's grip on his arm to hold him still. His breathing slackened.

"Stand right on the edge, like I told you." Hector pointed down at the rocks.

Luther obeyed his older brother. "I'm scared," he said. He heard his own voice quiver. His shoulders tensed. The pounding in his chest had him convinced his heart was sure to explode.

"Here come the dogs. You grab hold of that collar and hold on for dear life." Hector reached out and for a second grabbed Luther's hand, caught his stare, and nodded. "Just a swim in the river with a dog. Easy."

"What about the falls?" Luther cried.

"Like jumping off the big rock back home." Hector smiled at him.

Luther rocked back on his heels, ready to spring backward. He knew his brother was lying, but even so, the fib made him feel better. *I can do this. Hector says so. Just like jumping off the big rock back home.* The barking grew louder and his stomach heaved.

"This is it, Castor. We got 'em. Them niggers have got no place to go 'cept back to us." Bennett kicked his mare into a gallop and peered through the trees. "Our twenty-five dollars is as good as in the bank." He sneezed and then wiped his wet moustache with a dirty sleeve.

"Don't count your money before they're both in our hands. Get your carbine out of its ring. They'll try to bolt past us." Castor sat up in the saddle, holding his reins with one hand and aiming his carbine with the other. He licked his lips and his eyes bulged, waiting for two black figures to lunge out of the bush. A hero's welcome waited for him back at the plantation and he grinned, happy it was almost over.

The dogs raced along the riverbank, well ahead of the horses. The river curved and the forest grew thick down to where the rocks lined the shore again. In horror, Luther watched the hounds tear out of the trees and onto the rocks, their necks stretching toward their prey. The two dogs, one brown and the other white, had muscular shoulders that powered them forward. Their paws smacked the rocks three times as both bounded into a leaping attack.

Luther stood frozen beside Hector. They stared at the dogs, riveted, with their backs to the river. As the white dog struck, the force pitched Luther backward into the air. He gripped the dog's neck and leather collar, its teeth inches from his face, before the animal jerked aside hard, breaking his hold.

"No!" he cried as he smacked down on the water, straining to keep his head above the current. The dog crashed on top of him, a paw scratching his chest and pushing him away. This water ran much colder and faster than the river at home, and he shivered as his face bobbed under. He glimpsed Hector on the water's surface, holding fast to the brown dog as it attempted to paddle back for shore. Then, in an instant, both Hector and the animal shot off downstream.

Luther slid over onto his back, the water surging against his skin, as the current swept him into the centre of the river. Once, before he dipped under, he saw smoke rising above a slave catcher's musket. The man had fired, trying to hit a disappearing target already a hundred yards away. Luther grinned and for a second let himself believe that he had escaped, that he was free, and that all he had to do was keep floating — floating to freedom and heaven.

Castor reached the river first while Bennett's horse trotted in behind, both men too late to see the dogs vanish from sight. Castor dismounted, stared into the river and then back to Bennett, who was now at his shoulder.

"Where the hell are those slaves and where the hell are my dogs?" Castor scanned the current until he spotted two dogs and a man, three heads bobbing and twisting along in the fast current. So the pair of them had jumped, done the very thing he thought they'd never do.

"There's one of them — farther out." A black head came to the surface so Bennett raised his carbine and fired, his face flushed with fury. His ball had little chance of catching flesh, but he fired anyway, and then threw his bowler hat to the ground. He kicked the dirt to either side of the hat and turned to glare through steely eyes at his partner.

Bennett stood with legs apart, carbine in one hand, and the other

15

hand on his hip. "Now what, Castor? What the hell do we do now? These fool niggers think they can defy them falls, goddamn them." He stamped a foot hard on the rocky ground.

"They're dead men, those two, but we're nicked of the big bounty, that's for certain. And now I'm out two good dogs." Castor spit. "Sometimes life ain't fair. Nope, just ain't fair and that's all there is to it."

"Goddamn river and goddamn cheating niggers," Bennett hollered.

"I've told you before, don't ever take the Lord's name in vain," Castor ordered. "Just don't do it."

"Them bodies gotta come out somewhere downstream." Bennett jabbed at the current and mounted his horse. Castor followed his lead.

"All we need is a hide to get paid five dollars," Castor said. "We're not done yet. Let's ride."

Luther glimpsed the sky again before the water rushed over his face, pushing him under. He resurfaced, gasping for air. Passing through the rapids, his backbone creased off a rock, forcing his entire body to stiffen. "Argh!" he shrieked. This was nothing like swimming in the river back home.

Where was Hector?

He kicked his feet and stroked his arms against the cold current that carried him far across the middle of the river. Whenever his head went under, he fought by coiling his body and then springing with all his might, arms and hands waving desperately toward the surface, where his effort bought him one gulp of air. An island in the river flew past, and for a few seconds, he rolled from his stomach onto his back again. The water rushing by him sounded like cupped hands slapping over both his ears. His speed increased and the thunder of the falls reached a horrible crescendo. He was going over.

Nothing he did managed to control his direction. Snorting and wheezing, he coughed water just once before the gush powered him head first into the roaring abyss. He whimpered in terror and screamed, "Father," convinced he was about to die. Down, down he went with the flood, the devil gripping his limbs, dragging him down to hell. More than one hundred and fifty feet down he went, floating and flying amid the water. Luther choked for air and swallowed hard, gasping for breath — death surely a mere moment away.

He shot upside down through the white surge of the surface below. Then the water propelled him up again, tumbling him around like some rag doll. For an instant he was above the foam, in the air. He panted desperately before crashing back into the current that pitched him downstream, flinging his arms and legs out to each side of him. The force jerked him forward and then tugged his head downward. Its grip loosened and he careened over on his back, breathing, twisting along wherever the lesser currents wished to take him. He could think once again, as he stared around at the world.

Maybe he was in heaven and Hector was here already.

Luther coughed and spit before stroking toward the shore. Like after a beating, his muscles and bones ached with every weak swipe of the water. He rolled to his stomach, stretched his arm out for a rock, and then tried to stand. Numb with cold, his legs collapsed under him, so he dragged himself ahead until he could sit in the shallow water along the pebbled shoreline, his head hanging between his knees.

A soft whistling that carried a light tune entered his ears, before it suddenly stopped.

"Where the hell did you come from, fella?" An elderly black man wearing a straw hat stood holding a fishing pole out over the river.

"Hector," Luther whispered.

"Say your name's Hector?"

"Is this heaven? Where's Hector?" Luther wrapped himself tight in his own arms while his bottom jaw trembled, teeth chattering uncontrollably.

"You're not making sense, boy. D'ya think you're dead? Well, you're not." The old man hauled in his line and rested the pole down behind him. "Where'd you come from — and who's Hector?"

Luther raised his arm and pointed up toward the far side of the river. "Up there, we jumped in the river to escape the catchers." Luther let his head fall again between his legs and tried to breathe. "Hector's my brother." His stomach gave a sudden heave and he wondered if he was going to throw up.

"Miracles happen, but I ain't never seen one till now. There's tales of Indians getting washed over them falls and living to tell about it, but you must be the first African. My, my." The old fisherman took off his straw hat to brush away a mosquito. "You're in Upper Canada now, fella. Heaven and glory land — that's just old slave talk for Canada. Your brother probably didn't want you spilling the beans about where you was heading. Right now, you're a free man."

Luther looked up and took the man's outstretched hand to help guide himself away from the water's edge.

"A free man?" Luther asked. A grin spread across to his still-shivering features. "Free?"

The fisherman nodded and grinned back with bright, sympathetic eyes.

"My name's Luther," he grunted, bending his torso slowly to ease the pain. "I'm sore as can be. And I'm mighty cold."

"You've gashed your back some. We'd better get that looked at." The fisherman frowned and shook his head. "Right over Niagara Falls … I didn't ever think it could be done. You is something else."

Luther glanced toward the falls but jerked his head up too fast. He doubled over, dropped to his knees, and began to spit up water. His stomach gurgled and he heaved once more. This time he stayed down, spread out his arms, and threw up again. His hands shook, clutching at the coarse grass, but he couldn't focus his eyes sufficiently to even see them. He then realized that he'd lost all track of time.

Luther closed his eyes and leaned his head back, wondering how long he'd been running. "What's today?"

"Saturday, of course." The old man wrapped a worn grey blanket around Luther's shoulders.

"No, the month."

"It's May 1, 1812. You hungry?"

Luther felt a gentle touch on the back of his head, so he reached up and gripped the friendly hand.

"You're going to need a job, so you can eat, 'cause freedom also means you're free to starve." The fisherman laughed. "Did they teach you anything useful on that plantation — any skills? Ah, no matter, I got just the thing."

Luther tried to sit up straight, but again his head began to spin. "My name's Luther," he repeated. "Where's Hector ... my brother?"

He let go of the old man's hand and slowly laid himself down, the coarse grass pricking at his legs. His breathing calmed while he watched the fall's water swoosh by. Luther closed his eyes again and sighed, relieved just to be alive.

"You told me your name already, fella." The fisherman chuckled. "And I don't know where Hector's at. But you're what you call a little upside down 'cause you had one hell of a ride. If Hector rode over them falls too, he's probably dead — sorry to say."

The old man picked up his fishing rod, looked back toward the falls, and rubbed his chin in awe. "Pleased to meet you, miracle man. I'm Richard Pierpoint, but most folks call me Cap'n Dick. Welcome to heaven."

3
· · · · · ·

LUTHER STUDIED A SHORT, bulky man with a long sword who leaned up against the barracks wall. Unusual for any officer he'd seen during the last month, the man was hatless and wore a faded red coat. When he pushed away from the wall, the officer unbuttoned his jacket halfway down his chest. He had a stern face and a small mouth with lips pursed in permanent disgust. Luther knew why this man made him nervous. In his half-opened jacket, standing there hands on hips, this officer reminded him of a slave catcher.

From one end of the second rank, Luther peered down the two lines of black militiamen. Dressed in blue homespun shirts and well-worn grey trousers, they shuffled to straighten themselves into two lines of twelve men each, some in black boots but many with bare feet. Luther stared at his own large feet, still bootless and toughened from miles of running.

The front rank stood sharply to attention, while Luther's rear rank didn't know where or how to stand. Shoulder to shoulder, this awkward line banged together, each man's elbows nudging the others beside him. Every man carried his own weapon, usually a pitchfork or a shovel held upside down.

Directly in front of Luther, his friend Richard Pierpoint the fisherman stood to sharp attention with his musket tight at his side. He wore a low, flat cap, and a faded dark-green uniform trimmed in scarlet. The Cap'n had agreed to ask the officer a question on Luther's behalf — presented only at the right moment. And Luther prayed to hear a positive answer.

Scattered stumps littered the hot dry field around him that was to be the company's drill square. From the time he was a young boy, Luther had listened to his father tell stories of brave men engaged in murderous battles. There was nothing in the world he wanted more than to march in their ranks to prove to his father that he, too, could be a real soldier. And now here he was, set to learn soldiering.

Under a blue sky, Luther inhaled deeply to calm himself, twitching his nostrils at the strong scent of the newly cut grass. Heat shimmered in rising waves above the field. The officer stopped first in front of the Cap'n and then, with his hands behind his back, strutted down the line as he spoke. He might have been only in his early twenties, but he spoke with the confidence of a veteran.

"My name is Lieutenant James Cooper from the 2nd Lincoln Militia. Just like you, I volunteered for this … assignment," he said slowly, pronouncing all his words. "You see, the other officers, regular and militia, think that Negroes can't fight — that you're too stupid. But I know that men who hate can kill, and that's what I want, killers. Who here doesn't want to kill? Tell me now, and you can go home." He paused to see if anyone took up his offer.

A few men turned their heads to look to either side of them, but Luther didn't see anyone step forward. And he knew the reason. The lieutenant continued marching up and down in front of the little company.

"Why are we all here, today?" Cooper asked.

Right in front of Luther, Pierpoint took one step forward. "June 4 is King George's birthday, sir, the day militia gets training." He stamped backward into line, standing still at attention, eyes front.

"Smart fellow. Your name, private."

"Richard Pierpoint, sir, formerly of Butler's Rangers, but these fellas call me Cap'n Dick."

"Any more from the old Rangers?" Cooper stepped back and looked up and down the line again.

Almost the entire front rank, all older men, shot their hands up. In the rear rank, only Luther put up his hand and then took it down.

"Good. Better than I thought. But we're going to find out if you can still kill," Cooper said. Then he pointed to Luther. "You're too young for the Independence War, so why'd you raise your hand?"

Luther hesitated, unsure of the consequences his words might have. "My father fought with Butler, sir. The Rangers here all know of him. When I heard the name Butler, my hand just went up. Sorry, sir." Luther stared at his feet, his shoulders and biceps visibly tensing. His heartbeat quickened, and he wished Hector were beside him to explain.

During the War of Independence, some thirty years previous, his father had joined the British Army on the promise and hope of gaining his freedom. But like many other slaves who had the ill fortune to be recaptured by forces loyal to the new republic, his father had been dragged back to his former owner. Luther wondered if he would ever see him again.

"What's your name, boy?" Cooper did his best to smile but with an expression that was more like a smirk.

"Luther."

"Luther. And your father's?"

"Alexander, sir."

"Alexander? Not Alexander the Great?"

"Sergeant Alexander, sir," Luther replied with enthusiasm and a broad smile. He stood straight, inhaled deeply, and puffed out his chest.

"Now there was a killer — according to the stories I've heard." Cooper shook his head. "The big man disappeared after the war."

"He's Master Caldwell's property again, sir, in Virginia. An old Ranger friend of his passed through the plantation and told him how me and my brother might escape." Luther motioned toward the river and continued almost in a whisper, "We got help along the way."

"Where's your brother now?" Cooper glanced down the line.

"Maybe the catchers got him, I don't know," Luther murmured sadly. "Probably dead."

"So we know why you fight," Cooper said.

"If the slave catchers grab hold, they'll take me back. I'll be in for the whipping of my life," Luther said. His stomach churned at the thought of it. He remembered feeling sick at the sight of Hector's raw shoulder blades. "And, this time, they'll work me to death on that farm."

"And I'll bet that's why you *all* fight." Cooper turned to address the ranks. "Every last one of you must have an escape story. If the Americans win this war, you're back to slaving."

Up and down the ranks, sombre faces bobbed their heads in unison and muttered a low rumble of agreement.

"Then let's get started making killers out of you new men. And the old Rangers need practising." Cooper gestured to the front rank where the men nodded again. "War's coming and the rumour is that Major General Brock wants an all-African company. Thinks it'll encourage other slaves to revolt and come north." Cooper laughed. "That'll give the bluecoats no end of distractions."

By day's end, Luther reckoned he had enough of drilling. The old Rangers fell in and remembered all their manoeuvres within the first couple hours, but the new men, the men in Luther's rank, bumped and banged into one another at every opportunity. With drilling finished, the company spread out on the grass, some men sitting cross-legged while others leaned back on their elbows. A leaky water bucket with a wooden ladle was passed from man to man, and after his turn, Luther handed it to Pierpoint for a sip.

"Is now a good time?" Luther asked him, motioning with his head toward Cooper.

Lieutenant Cooper had dismissed the company and walked over to his horse. After he gulped from his canteen and mounted up, old man Pierpoint approached. Luther strained to hear.

"The company would like to thank you, sir, for drilling us and all. We won't let you down."

"You're a damn sight better lot than what I'm used to working with." Cooper assumed that look of disgust again. "It'll take time with the new men, but they'll catch on, eventually."

"Drilling's one thing, sir, but killing, well, that's another. Africans are different." He looked up at Cooper and patted the horse's neck. "We do things better when we have a chief … a leader who's one of our own. We don't expect no officer, no sir, but would it be proper to have a sergeant? And, if we could, maybe that man could be Alexander … Sergeant Alexander?"

"You might get a sergeant, and goodness knows we need one, but Alexander's in Virginia. You heard his son say so."

Luther took a step closer toward the two men.

"Each man here would fight like ten alongside Alexander, sir," Pierpoint persisted. "Once the war starts, maybe we could steal him away? That would set the fox among the chickens."

"That's impossible. Might as well try to kidnap President Madison." Cooper paused; perhaps it wasn't so impossible. He'd heard General Brock himself declare that the word *impossible* shouldn't exist in a soldier's vocabulary. "Fox among the chickens, you reckon. We'd have to send someone to break him out." Cooper inclined his head to peer skyward, holding that look of disgust on his face.

"Every slave down south might think of running to our side if Alexander escaped, sir," Luther joined in from behind Pierpoint's shoulder.

"I know an officer close to the major general … leave it with me. Perhaps a letter in the right hands?" Cooper nodded and spurred his horse.

Turning back to Luther, Pierpoint raised his eyebrows and shrugged. "You never know … but don't get your hopes up."

But Luther's hopes soared nevertheless and he clapped his hands. Lieutenant Cooper would consider the idea and that meant there was a chance to see his father again. Luther leapt in the air, touched his heels together and laughed. If his father could only get here, then maybe he'd bring Luther's friend with him too. Anything was possible when you were free.

From his saddle astride a white horse, Lieutenant Colonel Solomon van Rensselaer studied the man's smirking cherubic face. The insolent fellow stood in the sunshine, gripping the low rail of a white-painted veranda that skirted the entire front of his house. New York's quartermaster general, Peter Porter, was a vital partner in the supply and shipping business of Porter, Barton, and Company, a major contractor to the government. His interest in the war effort was therefore both professional, serving as part of the military, and for personal business — a wonderful arrangement that would ensure he'd make a fortune so long as the war proceeded apace. Solomon bristled, thinking how much he'd like to pound that smirk right off of Porter's chubby face.

With Solomon in front, three horsemen dressed in well-cut blue coats trimmed with gold epaulettes led a train of wagons, carriages, and soldiers marching on foot. A dozen dragoons riding on either side of him, he and the other riders pulled up their horses at the steps leading onto the grand veranda. He glanced up at Porter, waiting in the uncomfortable heat for a welcome.

Typical for a midsummer day in Buffalo, the humidity of August 10, 1812, drew patches of sweat to stain the underarms of his tailor-made uniform. Solomon remained silent as Major General Stephen van Rensselaer, commander of the United States Army of the Center, took off his hat and brushed back his well-groomed hair from a face that betrayed no emotion, only power and privilege. He unhooked a canteen from one side of his horse and tilted his head back for a long swig of water.

"Well, you've got your war, Mr. Porter. I hope you're satisfied." The major general waved his hat to brush away the heat. "Meet my cousin, Lieutenant Colonel Solomon van Rensselaer, and this is Major John Lovett."

Solomon gave Porter a curt nod, while Lovett offered a mock salute.

"Welcome to Niagara, gentlemen. My apologies for the heat." Porter shrugged. "War was declared almost two months ago and what have we accomplished? Not much," Porter declared, his boyish features forcing a smile that looked more like a grimace. "Your men can camp in that field over there. Come on in, you're almost late for dinner." Porter returned through the door opening onto the veranda without any further discussion.

The dining room possessed two walls fully lined with books,

another with an oversized unlit fireplace, and one with three large windows through which the afternoon light beamed. A silver candelabra holding eight tapered white candles sat in the centre of a table suited for twelve guests. Dinner brought an uneasy silence that Solomon knew wouldn't last. Sooner or later the assembled company would have to discuss the contentious business at hand, and that business was the war.

After consuming a sumptuous course of roast chicken, Solomon leaned back in his chair as the servants cleared the plates and poured them more wine. The men sat across from one another, arms folded, Porter and Stephen at opposite ends of the long table and Solomon directly across from Major Lovett. The humidity in the room exacerbated the tension, and the air thickened further after the four men lit their cigars.

Porter stared down the long table toward Stephen. "Have you heard from Major General Dearborn?" he asked.

"He's supposed to be running things from Albany, but the most I've heard from him is that he wants me to attack immediately," Stephen replied. "President Madison and the Washington crowd — your friends the war hawks — are pushing Dearborn so the pressure flows downhill to me. They've conveniently forgotten that the British control the waterways at either end of the Niagara River."

"You have fourteen hundred men to do something with. I'm building you longboats. Can we not attack somewhere along this thirty-six-mile river?" Porter gestured with his cigar toward the waterway outside.

"One-third of our men are ill and we have precious few medical supplies." Stephen ticked the end of each finger as he continued to make his points. "They even sleep under the stars because there are not enough tents. Not only do we have no engineers, but we have no more than ten rounds per man. If the enemy attacks, we can hold out for maybe an hour." He took a sip from his wineglass and held it up to the light. "That's *one* hour, I said."

"But—"

"But nothing," Solomon interjected. "My cousin is too much of a gentleman to say it plainly. We are not prepared for this war, and you know it. I have here your letter to our illustrious secretary of war." He took a paper from inside his jacket and smoothed down its edges on the table.

With a table napkin, Solomon wiped away the beads of sweat from across his broad forehead. He knew his dark eyes must be glaring but didn't really care if he showed his anger. Of the four men in this room, he'd seen the most military combat, and he'd now say his piece. He rubbed his narrow chin to calm himself somewhat.

"Back in April, you wrote, 'It would be an act of madness to declare war at this time.' These are your own words, yet you and the other war hawks have been relentless in your efforts to declare war. It must be convenient for you to have a business that supplies the war department while at the same time ordering the supplies as quartermaster." He spit out the last sentence with disgust.

Porter sprang up, bumping against the table, red wine spilling to stain his white linen. "You presume on my hospitality too much, sir." He'd been accused in his own home of engaging in a conflict of interests — even if it was true. "We can't tolerate the British seizing American seamen from our ships. The Indians want a buffer state between us and Upper Canada, and the Canadians are flooding in to trade furs with them. And why shouldn't we trade freely with France if we choose?" Porter hammered the table and his face flushed red. His voice cracked, "All these things must be stopped. The problem with you Federalists is that you have no alternative for the British bully except meekness. Do you want them running next through the streets of Washington?"

Solomon jumped to his feet, but Major Lovett, who had been quiet throughout the meal, stood first. Lovett was military aide, secretary to Stephen, and a lawyer by profession. Solomon wondered why it had taken so long for this man known for his dinner-party wit to say something.

"My dear Mr. Porter, you forget that Lieutenant Colonel Solomon here was promoted for his gallantry at the Battle of Fallen Timbers, so he is hardly meek." Major Lovett smiled. "And you forget, sir, that he is just as likely to seek satisfaction from you on the field of honour. And finally, you forget that we are all Americans, whether Federalist or Republican, and we'll have to work together to win this war."

"There'll be no duelling on my watch. Sit down, all of you," the major general ordered. "Well said, Major Lovett. All of us want to win."

Porter sat down as instructed, his chest heaving in and out. Solomon reached for his wineglass but stopped, knowing that his hands were shaking and he'd curse himself if he showed Porter any sign of his agitation. Instead, he sucked in a deep breath and folded his hands on the table.

His older cousin turned to him and smiled. "It's getting late and bickering doesn't help." Then directing his voice straight down the long table toward their host, Stephen said, "We need a thousand tents, Mr. Porter, and a hundred cases of ammunition, for a start. You can follow that up with some medical supplies."

"I'll get to work on that immediately, sir." Porter nodded. "You're all welcome to stay in this house as my guests. There's room enough." He waved a hand limply toward the rest of his grand house, but the gesture and the tone of his voice made it a reluctant invitation.

Stephen saved Solomon from saying no. "Thank you for your kind gesture, but I prefer we sleep out in the field, under the same conditions as our men. We'll only impose on your grounds for one night. Tomorrow, we march for Lewiston."

The dinner now ended, Solomon was relieved to escape the tension and confining heat of the room. He puffed on his cigar and then waved away the smoke as he followed his older cousin outdoors. Porter gave him a goodbye handshake, their animosity put aside for the moment, but he doubted that this quartermaster fellow would move with much speed to deliver their vital supplies. After all, the man was a Republican, therefore a scoundrel who had no real interest in seeing the Federalists succeed at anything. A successful duel would have been a more satisfactory ending to the night.

Porter watched the blue-coated backs of the three men, cigars in hand, stroll off toward a field packed with tents, horses, and scattered cooking fires. The Van Rensselaers were among New York's first families, rich beyond his imagination, yet they had volunteered to fight a war they didn't believe in: Americans doing their duty, but Federalists opposing the war. Odd. He wondered if they would fight as well as they talked. And why couldn't they see that it was in his personal interest to ship the supplies? The more supplies he shipped, the more money he made. His problem was actually finding and accumulating the goods, prior to paying for them, and transporting them. The stinking-rich Van Rensselaers were too used to having the world go their own way. Thank God they would be gone from his house and grounds on the morrow; otherwise, the initial shooting would not be directed against the enemy across the river but between Republican and Federalist.

The Van Rensselaers shifted their final camp to just south of Lewiston, out of sight of any British eyes peering at them across the river. Solomon, meanwhile, convinced his cousin to activate more militia units as his small force grew slowly. During the open-air service that Sunday, he prayed to God that the British did not attack. He prayed most of all for time, time for America to prepare for a war he didn't himself believe in.

The sun cleared the treetops and fell directly on the congregation, but just as the heat became insufferable, the service was dismissed and the rows of makeshift pews emptied. In the throng of fellow officers, Solomon felt a tug on his sleeve.

"Have the supplies arrived from Porter?" Stephen van Rensselaer asked.

"Not yet — might as well pray for them too."

"I thought as much."

"I've increased the drills, lasting morning to night," Solomon said. "And, come hell or high water, this camp will be clean."

"Keep the drinking water well away from the latrines," his cousin advised.

Solomon squinted in the sunlight and put a hand up to shade his brow. "Are my eyes playing tricks or is that a British officer with a white flag?" The congregation surged past him, temporarily blocking his view.

A moment later, Major Lovett appeared out of the crowd to nudge up beside him and study the same officer riding at a gallop. A hand resting on his sword, he grinned at the major general. "The redcoats are no doubt surrendering, sir."

"But why do we allow an enemy officer to ride unescorted into our camp?" Stephen frowned at Solomon. The officer had obviously crossed the river by boat and been offered a horse to carry him and his dispatch through the camp.

As the rider drew near, Lovett reached for the reins as the horse reared to a halt, throwing up a cloud of dust. Uniformed immaculately, a tall lieutenant of dragoons dismounted, saluted, and unstrapped a leather valise from his saddle.

"Dispatches for Major General Van Rensselaer, sir, from our Major General Sheaffe," the man announced, coming to sharp attention.

Solomon stepped forward, returned the salute, then accepted the valise and handed it to his cousin.

"This is the major general and I am Lieutenant Colonel Solomon van Rensselaer. What's contained in the valise, Lieutenant?"

"I'm not privy to the documents, sir, but my understanding is that Governor-in-Chief Prevost in Montreal is proposing to General Dearborn a temporary cessation of hostilities." The officer smiled. "We are to have an armistice it seems, sir."

Stephen turned a page, glanced up from the documents, and nodded in silent confirmation to Solomon.

"Major Lovett, take this officer back to the edge of our camp and give him some refreshments," Solomon instructed. "Our reply will come forthwith."

Once Lovett and the British officer were out of hearing, Stephen spoke in a hush: "I swear to you that this very morning I prayed for extra time and now God sends me this gift. Has Governor Prevost lost his mind?"

"I offered the same prayers, cousin. I'll send an express messenger to Dearborn with the documents and pray that he doesn't muck up our chances," Solomon said.

"Send him right away. Then tell this good fellow who brought us the news that we'll contact General Dearborn for his answer. And, Solomon, let's not have British officers riding freely around our camp. If we must offer them a horse, then they should be escorted. Otherwise, in the future they wait at the perimeter."

Two days later, inside the doorway to his cousin's tent, Solomon squinted to read in the shimmering lamplight. The document in his hand told him that Dearborn had indeed approved the armistice. A gift from God, surely, but one that was not quite complete. Could blood be squeezed from a stone?

"But it doesn't allow for any movement of men or material by water." Solomon turned to his cousin. "Does Dearborn think our cannons can fly of their own accord from the other end of Lake Ontario?"

"The British won't agree to let us use the waterways," Major Lovett interjected, as if he was making an obvious point. "It's not in their interest."

"I'm not here to defend their interests," Solomon asserted. "I'm here only to defend American interests, and we need those cannons."

"I suppose, but what makes you think — " Lovett shrugged, trying to make his point before being interrupted.

"If we don't ask, we'll never know! Let me try, cousin." Solomon shook the document in the air so that the light from the lantern wavered. He rubbed his chin, considering their position. "Perhaps your opposite number — what's his name — is instructed to make a deal, any deal. If we can meanwhile bring the cannon and supplies from Oswego by water, think of the difference it'll make."

The major general shook his head and paced about his tent, thinking. "I've heard General Sheaffe is a stern man, not a stupid one." Stephen turned and stretched his hands out to either side of him. "But there's no harm in trying," he added. "Go."

The following day, Solomon passed through a picketed V-shaped rav-
elin rising directly in front of the massive gates that swung outwards
from Fort George, the British stronghold that secured their northern
flank at the juncture of the Niagara River and Lake Ontario. Hustled
straight to a large building standing in the centre of the fort, he studied the wooden palisade connecting the six log bastions positioned
around the perimeter. Men stood sharply to attention beside their
guns in each of these bastions, armed with cannon and shot. He calculated that this show of readiness was meant especially for him.

As Solomon entered the officer's quarters, Major General Roger
Sheaffe, resplendent in full dress uniform, extended his hand and with
a formal bow offered his visitor a chair. The receding grey hair made
his forehead protrude, suitably to match a face of large Roman-like
features. Solomon sat in the spartan office ready to make his demand,
sure of himself but nervous nonetheless. His shoulders tensed from
the proximity of Sheaffe's officers seated directly behind him.

"You're here to approve the armistice?"

An arrogance in Sheaffe's tone immediately put Solomon in a defiant mood. The major general clearly considered him to be a mere
messenger, not a legitimate negotiator. He guessed that Sheaffe was at
least ten years his senior and now the older man was grinning, looking
confidant that he had a deal.

"There is one small detail missing, sir. As the roads are included
in our agreement for the transportation of supplies, so must be the
waterways." Solomon spoke the words as if both parties had merely
made an oversight that was easily fixed.

"Inadmissible!" Sheaffe bolted upright and turned his back to the
American. The officers behind Solomon also stood.

"Then there can be no armistice. Our negotiations are at an end,"
Solomon declared. He stood up to leave.

Sheaffe jerked his head around, his silver hair flying out at the
sides. The cords in his neck bulged as he strained to speak. "You take
the high ground, sir."

"I do, sir, and will maintain it."

An officer stepped forward to steady Sheaffe's hand hovering above his sword. "May I suggest we leave the room for a moment, sir?" The officer smiled toward Solomon as he led Sheaffe through the door.

Solomon sat down again, barely able to breathe. An armistice that would prevent Brock from attacking and yet concede the right for the Americans to use the waterways would enable his cousin Stephen to float heavy cannons the entire length of Lake Ontario while allowing for time to properly arm and train the militia. But any armistice was better than none, and now he'd chanced everything by grasping for too much. Squeezing blood from a stone … it was a bad idea.

Sweat trickled down his spine as he waited. Solomon closed his eyes. By God, the war in the Niagara Peninsula hung in the balance and he was risking the very advantage that could save them. He should never have come here. He shuddered, clasping his hands to his head and asking himself what he was doing. What was taking Sheaffe so long?

The major general returned moments later with his hair combed neatly in place and smiling again. Solomon then saw the stiff expressions of the officers escorting him and he had a sinking feeling in his stomach that his gamble had lost both the armistice and the time they desperately needed. His hands began to shake and he felt the blood drain from his head. He stood up from his chair to announce that he was sorry, that he had exceeded his orders, that his demands were withdrawn, but General Sheaffe, back in control of himself, held up a hand indicating that he wait.

"Sir, for amicable considerations, I grant you use of the waters." Sheaffe held out his hand.

For an older man, his grip was crushing and Solomon wanted to cry out in pain. So convinced was he that he had lost his gamble, he had no reply other than, "A deal, then?"

"The papers will follow," Sheaffe declared.

Solomon nodded, saluted quickly, and marched out of the bare room before Sheaffe could change his mind.

On his crossing back over the river, Solomon wanted to yell, "Thank you" to the heavens, but he waited until he was safely inside the command tent, face to face with his cousin and Major Lovett. The three men, all university graduates, proceeded to dance a jig in a circle, with arms extended over one another's shoulders.

"The twentieth of August, a great afternoon to celebrate with cigars and wine, the beginning of our life-saving armistice. Congratulations, Solomon, your cursed stubbornness has beaten them," Stephen chided. "Brock is going to be furious."

"Well, he has his idiot government to contend with, thank God," Lovett quipped, "but, then again, we have the Republicans."

Solomon laughed, slapping Lovett's shoulder before clinking his glass in a toast. His was the first victory gained in the Niagara campaign, and it had come in the form of peace. Now the race would be on to supply the United States Army of the Center before the British realized their colossal blunder.

4

· · · · · ·

Ensign Jonathan Westlake gripped the rail of the schooner *Chippewa*. He squinted as he stared across the glistening water at the enemy's shore, scanning for movement. The deck slanted under a westerly gust, and a rolling wave crashed against the starboard bow. The young man let the rail take his weight as he craned his neck over the side, his blond hair whipping in the wind. He retched again, but there was nothing left in his stomach to expel.

Whenever he needed to think, the ensign enjoyed watching the vast open space of the lake, but on this day his thoughts wandered and rolled along with the ship. He couldn't see a way out of his confusion. Dreams of a young woman, her bare shoulder and dark eyes, had driven him across half a continent of wilderness. He'd survived killer cold, vast mosquito swarms, a punishing canoe wreck and, in the end, he had slaughtered his enemies. Finally, Westlake's pursuit had ended when he'd caught up with Mary Collins outside Fort Detroit.

To his delight, she had declared her love for him, and for two entire days the world was bliss. He planned to escort her back to his family's home in York, to the stone house, Maple Hill, where he would introduce her to his mother, Elizabeth. But on the third day after they had dispatched their enemies to hell, Mary had gone quiet, distant, giving him no clues as to why. She no longer laughed at his jokes. In fact, she seemed to find him and his humour annoying.

Westlake had no idea what to do, and the fresh air of Lake Erie provided no answers. He couldn't tell if it was the rocking ship itself or the worry over Mary's cold shoulder that made him throw up. When his stomach heaved again, he spread his feet and squeezed the rail tighter. He grimly watched the ship plow through another breaker, then heard a shout from above him.

"Deck there, sail on the lee bow," someone bellowed in a gruff voice from high in the masts.

Westlake jerked his head up and searched the eastern horizon for a ship, but he could find no trace of a sail against the blue sky. He shaded his eyes and peered above him at the towering masts and crossed yards. His head began to spin just as the rugged seaman in the topmast stuck out his arm.

"It's the ship, *Lady Prevost*, zur," the man shouted down to the officer of the watch.

"Ensign Westlake, if you would follow me." Captain Edward Nelles, an officer in the 49th Regiment, had approached from behind him and now motioned with his hand.

"May I inquire, sir, how that man can know the name of the ship when I can't even see it?" the ensign asked.

Captain Nelles studied him, sighing. "Your eyes have gone from clear blue to blood red. Puking will do that, Mr. Westlake, and from your secure position down by the rail, it's little wonder you can't make out the other vessel. My guess is that fellow's trained eye and height above the water give him a distinct advantage." Nelles gestured up to the topmast with his thumb. "The question is, on this fine afternoon, does the *Lady Prevost* bring us good news or bad?" He smiled.

The announcement of another sail brought a flurry of activity in the rigging and soon, up a ladder from below decks, the ship's captain emerged. He too scanned the horizon. August 23, 1812 and, although Lake Erie was under British control, Westlake realized the war had made everyone extra diligent.

"Steady as she goes, zur! East by nor-east!" the helmsman called to the captain.

"How long, helmsman?" the captain demanded.

"In these light winds, zur, it'll be a good couple hours before she lays to, and that's no error."

"Call me if anything changes. Otherwise, carry on." The captain glanced again toward the oncoming ship and then returned down the ladder to his meeting.

Westlake inhaled, tasting the lake air, and for the first time felt the colour returning to his face. With his thumb and forefinger he stretched his eyelids, wondering if his blue eyes had really turned red or if Nelles was merely joking. Strange, he thought, he'd canoed across Lake Huron and all of Georgian Bay, hundreds of miles, and never been seasick. For an instant, he thought of Mary, and his stomach clenched again.

Maybe it wasn't either Mary or seasickness, he considered. Perhaps the continuous liquid celebrations after the fall of Fort Detroit had been taken to extreme and now affected his stomach. Yes, that must be it. *These hangovers are killing me.* He determined never, ever, to drink alcohol again. Westlake glanced up and closed his eyes against the sun, making a solemn promise to a God he wasn't sure existed. *I swear it; I'm finished with drinking.*

He stepped lightly down the companion ladder, after Captain Nelles, and stooped beneath the deck beams. The world closed in. His heart quickened in the cramped space and his throat tightened to the thick smells in a vessel packed with men — and one woman. The sweat, bacon grease, canvas, and damp mingled their weighted odours to twist his innards in the humid atmosphere below decks. He wanted to escape, to run.

With the sunlight gone, he could see only formless shadows until his eyes adjusted and the sentry opened the wardroom door. Compared to his own berth among the midshipmen, the wardroom was palatial. Lined with wooden compartments, it housed the lieutenants and the master, some of whom relaxed on padded chairs.

Westlake glanced through a window only to see rolling waves, and then jerked his head away to look at something more stationary. Was his stomach to have no relief? The floor was covered in a black canvas and the walls were painted stark white, but at least they weren't endlessly moving. Maps spread on a desk were held down with whatever was handy, including a decanter of claret.

Captain Nelles poured two glasses and returned the decanter to its place. He offered one glass to Westlake, who held up his hand to say no, but when Nelles glared at him, acting insulted, Westlake took the glass in hand. His resolution of abstinence, his oath to God, they had lasted all of ten minutes. He took a sip, and as the wine slipped down his throat, he started to gag but instead clamped his lips to hold it down. After a momentary burning in his stomach, Westlake felt a sense of warmth, as if all was well. He smiled reassuringly toward the senior officer present at the table.

Lieutenant Colonel John Macdonell of the York Militia had lost none of his Scottish accent. He ran several fingers across his forehead, wiping away the drops of sweat, then brushed back his curly brown hair. The man's youthful facial features concealed the sharp mind contained within. Although only in his late twenties, Macdonell had already been appointed acting attorney general for Upper Canada by General Brock. A regular confidant of the supreme commander, this powerful position made him the envy of many men his senior.

"Two thousand enemy over there, but surprise would be with us. A deserter, a militiaman, reported that they only have four rounds per man. Just four rounds!" He jabbed his finger at a spot on the map, then picked up a ruler.

"If we land our eight hundred regulars some distance upstream, we can assemble and march, rolling over the lot of them all the way to Fort Niagara. Mind you, there'd be a fight, I tell ye, but we can't expect them to surrender *every* time we ask." Macdonell laughed like a man flush with victory.

Yet Westlake was the only man in the room who had been present at the surrenders of both Fort Mackinac and Fort Detroit. He remembered the feeling of triumph, the sense of elation turning to relief. General Brock had ridden at the front of the column, right down the road that led to Detroit's cannons. Through his and Tecumseh's intense planning and harsh threats, the Americans had given up those two forts without a fight, leaving the British forces without casualties. The Niagara campaign would surely be more gruelling.

Captain Nelles had also taken a seat and he now slouched in his chair. A thin man, whose chin came to a rounded point, he had an intelligent face. In the casual atmosphere of the wardroom, he waved the sides of his unbuttoned coat in and out to disperse the heat. "There's a rumour General Brock wants to strike fast at Sackets Harbor, and maybe at Albany after Niagara. Can it be true? They must still be a good three or four hundred miles from where we are."

"If it's confirmed that Dearborn is collecting an army at his head-quarters to attack Kingston or perhaps Montreal, then why not?" Macdonell used the ruler to measure the distance between Albany itself and Newark, at the mouth of Lake Ontario. "With control of the lakes, we'll land anywhere that's to our advantage, and march the rest of the way. That'll cut the bloody trip in half."

Nelles lurched upright. "God's teeth, but he has indeed an ambitious plan."

"That one action could be enough to end the war, and besides, who else will act in the interests of Upper Canada?" Macdonell slapped the ruler across his palm.

His voice was sharp, almost angry, as if it shouldn't have needed two victories to prove Brock's brilliance to the Canadas and to the world. "After Detroit, he's being hailed its saviour ... the saviour of Upper Canada ... and deservedly so. Let's get on with our plans for Niagara."

Before Detroit's bloodless victory, Westlake had heard rumours that Governor-in-Chief Provost, in Montreal, wanted to abandon Upper Canada to the Americans just so he could better protect Lower Canada. Only Brock had stood in his way. And now, after victory at Detroit, Westlake figured such abandonment was unthinkable.

For more than an hour, he watched them debate the planning for an attack across the Niagara River. Boats, food, men, weapons — they were calculated in every detail. A knock at the door brought a young midshipman with a message that Captain Nelles was to repair immediately to the captain's cabin.

Before the boy could leave, Westlake inquired about the *Lady Prevost*.

"The wind's up, zur. She should close with her news within the half-hour, but you didn't hear it from me." The midshipman saluted, turned smartly, and scurried away before Westlake could even return his salute. Good news or bad, they would know soon enough.

Nelles placed his glass on a side table and buttoned up his coat. "That means you as well, Mr. Westlake. The major general would have a word, so you're with me." A drop of sweat fell from his long chin.

At that, Macdonell raised his eyebrows. "Something's up for you, laddie. Keep your wits about you and you'll do fine." He signalled a goodbye.

Westlake touched his forehead in salute to excuse himself and pondered why he would be summoned. While in his presence, Brock remained friendly, even cheerful, but he rarely addressed anyone unless it concerned delegating a task of some kind, and that included Westlake. The general's intense planning never stopped. The man seemed to live and breathe war.

A sentry snapped to attention outside the ship captain's quarters. The door swung open, pushed by a servant who bowed with one hand extended, to invite the way into the great cabin. A yellow lantern swung over a desk, illuminating a hand-drawn map curling upward at the edges.

His white shirt unbuttoned halfway down his chest, Major General Isaac Brock leaned back in the captain's chair, stretching out his six-foot-plus frame. The ship's captain stood beside him, arms folded, studying the map. No one else on board would have dared sit in the captain's chair, not even Macdonell, yet to Westlake, Brock sat comfortably as if it belonged to him.

And, in a way, it did. Before his forty-second birthday Brock had been named supreme commander and chief administrator for Upper Canada. Nothing military or political happened in the province without his knowing. Contrary to the wishes of his superiors in London and Montreal, he had used his power to attack and defeat Fort Mackinac in the north and Fort Detroit in the southwest. All the Great Lakes and most of the territory around them, including Upper Canada, were under his control: an area larger than France and England combined. Brock had laughed when he first realized it, wondering what Wellington would think when he heard the news.

"Good afternoon, Captain Nelles. Sit down please, Ensign Westlake. I see your tan has returned. Feeling better, are we?" Brock grinned.

"Sir." Westlake nodded and sat down in one of the two chairs positioned in front of the ship captain's desk. Did *everyone* on board know that he'd been throwing up?

"Glasses please, Captain." Brock nodded to Nelles and then turned back to Westlake. "Captain Nelles informs me that from your records he's learned this day is a special one. Are you even aware today is your seventeenth birthday?"

"I had forgotten, sir, but if it is August 23, then it is indeed my birthday." Westlake smiled.

Nelles had poured each of them a glass of claret and now he distributed the red wine with care.

Brock raised his glass, as did Nelles. "Happy birthday, Jonathan. I'm sure your mother and father would be proud of what you did at Michilimackinac and Detroit. Seven months an ensign and already two victories to your credit."

Westlake's mind suddenly jumped back to a beach, where four enemy soldiers lay dead at his feet. "Thank you, sir. I'm happy I played a small part in the victory." Westlake clinked Brock and Nelles's glass with his and then took a sip.

"At fifteen years old, I, too, was once an ensign, hard as it is for you to imagine." Brock grinned, glancing out the stern window.

And he was correct that Westlake couldn't imagine the larger-than-life figure before him being anything but a major general. Yet here was the same man wishing him a happy birthday. No wonder the rank and file loved the major general.

Brock put his wine on the table, signifying the celebrations were over. "Have you heard of our new militia, the Coloured Company?"

Westlake shook his head. "No, sir."

"Some former slaves and a number of old Butler's Rangers — a hodgepodge really, but they're enthusiastic to fight. We're adding another dozen or so, and soon so their number will be up to thirty-eight. They claim that if they had their old sergeant back from the Rangers, a man known as Alexander the Great, they'd each fight as ten men."

Westlake sat there impassively, wondering what all this had to do with him. The ship creaked to the wind and someone above dropped a heavy block so that the ship's captain glanced up at the deck beams with a frown. Someone's name would be taken for that interruption.

But Brock continued with the confidence of a man possessed with his plan. From previous encounters, Westlake knew that he had this way about him of raising your enthusiasm with his infectious smile and attitude. He could make men do things willingly that they would otherwise never even consider. Westlake determined not to be charmed so easily again.

"But Sergeant Alexander is a slave now back in Virginia, recaptured at the end of the Revolutionary War and working on a plantation. I want you to go get him ... and bring him to me."

Westlake's stomach tightened and he slid to the edge of his seat.

Smiles gone, Brock leaned forward with his arms extended across the desk. "You'll be out of uniform operating underground, so to speak. Naturally, no one must ever know that you are a British officer, so you'll travel as a fur trader again. Just get Alexander for us, and escort him back to Upper Canada. Straightforward, eh?"

"What about my trip home to York, sir? I've travelled over two thousand miles and surely earned a rest." The order didn't seem fair to him after being promised a period of leave. "And what about Walt Parrish?"

"Parrish will be going with you, to watch your back." Brock smiled and paused. "It seems a long time ago now, but it was only in February when I remember a young man saying he wanted to make a difference. Of course, you faced a hanging at that moment, so I'll forgive you if you've changed your mind."

Westlake remembered his exact words but was surprised that Brock, with all his responsibilities, could recall the wishes expressed by one insignificant young man. Maybe that was the reason other men wished to do his bidding. Maybe it was as simple as the fact that he cared.

"I still do, sir, but Miss Collins has nowhere else to go. I've already promised her that she can stay at Maple Hill." Westlake shifted his feet from side to side, uncomfortable at discussing his personal life this way in public.

After the fall of Detroit, Westlake had related Mary Collin's plight to Brock. With no other relations of her own, Westlake had promised her shelter at his family home in York. And now that she was the only woman on board the ship, he couldn't simply desert her in the middle of their voyage.

"Captain Nelles himself will escort Miss Collins to Maple Hill. If I know Elizabeth, I'm sure your mother will do the right thing. You can say your goodbyes from the ship. I want you to leave tonight, as soon as it's dark."

Suddenly, cannons boomed out a salute to Brock from beyond the cabin walls. The *Lady Prevost* had arrived and seventeen times her guns fired, rattling the empty glasses on the tray. Westlake tried to think what his impending mission meant. Escorting one slave to Upper Canada from Virginia was hardly the stuff that this strange war would turn on. Something more vital was clearly at stake, but he kept silent.

"This Alexander fellow will have with him a package of some kind. It's not clear what it consists of, but that's all the information I have. I'm sure you're wondering why all this fuss over one man," Brock said.

Westlake waited for the answer. The general seemed to know what he was thinking, and Westlake had come to know the man's style. Brock constantly put himself in the other fellow's shoes, so when he voiced their thoughts he seemed to be reading their minds.

"I want the enemy to believe that we'll free their slaves in order to win this war. Many in the north are abolitionist when it comes to slavery, and they also oppose the war. So let's give them something to cheer about … separate them further from their own government."

Brock crossed his arms and rested on his elbows as he leaned over the desk. He had a handsome, open face so that when he smiled, it was difficult not to smile along with him. "And, of course, I want our new Coloured Company to learn how to fight. Alexander is the perfect man to teach them."

Westlake gave half a smile. "I've never been to Virginia, sir." His home-cooked meal back at Maple Hill would have to wait.

"Good, that's settled then. For your excellent work up north at Mackinac, and later down here with Tecumseh, you'll be the senior on this excursion. Congratulations." Brock stood and offered his hand.

"Thank you, sir … I think." Westlake shook his head. Two glasses of claret had left him feeling too relaxed.

"I have to greet the officers from the *Lady Prevost*." Brock gestured to the deck above. "Captain Nelles will fill you in on the details of our … our underground railroad. Get to know this map well and then burn it. You have three stops along the way, three fine conductors to assist you on your journey, but I need not warn you to be careful. You'll be working in enemy territory."

Brock passed Westlake the map and offered his hand again before walking to the door. "Best of good fortune to you, Ensign Westlake. We need this man the sooner the better, so make haste. No unnecessary sideshows, understand?"

"Yes, sir," Westlake replied flatly, aware that Brock suspected he sought out confrontation wherever he went.

"Happy birthday, once again."

"Sir."

The shuffle of feet, orders to lay to, the piping aboard of officers were all sounds that Westlake took in from the captain's cabin. With assistance from Captain Nelles, he studied the map, learning the routes to travel and where to stop for aid. The code word for Canada among slaves was "heaven" or "glory land." This would identify Westlake as a friend, whereupon he would receive whatever aid the conductor could provide.

Nelles pushed a stack of U.S. dollars across the table so that Westlake could buy horses at the first station stop. There was also money to pay the next two conductors. The second stop would be at a German family's farm, where he could eat, sleep in safety, and get re-supplied if need be. The final station was to be a blacksmith in Virginia. Little information was known about the man, except that he knew the exact location of the target plantation. The blacksmith would then direct Westlake to Alexander the Great and his package.

There was a knock at the door and Ensign Robert Simpson, a young man just a year older than Westlake, entered the room and saluted. Even in the heat, his tailor-made uniform was buttoned right up to the neck. Hair carefully combed, and boots polished to a shine, Simpson snapped to attention.

"One last thing, Mr. Westlake. Ensign Simpson will be going with you," Nelles ordered.

"We don't need him, sir," Westlake protested, shaking his head emphatically. "With all due respect, he could jeopardize the mission's success."

"Can you speak any German? At your second stop, your farmer conductor speaks German and very little English. Simpson speaks that language well, and the man will feel much more comfortable dealing with strangers in his native tongue. Plus, three of you can protect one another better than two."

Westlake glared at Simpson and took a deep breath. "We're asking for trouble with him coming along, sir."

"I take that as an insult." Simpson pouted from a boyish face. He raised his chin and stuck out his chest, at the same time reaching for the handle of his sword.

"No, you will not, Mr. Simpson," Nelles commanded. "There will be no duelling or any such nonsense from either of you, understand?"

"And that's enough from you as well, Mr. Westlake. Mr. Simpson has been instructed to defer to your judgment. Unusual for a senior ensign to take orders from a junior, but with your past experience General Brock has great faith in you. And, since you'll be travelling out of uniform as civilians, he has ordered an exception to be made."

Simpson cleared his throat, scowling at his adversary. "I don't see the need for it myself — to take orders from you — and, of course, I would rather it not be the case. But those are my orders."

Westlake ignored what he said. Everything he knew about Simpson led him to believe the young man was an empty-headed twit. Whoever he was trying to impress, Westlake didn't care. But he knew that Simpson's actions were likely to endanger any mission, and especially one in enemy territory.

He shook his head in resignation. For a moment, when Brock had outlined the mission, it had crossed his mind to sneak home to Maple Hill despite his orders, but now, with Simpson along that was impossible. He was already dreading the task of relaying the news to Walt Parrish, a private in the 41st Regiment.

"One more thing, Mr. Westlake. Try to keep the death and destruction to a minimum. Like the general said, no unnecessary sideshows. Much easier that way."

"Of course, sir. We need to pack now and I should say goodbye to Miss Collins." Westlake stood up and saluted.

"Good luck, then. Just grab this fellow Alexander and hustle yourself back here. The general wants to get this war over with, so we'll probably see action sooner than later." Nelles offered his hand. "Let me know when you wish to visit Miss Collins." Nelles grinned. "And as before, happy birthday to you."

"Thank you, sir. I confess I won't be sorry to get my feet on solid ground again."

5

· · · · · ·

A FIRST LIEUTENANT'S quarters on a brigantine are private but tight for space, allowing a bed, a chair, and a closet the depth of a man's jacket and about as wide. Westlake tapped on the door and heard its occupant cough. He wondered which Mary Collins would greet him: the young woman of his dreams or the woman who had become reserved and distant. She pulled the door open a crack and, fortunately, smiled. Barely the height of his shoulder, Mary peered up at him with her dark eyes.

"Hello," she said with a grin that seemed to light up her plain, round face. Perhaps it was the edge of her smile or the glint in her eyes, but no matter the size of the room, her presence seemed greater than her dainty frame merited. She commanded attention.

Westlake remembered their initial meeting six months ago. On his return to York, he had rescued this girl from a beating at the hands of her stepfather. From the day he first saw her, she had filled his thoughts until he realized he was in love. Now his grand plan to take her home to York had been crushed by his orders to journey to Virginia.

"General Brock has ordered me away on a mission, Mary. I'm sorry."

"Is it dangerous? Where will I go?"

"Captain Nelles will escort you to my family's home on Maple Hill. I've written this letter of introduction to my mother." Westlake handed it to Mary. "She will understand, trust me." Westlake reached out to hold her, but she backed away quickly. The humid room seemed suddenly warmer and Westlake lifted his chin as he tried to breathe.

"I won't go there without you. I'm not prepared to meet your mother with just a letter." She coughed yet again and threw the letter on the bed. Her shoulders gave a heave and then she crossed her arms.

Reminded that her small frame disguised a steely determination, Westlake paused for a few minutes, to let her calm down.

"Please, Mary, you'll be safe there," he pleaded. "Why are you coughing? Are you ill?"

She turned away to face the bed. He tried to imagine what it was like to be so alone in the world, to be without a mother and father, friends from school, or even the relationships he'd formed in the military. Life would feel so empty.

After the death of her mother in London, Mary had journeyed from England to Upper Canada with her stepfather. In the depth of winter, the old man forced her to march north to Fort Mackinac and then later south to Detroit. All that while, he was her only companion, except for one other man, who travelled as their bodyguard. But the protector had turned murderous on her stepfather, and Mary had used every inch of her five-foot frame to fight him off alongside Westlake.

How could this same young woman be nervous about meeting his mother without his presence? To Westlake's way of thinking, females could be contrary, but this bordered on plain stubbornness.

"I'll feel like an intruder without you." She flicked her wrist in a dismissive manner as if to say his idea of a letter of introduction was ridiculous. "No doubt there are houses elsewhere than Fort George. I'll take rooms in Newark; that's where I'll wait for your return. Whenever that will be."

"Good grief, Mary, it's not my fault. I *must* go. My orders come direct from General Brock."

"And I had hoped for more than just a letter," Mary replied. She looked away from him and sat down on the bed.

"You mean me taking you there myself, but I've explained — "

"No, I don't mean that. Think!"

Westlake was confused, for her conversation made no sense. What was she hoping for that he had not agreed to? He wished she'd speak plainly. There were times she mystified him. The tension now gripped him more than the idea of going into battle; he tried to relax his clenched jaw. Finally, he sat down on the bed beside her and took her hand, its warmth disappearing between his palms. But when she stared into his eyes, the thought struck him like a glove to the face.

"Do you want to get married?" he blurted.

"Yes … Yes, I will marry you, Jonathan Westlake." She sprung from sitting motionless to an embrace that toppled him back onto the bed.

He had meant it as a question about her own intentions, not his, but it was too late to take it back now. Or was it? He had to say something before this went any further.

Westlake felt her lips pressing on his, and he returned her kiss. Then she was kissing his cheeks, his forehead, and then back to his lips. She was hugging his neck so tight it hurt. She smiled so that her eyes were lit up in a way he had never seen them before.

"I meant to say … " Westlake began.

"I love you, Jonathan. Tell me you love me too."

"Yes, I love you, but I — "

Mary silenced him with another kiss directly on the lips before a loud knock on the door interrupted. She leaned back on the bed.

"Mr. Westlake." Captain Nelles's voice boomed through the door. "Against my better judgment, I gave you five minutes alone together to say your goodbyes. You must come out at once."

Captain Nelles's determined knocking forced Westlake to his feet.

"That's an order," Nelles commanded.

Mary laughed and jumped up to open the door. "We're fine, Captain. Jonathan and I are to be married," she announced with a broad smile.

Nelles paused to look from Mary to Westlake. "Can this be true, Mr. Westlake?"

"He just proposed to me this very minute," she confirmed.

"Well sir, that is … " Westlake hesitated on seeing the happiness on Mary's face. He couldn't take that away, not now, not at the moment of his leaving. "It appears so, sir." He felt almost powerless as he stared into her eyes and tried to look away. "Yes, sir, we are to be married."

The skill of the oarsmen drove the longboat in silence through the night air. A few stars allowed the passengers to see one another's apprehensive faces, but just barely. As they glided along, the wind caressed Westlake's face, and only the odd slap of black water on the boat's hull reminded him that he was still on earth.

He peered through the darkness, wondering what they would face at the shoreline; meanwhile, his body tensed and he gripped his musket. Perhaps their boat was already spotted and he had only minutes to live? *Stay calm, keep control of yourself.* Determined to think about something other than landing on a hostile shore, he concentrated his mind on the events of the past few hours.

Mary Collins had refused passage to Maple Hill, even with the proposal of marriage. She would meet Westlake's mother with him present or not at all. He clasped his head in frustration. Captain Nelles had fortunately agreed to find her suitable quarters, close to Fort George in the small town of Newark.

Throughout his travels over thousands of miles, Westlake had dreamt so often of being with Mary, but now that he was committed to wedding her, he was nervous. Did all men feel trapped thus after proposing marriage? Initially, he questioned himself about having accepted Brock's mission, yet now he had come round to considering it a relief. After just a few hours on that little ship, somehow his whole life had changed.

Westlake had told the news to Private Parrish while they stood together at the rail of the ship, but the big man had ignored the marriage and cheered the mission. Clearly, he'd heard only what he wanted to hear. Thrilled to be independent again, Parrish said he regretted missing a good night's sleep in a real bed at Maple Hill, but anything was better than returning to parade-square drilling and regimental discipline.

Seven months previously, Parrish and his massive twin brother had been released from military prison for one purpose only — to keep Westlake alive inside enemy territory. The brothers had fought the King's enemies through two thousand miles of wilderness, and when Walt had completed the mission, he received a full pardon for his efforts from Brock himself. Now he'd grown accustomed to the freedom that came with his new life as a secret agent. He told Westlake of his plans for a future in farming after his army career was complete. His only concern on this mission was that Ensign Simpson might somehow get him and Westlake both killed. "How far is it to Virginia?" Parrish asked, pointing one big hand to the south.

"Did you not hear me say how I'm getting married?" Westlake cuffed Parrish behind his ear. "I merely asked her if *she* wanted to get married. It wasn't a proposal, but she took it as such and said yes. And then she started kissing me, so what else could I do?"

"Sounds a bit dodgy to me, sir. Women know what they're doing in these matters, 'cause they think a lot about things like that." With his forefinger, Parrish tapped the side of his head knowingly.

"I became the love of her life for those first two days in Detroit. Then it was as if I had developed the plague. You know — she loves me, she loves me not — this girl drives me crazy. Now what do I do? I'm stuck."

"You're in a right pickle for sure, sir. Look at it this way, you might be lucky and get yourself killed in Virginia." Parrish laughed at his own joke and slapped the ship's rail.

The longboat jerked its way across a sandbar, bringing Westlake back to the present. He turned his head to see Ensign Simpson sitting straight-backed on the opposite side of their vessel, his arms folded across his chest. On hearing the details of the mission, Simpson had voiced his objections to Captain Nelles. His idea of proper soldiering did not consist of dressing up in blue trousers and a grey homespun shirt, then sneaking into enemy territory and stealing a slave.

Simpson expressed his concern as to what his father would think of him if he were caught and shot as a lowly spy? Westlake hoped that Nelles would relent and leave the ensign behind, but he had no such luck. The second conductor, the farmer, spoke little but German, which meant that Simpson had to go.

Nelles's reply to Simpson had been unsympathetic: "If you don't want to get shot, then you'd better not get caught."

Westlake watched the shoreline take shape out of the darkness. The longboat crunched onto the stones, and the three passengers leapt over the side with their muskets in the air. While the seamen passed them their packs, first to Parrish, then to Simpson, Westlake surveyed the treeline. When he turned back, the longboat had pushed off without a sound.

In the United States again. Westlake tensed as the watery sand slid away beneath his feet. He crouched, trying to see where they were. On the map in the captain's cabin it looked easy, just head due south to make contact with the first "conductor" and his supply ranch. But now he had to actually decide to put one foot in front of the other, and it was not so simple to go this way or that.

"Pick up your packs and let's get off this beach. Quickly now," he whispered.

Musket in one hand, pack in the other, he stumbled across the sand with the other two men following, his boots slipping with every step. They reached some low brush that gave way to cedars as they stepped farther inland, and there they paused. Westlake glanced back at the dark water for one last time, but the longboats and their rhythmic oars had already disappeared into the lake's blackness.

"That wasn't too bad," Simpson announced in a huff.

Westlake put a restraining hand over Simpson's mouth, but it was already too late.

"Who goes there?" demanded a young voice from the other side of the cedars.

Westlake grimaced, glaring at Simpson. If only he hadn't spoken, the sentry might have passed by, leaving them unnoticed.

"A friend," Westlake called out.

"That's not the password. Hands in the air and come out of those trees."

The click of a musket's hammer told Westlake the young man was serious. With his hand, he made a circling motion to Parrish, then pulled Simpson by the arm through the cedars.

"I'm afraid the two of us have lost our way."

"Get your hands where I can see them, and lay those muskets on the ground," the sentry ordered.

The young fellow might have been no more than fourteen years old, but it was difficult for Westlake to judge in this darkness. The boy aimed his weapon at Simpson's chest, appearing determined enough. Dressed as a farmer, with a straw hat and overalls held up by suspenders, the guard, Westlake guessed, was part of the local militia.

"Where did you come from?"

A crack to the back of his head crumpled the militiaman to the ground, but not before Westlake snatched the musket from his side.

"You hit him too hard, Parrish. He's just a boy." Westlake bent down and lifted the boy's head, placing two fingers against his neck to feel for a pulse. When there was none, he put his hand over the lad's heart.

"Oh God, no, he's dead. There was no need for this. Just a boy."

"I'm sorry, sir. Cripes, I didn't mean —"

"You great bloody brute, Parrish. Why did you hit him so hard?" Simpson demanded.

"Shut your mouth," Westlake whispered harshly. "If you hadn't made a sound back there, this boy would still be alive. This is all your doing."

"I say, steady on —" Simpson began, his chest puffed out in indignation. But Westlake drew a foot-long blade from the side of his boot and pressed it to his throat.

"Say nothing more. *Nothing*. Do you understand how serious I am?"

Simpson nodded his head barely an inch, his eyes wide.

"We don't have time to bury him. Parrish, carry his body back to the water." Westlake sheathed his knife. "We'll have to fill his pockets with stones and sink the body a ways out. By eight bells they'll be searching everywhere for him, which gives us a minimum of five, maybe six hours head start."

"We should be fine, then," Simpson blurted.

"It would be a shame if I had to end up killing you, but I will do so to accomplish our mission." Westlake frowned. "Our pursuers will be on horses. We're on foot and in unfamiliar woods. They'll take to the road once they guess we're headed south." Westlake spoke only inches from Simpson's face. "The best we can hope now is that they won't find the boy's body for a while. In which case, we may find them waiting in ambush for our return. Still think we're fine, Mr. Simpson?"

Westlake didn't wait for an answer and instead grabbed Simpson by the arm, pushing him toward the water, where they floated out the body. They filled the boy's pockets with stones until he started to sink. Westlake pushed the body down until it was well below the surface, and then made his way back to the beach and the cedars. The men strapped on the packs and snatched up their muskets.

"We head straight south first to buy our horses. I'll lead the way, Simpson in the middle ten paces behind me, and Parrish the same distance back of Simpson to guard our rear." Westlake glared at Simpson. "There's no need for talk unless one of us spots danger. Let's march, double time."

Brock clasped his hands behind his back, squeezing so hard they pained him. The news carried by the other ship was worse than he could imagine. If he yelled it out from the captain's cabin, everyone aboard the *Chippewa* would know instantly that Governor-in-Chief George Prevost had betrayed him. In the cabin itself, the officers surrounding him kept their eyes to the floor. Even the ship's captain and Macdonell stared out the porthole window, preferring not to witness his rage.

With Brock absent from the Niagara frontier, Prevost had directly ordered Major General Roger Hale Sheaffe, Brock's second-in-command, to conclude a far-reaching armistice with the Americans. With the fighting stopped, all Brock's invasion plans across the Niagara River were gone in an instant. He supposed the Americans must have danced a jig to celebrate.

In the past, Prevost had held firm to the naive position that if he didn't antagonize the enemy, they would reciprocate and do nothing of a hostile nature against the Canadas. Brock argued vigorously against this reasoning, and thought the argument won after the American invasion at Sandwich. In his mind, Brock tried to be fair to Prevost, knowing that he was acting under instructions from London.

"Now they have time to mass their armies along the Niagara River, to hold Upper Canada by the throat," Brock protested. "And there is not a damn thing I can do about it — except watch."

Prevost seemed oblivious to Upper Canada's interests, at one point even suggesting that the province be abandoned to conserve manpower and better defend Montreal. Brock hoped to show that by defending Upper Canada, he could delay any attack on Montreal — and in this he had succeeded. That Prevost would now deliberately sabotage their momentum toward victory, after the American surrenders at Fort Mackinac and Detroit, was near treason to Brock's way of thinking.

"Christ, at the Canard River bridge they shot and killed our men!" Brock pounded the ship captain's desk.

The shoreline came into sharp focus and Brock paused at the stern windows, watching the waves of the lake roll away, their white caps disappearing like his plans for a Niagara campaign. His temples throbbed and he massaged them with his forefingers.

"Stand by to take in sails," he heard a lieutenant shout somewhere outside.

"Stand by to let go the anchor."

Brock marched out of the cabin and motioned for the captain to follow, leaving the other officers behind. On deck, he stared back over glittering water at the eleven other vessels in the flotilla trailing the *Chippewa*. Crammed into their hulls were more than two thousand American prisoners of war, the remnants of Hull's army of the Northwest, all waiting anxiously to disembark. Moments later, the mighty splash of the anchor brought Brock back to his immediate business.

"Thank you for your hospitality, Captain, but if you would prepare my boat," Brock urged.

"My pleasure, sir." The man saluted and marched away.

On deck, Lieutenant Colonel John Macdonell approached cautiously and stretched out his hands to grip the rail immediately alongside Brock. "I'd like to speak freely, sir, if you don't mind."

"You have my complete confidence, John." Brock gestured with a slight wave of his hand.

"I'll tell ye this, sir, it wouldn't have been so bad, but Sheaffe included the damn waterways. Now they can move by ship to resupply wherever they wish. That means men *and* cannon. It's almost a capitulation."

Brock nodded in agreement and swung his big frame off the rail. "You may have to stop me from strangling Sheaffe when I next meet him, so you'd better stay close." He removed his large hat to wipe his receding hairline with a handkerchief.

"On the other hand," Macdonell continued, "you can bet Sheaffe was acting on orders from Prevost himself. He sits comfortably in Montreal and thwarts our efforts at every turn. The man is a fool if there ever was one, and his disastrous conduct of this war will be the death of all of us."

"If hostilities recommence, nothing could be more unfortunate than this pause," Brock added.

The two men remained side by side as Brock glanced back at the *Nancy*, the ship that had carried him a good deal of the way to Detroit before the surrender. Those were the days when he had prayed for victory, full of anticipation and enthusiasm. But, now victorious, he was returning home, deflated. The world being turned upside down made no sense to him. Once again higher authorities, people who should know better, were working against the interests of Upper Canada.

"It's not just Prevost; it's London forcing his hand. Wellington needs New England's grain so he can fight the French. World forces are working against us."

"So what do we do, sir? That's the question."

"Prepare defensively; there's no choice. How long do you think we have before the Americans will be ready to invade?" Brock asked.

Macdonell hesitated, so he pressed him further. "Come, give me your best advice. This is crucial."

Macdonell slowly rubbed one side of his youthful face and peered skyward. "Forty-five days to supply and equip their army, and another fifteen days to organize the attack. Sixty days at most, sir, maybe sooner depending on how well their troops are trained. Sometime around mid-October would be my thinking," Macdonell said. "But remember, it's just a guess, sir."

"Boat's ready, sir." The captain saluted.

"Thank you again, Captain." Brock returned the salute and then turned back to Macdonell. "We'll make the best of it — more training, raising additional militia. And bring in that damn fellow, Norton, and his bloody Indians — at least five hundred of them. They scare the hell out of everyone."

Captain Nelles approached them, carrying a black valise.

Brock shaded his eyes with a hand to stare back at the ships following. "Captain Nelles, you're with me. You'll check in on the Coloured Company for me." From the rail, Brock waved his hat to someone on the *Nancy* and a great cheer grew out of the vessel.

"Our troops honour you, sir," Macdonell observed.

"They like winning." Brock smiled and offered a casual salute as the roar grew louder.

"It's more than that, sir. They're calling you the saviour of Upper Canada."

"Very generous of them, but I didn't gain those victories by myself — we did it together." Brock waved a last time. "Sixty days until battle, you say."

"Or less, sir."

6

......

IN THE MIDDAY LIGHT, from his perch on a ridge, Westlake studied the vast forest sloping away in front of him. Two dark parallel lines interrupting the trees below suggested the likelihood of a river and possibly even a road. He had to reach the river and follow it west, where a gap between three small hills would reveal their first station, a ranch that could sell them horses. Although he and his companions had marched ten miles south during the dark hours, their little path had drifted west, so that Westlake hoped the distance to the ranch would be less than the five miles Captain Nelles had described. He waved Simpson and Parrish forward.

"Down there, that's what we've been looking for. Let's go," he ordered. "If that's a road, be wary."

Muskets in hand, the three men clambered down the hill. Under the weight of a heavy pack, Simpson stumbled, and Parrish helped him to his feet. Westlake continued on downward, his head turning constantly from side to side, watching the trees for danger. In less than an hour, they reached the first break, a road, and then came to the river, where Simpson unbuckled his canteen and submerged it in the shallow water.

"I've drunk all my water. It'll just take a second," Simpson explained as he squatted by the river's edge.

"We've got to cross this river so make it quick," Westlake urged.

"There's a perfectly good road that'll get us there faster," Simpson replied.

"If there are patrols about, will they be more likely in the woods or on the road?"

Simpson gulped a swig before plugging the wooden stopper into his canteen. "More likely on the road," he admitted.

"Which is why we'll cross the river and approach our destination through the woods. We'll sacrifice a bit of speed just so I can get you there alive." Westlake glanced at Parrish for confirmation. Only a few months ago, after an April rain, Westlake had pushed for speed, and walked straight into an ambush that had cost a good man his life. Afterward, he promised himself — and Parrish — that he would never make that same mistake again.

The woods were dense on the river's southern bank, so Westlake had to navigate a route through and over fallen tree branches. They crossed a narrow path that ran south, one that Westlake made a mental note to use once they got their horses. By late afternoon he smelled a fire, and soon after, emerging from the forest at the water's sandy bank, he spotted a log farmhouse with a spacious barn beside it. Three hills rose to the back of the farm, which told him they were at their destination.

"Did you hear something?" Simpson asked Parrish.

Parrish paused and shook his head.

Westlake hadn't heard anything either, but that actually was the problem — for the forest had gone dead quiet. For a second, he studied the farmhouse and the road leading up to it. Then he heard the horses and spun around. "Back into the trees, quick," he hissed. "Keep down!"

"German ears." Simpson pointed to one ear. "We hear things others don't, makes us such good musicians."

"Shut up." Westlake glared at him. "And watch the road."

Six rough-looking men on horseback galloped along the road and dismounted at the farmhouse. They tied their horses to the porch rail before their leader jumped up the steps of the veranda and banged on a blue-painted front door. When it opened, the men barged their way in, except for one man who stood guard outside, searching the forest with his eyes, seemingly looking right at Westlake.

"Now what? We're too late to get the horses," Simpson complained.

"Good God, you are frustrating, Simpson," Westlake replied. "Spouting rubbish at every opportunity."

"We're not too late, sir." Parrish turned to Simpson. "We're right on time because, if we'd arrived ten minutes sooner, we'd now be fighting for our lives with those men."

Westlake said nothing but keenly watched the front door and surveyed the road for stragglers. A short time later, the guard changed, and a new fellow sat on the steps to scan the surrounding forest. After about an hour the five other men emerged, mounted their horses, and all trotted back along the way they came.

The setting sun's ball touched the edge of the treetops casting long shadows, but Westlake still stayed hidden. For another half-hour, he peered through the bushes at the nearby road and then back toward the front door of the farmhouse. Nothing stirred on either the road or at the farmhouse, and the normal sounds of the forest soon returned.

The twilight deepened as Westlake again waved his companions forward. They quickly splashed through the shallow river and scrambled up to the road, where they stopped once Westlake held up his hand.

"Parrish, make your way down this road," he ordered. "If they've left anyone watching the farmhouse — kill them. If they ride back this way, you'll have to hurry to warn Simpson."

Westlake turned and gestured to Simpson. "If you see Parrish running toward you, make like hell for the farmhouse." Simpson opened his mouth to protest, but the grim look on Westlake's face persuaded him to keep quiet. Parrish crept off down the road, and Simpson ran to the other side of it.

Westlake stepped up onto the farmhouse veranda, approached the blue front door and knocked, praying that his reception there would be cordial.

A well-groomed middle-aged man opened the door cautiously, and half stepped outside. He was small in stature and dressed like an English gentleman farmer, with a woollen tie, blue waistcoat, and tanned riding boots. "Good evening, sir. Where might you be travelling?" he said with a smile in a clipped English accent. The fellow appeared friendly enough, and not frightened in the least but, then again, he held a cocked pistol in his left hand and rested the point of the barrel against Westlake's chest.

At the sight of the weapon, Westlake's stomach clenched. "I need four horses, and I was told you'd sell them," he stammered. He took one step back, but the pistol remained pressed to his chest and now he noticed the short sword in the Englishman's other hand. If the pistol misfired for whatever reason, Westlake supposed he would be still run through.

"Delighted that you need four horses, but that does not really answer my question. I will ask you once more, and then I'm afraid I'll have to shoot you if I decide I'm hearing the wrong answer. Where are you going?" The man's face had remained in a fixed smile from the moment of opening the door, but now a frown pulled down the corners of his mouth. His piercing blue eyes squinted just enough to assure Westlake he was about to die if he gave the wrong answer a second time.

Westlake swallowed hard and inhaled deeply, finally blurting out, "Heaven … I'm going to glory land."

"Excellent, why didn't you say so? Foster's the name." He uncocked the pistol, tucked it through his belt, and extended his hand. "Anyone else joining us?" he asked, peering around his visitor's body.

Westlake exhaled and shook hands while Foster's eyes resumed the gaze of a kindly gentleman rather than a killer. "I've two guards a ways down the road, where they'll stay until I order them otherwise," Westlake said.

"Ah, best be off to heaven then, young man, before the devil knows you're missing." Foster laughed at his joke and then discarded his sword on a table by the entrance. He gave instructions to someone inside the house and closed the door before pointing the way to the stables.

"The horses need to be fast. I'll need saddles, and some food, if that's possible. We've some salted beef, but I'd rather save it," Westlake explained.

"That's wise, young fellow. I'd ask you to stay for a meal, however, your visit comes at a rather inopportune time … but I suspect you know that." Foster gripped the rail as he descended the veranda's steps.

"I had a rather nasty visit this afternoon from some upset militiamen. My guess is that they were searching for you. Seems for no reason, someone up north, murdered a young sentry right on the shoreline of Lake Erie."

Westlake jumped down off the veranda. "That's not true." He lowered his head, sadly remembering the dead boy's face. "He tried to stop us and got killed by accident. It was impossible in the dark to see how young he was … I'm sorry."

"Remorse won't bring him back. However, now you have a choice. You can continue south, where you'll have to contend with those militiamen that got ahead of you, and then hope to hell the rest of the militia following don't catch up and kill you anyway. Or you can hold up in those hills for a week, until things settled down." Foster gestured with a sweep of his hand to the three small hills rising behind his ranch.

"An entire week?" Westlake surveyed the undulations in the terrain, already judging the best place to hide.

"Probably ten days would be better. I've done this business before and doubtless you've stirred up a right hornets' nest. Every couple days, one hour after sunset — so long as it's safe — I'll have my wife hang a white sheet on the fence post. There'll be food left in a bundle at the foot of the post, but don't come near if the sheet's not there. And on no account must you ever again knock on my door."

Westlake shook his head and stared up at the hills. *Ten days!* He kicked at the dirt and swore silently under his breath.

When they reached the barn, Foster swung open a large door to reveal stalls packed with horses and feed. The sharp smell of animal sweat and fresh manure assailed Westlake's nostrils. Dry straw on the barn floor crunched under his foot, and the horse in the nearest stall grunted once or twice.

"These four up at the front are quickest. How about the money?" Foster turned up the palm of his hand and smiled. "Even goodwill runs on cash."

Westlake opened his shirt and from Captain Nelles's money pouch took a stack of US dollars designated for the first station. He passed the bills to Foster and then moved closer to examine the horses. Well groomed and muscular, they stepped nervously in their stalls. The saddles and blankets rested on the double partitions between the stalls. Foster opened a gate, placed a scarlet blanket over one horse, then heaved on a saddle.

Before Westlake could do likewise, a tiny woman appeared at the barn entrance with a red tablecloth tied around what he assumed was a parcel of food. Her grey hair was pulled back in a neat bun and she stepped lightly toward him, placing the food at his feet.

"Take this and good luck. It's a Christian act you do." She touched his hand, her face scrunching into a smile. Then she marched in small, quick steps back toward the farmhouse with her long brown dress swishing on the ground behind. There she stood and looked around for sometime, her head jerking from side to side as she scanned the surroundings for any threats, before slowly closing the door. Next, he heard a clunk as a bar fell into place inside the door. This set Westlake to wondering as he opened the stall directly opposite Foster. He threw a blanket over the horse, pulled up a saddle, and placed it on the horse.

"Why are you doing this?" Westlake asked.

Foster scanned him from head to toe but did not answer immediately. How much would this man give away? To be studied, under such close scrutiny, made Westlake uncomfortable.

"I could perhaps inquire the same of you, young man," Foster finally replied in his tight English accent.

"I follow my orders, sir."

"Don't trifle with me."

Westlake nodded. "You're right, poor answer. I defend my home and I want to make a difference." Westlake shrugged. "This seems to be the best way."

"Ah! You want to make a difference. A noble aspiration. Well, so do I." Foster slipped a bridle over the horse's muzzle, positioned the bit over its tongue, and then proceeded to the next stall.

"Well, I don't mind telling you the truth. I was once a horse trainer in Kent for a nobleman's family… but his lordship treated me dreadfully … as if I was no better than a slave. He even reduced me to feeling like it too." Foster threw the blanket and saddle on the second horse, threaded a belt through a buckle, and cinched the leather girth around the animal's underbelly. "He decided to visit an inherited estate in Delaware, and on board ship he stuck me in the stinking hold, alongside his horses, his favourite hounds and their filth. I was seasick most of the way to the New World."

"That sounds horrible." Remembering his own recent voyage, Westlake shuddered. Just the thought of being locked in the hold made his stomach clench. He began saddling a second horse while Foster continued his account.

"Once we arrived in New York, I had my chance to make off, so I did… For three years I trained stables of horses on a southern plantation, and saw how slaves were really treated … The owner paid me well, and when I set up on my own, I decided that I owed it to my good fortune to help anyone else trying to escape."

"Not many would do that, Mr. Foster," Westlake marvelled.

"Don't think I'm so noble. I told you, it's done for myself. I strike back at the world in order to feel free. Every runaway that my wife and I manage to help reaffirms that I can do whatever I damn well please, and to hell with the so-called lords and masters of this world."

"I've never thought much about freedom, sir. Haven't had to, I guess," Westlake replied.

"I'm not what you'd call a religious man, devoted to God and all, but I believe that in the Lord's eyes, men are equal — royalty included. And no man should ever be the slave of another. Period."

"Then why do you remain here in a country that condones slavery, when glory land is just to the north?"

"Haven't I made that clear? I hate the British and what they stand for, and besides, you're not building anything up there. Upper Canada is just little England, and I've had my fill of it with that lot." Foster shrugged. "With all our problems down here, there's still a sense that

you're part of something big, that you're building a new country —
that's America — a fresh start."

Foster had finished his task and now gathered up the reins of the
two horses he'd saddled. He led them out through the barn entrance,
handed Westlake the reins, and gave him a light slap on the back.
"You'd best be off, before the rest of the militia show up. If they start
heading for the hills you're hiding in, I'll fire a shot so you know
they're coming."

Then Foster shouted after him, as Westlake continued walking
away with the horses. "I didn't catch your name."

"I didn't offer it, sir. You're a good man, Mr. Foster." Westlake
smiled and held up the reins in one hand and the food in the other.
"Thanks for everything, to you and your kind wife. I'll look out for
that white sheet and rest assured that we'll follow your instructions
exactly."

Just when he thought the situation was turning in his favour, the news
of Hull's surrender of Detroit destroyed any joy that Major General
Stephen van Rensselaer had felt over the signing of the armistice. But
that was a week ago, and now he sat with his cousin Solomon and
Major Lovett staring into a weak fire. He watched Solomon reach
into the woodpile and throw another log on the embers, its outer bark
bursting into flame. Pressure to attack across the river grew by the
hour and Stephen rubbed the back of his neck. He knew the other
two men were thinking the same thing as him. If not now, then when
would they be ready to do battle?

"Any news from Porter regarding supplies?" Lovett asked.

Stephen shook his head to say no.

"But men and supplies are still coming by boat from Oswego.
That'll help," Solomon added. In the blistering heat of August 27, with
a grey wool blanket wrapped around his shoulders, he shivered visibly. Illness was spreading in the camp, yet their soldiers were still not
properly trained to attack. Without Solomon in full health, Stephen
judged their chances of success to be slim. His cousin possessed the

most knowledgeable military mind in the camp — far more experienced than his own.

"Do you ever wish you'd never taken up Governor Tompkin's offer to run this campaign?" Lovett suddenly asked.

The major general thought about it for just a second. New York's Republican governor had asked him to command the Niagara war effort. The governor knew the Van Rensselaers were Federalist, anti-war, and itching for the chance to challenge him in the next spring election. Stephen had felt politically trapped. If he turned down the offer, he'd be known as unpatriotic; if he accepted it, he risked failure. And now, how could he campaign back in New York against this war when he himself directed it?

"Who else could do it? After all, I'm an American and our country's at war," he replied to Lovett. "We all have to do our part."

But they had not enough boats, not enough food, not enough tents, not enough anything. And he knew his own planning was deficient. He stabbed at the outer edge of the fire with a stick. What else could go wrong, he wondered.

And not everyone was playing his part. They had not heard from Dearborn since he'd travelled to Boston to try to convince the New England states to join the war effort. Rumours flew around that he'd been flatly refused, and Stephen shook his head in frustration. Dearborn had been wasting everyone's time.

A single rider approached them at a gallop. Captain John E. Wool of the 13th Infantry slid out of the saddle as his horse came to an abrupt halt in a cloud of dust. The man had a small but intelligent face with penetrating round eyes below bushy eyebrows. As he came to attention and saluted, Solomon stood up and returned the salute, the blanket sliding from his shoulders.

"May I suggest, sirs, that you follow me down to the river, where you will witness a spectacle the likes of which you'll hope never to see again," Wool announced. He stared at Stephen. "Prepare yourself accordingly, sir."

"Spit it out, man! What have you seen?" Solomon demanded.

"General Hull's shattered army is passing along the opposite bank," Wool cried. "Our men are lined up on the shore in tears."

The three officers mounted their horses to accompany Wool. Stephen set the pace at a trot, not a gallop, so that the high command didn't appear panicked at the sight of a defeated American army. He crested a rise and surveyed across the Niagara River. Wool's account had been correct. His stomach wrenched. Stretched out for a half-mile on the far side, he witnessed the tattered American Army of the Northwest limping along.

"We watched them disembark at Fort Erie, then take the River Road north toward Fort George," Wool continued. "Rumour has it that they'll be shipped across Lake Ontario, to be imprisoned in Quebec."

Every man marching wore the uniform — or what was left of it — of the U.S. 4th Army. Regulars all of them, they shuffled along with their heads bowed in shame or just from plain weariness. Stephen surmised the militiamen must have been sent home after promising not to take up arms again.

"Good God, half of those men are without shoes or even coats!" Major Lovett exclaimed.

Stephen van Rensselaer urged his horse down the embankment, closer to the river's edge. When a few of his men waved to the other side but received no response from the wretched prisoners, a low murmur passed through his watching militia. He stared at a broken army, a remnant with no will, no spirit. A quiet sadness descended over all present, and the major general found himself listening to a conversation between two soldiers in front of him.

"They don't wave back 'cause they're ashamed. I've heard the stories of what happened to them."

"You won't catch me going over there, not to end up like that," another intervened.

"That traitor, Hull."

"And plain treachery from his officers, if you ask me."

Solomon and Lovett came up on either side of major general's horse, where Solomon uncased a glass and studied the prisoners of war on the far side. "You'd better take a good look for yourself, sir. Focus toward the back of the line ... in the carts." Solomon handed the glass to his cousin.

"Poor devils are loaded in open carts. Just the sight of wounded men being treated like that'll wipe out whatever morale we have remaining," Stephen declared. Some men hobbled, but he couldn't discern if it was due to injuries received or simply a lack of boots. He sighed on hearing the distressed men in the carts give a moan every time their vehicle crossed an obstacle in the road. A cart would roll, the wheel bumping or jamming, and a man would scream out in pain. From this distance, the bloodstains on their white shirts were clearly evident.

The militia standing nearby began to drift away without a sound, dejected and defeated even before their own battle had started. Stephen watched them go, heads down, dragging their feet, hands buried in their pockets, appearing much like the destroyed army opposite them. *Where would this lead?* His breathing quickened, and he released his grip on the reins to shake a fist.

"Brock's up to his cunning tricks. Well, he'll not 'Hull' me," the major general whispered between his teeth.

"Really, cousin, I've never seen you so agitated," Solomon said.

"Excuse me, sirs, you know best I'm sure," Wool interjected, "but the other officers here want to attack forthwith." His round eyes glaring in anger, Wool had been urged by his fellow officers to deliver the message to the high command, and he had not shrunk from his promise to do so.

"Do you really think our men are ready for battle?" Major Lovett demanded of Wool. He gestured with a wave of his hand toward the water. "Ready to cross that river and then defeat the British forces opposite?"

Wool glanced at the backs of the militia skulking away from the riverbank. He hesitated with his answer. "No, sir, but the officers and myself ... we want to strike back, now."

Stephen van Rensselaer eyed the young man. "You'll have to wait. Listen carefully and perhaps you can help us." He turned to Solomon, and knowing the answer to his question, he asked, "What do we need to do?"

"Drill and more drill, sir, until our army is a proper killing machine: three rounds a minute without fail," Solomon replied. "Yes, drill this bloody sense of shame right out of them, sir, morning, noon, and night, until they hate the British with a passion that will drive them to a killing frenzy. That's what we need to do."

"Major Lovett, do you have some assistance arriving soon to aid Captain Wool?" Stephen asked.

"Captain Wool, would two thousand men, and several cannons, help you and your anxious officers?" Lovett asked.

Wool smiled and gave a whistle. "Very much, sir."

"That's settled, then. No attack today, but we'll be attacking soon enough. Let's get down to training, hard physical training," the general exclaimed. "Brock will need more than a few theatrics to get the better of me."

7

· · · · · ·

As he did every morning, Luther watched Lieutenant James Cooper, 2nd Lincoln Militia, stand sweating in the late August sun, boots planted two feet apart and arms folded across his chest. Except for his expression of disgust, to Luther, Cooper never looked much like a normal officer, wearing a faded uniform unbuttoned halfway down his chest. But with low expectations for the Coloured Company, nobody really cared what the man did. On a dusty parade square, Luther and twenty-three black militiamen marched in two ranks of twelve, carrying in hand their weapons — shovels, pitchforks, and the odd musket. One rank marched almost perfectly while the men of the other, the one including Luther, still jostled one another at random intervals. He had to get this right to become a proper soldier, and Luther was determined to give it his best efforts.

"Halt!" Cooper bawled. "We have old Butler Rangers who *can* march and we have new men who can't seem to manage. We are now going to reform four deep, so I want every old Ranger in the front section with new men in the rank behind. Then another four of Rangers, followed by a section of four new men."

Luther thus found himself behind Richard Pierpoint, while Pierpoint himself led the first rank. Luther grinned and nodded to the old man known as Cap'n Dick. Pierpoint did not grin back. Luther's efforts to make a good impression through smiles were not well received.

"That's it, a former Ranger at the front with a new man behind him — repeat that through all six sections. Now we have experience leading inexperience. This should work," Cooper said out loud, mainly to himself, then took a deep breath.

Luther stared at the back of Pierpoint's head and wondered if this was actually going to work, or would the whole thing fall apart again like every other time. When he watched the regular army march, it looked so easy. If Hector were here, he'd know what to do because he always did. Luther began to imagine his brother's smiling face until the sound of Cooper's voice startled him back to the present.

"Good. Remember what I told you about always leading with your left foot. Here we go: easy twenty-four-inch steps." His voice rose to issue the command, "At the ordinary, march!"

The front rank lurched into motion. Pierpoint led with his left foot, sharp and smooth. Luther trod in behind with his left foot, but somewhere back of him, a man who was obviously used to walking away from his bed every morning with his first step on the right, trampled on the heel of the still-stationary right foot of the man in front of him, causing the fellow to stumble. And, as a result, he thrust the man in front of him, who shoved Luther, who crashed into Pierpoint, who flew spread-eagled to the ground. The line was a shambles in seconds, with weapons strewn around sprawling bodies. The other sections continued to march away, until Luther heard Cooper shout, "Halt!"

A dozen regulars of the 41st Foot, lounging by the barracks, snickered and guffawed. They had been given leave from their duties and, while a few wore their uniforms, at least half of them were dressed in barrack coats. No one carried his musket.

A man nicknamed Trash pushed himself off the wall and called out to his friend just loud enough for Luther and the others to hear, "Mad Dog, you could say they are bumping along." With that, their fellow regulars lounging on the grass broke into howls of laughter. "Might as well try to teach monkeys to march," Mad Dog crowed in return. "I knew they were a mistake. They'll never be able to fight."

Luther shoved away the old Ranger who had bumped into him, and the man swung a fist. Luther leaned away from the swing, and the man punched wild. "Fool. You shoved me," Luther growled.

Pierpoint pushed himself up from the ground, brushed himself off, and stepped quickly in front of Luther. He stuck out an arm between the two men and commanded, "Stop. Stop, I say, both of you."

The three of them snapped to attention as Lieutenant Cooper approached. Luther knew he could be lashed for assault, but heat and frustration was getting the better of him. Hector. Where was Hector now he needed him? A bead of sweat trickled down from one eyebrow into his eye, but he held himself to attention.

"Pierpoint, I'll have none of this brawling among ourselves!" Cooper thundered, his face flushing red. "Do you hear me?"

"Sir." Pierpoint nodded in agreement.

"Those two men who called you monkeys are particular trouble. I can complain to their officer for punishment on your behalf or we can continue as before and get it right. I'll leave it to you," Cooper said.

"That's very fair of you, sir, but our men are working against themselves. Let's try again. There's enough bad blood right here within our own company, and we don't need no more bad blood between us and the 41st."

"Suit yourself. Right, form up in fours as before, facing me."

Luther stepped back into line behind Pierpoint as the rest of the men formed up in their sections.

"Atteeenshun!" Cooper shouted. "Elbow to elbow. You're looking good so far. Now, each of you remember, for God's sake if not for mine, lead with your left. At the ordinary, march!"

Luther watched the feet of Pierpoint and moved his left foot exactly in time. The company managed a score of paces before someone's over zealous stride caught the man in front, so Pierpoint went for another tumble. They had made progress but again, the men of the 41st were calling out, "Monkeys, monkey militiamen." Mad Dog strutted about stiff-legged and purposely banged into his friend Trash, all the while laughing.

Luther felt Pierpoint's hand on his shoulder, then heard a whisper in his ear. "It'll be different this time. Just do as you're told." Pierpoint move down the line, speaking quietly to each man and ending with Lieutenant Cooper.

Cooper marched over close to where the regulars were howling in mockery and turned his back on them. "Coloured Company, form two ranks in front of me."

The men scrambled into their two ranks; only this time they were directly facing their hecklers. Two ranks of glaring, sweating black men, who stared angrily with big white eyes. Luther's own face contorted in rage.

"Coloured Company, atteeenshun."

Luther snapped his heels together, pitchfork upright at his side.

"Shoulder arms."

"Coloured Company, port arms!" In one motion, both ranks brought their shovels, pitchforks, and muskets to their front, sloping across their bodies.

"Charge bayonets!" Cooper ordered.

Luther pointed his pitchfork at the prospective enemy and looked along his line. Every man in it had lowered his weapon ready to charge. Mad Dog and Trash jumped to their feet, followed by the rest of the lounging 41st, the laughter now silenced as if sure they were about to be impaled on a pitchfork or shot through by a musket.

"Coloured Company, why are you here?" Cooper shouted.

"To kill!" the company shouted in unison.

Luther stared as the regulars took a step backward, then another. The concern on their faces surprised him. White men had always seemed so confident to him, and yet here was an entire dozen, scared and ready to run.

"I can't hear you," Cooper said. "What are you going to do?"

"Kill!" Luther screamed with the others.

The regulars continued to edge away from the line of trainees. Trash stumbled to the ground and two of his fellows rushed to pull him to his feet.

"Advance," Cooper ordered. The line took three sharp steps forward before the regulars finally spun about and ran. In his haste, Mad Dog snarled at the man in front of him to get out of the way. Luther watched their backs jostle and then disappear around the corner of the barrack.

"Coloured Company, halt. Stand at ease. Fall out." Luther could barely hear Cooper's words above the cheering. The men slapped hands and laughed. Luther held his pitchfork above his head and yelled, "Kill" for a final time. He looked around for Pierpoint.

"We've won our first battle, sir, without a single casualty." Pierpoint grinned at the men. "Ain't that something, they made white men run. Now they'll work well together."

"God, look at them; you'd think it was Agincourt." Cooper slapped his knee, laughing. "I'll probably catch hell for that little trick. Won't be the first time I've been in the soup, but it was fun to see those bastards run."

Luther grabbed Pierpoint's elbow and swung him round in a victory spin. When they were finished he took a step toward Cooper.

"We want to march straight, like proper soldiers. Make ourselves proud and you too, sir," Luther said. "We'll get there. I promise you.

"General Brock has brought muskets and ammunition from Detroit," Cooper announced, clearly pleased with his news. "Should have them for every man here next week. What do you think of that?"

"Cap'n Dick called him the saviour of Upper Canada, sir, and I know I'll do better with a real musket," Luther replied.

"You'll be a killer yet." The white man lifted his head so everyone else could hear. "Have no fear, with real weapons I'll make killers of you all, or my name isn't Cooper."

"Still, we'd all feel a might better if Alexander the Great were here. Like old times," Pierpoint said, smiling sadly.

"I sent off the letter to Captain Nelles" — Cooper shrugged — "but who knows what will come of it."

On hearing his father's name mentioned, Luther felt a lump rise in his throat. The lieutenant had actually sent the letter. If there was the smallest chance that his father could escape, then he was as good as home.

Alexander stood shirtless in the shade of an oak tree, his wrists strapped tight together. He studied the movements of Master Peter Caldwell, who paced the large white veranda with his hands clasped behind his back. Those hands had to move before the special signal could be given … one that Alexander had witnessed before.

The pale-skinned master had fleshy purple cheeks, with a wide, clean-shaven chin, and even in the heat of this August day, he wore a blue suit, white shirt, and blue cravat. His hair was pulled back and tied with a ribbon. Suddenly he turned purposefully to grip the veranda rail, but not before motioning up with a forefinger — the signal that prompted Alexander to take a deep breath. That one raised finger, just the slightest motion, sent the two slave catchers rushing to hoist Alexander below a low-hanging tree branch, so that his upstretched arms and body hung limply, with just a couple of toes brushing the ground.

Although in the shade, sweat ran down his bare back from the afternoon heat. He turned his head from side to side to glimpse George Castor and Fred Bennett standing on either side and just back of him with whips in their hands. They were big, muscular men who both looked eager to begin, and he wondered if he might faint in the next few minutes.

Castor took off his black hat and sat it carefully on the veranda railing. A large man with a barrel chest covered by a black leather vest, Alexander caught a glimpse of him grinning before he heard the snap of the uncoiling whip. He jerked his head around to locate Bennett, but the other man was out of sight. Where the hell was he? Alexander's heart quickened now, the agony just moments away. There was nothing to be done except endure the pain.

For an instant, he thought of Luther and his constantly smiling face, now most likely dead, and then of Hector's broken body, which the catchers had hauled back from the Niagara River. They had hung his bloated corpse from this same knotted branch for all to witness as an example of what happens to slaves who run away. The thing had twisted this way and that at first, until the ropes straightened themselves and then finally came to rest, the body stilled.

The only reason Alexander didn't go insane with rage was that the boy's corpse looked more like something foreign and not his son Hector. The stinking cadaver seemed even more degraded by the hordes of buzzing flies that relished its decomposing flesh. On the next Saturday night, just before the Sabbath, the cords were cut through and the corpse dropped into a cart, where it bounced along the roadway to the slave cemetery. At the burial, many of the other slaves wept, but no one spoke.

Tears came to his eyes for his two boys, and Alexander swore revenge for the thousandth time. He'd hoped the boys would make it to freedom, but Castor claimed the river had swept them over the falls. *They must have taken a wrong turn.* Alexander let his head droop between his arms, chin resting on chest, and tried to put the memory of Hector's dangling corpse out of his mind. The tears running down his face and into his mouth left a bitter taste of salt.

A crowd of workmen and three dozen slaves — men, women, and children — shuffled into a semicircle beside the veranda to witness his punishment. A dusty, winding road divided the plantation into east-and west-lying fields, and now the six overseers from each side wandered to the edge of the gathering. They were all there for only one purpose: to witness him suffer.

Percy Caldwell, a young man a couple of years younger than Luther, whistled a tune and strutted over to the tree where Alexander hung. With a snap of his head, he spit hard on the captive's chest. "Gimme." He held out his hand with authority for Castor's whip. Tall and thin, like many in their mid-teens, the boy's white face was so pale as to be almost sickly. Copying his father, he had tied his blond hair at the back of his neck, and wore the same coloured suit and cravat.

Near Percy's buckled shoes and disregarding the crowd, a proud rooster cocked its head and seemed to imitate the juvenile Caldwell as it pecked its way forward through the dirt.

"No you don't. I don't care how old you think you are, no son of mine is going to whip niggers," his mother commanded from behind one of the white veranda columns. "It's not a Christian thing to do. Let them catchers do the whipping. That's what they're paid for." She then stepped back behind the master.

"The fellows blubbering already. Not so great now, are you, Alex?" Percy flicked his wrist as if to strike, then laughed when Alexander winced at the crack of the whip. But, instead of lashing out, the boy followed his mother's instruction and returned the whip to Castor. He continued whistling his tune and strutted off.

Master Caldwell unbuttoned his suit jacket and raised a forearm to prop himself against one of the columns. He pursed his lips, his eyes glinting in anger. Alexander could barely breathe for wondering how many lashes Caldwell would dictate.

"It doesn't feel right, damaging our own property, but what can I do?" he said to his wife. "An example has to be made, or maybe some other slave will get ideas of running."

"You have to do what's right. Give him what he deserves," his wife said from behind his back.

The master walked to the edge of the steps and called out, "Those two boys of yours would be alive today if you hadn't encouraged them to take off." Caldwell had raised his voice to make sure his words reached Alexander. "And don't say you didn't push 'em to it. You did it once before and then you did it again. You've brought all this on yourself, and put me and Mother here in this position." Caldwell looked down from his stance on the top step, scanning the crowd in front of him to locate a specific slave among them before he concluded his statement.

"I've thought about this for months. Running can never be encouraged. And this is what'll happen to you too, Precious, if you try to run."

Alexander thought back to several winters ago, when the young girl's parents had died only a month apart of the ague and she had adopted him as her protector. Now his eyes watched Precious shrink down on her knees at the front of the semicircle, her head bowed and her arms clasped together. He had taught her all the things a parent should teach, and also how to read from the Bible and even write some. He was her only family, and the single person she cared about other than her secret lover, a man only Alexander knew of. When would she ever see her young man again? He shook his head sadly for the poor girl.

Percy had faded back into the crowd of slaves and workmen and now crept up behind the girl to grip her narrow shoulders with his bony hands. Alexander watched her shudder as Percy whispered something in her ear. He guessed another nighttime visit was demanded because his beautiful girl began to sob. He almost didn't hear the master finally speak.

"You didn't run yourself and for that I'm trying to be fair. Six lashes for each boy who ran and six for each of the dogs lost. Get started, Castor. Twenty-four lashes." Master Caldwell motioned with his finger.

Alexander's eyes shot around to his right, where Castor stood legs apart, tapping the whip's small handle that he held in his thick hands. Alexander knew this man wanted revenge — revenge for his lost dogs. His heart pounded in his ears and he struggled to breathe while bracing himself for the first vicious bite of the lash.

"Only six lashes for each dog, hardly seems fair," Castor grumbled to Bennett.

"This bastard and his goddamn sons cost me a whole month's wages," Bennett said between his teeth.

Alexander turned his head the other way to see Bennett press his bowler hat firmly into place. The man spit once on the ground, uncoiled his whip, then drew back his arm. With all his might, he cranked the whip forward, the measure of his spite sounding in the *crack*. Alexander winced, groaning in pain.

The first lash stung like a knife cutting across the flesh of his back. *Lightning* was the next thought that came into his mind. He'd been struck by lightning. He tilted his head back and saw patches of blue through the tree leaves before the second lash struck, and then the third, setting his back on fire. "A – a – ah." His teeth clenched and bit down so hard that his jaw ached.

When Castor's turn came, he pulled his lash so the tail end of it cut deeper into Alexander's flesh. By the seventh lash, Alexander's back blazed and when he rolled his head forward he caught a glimpse of Precious kneeling, crying. Hate for the Caldwells and love for Precious were the only two things that kept him conscious. He fought to breathe, but the searing pain wouldn't let him.

His back already shredded, on the eleventh lash his knees buckled under him, lifting him off his toes so the leather ties bit into his wrists. *"Oh, God, save me."* Finally, he lost consciousness for a time and didn't feel lash number twelve. By number twenty-four, when the whipping was over, his vision had long faded and the staring crowd wavered like figures in a nightmare.

A couple of slaves rushed forward and he felt their hands supporting him under his arms. Alexander made out a blur where Caldwell motioned with his finger in approval to slice the cord holding him to the tree. Caldwell turned away without further comment and opened the imposing front door so his wife and he could pass through. The door closed, *click*, and they were gone. It was finished.

The spectators shuffled back and a young slave pointed the way through the semi circle as it parted for the men carrying Alexander. "Take him round the back, to the old horse trough," Mathew instructed. "It's been filled with fresh water." Just hearing the young man's familiar voice brought Alexander some comfort. When his son Luther was a youngster, the two boys had played together and become best of friends. Now, Mathew held a ladle of fresh water to his lips and he swallowed.

Away from the white men, they carried his limp body around to the back of barn and then gently lowered him into the trough. He heard himself whimper as the water seared his back with renewed pain and everything went dark, even the hatred. Surely, he was dead.

Then he felt soft hands and someone was speaking to him. "You're strong and you will live forever." He heard the words but they were more like an echo of words mixed together. His mind floated. *Revenge. Hatred. Be careful. Run. Run away. Kill.*

Precious caressed his head, and the pain throbbed on his back while he lay soaking in the water. After a while — he couldn't tell how long — the men lifted him up and carried him to the straw mat in his cabin where Precious dried him off with a clean towel, dabbing around the open slits in his back. He drifted into semi consciousness.

"Shush that silly talk. You be getting us into trouble. 'Sides, you taught us to forgive," he heard Precious speaking. She began feeding him from a large wooden spoon, and he tasted lukewarm pea soup as it trickled down his throat. His jumbled thoughts gradually stilled and he began to think clearly.

Well into the evening, she regularly pressed a cool damp cloth to his forehead until the door burst open. Percy strode in and whistled.

"Leave him. A brute like that won't die from a whip's tickle. You're mine tonight." Percy laughed and grabbed her by the wrist when she backed away. "C'mon, my little Precious, don't act like this is your first time. I've a special cabin set up … a real bed for our fun."

Alexander rolled his head enough to see the door remained open into his empty room. He closed his eyes, imagining what Percy would do to his girl and then heard himself whimper as the cuts in his back stretched and bit with each breath. Alexander the Great had finally broken, only not in the way Master Caldwell, the catchers, and the others imagined.

Death would now be better than existence. *Anything is better than this … anything other than slavery.* His two sons gone, Precious raped nightly, his hatred turned into thoughts of killing.

The searing pain in his back was almost forgotten when he thought of what he would do to Percy, maybe to all the Caldwells, if ever he got the chance. When these cuts healed, when he could stand again and be strong, Percy Caldwell would die and he would run … run with Precious at his side.

8
······

In the morning sun, General Brock surveyed the ten-foot-thick stone walls packed with earth. The powder magazine, sixteen paces long and four wide, contained eight hundred barrels of gunpowder: enough to blow up Fort George, all its men, and half the town of Newark that lived outside its walls.

Inside the magazine, two soldiers caught sight of their major general. They laid down their barrel with care, snapped to attention and saluted. Brock returned a casual salute and noticed they worked in their stocking feet. There would be no sparks here.

"Carry on."

He motioned the officer with him to come along and stepped through the copper-sheathed doors, scanning the powder barrels ranged in rows of wooden racks. With a copper mallet, a soldier drove in a wooden plug to bung the end of a barrel marked FG in black letters, initials indicating fine-grain powder. Even the nails securing the floorboards had been replaced with wooden pegs. Above him, Brock scanned the giant crossbeams supporting a tin roof that was in theory expected to withstand heavy punishment from enemy artillery.

"Can it take a proper pounding?" he asked.

Captain Vigoreux of the Royal Engineers stared up at the vaulted ceiling and nodded his head.

"A direct hit with heated shot might do some damage, sir, but otherwise you're standing in the safest place in the fort." Vigoreux knew his business and had worked his engineers tirelessly to improve the fort's defences. To show his trust, Brock gripped the man's shoulder. "Thank you, Captain. Well done."

Vigoreux smiled with pride.

Lieutenant Colonel Macdonell strode across the grounds to the magazine with the youthful vigour of a man in his late twenties. In his right hand he clutched a bundle of papers. Major General Roger Sheaffe, second-in-command to Brock and more than twice Macdonell's age, picked his way along behind.

Brock dismissed Captain Vigoreux and accepted the four pages from Macdonell's outstretched hand. The wind blew hard and he held tight both edges so he could read. From American deserters crossing the Niagara River, Macdonell had learned that the enemy possessed little food and less ammunition. Sickness was causing havoc to their training and men in the hundreds were threatening desertion due to lack of pay.

The second page reported that a Lieutenant Colonel Fenwick had arrived in the American camp by boat with two hundred regulars, and also cannon consisting of two six-pounders, two twelve-pounders, and two eighteen-pounders. More cannon were apparently on the way. The total number of enemy regulars reached eight hundred. The day following Fenwick's arrival, an additional four hundred militia had marched into the camp. Brock jerked his hand in disgust as he offered the same page to Sheaffe.

Sheaffe's first meeting with Brock after signing the armistice had been stormy. Macdonell had politely intervened when Brock accused Sheaffe of working with Prevost behind his back. Generally considerate of his subordinates, the release of the waterways to the Americans was too much even for Brock. Now Sheaffe appeared nervous, patting down some grass with his boot while waiting for a reaction from Brock's perusal of the reports. Sheaffe took the page offered him by Brock and, without reading it, tucked it under his arm.

"I've seen it, sir, I'm sorry." A proud and formal man, Sheaffe hung his head, the blame for the armistice weighing on his shoulders. The wind had dishevelled his grey hair and with one hand he pushed it back in place, anticipating another drubbing. He brought himself up almost to attention as Brock began to speak.

"It's not your fault, Roger. You only followed orders from Montreal.

I understand." The time for recriminations had passed, and Brock was aware that Sheaffe had not acted alone. "Others should have known better, but I doubt they even stop to consider Upper Canada's interests. Thank God that Dearborn cancelled the damn thing."

"I'll bet the Van Rensselaers are furious, eh?" Macdonell added. "Their own higher-ups, working against them ... sort of like us." Then everyone there saw the irony of it and laughed. "But that is just the bad news, sir. I do carry something that will cheer you." Macdonell handed another document to Brock.

Three hundred Mohawk Indians had arrived in Queenston while another two hundred were currently on the way with Chief John Norton. "It's about time these Mohawks came on side. Five hundred will do nicely. When Norton gets here, bring him straight to see me," Brock ordered. His force was building. He had recalled all the militia and sent for the 3rd York Regiment.

"But read on, sir. That's not all," Macdonell urged.

The bottom half of the page reported that six companies of the 49th Foot, officers and men from Brock's old regiment, were on their way by water to Fort George under the command of Captains James Dennis and John Williams. These regulars would be well trained, disciplined, and reliable.

Brock made a fist, looking up at the sky, and punched the air. "These men are good officers." He twice tapped the page where their names appeared. "Put their two companies at Queenston, where we're weakest. The others can go to Fort Erie. I don't want the Americans turning our flank."

"Speak of the devils, sir," Sheaffe said.

Marching across the open ground toward Brock appeared two figures in black capes that flapped in the wind. Underneath his cape, each man wore a red jacket with white cross-belt and a red sash. The pair strode with the type of confidence that Brock recognized immediately. He pursed his lips in a grin as they came to an abrupt halt, staring straight ahead, and snapped a salute.

"Captain Dennis and Captain Williams reporting, sir."

"How did the likes of you two get past the guards, and where on earth did you get those flashy capes?" Brock grabbed hold of Dennis's cape, turned it over, and rubbed the smooth lining between his fingers. "Are they silk-lined?"

"We told the gate we were all the way from Holland with a message for His Majesty the King, sir." Captain Dennis laughed and accepted Brock's hand. "Do you really want to know how I got these?" Dennis held out the edge of his cape.

Brock shook his head. "Perhaps it's better that I don't know, then I won't have to arrest the pair of you." He laughed. "I can't tell you how good it is right now to see old friends. And I'm in great need of some competent officers."

Captain Williams then spoke out, reminding Brock of the time when they were lieutenants together in Holland. "The lead was raining down on us like pellets in a thunderstorm. They knocked you down in that battle." Williams laughed. "Remember, the spent bullet that caught in your clothing."

"My silk cravat saved my life, but that ball bruised me like a hammer to the chest." Brock rubbed his breastbone, reliving the pain. "They nearly killed you, Dennis." He slapped the man on the back.

"Yes, they did at that, sir. I thought I was done for." Dennis's face became serious as he thought back to his wound. "Never mind, sir, none of us are so foolish as we were in the old days, right?"

"Let's hope not," Brock replied.

"When do we start thrashing them, sir?" Williams asked. "My men are anxious to get this over with."

"I firmly believe that I could at this moment sweep everything before me from Niagara to Buffalo." Brock turned his gaze toward the Niagara River.

"That's what I wanted to hear," Dennis said, pulling in his cape from the tug of the wind. "So, tomorrow, next week — when do we attack?"

Brock let out a sigh. "Gentlemen, I'm afraid I have orders from Governor General Prevost that, even with the armistice ended, prevent us from doing anything that might be considered offensive to the Americans." He looked up at the scudding clouds to hide his embarrassment at the situation over which he commanded.

"You're pulling my leg, sir." Dennis laughed, but Brock didn't laugh along with him. The man looked to Sheaffe, who with pressed lips shook his head. Dennis lost his smile. "This is too dangerous. What are we supposed to do, sir, just sit here and wait to be killed?"

"Lieutenant Colonel Macdonell here" — Brock shaped his hand into an imaginary pistol and fired at Macdonell — "assured me that once the armistice was over, the Americans would attack us in mid-October —"

"Or sooner, sir," Macdonell interjected. "But as you will recall, it was just a rough guess."

"They've been resupplied by water. Therefore, we can assume they're training every available day. Today's September 10, so I'm sure the pressure over there is building for a battle," Brock continued. "Ever been to Queenston Heights? Come with me and I'll show you to your new quarters. It'll be like old times."

"How many days do we have to wait?" Williams persisted, his cloak rippling in the wind.

"Less than forty-five is my guess," Macdonell replied.

"Better sooner than later," Dennis said.

Then Brock heard the crack of muskets.

Sergeant Nathaniel King and Private Josiah Green, both of the U.S. Twenty Third Regiment of Infantry, sat on a log some three hundred yards south of Fort Niagara, cradling their muskets. Since the armistice had ended a few days before, they were part of an American patrol that bored themselves rigid by keeping watch on the west bank of the Niagara River for any signs of a British invasion. King stared across from the river's edge as the wind whipped the rolling white caps and pushed away the mid-September heat.

His less witty and easily offended friend, Oliver Ambler, marched over to join him and Green. Ambler sat down, removed his hat, and wiped the sweat from his brow with the back of one hand before resting his musket down by his side. He took out a carrot from inside his jacket and his teeth crunched down on it.

Not far south from Fort George, a British patrol appeared on the opposite side and called out across the water. The words were lost to a gust of wind, but the accent was clear and the tone meant that something nasty had been said. King poked Green in the side with his elbow as if to say, "Play along."

"Oliver, did those rogues across the way say something about your mother? I didn't catch the name. Was it M ... Ma ...?" King asked.

"Gweneth? They didn't say Gweneth," Ambler replied.

"They did too, because I heard them," Green said. "Listen to the bastards. We should shoot the lot of them."

The British called across again, offering a soldier's salute with their middle fingers. The group of four strong was soon joined by another four redcoats, who added their insults to more shouting that was followed by bouts of laughter. This time they gestured straight up with their muskets, instead of their fingers, and then all fell backward together on the ground, howling in laughter.

"That was clear as a bell. Surely you heard it?" King asked. "'Gweneth, why don't you —'?"

"Don't say it, King. Don't say a thing about my mother." Ambler flushed red and cupped a hand around his ear.

"But how do they know her name? Do you happen to know those redcoats?" Green persisted. "Listen, there they go again, 'Gweneth, why don't —'"

"Shut your mouth, Josiah. I don't know how they would know my mother." Ambler reached for his musket and then opened the cartridge pouch hanging on his right hip. "But I know what redcoats are like and I can see them laughing."

The British patrol was back on its feet and yelled in unison, "Bloody cowards." The wind had died, and the words carried clearly across the water toward the three soldiers of the Twenty Third.

"You must have heard them call you a bloody coward. Even your stuffed ears picked that out." King said. Then he realized that the barb was meant for him too — and for all Americans.

They were the only words uttered that reached clearly across the river that day, and it bothered King almost as much as it did Ambler. For days the regular army had been urging action, but the Van Rensselaers had declined, sure that the British were planning an invasion.

The redcoats again did their trick of raising their muskets before they collapsed over backward.

"They called us cowards, Nathaniel!" Green complained to his sergeant.

The crack of a musket close to King's head was like a slap to the ear. Both he and Green leapt in the air at the unexpected sound. King snapped his head around to see gun smoke drifting past Ambler's face. The man was already reloading by the time he and Green decided to join him in blasting away. They jerked up their muskets and fired quickly, the sound echoing upriver, bouncing between the two forts.

"Take cover behind the trees," King shouted.

The shore was spotted with maples, where he hid while reloading. Ambler remained standing in the open, legs apart as he fired again. This time the redcoats fired back, their lead balls clipping the maple leaves overhead, but coming nowhere close to their intended targets. They had fired high, hoping the balls would arc downwards to kill when they reached the far side of the river. King crouched low, praying that a stray ball wouldn't find him.

Lieutenant Colonel Fenwick heard the sound of musket fire and decided to investigate. As he rode his horse at a slow trot through the gates of Fort Niagara, in his right hand he clutched a flask from which he took a gulp, before tucking it inside his left breast pocket. Then he spurred his mount into a gallop.

A few minutes later, he spotted King and Green jumping out from behind some maples to shoot, then jumping back to safety. Private Ambler simply stood out in the open and continued to fire.

Before Fenwick could say a word, Lieutenant Colonel Solomon van Rensselaer galloped to a halt beside him and demanded to know what caused the commotion. Seconds later, he was joined by young Captain Wool, reining in his horse while still holding on to his hat.

"They were shouting about my mother, sir," Ambler said.

"Who fired first?" Van Rensselaer asked.

There was silence as the three soldiers stared at one another. Before Ambler could sink them by telling the truth, King answered, "We was on patrol and they fired at Ambler, sir, and we returned fire. Seemed like the right thing to do."

"Is that what really happened, Ambler?" Wool inquired.

Fenwick swayed in his saddle, the flask pressing against his chest under his jacket. He watched Ambler stare down at his boots, not wanting to lie. Across the water, the redcoats were busy reloading.

"When I arrived, sir, the redcoats had just fired, then all of them fell over backward, laughing," Fenwick said. "Our men simply returned fire." He studied the far bank and noticed the enemy patrol ramming their charges home, so he spurred his horse into cover behind a stout maple.

"They called us cowards, sir," King said, watching the redcoats raise their muskets and point. He stepped sideways behind his tree and nodded his head to the opposite bank.

Fenwick followed the direction of King's nod across the water where the redcoats raised their muskets in preparation for volley fire.

"Sir, we had best guard ourselves. Take a look yonder." He pointed to the enemy just as their muskets banged out in unison. Some of the balls shattered a branch overhead but otherwise caused no damage.

Van Renssellaer jerked his head upward at the sound of the blast as puffs of smoke rose from the British weapons. The enemy pointed their muskets vertically, raising them up over their heads as if in a giant one-finger salute, shouting, "Cowards" before they proceeded to topple backward to the ground again, laughing wildly. Someone on the other side obviously thought they were being very funny.

"You see, sir, we couldn't just do nothing," King said. "'Cause we're not cowards, are we, sir?"

"You men will cease fire, immediately! Of course you're not cowards, but I'll not have any of us taking random shots at the other side willy-nilly. Captain Wool, see to it that this type of behaviour ends," Van Rensselaer ordered. "You men get back to your patrol. And no more shooting."

"When are we going to attack, sir? Everyone is asking, now that the armistice is over," King asked.

"When we're good and ready," Wool interjected from horseback. "Get moving, now." He followed the men as they marched back toward the fort.

The redcoats were reloading when three British officers appeared among them on horseback. Fenwick lingered behind his tree and took another sip from his flask before tucking it under his jacket again. His horse then stepped up beside Van Rensselaer's and Fenwick watched as one of the British officers issued orders and pointed. The soldiers shouldered arms, as if on a drill square, and marched away.

"You may have stopped our boys firing a touch too soon." Fenwick grinned. "I believe we are looking at Major General Isaac Brock. They might have got in a lucky shot."

The younger Van Rensselaer studied the opposite bank. "We don't take potshots at each other," he said sharply. "Are you much drunk, sir?"

"Not in the least."

"Good, then you won't mind taking the roof off the Castle and hauling up the nine-pounders and a howitzer. When the fighting starts, I want to pour shot into Fort George, and that's the highest spot for a battery."

Fenwick considered the task. The oldest building in the interior of North America, the Castle guarded the river approach from inside Fort Niagara. Any deconstruction of it would be heavy work.

"Can it take the pounding it will receive when the British return fire, sir?"

"It'll have to," Solomon replied quickly.

He was obviously unconcerned about the dangers to the soldiers who would man the battery, Fenwick guessed. As he looked back toward the fort to study the Castle, a few drops of rain touched his face and he felt the wind pick up speed. Originally constructed by the French eighty-five years previously, to resist Iroquois attacks, the Castle resembled a tall, stone trading house.

"How soon will you need the battery, sir?"

"You're asking me when I will give the order for battle. Well, I can't tell you when either the British will attack or when we will attack them, but I can tell you for sure that we'll have one hell of a hard time without more ammunition."

"Sitting around makes soldiers anxious, sir. We need to do something if only to relieve the tension," Fenwick said. "The regulars want to start fighting now, and the militiamen are threatening to go home if we don't attack soon."

"Do you not think I know that?" Van Rensselaer said sharply. "The militia is still untrained, and the army is uncoordinated. Quartermaster Porter had damn well better deliver our supplies, otherwise we'll be using our muskets merely as clubs."

"How are you feeling, sir? Got over the ague?"

"If this weather doesn't improve, I'll stay sick, but the truth is that I'm feeling much better today, thank you."

"The officers know we can't attack without you, sir … that you're the sharp end of the Van Rensselaer stick. We all wish you well."

"Just get that battery built on top of the Castle; we may need it sooner than you think. And Fenwick, stay off the drink." Solomon reached up to grip his hat and then spurred his horse away.

War, sooner than you think. A stiff drink would go well now. Fenwick glanced at a blackening sky, slid his hand back inside his jacket, and turned his horse in the direction of Fort Niagara.

9

. . . . . .

THE OLD ENGLISHMAN FOSTER had been exactly right. His ranch was investigated four times during the next ten days while Westlake and his party hid in the hills. The other good thing about hiding out there was the food that Mrs. Foster left for them regularly at the foot of the fence post. As he feasted on mutton, rabbit, peaches, and a host of vegetables, Parrish longed to stay on another day just for the meals.

"Have you noticed how those militia patrols always visit around mealtimes?" Simpson remarked. He lay down and pulled a blanket over himself. "Foster doesn't realize it, but he's drawing them to his farmhouse like bees to honey."

Westlake rested the back of his head on a saddle. The sun had dipped below the horizon two hours before, and now a few stars appeared in the northern sky. During the time they remained hidden, he'd thought about Foster and how the man had worked like a slave for his English lord and master. Now he aided runaways in an effort to set himself free, and to strike back at a world that had once enslaved him.

"He knows precisely what he's doing, Mr. Simpson," Westlake replied. "His wife's excellent food acts as a distraction. It's why the militia doesn't bother patrolling farther into these hills. Foster just tells them no one has passed by his ranch and they want to believe him."

"So we have to leave tomorrow?" Parrish asked.

"No militia has appeared for a day back. Time to go." Westlake turned away under his blanket to signal the end of their conversation. He was anxious to begin their journey again with the dawn's first light.

In the cool morning air, Westlake circled his horse south off the road, then through the river and down the Indian path they had crossed on their original approach to the Foster ranch. He resisted the urge to say goodbye to Foster and his wife and instead kept his word by staying well clear of their home. Grey clouds rolled in from the west and Westlake hoped the weather would hold so they could make up for time lost.

Simpson and Parrish urged on their horses to stay close behind him before he gestured for the two men to spread out and keep quiet. He pointed to his eyes, to emphasize the message he had given them before breaking camp. *Keep watch!*

Riding a trail through thick forest for most of that day, they saw no sign of the militia patrol that had inspected the Foster ranch only a couple of days before. Westlake was happy to be back travelling again. Around midday a constant rain started to fall, slowly filling their rutted path with water and turning it to mud. His horse's hooves began to make a sucking sound with every step, and their progress diminished to a sluggish walk.

As the forest encroached farther on the path, a canopy formed overhead that kept the travellers dry while the rain gathered on the leaves above. Westlake edged his horse up the bank and then spurred the animal forward until he found himself in a clearing. Again a memory struck him from a few months previously: an ambush, a musket blast, and death.

He shot up his hand to signal the others to stop. Westlake studied the trees all around, peering through the slanting rain, watching for any unusual movement. He found nothing to give alarm and lowered his arm, yet his heart pounded in his ears. A second quick scan again revealed nothing. At a gesture, his troop urged their horses forward.

In open ground, the wind increased and the rain came down harder. When he tried to keep his head up, the pellets lashed across his face. Through the trees, Westlake glimpsed the outline of a structure some twenty paces into the forest, and spurred his horse in its direction. On a slight rise, a lean-to large enough for at least five men rested against the sheer face of a giant moss-covered boulder. The roof was bark-shingled and a thick breastwork composed of branches formed a semicircle extending ten paces out from the central structure. To sleep in some security, someone had taken great care to protect his temporary home.

Westlake dismounted and crept through the breastworks, approaching the open doorway from one side. Behind him, he heard Simpson and Parrish cock their musket hammers into place. If there were someone inside, he would have to withstand three balls if he expected to overpower the intruders.

Westlake poked his head inside the doorframe and then quickly pulled back. Nothing.

"Perfect." He waved for the others to follow. "We'll camp here and get some sleep."

"Should we not push on till dark?" Simpson asked.

"The advantage of ambush is always with the attacker, Mr. Simpson, and even more so when the prey can't keep his head up high enough to see. Better to go slow and get there alive than push for speed and end up buried in the forest." Westlake glanced at Parrish but saw no change of facial expression there. "Besides, we're unlikely to find better quarters than this further ahead."

"Who's got the first watch?" asked Parrish, who had dismounted and was already unsaddling his horse.

"Mr. Simpson seems eager," Westlake said with a grin, "so give me four hours and then wake me. Parrish, you can sleep through till the morning." He hauled the saddle off his horse and swung it inside the lean-to, to rest on the dead grass within. Beside his saddle, he threw his pack on the ground and unrolled a blanket. "Watch that damn path, Mr. Simpson, and keep your firing pan good and dry under your armpit. Yell if you see anything. Goodnight."

Westlake lay back with his head on the saddle, pulled a blanket over himself, and briefly wondered how Mary was passing her time. Then the coarseness of the wool against his face made him think longingly of the soft quilt that covered his bed back at Maple Hill. Before drifting into sleep, he imagined his family home and in his mind's eye saw every detail of his old bedroom.

The evening rain tapered off into a light drizzle, allowing Simpson and then Westlake himself to stay mostly dry by huddling under the breastwork. At first light, the storm was back in force and the rain drenched the roof of their little home but without too many drops seeping inside. Westlake peered out through the gaps from under the lean-to, watching the sheeting rain waver with the wind.

"Parrish, remain in here and keep watch. You can see the trail well enough during the daylight."

"Shouldn't he go outside to see better?" Simpson protested.

"It's pouring. I'd rather have a healthy Parrish to defend us than a sick one. Besides, it's doubtful anyone's tracking us in this weather," Westlake replied. "And I would also ask you to stop questioning every one of my orders."

"I am the senior here."

"And you've been told to do as I say. End of discussion, Robert." Westlake unrolled the food bundle provided by Mrs. Foster and spread it on the ground between them. Several carrots and three fresh tomatoes, three loaves of bread, an equal number of cheese chunks, and an entire cooked chicken. He looked up into Simpson's eager face and raised his own eyebrows at the feast, then broke one loaf into three and gave each man a portion of cheese and a large piece of chicken.

Parrish ate his meal staring out at a forest dripping with the rain. Simpson washed his down with regular swigs from his canteen, while with every bite Westlake thought of home-cooked meals.

"As long as the storm holds its strength, we'll camp here. We wouldn't make much progress in the mud anyway." Westlake glanced at Simpson, expecting an objection, but none came. "We might as well get some sleep meanwhile. We've a long way to go once it clears."

"Why did you volunteer for this mission, Mr. Westlake?" Simpson asked. "General Brock would not have forced you to go." Westlake's face stiffened before Simpson added, "I mean, I know why I'm here, but I don't understand why you are if you could've gone back to York."

The question came as a surprise. What difference did it make to him? Westlake wondered. Parrish turned round, gave Simpson a glance, and then turned away with a shake of his head.

In truth, Westlake had asked himself that same question, but he was not sure of the answer. In the previous twelve months, he had travelled more than two thousand miles, twice to the heart of the continent and back again, and now he would have much preferred to be at home on Maple Hill with Mary. But he had volunteered, nonetheless.

"Why does anyone choose to leave home? You say you know why you're here, so tell us," Westlake suggested before biting down on his chicken.

"Apart from one of us needing to speak German, I'm simply following my orders. I want promotion and the best way to get it is by undertaking successful missions, even if I have to dress like a ragamuffin." With his mouth stuffed full of food, Simpson spread his arms out as if to say, *"See this; I look pathetic."*

"Following orders doesn't explain why you're here, in North America, risking your life when your family is safe back in England," Westlake said.

"My father is English, but my mother is German, connected to the House of Hanover. She is a distant third cousin to the King, so that's why you have these rumours in the ranks that I've influence at the royal court. Don't think I don't know about them, Parrish." Simpson washed down another mouthful with a swig from his canteen.

Parrish turned away again and shrugged. It was true about such rumours, but he wasn't going to admit it to the likes of Simpson.

"My mother would have me attend high-society gatherings in London to find a bride and my father thinks I'm a useless sissy. I'll show them both wrong." Simpson pulled on his cuff and raised his chin.

Westlake wondered if the fellow's father was close to the truth but kept such thoughts to himself.

"Already I've ridden at the head of a column with General Brock and commanded his longboat on Lake Erie," Simpson continued proudly. "Bloody thing nearly sank during the storm. We got stuck on a sandbar and the general jumped into the water with the rest of us to push the damn vessel off. Do you know he gave each man a ration from his personal liquor case?"

Westlake had indeed heard the story of the boat and even the rations. It had spread like wildfire through the ranks. As a result, the men from Brock's longboat considered themselves a special group, the chosen few. Since that day, General Brock's personal status had soared to the Olympian heights of some godlike figure. It was unheard of for a major general to share his liquor supply with common soldiers and he was loved for it.

"You have still not said why you are here, Mr. Westlake," Simpson persisted.

"To make a difference. Try my best. Nothing so deep as proving my father wrong or showing my mother anything." Westlake knew this was a lie; he'd worked for more than a year to redeem himself in the eyes of his parents and General Brock. Now, when he looked in the mirror, he was no longer ashamed of being thrown out of school for displaying violent behaviour. But since then his ambitions had grown beyond those of a young adult. "I wish to defend my home and be of assistance to General Brock."

Westlake grinned and poked Parrish in the ribs. "So tell us why you are here, Mr. Silence."

"Beats highway robbery, which is what we was doing before we joined the army. Me brother and me thought if we had uniforms, we'd be free of hardship." Parrish shrugged. "Ain't that the dumbest idea for two thieves? So it was either this secret agent business or military prison, as I recall. After Mackinac and Detroit, the general cleared me of the prison sentence and now he's given me the one job of keeping you alive." Parrish laughed and nudged Westlake in return.

"Besides, I'm saving up to be a farmer. When I've done my seven years, I'll have meself some money and land from the army. Only five bloody years to go and I'll have me one of those big, soft farmer beds too. S'truth, I was gobsmacked to be sleeping in that bed back at your family's home on Maple Hill."

The conversation ended, Westlake lay back on his saddle pillow. At intervals the wind gusted to lift and smack the birchbark shingles, making sleep difficult. As Westlake dozed, he found himself thinking of Mary and of marriage. He wasn't sure at all that marriage was for him. *Why was I stupid enough to ask her? She said yes so fast. Was getting wed all that young girls thought about?*

He rolled on to his side and listened to the slashing rain, aware that they were losing too much time and had to get moving again. As soon as the weather changed for the better, the race to rescue Alexander the Great would begin again in earnest.

The rain continued for another day but stopped at last sometime during the third night. With its end returned the heat, and by first light, as the trio passed out through the breastworks, the ground was giving up its dampness to form a thin mist that hung in the air. Westlake turned around in the saddle for a last look at their little home, happy they were finally on their way.

They travelled straight south, single file, along a pathway that in places was at least three inches under water. Shafts of sunlight stabbed through the mist to reach a drenched forest floor. Westlake ordered the two men to ride twenty-five paces apart. Where possible, he shifted his own horse to wherever it was dry, on higher ground beside the trail. At one point, the path dissected a large clearing where the grass grew tall before a forest of thick cedar and pine closed the circle around them. He felt the wind on his cheek as he watched the mist wavering above the tips of the long grass.

Gradually the wind lifted the mist to reveal the far end of the clearing crowded with Indians. Westlake squinted, not believing his eyes. His stomach clenched and he gripped his reins tight. There were at least a hundred warriors blocking his path. They stared, perfectly still, six of them mounted and the rest on foot.

Painted for war in streaks of black and white clay, one warrior's head was completely shaved and stained red while another's scalp was bare except for a four-inch-wide tuft of black hair running from his forehead to the nape of his neck. Westlake recognized this immediately as a war party because in addition to the war paint, each man carried weapons — muskets, bows, war clubs, and tomahawks. His heart beat faster and his throat tightened. He pulled in his reins and held up a hand for Simpson and Parrish to halt likewise.

One warrior dismounted, keeping the reins of his horse in hand. He walked forward and stopped well in front of Westlake. Westlake dismounted to talk with the man who was almost as tall as he and whose face was painted with two red stripes across each cheek. This warrior, who had a neck like an ox, kept his distance.

"Who are you are?" he demanded in perfect English. Other Indians pressed forward to listen but stayed a good ten paces back, gradually forming a circle around the two men.

"We trade for furs and now travel south," Westlake replied.

"You use a path well worn by our warriors over many seasons."

Simpson rode forward and declared from his mount, "Welcome."

Westlake looked up at him and frowned. Several warriors crept closer, one reaching for the reins of Simpson's horse while two other Indians began walking Parrish's animal forward too. They held on to either side of the bridle while Parrish kept a tight hold on the reins and also those of their fourth horse. One Indian patted the horse's leg as if judging its strength, but the animal nervously sidestepped, knocking him over.

"We thank you for the use of your path." Westlake then pointed to the assembled natives behind. "Which people are you?"

"Not all our warriors have horses, and you have more than you need." The spokesman gestured to the pack-horse.

Westlake considered an appropriate response, but before he could speak, Simpson blurted out, "This is Jonathan Westlake, who is the friend of Tecumseh."

Warriors had surrounded Simpson's horse, standing directly to the back of Westlake.

"I am Chief Brown Jacket," the leading man declared. "We are from many tribes, Shawnee, Wyandotte, and others, warriors who do not fight beside Tecumseh. We here are just one hundred of almost two thousand strong, and we fight alongside the bluecoats."

A warrior stepped forward beside the chief. "I know this man; he challenged us in Detroit. He is our enemy." Black feathers hung from leather straps tied around his biceps, and on his face were painted black stripes running from cheeks to chin. During his time with the

Shawnee, Westlake had learned such war paint was just for show, but it unnerved him all the same.

"You are Kawika, friend of Paxinos," observed Westlake, who had met this young Indian brave before. "I, too, am friend of Paxinos. Do you let the American war divide Shawnee friends?" he asked.

"But you are not Shawnee. You are my enemy and we want your horses." Kawika took another step forward, a hand poised on the tomahawk that rested in his belt. As he whispered in the leader's ear, the chief considered his words and studied Westlake closely.

"I am told you have killed many men," Brown Jacket said. "But we need your horses. There are too many of us for you to kill so give us your horses and you may live to travel south."

From his horse, Simpson cleared his throat to speak. Westlake realized they could all die if Simpson said something foolish. At Westlake's back, a warrior stood between him and Simpson's horse. He turned to order Simpson to be quiet but looked up to see Simpson's eyes suddenly widen even as his mouth opened.

Westlake dived for the ground as Kawika tumbled over the top of him with his tomahawk slashing forward. It struck the warrior behind Westlake full in the chest and the man bellowed in surprise as he collapsed. Not pausing for an instant, Westlake sprung off the ground, reaching for the knife strapped to his boot. Before Kawika could move farther, the knife's edge was pressing under the Indian's throat. Kawika stood absolutely still, his neck stretching backward as Westlake gripped him from behind.

"Yes, I have killed many men, all white and never an Indian — until today, if you force me," Westlake declared angrily. His jaw clenched and he breathed hard. The knife pressed against Kawika's skin, drew a tiny drop of blood, and forced him to his toes. "Choose," Westlake shouted at the chief. "We meant you no harm. Let us pass ... with our horses ... or this man dies and so will you."

The chief staggered backward and held up both hands. The other warriors in the circle stepped away with their chief, leaving Westlake's party and Kawika alone in the centre.

"Choose now!" Westlake demanded. "Your decision!"

"You may pass unharmed. You have my word."

"Simpson, fetch me my horse. Parrish, ride over to the far edge of the clearing with the other horse. You will follow him, Simpson." Westlake held the knife tight to Kawika's throat, where blood was dripping on the blade.

"But, sir," Parrish protested, "I promised I wouldn't leave you."

"Do as you're ordered, damn you," Westlake hollered. "Once I'm in the saddle again, ease your way south through the trees."

The Indians parted to let the horses step their way through. Westlake waited until Parrish and Simpson were well clear and on their way. He took one step away behind Kawika, withdrew the knife from his throat, and, with a foot placed against his back, pushed the man forward. He had one foot in the stirrup, and leapt in the saddle, before Kawika stumbled to the ground.

Westlake spurred his horse and trotted toward Simpson and Parrish. His back was turned and this was the moment he feared most. He prayed the chief's word would last until he reached the trees.

As soon as he got there, instinctively he peered back to see if he was being followed. He heard whoops and screams. In a matter of seconds, the angry warriors were charging after them.

"Ride for your lives and don't stop for anything. Now go!"

Westlake spurred his horse to one side of the path where the animal could gain better footing. Immediately, an arrow shot passed him, thudding into nearby a tree. Then others whizzed overhead or arched into the ground beside him. He rode on with his head down, hunched over, as if to make himself smaller.

The others followed at a gallop and even Parrish, who struggled with the extra horse, managed to stay well ahead of the warriors pursuing them on foot. Only one Indian followed on horse, and he hung back toward the rear of the attacking warriors.

Westlake glanced over his shoulder to see the Indians falling behind. Suddenly there were no more arrows, and after ten more minutes of hard riding, Westlake judged that he and his men were safe. He slowed his mount to a trot, took a deep breath, and waited for the others to catch up.

"Great Scot, I thought the Indians were meant to be on our side," Simpson complained from behind.

"Every tribe has its dissenters. In that, the natives are no different from the British and Americans," Westlake replied.

"But some of them were Shawnee. And what about Tecumseh? Stealing horses is a bit much," Simpson protested.

"We slept in their shelter, Mr. Simpson," Westlake argued. "And we've used their path during a time of war. They have every right to payment. And next time we meet anyone, hostile or otherwise, keep your mouth shut," he ordered.

"How did you see that tomahawk with your back turned?" Parrish asked.

Westlake swung round quickly in his saddle to make sure that the warriors were not still following. The first few drops of a light rain hit his cheek again, and looking up at the sky he swore. "Mr. Simpson's eyes grew to the size of apples so I knew there was trouble behind me." Westlake shook his head and grimaced, his heart still pounding in ears. "But it was close, eh? I was lucky."

"Too damn close, if you ask me," Parrish said. "Blimey, look what I found." He tugged free an arrow that had lodged itself in his saddle-bag and held it in the air. "Like I said, Too damn close."

"You can bet they're still coming," Westlake interjected. "We'd better get on and find our German friends." He again spurred his horse and glanced back for a final time. Just trees, and the wind, and a rain as fine as mist.

10

......

GENERAL BROCK scanned the letter to his brother before signing. To save his brothers from financial ruin, he would offer them all he earned. The war demanded that family problems back home be resolved quickly.

> "...You know the position to which I am lately raised. It will enable me to give up the whole of my salary, £1000 yearly, and I shall enclose a power of attorney to enable you to receive it — do with it what justice demands — pay as fast as you receive, unless indeed want among any of you call for aid ... "

Stave off the creditors and buy time, he hoped, as he signed and sealed the letter.

Captain Edward Nelles, personal aide to General Brock, knocked on the door and opened it wide enough to squeeze through his narrow face. "The guest you've been expecting is waiting outside, sir. May I bring him in?"

In his spartan office, decorated only by the Union flag on a pole, Brock looked up from the maps spread on his desk and nodded. Nelles closed the door.

General Sheaffe, second-in-command of all armed forces in Upper Canada, had waited for him to finish his writing and now jabbed one map with the tip of his finger to a spot in Newark, the town lying adjacent to Fort George. "We have no space remaining in the fort, so incoming supplies are stored here, sir, near the town." He brushed back his grey hair. "Also, the newly arrived regiments are camped in fields here and here, guarding the supplies." His Roman-like features suggested the discipline of a hard officer comfortable with the responsibilities of command.

Brock considered for a moment. "We'll greet our guest and then go have a look for ourselves. I've been cooped up in this office far too long. We're up around two thousand men, I'd say. Time for me to see what's going on."

Another tap on the door, and Nelles escorted Chief John Norton into the major general's office. The new arrival wore a blood-red sash, a green scarf wrapped around his neck, and a cream-coloured headband drawing up his hair to reveal a large forehead. His narrow features boasted thick eyebrows, long sideburns, and a full mouth that broke into a grin on seeing Brock. Two loop earrings swung from each earlobe as he stepped forward.

Brock already knew a great deal about his visitor. Born to a Cherokee father and a Scottish mother, Norton had been schooled in Scotland. He had since been a soldier, a teacher, and even a fur trader. By using his language skills, he'd managed to ingratiate himself with the Iroquois living close by on the Grand River.

"Well, what have you got to say for yourself?" Brock demanded, remaining seated.

"The Six Nations send ye their congratulations on your great victory at Detroit, sir," Norton replied in his Scottish accent.

"Little thanks to your people. Indeed, as I recall, sixty warriors was the limit of your commitment to assist me at Detroit. I hope you'll be making a better effort this time."

"For us to fight beside the British means that we must contend with our own people who side with the Americans, sir. And if the British should lose again, King George may forget the Iroquois nations and leave us to the mercy of our enemies."

"Damn your skin, Norton, you're either with me or you're not." Brock finally rose from his chair, his face turning crimson against his white shirt. Neutrality was almost treason, as far as he was concerned.

"Aye, *we were with you*. Sixty were sent when many other tribes were reluctant to choose sides."

Brock nodded, acknowledging this was true. When he had left the Grand River reservation, four months previously, and before his triumph at Detroit, the Iroquois had decided to assist him in the battle to come. Perhaps just choosing to support the British side was the most he could have expected. It was victory enough. That thought calmed him and he sat back down.

"This time I've brought three hundred warriors, with two hundred more coming soon. When do we invade the United States?" Norton eyes cut to Sheaffe, then to Nelles, and finally moved back to Brock.

A momentary silence descended on the room. Norton offered Brock all he hoped for.

"That's better, my man!" Brock jumped up from his desk, striding round to take hold of Norton's hand. "No more waffling, eh."

"Good show," Sheaffe added and also shook Norton's hand.

"What would you have us do now?" Norton asked.

"Show yourselves along the shore to our enemy and scream a lot," Brock replied with a grin.

"Scream, sir?"

"It scares the hell out of the Americans — the rest of us too, for that matter." Brock stroked his chin. "Last month, at the Brownstown River, Tecumseh won a marvellous victory against ten-to-one odds because his warriors were screaming like devils," he continued. "The Americans ran like rabbits. So, yes, I want you to send all your warriors down to the riverbank and scream. I'll bet half their troops won't cross the river out of sheer fright." He laughed.

"My men will need food, sir."

"General Sheaffe and I are off to inspect supplies. Would you like to join us? I'll leave the food organization to your care." Brock glanced at Sheaffe, who nodded in return.

"Consider it already done, sir," Sheaffe declared.

"Thank ye, sir." Norton bowed.

"Captain Nelles will also join us," Brock ordered.

Nelles held open the door and stepped to one side as the other men filed through.

After a short ride, Brock and his party of three came to the edge of Butler's Field, where he held up his hand to halt them. "Keep your horses back for a moment, gentlemen. I want to see this." He peered through a thick line of cedars to see down a gentle slope where, some thirty yards away, the Coloured Company milled about in the mid-September heat. A few wore faded redcoats but, except for their leather cross-belts, most were dressed in homespun civilian clothes.

Two tables stood side by side, one laden with long boxes and on the other a mound of leather pouches. Every few moments, a man would carelessly saunter too close to a table, only to be driven away by a stout sergeant who seemed to enjoy jabbing them with the point of his hardwood staff. The man chuckled to himself each time the staff caused some pain.

Brock watched an officer on horseback approach the circle of men. "Fall in. Form a single line to the right of the first table." Lieutenant James Cooper drew his sword and pointed down the field. "Welcome to Butler's Field, gentlemen." He swung his sword back toward the sergeant who now sat behind the first table and winked uncontrollably a half-dozen times. "Sergeant Puffer there has brought us some presents from General Brock. Today, the Coloured Company is to receive muskets."

Brock heard a cheer and some of the men locked arms while their friends clapped hands before Cooper shouted to them, "Back in line." Brock grinned at their enthusiasm and waited to see the drill begin.

Luther couldn't believe what he had just heard. Standing second in line, he watched the lid of the first box of muskets pop open after the nails holding it shut were pried lose. Sergeant Puffer snatched up a musket, handed it to the man in front of Luther, and moved over to the second box, where he withdrew a bayonet. Then it was Luther's own turn.

"Make your mark here." Puffer pointed a dirty finger to the spot on a page that Luther marked with an L. "Know your letters, do ye? Don't get above yourself, or I'll have to hurt you good." Puffer winked and handed Luther a musket and bayonet. "Grab your cartridge pouch now and try not to shoot yourself ... or me." Puffer winked again, then shook his head. "Arming slaves, this is going to go bad."

"What's that, Sergeant?" Cooper demanded.

Puffer's eye closed again in an involuntary wink. "I said he looks a right good lad — yes, a good lad, sir."

"Just attend to your duties, and keep quiet."

"Sir." Puffer winked once more.

Luther attached the bayonet to his left hip and the cartridge pouch to his right hip, just the same as he'd seen done by regular soldiers. He rested the musket on his shoulder gently, as if it would break. His eyes widened, lifting his eyebrows, and he smiled, showing all his teeth, until his cheeks ached. His own musket. Finally.

Heavier than he had guessed and smoother too, Luther slid his hand down the barrel. Already excited, he imagined himself firing, and hoped he didn't have long to wait. He stroked the musket again.

Luther stood and watched the others receive their weapons, reacting much the same as himself. Muskets were caressed as if they were newborn children. He aimed his own across the hundred-yard clearing of tree stumps surrounded by thick forest and underbrush. That morning, they had marched only a mile from Fort George, yet with no one in sight. Luther leaned on his musket and called out, "Where are our targets, Cap'n Dick?" But before Pierpoint could answer, Lieutenant Cooper began on his lesson.

"Whether with General Wellington's army in Spain or General Brock's army on the banks of the Niagara River, you do not aim a musket so much as you point it, and with our mass volley, together we hope you'll hit something." Cooper studied Luther's face for some sign of understanding but found none. His eyes scanned the blank faces of the other men and he proceeded to explain.

"I don't have to remind you that almost everyone in this man's army has doubts about whether former slaves can fight." Cooper motioned with his sword toward the river and the American shore. "A battle is coming and the only way to convince white soldiers that

Africans aren't stupid, and to prove they can count on you when the fighting starts, is to show 'em. Fire three rounds per minute and they'll love you like brothers — so we'll do the prime-and-load drill until you can do it with your eyes closed."

Cooper ordered sharply, "Form two ranks."

The men shuffled into place.

"Tenshun! Come on, dress the line. Elbow to elbow. That's better!" Cooper tapped his left shoulder with the flat of his sword.

Luther snapped to attention and glanced to his side to see that everyone else stood in line. He had been drilled with a pitchfork and watched the prime-and-load drill a hundred times, but now that he had a real musket in his hands, his palms were sweating and he swayed a little in anticipation of the first few orders.

"Now, Cap'n Dick has demonstrated this drill to you many times, but can you do it for yourselves? We're going to find out. Muskets at half-cock, pans closed. Prepare to load!" Cooper ordered.

Twenty-four men brought their weapons across their chests and opened the musket pan.

"Handle cartridge," Lieutenant Cooper ordered.

Luther withdrew a paper cartridge from a small box that hung on a leather strap over his left shoulder, resting against his right hip. He bit off the cartridge's end.

"Prime!"

He poured a small amount of powder into his firing pan and snapped shut the frizzen to cover it.

"Cast about!"

Luther brought the musket vertical to rest on its butt and then stared down the line. He poured the balance of the powder, the ball, and its paper casing, down the barrel of the musket and listened for the next order. Everyone appeared in position. In front of him, Pierpoint was poised and ready, standing still, waiting for the next command.

"Draw ramrod."

Luther slid the ramrod out from the under the musket and tucked it just inside his barrel, waiting for the next command.

"Ram down cartridge."

He slid the ramrod twice down the bore, to jam the cartridge in. Too busy to watch others, he knew that they were out of sync just by what he could hear. The former Rangers in the front rank finished ahead of the rear rank on every motion, and Luther panicked as he tried to keep up.

"Return ramrod." Cooper seemed to be going faster. "Shoulder arms!"

He snapped the musket to his shoulder, inclined vertically to his body.

"Front rank and rear ranks, make ready!"

Pierpoint raised his musket and pulled the hammer to full cock. The man was ready to fire and glanced down the line. Luther followed his eyes.

"Front rank, present!"

The front rank consisting of older, more experienced soldiers pointed their muskets downrange, but when Luther peered across his shoulder, he saw the rear rank still fumbling.

"Fire!" Cooper shouted.

Pierpoint pulled his trigger, and like most of the others in line, his musket crashed out in flame, spitting the ball downrange. Luther glanced at the man directly beside Pierpoint because no sound had emerged from his musket except a distinct click when the hammer flicked forward. One in five muskets usually misfired and the percentage got worse on rainy days.

"Rear rank … my God, rear rank, we're all going to die." Cooper shook his head and sheathed his sword. Luther's heart sank, knowing the new recruits' lack of training was all too evident.

One man had dropped his cartridge, another fumbled on the ground for his ramrod, and Luther was horrified to find that in his panic to shoulder arms promptly, he'd left his own ramrod inserted down the barrel. He withdrew it quickly, locked it in place under the barrel, and returned the musket to his shoulder.

Cooper approached to scrutinize him up and down. "Are you finally ready, young man?"

Luther stood to attention and nodded. "Sir."

"Rear rank … make ready!

"Present!"

"Fire!"

As Luther pulled the trigger, his musket fired and recoiled hard into his shoulder, the pain instant and sharp. He took an unbalanced step backward and moaned out loud, surprised at its fierce kick. The breeze blew the smoke of the discharge directly back into his face. He turned his head away but not before inhaling the acrid taste of burnt gunpowder. Other men in his rank were busy coughing and rubbing their shoulders.

The front rank had fired within thirty-five seconds of receiving the first command — not bad on their first attempt that day, according to Cooper. Now he suggested a plan to fix the rear rank. The men would stand side by side with their counterpart in the front rank and imitate all their motions until they had it right.

Pierpoint worked with Luther. Thirty times in as many minutes, they repeated the prime-and-load drill until Luther could do it on his own without Pierpoint calling out any commands. Yet the first time Lieutenant Cooper shouted the orders, Luther's clumsiness returned, and he dropped his musket on the initial command.

"This won't do at all. Is there anything you're good at, young man?" Cooper asked.

Luther recognized the threat here. Cooper could dismiss him from the company to dig ditches or to be assigned to other menial work. "I want to fight, sir," Luther pleaded. "I'll get it right."

"Will you, indeed? You can march fine; I give you that. I'll let you fight when the time comes, but at the moment you're breaking up our firing line. You need to train separately."

"He's a tinsmith by trade, sir," Pierpoint said, "but he's very keen to fight."

"You say you're a tinsmith?" Cooper's eyes widened. "By God, we're in desperate need of outdoor lanterns. D'you know the kind I mean?"

"Ones that don't blow out in the wind," Luther said. "But I want to fight."

"I'll musket-drill him in between making lanterns, sir," Pierpoint offered, "but like you said, he gets his chance to fight."

Cooper nodded in agreement. "Did you just say you can a make lantern that doesn't blow out in the wind? That's impossible. And where the hell did you learn tinsmithing?" Cooper demanded.

"The master always said slaves is cheaper than white folks. So lots of us are learning trades 'cause we's a lot cheaper. Yes, sir, Master Caldwell was a mean man, but he was plenty smart."

"I'd like to see one of those fancy lanterns. And you'll get your chance to kill sooner than you think. Meantime," Cooper raised his voice and addressed the company. "We're back to our prime-and-load drill. Tenshun!"

As Luther stood to attention, he wondered how long it would take Pierpoint to turn him into a killer.

Brock edged his mount forward through the trees, and made his way slowly down the hill, reflecting on Lieutenant Cooper's understanding style of command. The junior officer had just what the Coloured Company needed: obvious good judgment. The first quality he looked for in every officer. The horse began picking its way through the tree stumps and Brock turned to Nelles. "The young man who dropped his musket?"

"The same one who went over the falls, sir? Yes, that's Alexander's son."

"Damn lucky fellow, if you ask me," Sheaffe said.

"Ever been for a swim in the Upper Niagara, Mr. Sheaffe?" Brock asked.

"Never, sir."

"You should try it sometime. Do you a world of good." Brock said it with a grin and then laughed at his own suggestion.

Sheaffe frowned. "For that matter, the lot of them are very fortunate you've allowed them their own company."

"They'll fight better together, so they deserve their own company. It's not a favour I do them, Mr. Sheaffe, and you would do well to remember that. Just give them an opportunity."

Brock saw Lieutenant Cooper bring the men to attention as soon as he saw the party of officers approach. The Coloured Company did not wear the bright red coats of British regulars, but even with just their cross-belts, Brock could sense their pride. He also noticed the rivulets of sweat running down the face of Alexander's son.

"Sergeant Puffer, what are you doing here? Shouldn't you be at York garrison, with the quartermaster?" Brock asked.

Puffer snapped to attention, staring straight in front, and winked. "Just doing my duty, sir — on the King's business, I am. Wherever the King sends me, I'm happy to be of service." Puffer saluted.

Brock ignored the response and turned his attention to the lieutenant.

"Good work, Lieutenant Cooper. Keep it up. I'm expecting fine soldiers out of this lot," Brock said with a smile, and loud enough for all the men to hear.

"Great honour to have you here, sir. They'll all be proper killers whenever the time comes."

"Well, you shouldn't have to wait too long." Brock steered his mount to one side and beckoned to Cooper. "This son of Alexander's …" he began in a low voice.

Cooper nodded.

"Watch him for me. I don't want anything untoward happening to him. Do you understand?"

"How about just making lanterns and separate musket drills, sir?"

"Fine. Captain Nelles, give Cooper a hand with any necessary arrangements."

"I've heard that another dozen Negroes will soon be joining us, sir. So I could do with a real sergeant, other than Quartermaster Puffer." Cooper glanced back toward his black company. "It's none of my business, of course, but how is Sergeant Alexander to get here?"

"You're a good man, Cooper, to have volunteered for this job. I want a crack company here, and you're the man to do it." Brock motioned for Nelles to remain with Cooper, then turned to the others. "General Sheaffe, Norton, you're with me. Let's go see these supplies."

Nelles rode in close beside Cooper. "Alexander is making his way here on a railroad of sorts," he explained, wiping the sweat from his brow with the back of his glove.

"A railroad, sir?" Cooper stood, looking puzzled.

Brock spurred his horse and chuckled, shielding his eyes against the blazing mid-September sun and scanning a blue sky. *A great day to be a soldier*, he thought.

He'd turned his horse away, but was still within hearing distance when Nelles gave Cooper a strange reply. "Yes, Lieutenant, on a new railroad. Alexander the Great is coming on Brock's railroad."

11

· · · · · ·

ALEXANDER DRAGGED HIS FEET along the path leading to his cabin. On the way, he passed the main stable, where a half-open barn door swung lazily in the humid air. The end of another hot day spent in the field, the dry earth billowed into dust clouds behind him. Now the big man was thirsty and heading home for a drink of water. The long gashes on his back where the whips had ripped deepest were for the most part healed and had thickened into red welts of bruised flesh. Still, if he lengthened his stride or twisted the wrong way, the damaged skin would crack open again, the pain of it jolting him upright. He winced, wondering if his back would ever feel normal.

During his recovery, Alexander had spent every hour he was alone planning his escape. After considering all the pros and cons, he made a decision. While a runaway slave who stole a horse would often be hanged, there was no alternative if he was to escape with Precious. They couldn't cover enough ground without horses, so this meant their ride would mean freedom or death. He glanced inside the barn to where the horses stood in their stalls, but due to the brightness outside he could see nothing of the interior beyond a few feet. He squinted, heard a rustling of horses and straw, but it was no use trying to see.

Castor called out to him from the darkness inside, and Alexander instinctively jumped back a step.

"Don't you go thinking of stealing any horses, boy. Else we'll be hanging instead of whipping you." Castor approached the open door, brushing dust from the bottom of his black vest.

"No, sir."

Then again, if he was going to die for horse thieving, he might as well finish off young Percy first, like he had planned. *They can only hang me once.* Alexander smiled, for the thought of revenge, of slitting Percy's throat, gave him great satisfaction. Percy's nighttime visits to Precious's cabin were infrequent now. The young man had since found an even younger slave and she took up more of his time. The good thing, however, was that the overseers knew Precious belonged to Percy and so they left her alone.

"And don't you go grinning like that either. It's the law here and I enforce it. There's slaves, there's white folks, and there's slave catchers. That's me. I uphold the law on behalf of society and God," Castor declared proudly. He folded his arms over his chest and nodded to himself.

"I'm sorry, sir, but I couldn't hears you right," Alexander said. "You and God?"

"You heard well enough. Me, God, … and the natural order of things."

"Some black folks is free now … working for themselves." Alexander halted, waiting for Castor's reply.

Castor paused and Alexander suspected that this thought of a changing world worried the man.

"If it's okay by the law, then I guess it's okay by the Almighty, and I abide by the Almighty," Castor said, putting his hat firmly on his head.

Men made the laws and the Almighty had nothing to do with it, Alexander reflected and began walking.

In his mind, he was already working through the details of his escape, just like he would do if he were still back in the military. Speed was the key, so before any mayhem started, the horses would have to be saddled and ready to go. The problem was that since the morning after Luther and Hector had run, both the barn and the main house were guarded day and night. The sentry posted at the barn would have to be restrained, or even killed to keep silent. That decision would need to be made at the time.

Alexander glanced back at Castor and saw that Bennett had walked out from the barn to stand beside him, pulling and looping a rope in his hands. Bennett was not wearing his bowler hat, and now his mostly bald head shone in the sunlight. That, combined with his exaggerated moustache and protruding eyebrows made him appear like some evil clown. Just the sight of Bennett swinging that length of rope made Alexander's heart quicken. The barn door swung and slammed back with an unexpected gust of warm September wind.

"That's all bullshit, if you ask me. Society." Bennett spit and announced, "We're leaving tonight to go help a neighbour, friendly-like." He gestured down the dirt road leading to the neighbouring plantation. The wind had thrown up the surface into a cloud of swirling dust. He glared at Alexander. "Some fool nigger's gone running over there, but I'll get paid more if I bring back a slave *and* a horse, so I hopes you do try to steal one. Then I can bring you back dead … like I brought back your stupid toad of a son."

Alexander spun round, teeth clenched and hands balled into fists. Bennett was trying to provoke him, and the man had frozen still beside Castor, the rope looped in his hands. Alexander knew he could grab that rope, wrap it around Bennett's neck, and strangle him. But then what? He'd have to kill Castor where he stood, and by the time he was finished, the overseers would have him; better to stay calm and wait his chance. His battle with Bennett would come, but not today. Alexander took a deep breath and turned back along the path.

"Good decision," Castor yelled. "Go on home. It's Monday, get your weekly rations and you'll feel better."

Alexander ignored him, thinking back to the time they'd brought home Hector's corpse and displayed him openly like a dead fish. *My son.* Alexander looked down at his hands, still balled into fists. His heart continued racing.

He vowed to himself that he'd force Caldwell to feel the same sickness in his stomach — what it was like to lose a son. Tonight, with Castor and Bennett away, he knew where the guards would be posted, but he needed to be certain of Percy's whereabouts. He'd only have one chance to escape, and therefore Precious would have to play her part.

He dreaded involving her. How could he ask her to do such a

thing? Behind him, he heard the heavy locking bar of the barn door fall into place.

Guards; horses; Percy; mayhem; and a distraction to buy time. The old Ranger who had passed through one day had told him of the first stop on the journey to freedom. If Precious could manage to ride that far, then they had a chance to get to "heaven," even if only a slim one. Just the thought of glory land brought a smile back to his face.

Strange how someone could get so used to abuse that the nightmare of it becomes tolerable or at least possible to live with, but maybe Alexander didn't understand that acceptance and never would. Then again, what choice did Precious have but to live through the ordeal night after night? Perhaps her mind went somewhere else during the act because when he asked her to keep Percy occupied in his special cabin, Precious readily agreed. Alexander made a solemn promise to rescue her the instant the horses were saddled up and ready to go.

That same evening, at ten o'clock sharp, Percy kicked open the door to Alexander's cabin and whistled for Precious to join him.

"Where's my whore? Can't live without it now — can you?" Percy gripped his crotch and motioned to it with his other hand. "I saw you wink at me today, so I want something extra tonight." With a snicker he grabbed Precious by the wrist and pulled her out through the door, totally ignoring Alexander. In an instant, she was gone.

"How could I ask her to do this?" Alexander reproached himself out loud. But now he knew Percy's exact location, and with a guard already keeping watch on the Caldwell veranda, he felt sure that Master Caldwell would stay indoors.

He leapt from his mat and tied the two bundles of rations for the week around his waist. With the door pushed open a crack, he peered through. Marching Precious alongside him, Percy had passed the halfway point toward his cabin of shame, which stood close to the Caldwell residence. There was no turning back after Precious was taken in Percy's grasp. His heart beat faster.

Before Percy even reached his cabin, Alexander stole out the door and slipped down one side of the hut. A sixty-second dash through the dark behind the slave shanties found him at the rear of the barn. He crept around to the front, where he heard a horse shuffle and whinny once … twice, … and then again. Someone was already in the horse stalls.

The guard named Robinson obviously heard something too because from the front corner of the barn, Alexander watched the man rise from his chair, lift the locking bar and pull open the door.

"Who's in there? Come out at once." Robinson drew one of the two pistols from his belt, lifting the lighted lantern in his left hand. "You'd best show yourself right now before I shoot."

Aiming to follow the guard inside, Alexander sped to the open door. He had to get hold of two horses fast — or his plan would collapse and Precious would have been molested again for nothing. *Oh God, what have I done?*

From over the gate of the fifth stall, young Mathew raised his hands in the air. "It's just me. I fell asleep on the straw."

"Open the gate and step out." Robinson waited till he did so, then peered inside. "Now close it up. I swear, you're the dumbest nigger I ever met. Why's this horse saddled if you fell asleep?" he demanded.

Mathew's lips remained pressed tight as he stood rigid the moment he saw Alexander approaching with long, quiet strides.

"They'll whip you silly for trying to run. And for stealing a horse to boot — dumb, dumb, dumb." Robinson shook his head. "You was going to sneak out the back way. Young bastard." In the flickering light, he squinted in surprise as Mathew took a sudden step forward.

At that moment, Alexander seized the guard from behind, pressing a table knife to the man's throat, just enough so that it stung. "Lower the pistol and ease the lantern to the floor or this'll be your last breath."

The man froze stiff before slowly bending down with the lantern. Alexander guided the pistol from his hand. "Mathew, take that other pistol from his belt and lay it on the ground behind the lantern, then run and shut the main door. Now, Robinson," Alexander jabbed him in the ribs with the barrel of the pistol, "you know I mean business. They'll hang me this time round, so I've nothing to lose by killing if you act foolish. Right?"

Robinson nodded and rubbed his throat. "Even if you murder me, you won't get far. You're a dead 'un, already."

"Shut up and do exactly as I say." The guard and Alexander were about the same height and now the escapee stared at the man's new boots.

"Head over to that post, sit on the floor, and don't make any noise. You won't be needing this." Alexander took Robinson's sheathed hunting knife and tucked it securely into his own belt, then pulled the knife from its sheath. He placed his pistol beside the one on the ground and relieved Robinson of his cartridge pouch. "And I'll be needing those too." Alexander pointed at the man's feet.

Sitting on the straw-covered floor, Robinson reluctantly slid off his new boots. When finished, he sat with his hands up, glaring at his boots. Alexander chucked the table knife over a stall door while keeping the tip of the hunting knife pressed to Robinson's back.

"Mathew, saddle up two more horses. Hurry! I want that big one — the brown mare in the end stall." The young man ran to do his work.

Alexander tethered Robinson to the post with leather saddle straps, binding his wrists and covering his mouth. Sitting there on the straw, with his bare feet extended, the man could now neither move nor yell. Alexander slid into the boots, reminding him of being back in the army. He picked up both pistols and the cartridge pouch, and jammed them into a saddlebag. With the bag in hand, he ran along to the end stall and helped Mathew cinch the last few straps securing the saddle in place.

"I don't know what the hell you thought you were doing, boy, but you're well in it now. Take all three horses quietly to the rear of Percy's cabin and wait for me."

Mathew started to open his mouth, but Alexander held up a hand. "Don't bother to speak. Just do exactly as I order. Unlock the back door of the barn and leave it open. I can't stop now to explain." He untied the rope around his waist attached to his bundles of food and swung it over the saddle so that they hung down on either side.

He led out the big horse, patting its neck, and Mathew ran to get the other two. Odd, Alexander thought. From the moment he grabbed Robinson, his heart was beating normally and his fear vanished. He grinned to himself, happy to be in action, a soldier again. "And I've only just started."

He left Mathew to care for the animals and then sprinted to Percy's cabin. On reaching the door, he put his shoulder down and broke the thing off its hinges. Without stopping his charge, he raced for the bed, where Percy Caldwell was throwing a bare white leg over Precious.

The boy jerked his head toward the door, in time for his face to meet Alexander's fist delivering a savage punch. Alexander felt Percy's nose shatter under his knuckles while the force of the punch threw the young man clean off the bed.

"Get yourself dressed. Mathew has horses ready at the rear of this cabin," Alexander urged Precious.

"What are you going to do? Don't kill him," Precious said as she quickly dressed. She stared at her tormentor lying unconscious and naked on the floor.

"Never you mind. Get round to the back of the cabin." If he had arrived seconds later, Precious would have been raped again. Angry at the thought, Alexander yanked Robinson's hunting knife from its sheath.

"If you kill him now, you'll only remember Hector hanging from that tree. And you'll be no better then them." Precious ran through the door.

Alexander stood over Percy with the knife in hand. Every desire urged him to take the boy's life in revenge. *Revenge.* He couldn't get the sight of his son's body out of his mind. He had planned for this very moment, this moment of satisfaction. He gripped the knife tighter until his fingers shook.

But he knew in his heart the girl was right; he could not actually take the boy's life. She'd repeated exactly what he had taught her about revenge — forgive, let it go. He reached down with the knife and took Percy's exposed testicles in one hand. The young man would live, "but you're not raping anyone else, ever again."

Percy's eyes flashed open as the knife did its work.

"Know what woke you up?" Alexander grinned a nasty smile. "Someone just cut off your balls." Before Percy could scream, Alexander punched him again, quick and vicious right under the chin. "Son of bitch."

He was unconscious again, but for how long Alexander couldn't guess. It didn't matter, because his little troop of escapees would be gone in minutes. He opened Percy's fingers and put the severed testicles into the palm of his hand before closing it into a fist. He then stuffed the bedsheet hard into the young man's groin, to stem the flow of blood.

Alexander sprinted out the door and around to the back of the cabin, where he found Mathew and Precious waiting for him on their two horses. He mounted the big mare and wheeled her around to face the barn. A trickle of sweat rolled to drop off the end of his nose and he wiped his forehead with the back of his hand.

"Ride down behind the main house, and at the end of the lane, take the road heading north," he ordered. "I'll catch up with you."

Mathew's eyes, wide with fear, flashed from Percy's cabin to the barn and then to the big Caldwell residence. He gripped the reins close to his chest and the horse reared back, sensing the nervousness of its rider.

"Mathew, are you listening to me, boy?" Alexander inquired in a harsh whisper.

"The road north — I heard you."

"I ain't never been on no horse before," Precious cried.

Alexander reached over to touch her quivering shoulder, and he smiled, as if they were starting out on a quiet picnic. "You can do this," he said.

She took a deep breath and nodded.

"Got hold of the reins? Good, so just grab on like this, if you have to." He spoke as if he had the whole night to explain. He took the fingers of her other hand and wrapped them around the saddle's edge.

"Mathew will lead and your horse will follow." Alexander gestured for them to go, but the two runaways still appeared anything but confident.

"Listen to me, both of you," Alexander demanded. "You've got to wake up! They'll hang us if we're caught. Understand? Now git, and don't stop for nothing!"

"Yes, sir," Mathew whispered.

Mathew spurred his horse and for a moment Alexander was left staring into the eyes of Precious. Once more he nodded reassuringly, then slapped the hindquarters of her horse. The pair of them trotted away in the moonlight, down the winding path that hugged the rear of the buildings.

Alexander gave a tug on the reins and rode for the barn. There remained a few things to do on this evening's agenda, and he checked them over in his mind.

The orange light of the lantern flickered as Alexander peered inside the barn. Robinson still sat upright on the straw-covered floor, his back to the post. Alexander dismounted, tied his horse to a rail, and pulled out the knife. He sliced through the ties that bound Robinson to the post, then hauled him out through the rear of the barn, across the path, and retied him to a tree.

"You'll be safer here. Young Percy's lying in his cabin, bleeding. Tell someone about him once they find you."

Robinson scowled up at him, then glanced down at his prized new boots on Alexander's feet.

Alexander dashed back to the barn and unbolted the door of every stall on one side and then on the other before opening wide the external doors. He scooped a handful of straw from the floor and lit it with the lantern's flame. The straw burned brighter as it flew through the air before landing on a bale of hay.

The dried-out bale burst into flame and fire scooted along the floor of straw. Soon a thick grey smoke wound its way upward from the burning bale. The horses whinnied and danced in their stalls, then together they pounded past their gates, escaping out through the open back door.

Nobody's chasing us for a while. Alexander covered his mouth with his shirt to check that all the stalls were now empty. Smoke surged through the cavernous barn as he picked up the lantern and ran out through the rear. He mounted his horse with the lantern still in hand. "Now let's see how we can use this for one last job."

He galloped down the back lane, past the cabin of shame, and toward the main residence. There he stopped for a moment, waiting, before he guided his horse along one side of the big house. *Mayhem.* He chuckled to himself. *Soon there would be mayhem.*

"Fire! Fire!" The guard sitting on Caldwell's veranda must have smelled the smoke or noticed the flames flickering inside the barn because he jumped out of his chair. "For God's sake, fire!" He leaned his musket upright on the side of the veranda steps and darted for the barn, waving his arms in the air.

Alexander let the man run some distance before urging his horse calmly around to the front of the house. With a mighty heave, he tossed the lantern hard through the big veranda window, shattering the glass. The curtains flamed in seconds, casting a baleful glow inside. He reached down and grabbed the guard's musket as he heard people start running toward the barn shouting, "Help us! Fire!"

Suddenly, Master Caldwell himself jerked open the front door, rubbing his eyes in disbelief before stepping out on to the veranda. Clad in his white pyjamas, Caldwell twisted sideways to see flames pouring out of his own front window and already licking the veranda ceiling. Alexander pointed the musket at the confused plantation owner who was waking to a nightmare.

Caldwell's eyes opened wide and he stiffened in fright, like a man about to meet his maker.

Holding the musket level, Alexander paused as the man who had ordered his savage whipping stood quaking before him. Yet, in his mind, he heard the warning voice of Precious and he pictured the girl's face.

"You'll be no better than them."

Caldwell stared at him, trembling, then peered down where a puddle of urine had pooled around his feet.

"On your knees," Alexander ordered.

Caldwell tried to bend to one knee but collapsed altogether in a heap, his pyjamas soaking up the noxious pool. The master had fainted into his own piddle.

"Precious was right. You're not worth it." Alexander lowered the musket, his arms relaxing, the hatred draining away. *Time to get free.*

He dug in his spurs and the horse took off in a gallop. One hand grasped both the reins and the musket while the other reached up and pulled the wide-brimmed hat tighter to his head. The moon shone just enough to light the path as horse and rider pressed forward. His shirt ballooned with air and the wind swirled across his back, tickling the scars. Yes, the glorious feeling of freedom — again.

At the end of the lane, and without breaking the horse's stride, he glanced back over his shoulder. Smoke and flames now billowed from the barn roof and he could see dark shapes running about in the fire's light. The main house was burning too and a gang of men ran to and fro with buckets. They'd have to choose between the barn and the main residence, so Mrs. Caldwell must have given orders for them to save her house.

Someone let out a desperate scream and Alexander laughed. He guessed the woman had found Percy.

"Tell him to whistle now," he shouted as he rode, brandishing the musket in the air. "Son of a bitch."

12

......

WESTLAKE WALKED HIS HORSE through the trees, up a small rise that gave way to a long, sloping field. At the bottom of the hill, not less than three-dozen buildings — houses and stores — lined the main street of Woodville. He pointed to an overgrown trail that circled around the town.

"Are we to avoid civilization altogether?" Simpson asked.

"Our German conductor lives in the second farm we'll come to on the far edge of this town," Westlake replied. "And we need no distractions before we get there. Mount up, we've a ways to go yet."

The path led halfway down the hill, then swung past the town itself before continuing to the west, where again the trees grew thick. Westlake roused his horse to step out into the open, glancing to either side before spurring the animal into a trot. They crossed a shallow river that must have supplied water for the town. A large stream diverged away, leading south, and he steered his horse into the current.

Within minutes, they were past the town and at the edge of a field where the forest stopped and a bounty of corn stalks began. Westlake scanned the ground toward the town but saw nothing to concern him. At least no one had followed them.

He pulled on the reins to halt his horse, and standing up in the stirrups, he pointed to a cluster of buildings well ahead of them. Smoke drifted above the trees, grey against the blue sky.

"Our conductor, gentlemen," he announced with a satisfied grin.

"Farmers need water so I knew he'd be living somewhere alongside this stream," Simpson chimed in.

Parrish moved his horse up beside Westlake's. "Well done, sir. We've dropped a long way down from up north and for our penny to hit the mark, you should be right proud. And it's good timing; I am starving."

Both house and barn were constructed of sturdy square beams, but the small front porch had collapsed on one side. A few rails around the porch had fallen so that their ends now rested on the ground. And moss had begun growing on the roof of the barn, which clearly needed repairs to one wall.

Westlake pondered why such prosperous-looking fields didn't ensure buildings of a better appearance. As he dismounted and tied his horse to a slanting porch rail, his nostrils twitched from the aroma of something cooking.

Before he could knock, the door opened and a thin man with receding grey hair stepped out, each hand clutching a carbine musket. He stood bolt upright, like a body nailed to a cross. The lifeless skin of his face made him look tired, maybe even angry.

Two young women, their full figures dressed in blue cotton dresses and wearing brown hats with wide brims, stepped into view behind him. The one closest to Westlake appeared to be the younger of the two sisters, a girl about his own age. A strand of blond hair fell from under her hat to touch her shoulder. Her liquid blue eyes had a mischievous look and Westlake thought he detected a slight grin. But, he wasn't distracted from the long barrel musket she aimed directly at his chest.

Simpson and Parrish had remained on their horses, and Westlake motioned for them to dismount. The man with the carbines ordered, *"Stehe!"*

"Sprechen sie Deutsch?" Simpson asked.

"Ja, but I also speak English." The farmer had a strong German accent, but his English was perfectly understandable. It seemed Westlake had dragged bloody Simpson along for nothing.

"Where are you going?" the man asked of Simpson.

"We were — " Simpson began, but Westlake turned his head and pointed sharply for him to be quiet.

"We were told you only spoke German," Westlake said.

"I don't care who told you anything," the man shouted. "I am German, but you must tell me this very second where you are going or I'll pull the trigger."

"Heaven," Westlake said, eyeing the sister with the blond hair. It struck him that he might already have arrived. "We're going to heaven, and we're hungry."

The farmer didn't move but instead studied Westlake up and down. He motioned to the two girls to lower their muskets and extended his hand. "You have no accent from around here. That's good. But where are you from? I'm Gerhart Bauer. This is Katharina, and here is my youngest, Seffi."

The girl tucked the loose strand of her hair around one ear.

Westlake shook Bauer's hand, then smiled and bowed to the sisters, whereupon each curtseyed. "Mr. Robert Simpson and Mr. Walter Parrish, sir." Westlake gestured up to them with his thumb. "May they dismount?"

"*Ja*, and for dinner you are just in time. Put your horses in the stable." Bauer pointed to another building, behind the barn. "After you feed them, you can join us. Your name, sir?"

Westlake glanced at Seffi, who had not taken her eyes off him. He wondered where the menfolk were, or if these two girls and their father managed the farm by all themselves. "We're from Upper Canada and my name is Jonathan Westlake. It will be our great pleasure to join you, sir."

Seffi's round cheeks rose up as she smiled ever so slightly. Her blue eyes held his own until Westlake felt his heart pounding and he forgot that Bauer was still shaking his hand.

"Very pleased to meet you and your friends, Mr. Westlake. Dinner is in less than one hour," the farmer announced.

"Yes, sir ... Mr. Bauer," Westlake replied. "We'll be ready."

Bauer swung his shoulders and torso away stiffly, his entire body turning together as if he had sustained an injury of some kind.

Like his two companions, Westlake worked quickly to unsaddle and water his horse. A bar of soap on a railing inside the barn gave Westlake an idea. With two horses to cope with, Parrish had twice the amount of work, but this allowed Westlake time to grab his blanket and head to the river running past the back of the stable.

He stripped off his buckskins and waded into the water, shudder-

ing at the cold. Westlake scrubbed himself fast with the soap before
dunking his head and coming up face first so that his blond hair fell
straight back off his brow. When he stepped up to the grassy riverbank, he wrapped the blanket around himself and dashed for the
stable, changing into the one clean shirt that remained in his saddle-
bag. The white shirt contrasted with his tanned face and as he studied
his reflection in the horse trough, he shrugged.

"It'll have to do," he said out loud to himself, wondering what Seffi
would think of him. He couldn't think of anything but her smile until
Simpson interrupted his thoughts.

"Those weeks of canoe paddling have served you well. You've
become a regular Titan."

"I can hold my own if I have to." Something in Simpson's tone had
told Westlake to be wary.

"That Seffi's a real beauty, not to say anything less of Katharina…
a little plump maybe. It's too bad you're almost married."

Westlake's stomach clenched as the image of Mary's face came into
his mind, round and plain with dark eyes that had once melted his
heart. On the other hand, Seffi's face was of the kind that men saw in
their dreams, and beneath that blue dress, he imagined a body equally
beautiful. He considered his dilemma and felt suddenly trapped.

Dinner was a quiet affair. Westlake stationed himself at one end of
the table, with Simpson and Parrish on either side of him. Bauer sat
at the other end, and after the two young women served dinner, they
took their places beside their father. With her hat removed, Seffi had
pulled her hair back into a blond bun, but Westlake pictured what it
must look like when it fell loose and touched her shoulders. He forced
himself to shift his eyes away from her and scan the room.

The wooden floor was uneven but swept clean and the furniture
plain, but functional. He couldn't see the bedrooms, and assumed
that they lay at the back of the building. Compared with his home on
Maple Hill, this house lacked any luxuries. At least the few windows
allowed in enough of the fading light.

From her place beside her father, Seffi smiled openly at Westlake, with her round cheeks and a mouth that he imagined wanted to kiss him. Either it was the heat of the kitchen or the presence of the girl — it didn't matter which — but he could barely think straight. With the edge of his thumb, he wiped a bead of sweat from above his eyebrow and tried to focus on anything else but her blue eyes. He succeeded for only a short time. *Focus on the rabbit stew, the corn cobs, on listening to old Bauer — anything, but stop staring at this girl's face. Remember your mission!*

"We're in need of supplies. Mainly food," Westlake blurted. "And, of course, we can pay. Also, we need directions to the next conductor … someone to help us, like yourselves."

"Is that what they call us?" Katharina asked.

Westlake nodded.

"All that can be arranged," Bauer said.

"Where is Mrs. Bauer?" Simpson asked abruptly.

The table went silent before Bauer replied, "She died some years back of a terrible illness, inside her." Bauer gestured to his own chest. "No doctors here could help her. But an African heading north stopped by to concoct some mixture of … of I don't know what, gathered right out of our garden. He claimed it would calm her, *ja*." Bauer nodded to himself. "That was the only peace she had during months of suffering. Days later the slave catchers came by with the same man slung across one of their saddles. They'd murdered the poor fellow, the fools."

"Hardly your fault," Simpson said.

"If that Negro hadn't stopped to give aid to my ailing wife, maybe he could have stayed free," Bauer said sternly. "Anyway, from that day on, standing before my wife's grave, I swore to God that we'd help every escaping slave who came by. We don't have much here, but food's at least plenty." Bauer shrugged.

Katharina added, "And being at the Pennsylvania border, right on their road to freedom, so to speak, makes it convenient for us to help. Maybe that's why God put us on this land." She looked to her father for permission to continue. "I do the cooking while Seffi helps with the farm chores."

Seffi pulled her hands off the table and tucked them under the tablecloth. Westlake felt the tension and saw her embarrassment. While she had the face of an angel, her hands were those of a farmer. For the first time her eyes, which looked straight down at the table, held no happiness. Westlake glanced at Parrish and then at Simpson. No one was willing to ask the obvious question about other menfolk.

"Our horses are blown so I was hoping we could stay the night … in the stable, of course," Westlake said. "And perhaps there is something we could do to help you meanwhile?"

"You can stay, but we don't need your help," Bauer replied.

And just as fast, Seffi said, "Yes, we do."

Bauer glared at her, but she continued, "We need a fence post dug, and the fencing strung. And we need more wood chopped. Father can't swing the axe with his back the way it is."

Bauer remained silent, but Westlake could tell he wouldn't object.

"That's settled. Mr. Simpson, Mr. Parrish, you find this fence post, dig the hole for it, and fix the fence properly. I'll chop the firewood. Miss Bauer, can you show them where you want the post dug?"

She nodded vigorously. "Of course," and her eyes were alight again.

It was safer for him if she went off with Simpson and Parrish. Westlake knew he'd cut down an entire forest for the smile on that face. "Drink up, gentlemen, dinner is over. I want the jobs finished before the sun goes down."

"I could — " Simpson began to suggest something before Westlake cut him off.

"You'll dig," Westlake ordered.

Just after sundown, Westlake found himself back in the river. He'd taken off the clean shirt before chopping the four-foot-high pile of wood. Now he stripped off his breeches too and plunged straight into the cold water. In minutes Parrish joined him on the grassy riverbank, and then Simpson followed a few steps behind, both grumbling about the other's poor effort.

"Did you get the hole dug and the fence mended?" Westlake demanded, standing hip deep in the water.

"Yes, sir," Parrish replied.

"Fine, then both of you keep quiet," Westlake said. He stepped out of the water just as the two men were getting in. "It looks like we each get our own stable stall, so don't bother me until morning."

Wrapping the blanket around his shoulders, he carried his clothes in one arm and boots in the other and walked gingerly toward the horse stall in his bare feet. When Seffi suddenly appeared at the stable, he pulled the blanket tighter around him but fumbled his boots. They dropped to the ground and he stared down at them.

"Aren't you going to pick them up?" She smiled.

"No, Miss Bauer. I mean, I can't, not without … maybe losing my blanket, and then what?" Westlake's face flushed red.

"That's why I asked." She laughed and took a step toward him.

He stepped backward and stumbled a little but held his grip on the blanket. His heart was racing, and he couldn't think of what to do or say next until he blurted, "My friends are coming back any minute." *Why did I say that?*

"I know," Seffi said. "Remember where you laid down your blanket at the river? I will go there tonight, when everyone is asleep."

"You saw me come out of the river?" Westlake said.

Seffi raised her eyebrows and grinned. "Will you come tonight?"

Westlake paused before nodding. "I will meet you." He sighed, aware that he should have refused.

The next four hours turned out to be the longest hours of his life. He tossed and turned on the straw in his private horse stall, first thinking of Mary and how she had trapped him into proposing marriage, but knowing in his heart that he'd made the promise of his own free will. There was no way out now.

His problem was that he loved Mary but was smitten with this German angel. He couldn't think of Seffi's face without experiencing a shiver. Westlake convinced himself that meeting her at the river would just be to talk, a rendezvous between friends. That was it, a discussion about extra chores … for the good of the farm.

He guessed it was just before midnight when he spread his blanket on the same patch of grass as he'd occupied in the daylight. No sooner had he sat down than she was there beside him. A sliver moon glowed in a sky packed with stars, enough light to reveal her blue eyes. She put her face close to his and kissed him on the cheek. He touched the spot with his fingers, feeling for the soft imprint of her lips.

"I have commitments," he said. He needed her to invite him and make it easy. She did better than that.

"We all have commitments, Mr. Westlake. Just kiss me," Seffi ordered.

He kissed her on the mouth, and she kissed him back. Her mouth was warm and moist, and she kissed in a way that he had never experienced. This wasn't merely a schoolgirl kiss. She wanted him *now*, and his heart thrilled at the thought. He closed his eyes, her warm body next to his, a sense of euphoria captivating him while he held her tightly in his arms.

"I've been waiting for you ... someone like you. I've waited for months and months." She leaned back to gaze in his eyes.

"But I must leave here and I am committed," Westlake said. "You can't fall in love with me." Yet that's exactly what he wanted from that first second he saw her appear in the doorway, with that strand of blond hair falling to her shoulder. He felt selfish and ashamed. She had to tell him that she accepted his situation or he would have to stop right now. Yet he wanted to go on; he wanted to make love to her and hold her forever.

Westlake waited for her reply, and in the darkness he sensed Seffi was hesitant to speak.

"Then I just want tonight, right now, so I'll never forget, and maybe one day ... maybe." She shrugged and untied her hair, which slid down to spread across her shoulders. Prettier than he ever imagined, she *was* an angel — or he was dreaming.

Even in this barest of light, Westlake saw her beauty as she knelt beside him. He touched her flowing hair with one hand, then ran his forefinger along her neck. She pulled him down on top of her, and he could feel her hands gripping his shoulders, and then his arms, feeling and searching his body.

"We need to stop," Westlake said. "I can't do this."

"Hold me," she whispered.

He cupped her buttocks in both hands, feeling her body move in response. Then her legs were wrapped around his thighs as she made a slight moaning sound. He kissed her mouth and felt her move against him.

They lay together like that for hours, just touching, kissing. Westlake did not want this night to end but knew that he had to get some sleep before the long ride tomorrow. Seffi must have read his thoughts because she suddenly stood up.

"Be careful going back or your father will kill me."

"Why? Nothing happened. Besides, my father knows I am here. One day I will tell you the story of my first marriage."

And then Westlake understood. She had learned to kiss that way with another man, in another time. Like a fool, he had assumed that he was the first. He felt clumsy and awkward.

Again, she divined his thoughts. "You were wonderful," she said, taking his hand. "And you are so handsome too." With her other hand, she ran the back of her fingers along his chin. "What my father doesn't know is that Katharina is now with your friend, Mr. Parrish."

She leaned down, brushing back his blond hair, and kissed him on the forehead. "Thank you. Do not feel guilty. You were honourable. Know that I could love you forever, if you give me the chance."

Westlake watched her turn away and fade into the darkness. He was just a heartbeat away from falling in love, again. And he could barely resist her.

The following morning, Westlake carried in two armfuls of wood for the kitchen fire. After piling them in a corner bin, he drew two pails of water from the well and set them close to the pantry wall. He'd risen soon after sunrise and tried to keep himself busy until he could next see Seffi.

Raw carrots, potatoes, and green beans arranged in small piles covered the kitchen table. He peered out through the window at a blue sky as his thoughts wandered back to Niagara. The smell of coffee filled the house, and he poured himself a cup, wondering if Mary was also enjoying coffee at this very minute.

Just as he sat down at the table, Bauer came in the front door and took the seat opposite him. Westlake tried not to make eye contact.

"Your friends have been picking vegetables for Katharina since dawn. You look tired. Late night, Mr. Westlake?"

The man wants some acknowledgment.

"I guess so, sir... yes, definitely a late night." Westlake stared down at the cup in his hands.

"How did you sleep?"

Westlake's first thought was to say "Your hospitality knows no bounds," but he remembered the intensity in Seffi's face.

"Best night of my life, Mr. Bauer, but I have a mission to complete and commitments. I have no choice but to move on." He looked up into Bauer's lined face. "Though I sincerely wish it were otherwise."

"A man like you could make a fine living here on this land." Bauer waved his hand toward the window.

"I cannot change my situation. There's a war on and I have a duty — and a home to protect back in York."

"This war won't last forever."

"And I must keep a certain promise, sir. Please believe me, I wish it were not so. But duty and honour ... " Westlake stood and gestured to the produce on the table. "I'll store these vegetables."

Bauer slumped in his chair with arms folded across his chest and his long sinewy fingers wrapped around his biceps. Westlake gathered up each bundle of vegetables and stored them in their appropriate bin along the wall, before returning to the table where Bauer remained seated.

"Is there any heavy lifting or other such chores that my men and I can do for you?" Westlake asked.

Bauer shook his head but did not look up. Katharina entered through the side door and began to prepare breakfast. Apart from the occasional banging of pots, she worked in silence.

Simpson and Parrish soon joined the two men to discuss how they would reach the southernmost conductor on their journey. The four sat around the table planning the safest route. With the nighttime adventures still on his mind, Westlake shifted uncomfortably in his seat and noticed that Parrish and Bauer did the same.

A blacksmith's forge located on their side of the mountains was their last stop. There they would be fed and rested in relative safety. Also, this last conductor knew precise directions to the plantation where Alexander the Great toiled away.

It sounded easy: straight south along the trail until they hit the mountain foothills, where they would come to Deer's Gap, a town of several hundred residents. They were to look for a black shanty inhabited by a free Negro. No, Bauer had never learned the man's name, just the town, his occupation, and colour of his residence. He stared down at the table with shoulders slouched like a man dejected.

"Horses saddled?" Westlake looked to Parrish who nodded but didn't make eye contact with his friend.

Along with the strong coffee, Katharina served hot porridge and eggs for breakfast and Westlake noticed that the plate given Parrish had an extra egg. Parrish ate in silence while Simpson chatted with Bauer in German.

By the time Seffi appeared from the barn, the men were mostly finished. She sat down with a glance at Westlake, but didn't speak until she finished breakfast. The young woman held herself erect, the tension evident in her shoulders as she rose to place her empty plate in the washbasin. Immediately afterward, Seffi rushed out the front door.

Simpson and Parrish continued speaking with Bauer, pretending to listen to him when really all they both wanted was Katharina's attention. Westlake eventually pushed back his chair and followed Seffi outdoors.

"Seffi," he called out from behind. She headed down one side of the house, out of sight. He ran to catch her, taking her arm gently at the elbow. "I wanted to say goodbye in private … and to say I'm sorry."

Seffi turned to him, tears welling up in her eyes. "You've done nothing to be sorry for. I came to you of my own accord and if you can't love me" — she shrugged — "then I had a beautiful night with a lovely man, that's all. Thank you."

"Please don't say it like that." He grabbed her in his arms and hugged her, feeling the slender body that had driven him wild with excitement.

"I may already love you," Westlake continued. "It's been so fast that I'm not sure. But I can't stay now." He kissed her lightly on the mouth. "The strange thing is that I can love you, but you mustn't love me. That would only lead to sadness for you, and I'd be ashamed if I let that happen. If I hurt you ..." He shook his head.

"Is there any chance, even the slightest, that you might come back here?"

"If there is one thing I've learned during this war, it's that anything is possible. We ride south now only to travel back north, heading directly past your farm. But, to be honest, one never can promise, so please don't hold on to any hope."

"Then say goodbye, Jonathan. And always know that I could make you happy."

They held each other for a moment longer. "I don't doubt that for a heartbeat." Westlake squeezed gently on each of her hands before letting go, then turned away just as Parrish appeared around the side of the house.

"Time for the horses, sir?"

Westlake nodded. "Let's go and find our last conductor — and our new sergeant."

Parrish walked the four horses around to the front of the house and handed the reins of two of them to his companions. Westlake patted his mount's nose, put a foot in the stirrup, and swung his leg over the saddle. Bauer and his daughters raised their hats and waved to them from the doorway.

"Thanks again for your hospitality." Westlake saluted from his horse.

Simpson waved and shouted, *"Danke für Ihre Gastfreundschaft."*

Parrish tapped his thick fingers over his heart. Then four horses wheeled around and trotted away.

"I think that Katharina girl fancies me," Simpson said with a smile.

"No doubt, Mr. Simpson. You will take the lead today. Thirty paces ahead, if you please," Westlake instructed.

Once Simpson's horse carried its rider out of earshot, Westlake rode up close alongside Parrish. "I know about you and the woman, Katharina, so I hope you didn't make any promises to her that you can't keep."

"She packed the bags full of food for us, sir." Parrish pointed to their spare horse where two large canvas sacks hung from the saddle, one on each side.

"What did you say to Katharina? Did you promise her anything?"

"They're both in desperate need of husbands, so they are, sir. I think Mr. Bauer may be dying, but he'll never admit it." Parrish twisted round in his saddle to look directly into Westlake eyes. "When he dies, they'll be left almost defenceless out here in the middle of nowhere ... all on their own. Finding husbands are a matter of life and death for them."

"And the promises you made?"

"Well, nothing really, sir. At least ... none for today," Parrish said.

And right then Westlake knew that Walter Parrish was indeed going back — not today, but one day he would go back to the Bauer farm and to his Katharina. The only question in Westlake's mind was if he himself would be going with him. The temptation to revisit the farm on their return journey would be immense.

At war with America, yet he'd fallen in love with an American — even though he had already promised to marry another woman. And he was sure of his love for Mary. How could this happen to him? One thing was certain: his heart pulled him in two different directions, and the confusion overwhelmed him.

13

· · · · · ·

Alexander opened his eyes and felt for the security of Robinson's two pistols resting heavily across his chest. After working all day in the field and then travelling all night, the three escapees were exhausted and slept with no one acting as lookout. He'd never allow it to happen again. He sat up with a jerk and scanned his surroundings. Other than their horses, nothing living showed itself. *Lucky. We'll need some luck to make it to glory land.* He laid his head back on the saddle and peered over at Precious, who lay sleeping between himself and Mathew.

They had ridden the horses hard for a good mile, but to gain the maximum distance, they had slowed to a trot before the animals were blown. Keeping with the road that led north toward the foothills of the mountains, they had finally dismounted and walked in the moonlight until dawn. Alexander directed his fellow runners off the road and headed deep into the forest. He'd take no chance at all of being seen by anyone.

The burning straw in the barn jumped to mind and he hoped the other horses got well away. With no horses for their pursuers, maybe he bought himself an extra day. Percy would need lots of medical care, but Castor and Bennett would be coming after them for sure. It was only a matter of time before they caught up on the distance by using the main roads all day. He had to slip through to the other side of the mountain pass, where help awaited him.

Without yet opening her eyes, Precious said, "Good morning. Did you remember to bring that food I bundled?"

"How long have you been awake?" Alexander asked in surprise.

"A while now. Ain't going nowhere without you, so I just laid here resting before we start travelling again."

"Always were the smartest darn kid around, I'll give you that."
Alexander laughed. "Food's still in those two bundles, just as you
wrapped them." He pulled over a cloth-covered bundle that rested
beside his saddle. After undoing the knot, he laid out two loaves of
corn bread.

"I had a good teacher," Precious said, grinning. She turned around.
"Wake up, Mathew, it's time to eat." She gave the lad a poke in the
side.

Mathew groaned and stretched out his arms. He rubbed his eyes
and sat up. "How long have I slept?"

"We'll eat now and get moving right after," Alexander replied. "The
catchers won't be getting here just yet. Them farm boys have been up
all night fighting the fire and they don't have any horses. Leastwise
not until they chase 'em down." He inspected their rations, consisting
of two loaves of corn bread, rice, lima beans, potatoes, and three ripe
tomatoes. "I don't recall getting 'us no tomatoes," he remarked with a
glance at Precious.

She grinned and tore a chunk off a loaf of bread. "I borrowed
them from the veg garden of the big house for our trip. I grow 'em, so
they're sort of mine, anyhow." Precious tossed a tomato to Mathew.
Then she retied the cloth that held the rest of their food.

"My, my, girl, you is something else." Alexander reached over and
squeezed her shoulder. He noticed Mathew surveying the trees around
their camp. If he'd been caught in the act of horse thieving, the lad
would have been tied up to the whipping tree. Just a minute later
to that barn and Alexander's entire plan for their escape would have
ended in disaster. He shuddered at the thought. Both of them caught
and Precious raped again for nothing.

"I suppose you didn't think to bring any food for yourself?"
Alexander asked.

Mathew shook his head.

"What were you thinking?" Alexander blurted out. "To steal a
horse and run all by yourself?"

"I just want freedom — the same as you do." Mathew shrugged

and pulled up his shirt to show a back covered in purple bruises. "My overseer carries a long pole." He continued to scan the perimeter of the camp.

"Walk out that way, fifty paces, and relieve yourself there." Alexander gestured. "Then run a big circle around us and make sure there's no one around. If you sees someone out there, you hightail it back here quiet as a mouse. Understand?"

Mathew nodded and strode off toward the trees. A good lad, Alexander grinned, as he recalled Mathew and Luther as children, pushing each other under the water in the river back home. *Luther's gone under in a different river, forever.* He sighed at the thought and laid his head back on the saddle.

"No one around," Mathew said upon his return, puffing. He plunked down on his blanket. "I've been wondering, what did you do to Percy?"

"None of your business. We have to go now." Alexander stood up.

"Did you forgive him, like you taught us?" Precious asked.

Alexander reached for the canteen that rested beside his saddle, considering what to reply. He uncorked it and took a swig. Just the thought of Percy Caldwell made his stomach wrench. He hated that boy and wished he'd slit his throat, but those thoughts, he decided, were better kept to himself.

"We want to know." Mathew waved a hand toward Precious. "Did you kill him?" The young man bit down on his tomato.

Alexander shook his head. "Just cut off some of his private parts. No more raping for skinny Percy. Come on, eat up. If we're to stay free, we have to keep moving." He motioned for Mathew to stand, but the lad wanted to continue. "Are you listening to me, boy?"

"Oh, man, that'd hurt something painful." Mathew crossed his legs involuntarily and grimaced. "Got what he deserves, right, Precious?"

The girl had sat impassively, eating the odd mouthful, as Alexander and Mathew bantered, but now she sat up straight, eyes glaring. "I can't never be free if I wake up every morning seething with hate for Percy." She balled her hand into a fist and shook it at Alexander.

"Why can't you understand what it's like?" She choked out the words and began to sob. "You always said we have to forgive, but you don't believe it. You hate Master Caldwell, his family, and everyone who works for him. You're not free."

"Them's just words from that Bible book. Forgive, phewy," Mathew said. "How you can you forgive Percy?" He turned to stare at Alexander, expecting an explanation. "There's no way she can forgive."

What could he say? He felt free because he didn't have to slave in the fields today. No master could whip him any more. Then he thought of Hector hanging from that tree, and in an instant the hatred returned. *Kill them all.* Yet maybe the girl was right. No, to hell with that thinking. Caldwell no longer owned him and he could now go where he pleased … so long as it was north. *Maybe I'm not entirely free just yet.*

"Now's not the time to jaw about freedom," Alexander said. "I know what I said about forgiving, but sometimes it's hard. Right now, I just wants to *stay* free." He stretched and bent over to lift his saddle. "We'll only be free for good when we get to glory land." Alexander pointed north. "Let's go."

"You're wrong," Precious replied. "It's not that easy." She stared at Mathew. "And you're wrong too; I *can* forgive."

"If we don't get going soon, for sure we won't stay free," Mathew said. "We just head through the mountain pass, right?" He rolled up his blanket and carried it with his saddle toward his horse.

"But not on the open road during the day," Alexander insisted. "We'll make our way through the bush until the sun goes down and then risk taking the road to make up for lost time."

"What's on the other side of those mountains?" Mathew asked.

"According to my old Ranger friend, a place called Deer's Gap and plenty of food," Alexander replied. A cool wind blew through their camp and he shivered. He hoped the weather held out long enough for them to travel.

Precious carried the saddlebags to the horses. "That Castor fella will be coming with his nasty partner, won't he?" she said. "Will he catch up with us?"

"Might." Alexander shrugged as he placed the saddle on his horse and reached under its belly to cinch the strap.

"What will we do if he catches up?" Precious asked.

"Kill 'em all, or die trying. It's that simple," Alexander replied. He looked at each in turn, making sure to catch their eyes. "Kill 'em, or die trying."

In the former entrance to the barn, George Castor stood with his hands on his hips and scanned the smouldering remnants of fallen beams and charred ruins. Smoke drifted up between three of the horse stalls that, though singed, were otherwise strangely untouched by the fire. The roof was totally gone, burnt away, and he peered up at a grey sky beyond the scorched ends of a couple beams sticking out from the one wall that remained standing.

The odd flame still burst from the blackened wreckage as men scurried about with leaky water buckets to douse them. Whenever the wind shifted in his direction, the acrid smell of charred timbers caught in the back of his throat, making him cough and spit before jerking his head away.

What hellish fiend would have done this? Castor wiped his mouth with the back of his hand, turned, and hurried over to the main residence. For the most part, the effort to save the house itself had been successful. From the outside, the only evidence of fire was the soot staining the white ceiling of the veranda. Black fingers fanned out from the shattered window to stain the pillars that supported the roof.

Castor knocked on the front door and soon a servant escorted him to the living room, where the same heavy odour of smoke assaulted his nostrils. The room was sunlit because the curtains were gone, but the window frame and adjoining ceiling were covered with thick black ash. Little puddles of water gathered on the floor and Castor looked down to find himself standing in one. On closer inspection, he realized that the entire room was dripping wet.

"… not civilized to live in a house that reeks like this," he heard Mrs. Caldwell cry from the hall.

"I'm doing my best, Mother," her husband replied. "We could have lost the entire house. It's not so bad."

"Should've whipped that nigger to death but, that's your problem, too soft," she said. "This is your fault."

Master Caldwell walked backward still facing his wife, into the living room. "That's a little harsh, Mother. Please, I'll make everything right, you'll see," Caldwell pleaded with his hands extended. "You can hardly blame me and my good intentions for the crimes committed by that savage brute."

Castor watched Mrs. Caldwell appear next in the entrance to the living room. She gripped the door frame with one hand while the other wagged a finger at Castor like he was somehow responsible. Her eyes squinted in the light, and for the first time Castor noticed her crooked, bony fingers.

"My beautiful carpet from India destroyed, and our curtains from New York are burnt to nothing. Look, my blue satin pillows — they're black," she shrilled. "And dear Percy's lying upstairs without his manhood, for goodness' sake. What sensible woman will marry him now, poor boy?"

To Castor, there was something terribly funny about hearing this woman talk about the suffering of her beastie little rooster, but he dared not laugh. "I'm sorry, Mrs. Caldwell," he said with feigned sincerity. The truth was that like most of the other overseers, he thoroughly disliked their son and heir. Always so cocksure, Percy seemed to think he could do no wrong.

"Sorry? Don't you waste time being sorry. Just go and catch that nigger and the other two." She suddenly swung her arms around her head like she was suffering from a fit. Castor took a cautious step back. "Hang him, that Alexander, and bring the young'uns back here. We'll work that boy to death, and she'll be kept pregnant for the rest of her childbearing life."

She ended almost screaming. "Someone has to pay for all of this."

Then she turned back toward her husband. "And don't you come back either till they're caught. You hear me?"

"Yes, Mother, of course, whatever you say is best," Master Caldwell replied quietly. "Saddle the horses, George, and round up ten men … I reckon that's more than enough to catch them. After all, he's traveling with that young girl."

"First we have to recapture enough horses, sir," Castor explained. "They lit out with the flames and we still got to go get 'em."

"Then go, now! Don't just stand around here," Caldwell shouted into Castor's face before prodding him in the shoulders toward the front door and away from his wife. Once they were outside on the veranda he closed the front door. "Lock up the slaves in their cabins tonight. See that no one gets out. You tell the overseers it's an order from me. I want to sleep knowing that I won't be burnt beef by morning."

"I thought we were riding tonight, sir?" Castor asked.

"That was just for Mother," Caldwell said, glancing over his shoulder. "The barn's still smouldering, for gosh sake. And by the time you chase down all those horses, bring them back, and saddle'em up, it'll already be pitch black. After last night, I'm desperate for a good night's rest. We leave at first light tomorrow morning."

"Yes, sir." Castor nodded in relief.

Master Caldwell had been right. It took the rest of the day to finally douse the barn and round up the last of the horses. By day's end, the men were exhausted. Castor went to sleep thinking of how Alexander had broken the order of things. The man was a menace to society, deserving of no mercy. And even if he had never liked the rooster Percy — indulging in forced sex with slave girls was not part of common decency — no man on earth deserved to have his privates cut off. Castor winced at the thought.

When he woke the next morning, he considered how he might bargain with Master Caldwell. In normal circumstances, the return of a live runaway brought at least twelve dollars fifty. The rate dropped to five dollars if the slave was brought back dead. He'd split the amount equally between himself and Bennett. It seemed like the fair thing to do, and Castor reminded himself he was a fair man.

At breakfast, Bennett urged him to demand more money, since a large posse was required to bring in three slaves, especially when one of them included a man like Alexander. While the farmhands would never expect an equal share, any amount at all paid to them would reduce his own pay. Maybe, in his anger, Master Caldwell would offer a big bonus. Castor grinned, looking in the mirror as he thought about the prospect that stupid Alexander had done him a favour.

But there was nothing funny about what they found hanging from the same knotted oak tree where he'd strung up Hector's body and where he'd whipped Alexander. From the edge of the veranda, he called out softly to Master Caldwell, once and then again. Never taking his eyes from the tree, he knocked on the door. "You have to come out and see this for yourself, sir."

Castor stared up in disbelief at Percy's naked body twisting on the rope. After wrapping the cord around his neck, the boy had climbed up the tree, tied the other end to a branch, and then jumped. His neck was stretched and his tongue, protruding through his lips, had gone loose at the side of his mouth. Blood dripped from both his heels and Castor's eyes followed the red trail up to the boy's groin. He jerked his head away.

Master Caldwell at last opened the door.

"This is going to be an awful sight, sir," Castor warned him before stepping to one side. "Prepare yourself."

"Oh my God, what devil nigger has done this to my boy?" Caldwell dropped to his knees. "No! No! It can't be," he cried, rocking back and forth, hands clasped in front of him.

"They was all locked up, sir. I'm afraid the boy did this to himself. I should cut him down before Mrs. — "

At the sound of a scream, Castor hunched down. Mrs. Caldwell had crept in behind them. He swung around to watch her faint, her head hitting the veranda floor with a thump as her eyes rolled back in their sockets.

Master Caldwell crawled on his knees to cradle her head. The woman's face was stark white. Caldwell glared up at Castor. "I'll get my son cut down myself. Round up your men and go. You don't need me. Kill the big nigger on sight." He shook a fist, his face turning from purple to bright crimson.

Castor glanced up at Percy's body and then down to Mrs. Caldwell. He hesitated now to raise the subject of money.

"And bring the other two niggers back here." Caldwell choked out the words, the veins bulging in his neck. "Every man gets a full share each, twelve dollars fifty per slave. You and Bennett get double each, whether they're dead or alive. This isn't about the money. It's about setting an example." He stared up at his son's twisting body, limp in the morning light. "And upholding the law of the land. Now git."

14

· · · · · ·

FROM THE EDGE of Pennsylvania's border to Deer's Gap involves three days' hard riding toward the foothills of the Allegheny Mountains. Westlake saw the smoke rising from the houses of the town long before they got close. Dusk had arrived already and this suited his purpose well. By the time they clambered across the bridge that led through the town, the darkness made it impossible for anyone to recognize their faces.

The blacksmith's forge lay at the far end of town and Westlake's horse maintained a steady trot along the main street. The old houses and small storefronts reflected the poverty of the place. Nothing was painted so the original logs showed the worn exteriors of every building. Westlake's stomach churned at the smell of cooking grease from one of the houses and he immediately thought of breakfast at the Bauers' and of Seffi's face. From the moment they had left the farm, he'd thought of nothing but Seffi — all the while knowing he shouldn't.

A sign proclaiming SMITH was displayed on the last shack they came to, a blackened structure whose shabby front entrance faced on to the main street. A railing allowed the three riders to dismount and tie their reins. Westlake knocked hard on a shaky door and waited, but no one came to open it.

Then he heard the rhythmic banging of steel on steel and assumed someone was at home. Westlake cocked his musket and motioned for Simpson to stay put. He tugged on Parrish's sleeve to accompany him around the side of the building. Under a sagging awning that stretched out from the main house, a black man hammered on what looked to be a long piece of flat steel. His dark skin gleamed with sweat in the glowing light of the furnace fire.

"Gonna be a sword. Don't ask more. State your business." A short man with a thick neck and defiant eyes, the blacksmith flared his nostrils. He maintained his steady blows, producing a *ping* with every strike, and barely glanced toward his visitors. "I don't talk with strangers."

"Heaven. We've come from heaven, and once we've done our business, we're going back there," Westlake replied.

The blacksmith said nothing in return.

"We have to travel through the mountains to the Caldwell plantation, to visit a friend there named Alexander. We'll be seeing you on our return." Westlake turned to leave. There was no point staying here if the man wouldn't converse.

"Wait." The pinging stopped, but the man kept the hammer in one hand while holding the red hot sword in the other. "What if I told you that you didn't have to climb through those mountains — that your friend was close by?"

"Don't play games, blacksmith. Where's your master? Either you know something or you don't."

"My master's long dead. He gave me my freedom and all you see." The blacksmith's muscular right arm waved the glowing sword in a proud sweep at his shop. "I have a paper to prove it," he added almost like a challenge.

"You don't have to prove anything to me," Westlake declared. "Just tell me the whereabouts of my friend."

The man put down the sword, lifted the oil lamp, and stepped out from under the awning. He swung the lamp from side to side twice and then moved it up and down. At first, nothing happened, but after a few moments, out of the treeline some fifty paces away, a man revealed himself, first remaining still and then walking slowly alongside a huge horse. In the dark, Westlake couldn't see the man's features and so he squinted as the figure drew closer.

"Parrish?"

"Looks unarmed, but it's too hard to see much," Parrish replied.

Westlake stared warily, hoping this man was their objective. His premature escape would cut days off their trip. The fellow slowed as he reached the midpoint and then he stopped ten paces out. Westlake stepped forward and offered his hand, but the man still didn't move.

"Who are you?" Westlake asked.

Something was strange here and Westlake tensed in anticipation. Why did the fellow delay? Too late, he realized the trap.

Behind him, he heard the click of a weapon and then another. The blacksmith stepped away, gripping his sword. Westlake turned sharply to see a large black man standing with two short pistols trained on Parrish and himself. Whoever this man was, he had snuck in behind while they were distracted by the man and horse in front.

"Don't either of you move a muscle," he growled in a deep voice. "Who is it wants to know who we are?"

"I'm Jonathan Westlake of the British Army."

"You don't look like no army man to me."

"And you don't look like a sergeant either, but life takes some strange turns. Put the pistols to one side, please. They have a nasty habit of going off." Westlake offered his hand again.

The big man peered around at the empty workshop. He was the same build as Parrish but at least twice his age. Now he studied Westlake and Parrish closely before moving nearer. The blacksmith nodded his approval.

"Why are you here and how did you know that I was once a sergeant?" The man kept both weapons level with Westlake's chest.

"I could ask you the same question. Why are *you* here?" Westlake replied. "But if you're really Alexander Johnson the slave, otherwise known as Alexander the Great, I've been ordered on behalf of His Majesty's government to escort you safely to Upper Canada — to heaven. This man here is Walter Parrish."

"How did you know where I was?" Alexander finally uncocked the muskets and took Westlake's hand in a tight grip but didn't let go. He bobbed his head in acknowledgment to Parrish and over Westlake's shoulder, scanned the shop yet again.

"My instructions are to take you safely back to Niagara, where you'll resume your duties as sergeant of an all-coloured company. And I didn't actually know you were here — you're supposed to be on the Caldwell plantation." Westlake's hand began to ache in the other man's crushing grip.

"They remembered me? The British Army remembered me?" Alexander grinned, showing all his white teeth. "My goodness, maybe there is a God after all."

He still hadn't let go of Westlake's hand, but Westlake felt the grip relax and then a tremble as the man's eyes filled with tears.

"It gets much better, Mr. Johnson," Westlake explained. "I bring you greetings from your son Luther, who awaits you at Fort George."

In the darkness, Westlake couldn't tell for sure, but he thought he heard Alexander suck in a deep breath and hold it. The man dropped to his knees and bowed his head, still holding on to Westlake's hand. He raised his other hand to grasp Westlake's wrist, and he appeared to sob. Westlake looked for guidance to Parrish who just shrugged his shoulders.

"Mr. Johnson, sir, we must go now. In my orders, I was told that you have a present or a parcel of some kind to bring with you. If you have it in your possession, I want for us to leave this instant."

"I'm sorry." Alexander stood up and wiped his cheeks with the back of one hand. "They told me Luther was dead. This is all too much." Alexander the Great was still trembling. "Call me Alexander and meet my friend Mathew, who escaped with us."

The man with the horse stepped forward and Westlake shook the young fellow's hand, but now he was confused. "Us?"

Alexander turned away, still emotional, so that his shoulders rose and fell with every breath. He motioned for the blacksmith to raise the lamp. A few seconds after the signal was given, Westlake saw another figure appear from the same section of the treeline, walking cautiously forward with two horses in tow. This time it was a young woman who appeared scared half out of her wits.

"This is Precious," Alexander announced.

"There's three of you?" Parrish asked.

"We set fire to the Caldwell house and barn, after we let the horses escape," Alexander said.

"Precious is the 'present' they mentioned?" Westlake guessed out loud and then shook his head. "It doesn't matter how many of you there are, my orders are to get you over the border." He turned back to Alexander. "So mount up, we're going. They're sure to be tracking you."

"We left in the middle of the night and there'd be no horses until the following day. Anyway, they'd have been busy trying to save the house."

"That gives us a head start of a day, maybe two."

"That's the way I figure, also."

"Follow us," Westlake instructed.

He hurried around to the front of the building and mounted his horse, with Parrish trailing behind. Simpson started to speak, but Westlake shook his head. "Later. We'll talk later. Untie that other horse and let's move."

The blacksmith stumbled between the horses, and wringing his hands he looked up at Westlake. The escaped slaves followed him.

"What am I to say if the catchers come?" the smith asked.

"Do you know the next stop north of here?" Westlake asked.

"Maybe ... the Germans, in Pennsylvania." The smith looked down at his boots, still reluctant to give too much away.

"Which German family? There are hundreds," Westlake said.

"Just a general area is all I know."

"Save yourself then ... it makes no difference to us. They know we travel north. Tell them exactly what you saw and heard, but take your time and delay them." Westlake gave the man a mock salute. "And you can tell them that the British Army is helping slaves to escape." He turned his horse so as to face Simpson and Parrish.

"Mr. Simpson, this is Alexander the Great — these are his friends, Precious and Mathew."

Simpson frowned at seeing the trio of escaping slaves. "There was to be only one man ... and a package of some kind."

"Well, now there are three of them, and he won't go anywhere without the other two. Remember our orders — your orders — to deliver Alexander to Captain Nelles at Fort George, alive."

Westlake paused to stare down the deserted main street of Deer's Gap.

"Just in case of an attempt to surprise us, you will shoot and if necessary kill anyone who gets in our way, understood?" Westlake announced.

Simpson nodded to Alexander and doffed his hat off to Precious. "My pleasure, madam," he said. "Seems a little extreme to me, Mr. Westlake," he murmured as an aside.

Parrish leaned back in his saddle and remarked to Alexander, "That's what I like about Mr. Westlake: no half-measures, just kill the bastards."

"We are kindred spirits then." Alexander grinned.

Westlake motioned them forward. "Your friends are sure to be coming hard after us. Let's ride."

The following morning, Westlake woke to the sound of someone throwing up. In the light of a half-moon, they had galloped through the lifeless town of Deer's Gap and crossed the bridge, this time heading north. Two hours later, as the horses tired, and drifting clouds made it impossible to see, Westlake led them off the path and well into the forest.

He had chosen the first two-hour watch, with Simpson taking the second, and now Parrish was nudging his shoulder in the dawn's first light. Again, someone nearby retched and moaned. Westlake strained to open his eyes.

"Miss Precious is being sick, sir," Parrish explained. Westlake sat up to see Alexander hustling to help her.

"Circle the camp a hundred yards around. Make sure we're alone," he said to Parrish. "There will be no fire this morning. We eat and then ride."

Alexander approached him with an expression of concern on his face. "This has happened for the last few mornings. She believes she's with child."

"Can she ride?" Westlake sat there, not knowing what to say or do. "It doesn't seem like the best thing to do in that condition."

"Precious has no choice; it's either ride or go back to slaving."

"She likely can't eat, so we'll be on our way immediately," Westlake said. "We'll ride hard and stop only when the horses need a rest. That's when we eat."

"I can do this," Precious appeared from behind Alexander. "I ain't never going back to slaving."

Alexander hugged her by the shoulders just as Parrish came in from the bush.

"Whew! That was a run. No one about, sir. I'm ready to eat." Parrish rubbed his hands together and grinned.

"Change in plan, Parrish," Westlake said. "Wake the others. We're riding now, and eating when the horses need a rest."

Parrish made to protest, but he must have changed his mind, because he turned away and grumbled to himself, "Crikey, I'm bloody starving."

By day's end, Westlake was satisfied that they'd covered as much ground as humanly possible. They headed north on the trail that would eventually take them past the Bauer farm. The horses slowed to a walk and his legs ached after the long ride. Slumped over the saddle of her horse, Precious continued to urge the animal forward. The sun soon began its descent below the treeline, casting long shadows.

Away from the trail, and through an alcove of trees, Westlake found a campsite that had been used many times. A few split logs were arranged in a circle around a fire pit. He held up his hand for the others to halt.

"We'll risk a fire while we still have a bit of daylight. Parrish, get it going and warm some stones for the lady's bed," Westlake ordered. "Mr. Simpson, go back to the edge of that alcove and stand guard, though I doubt any catchers can be too close behind, but let's err on the safe side. Mathew, help me with the horses. They need feeding and watering, just like you and I."

"I'll look after our girl here," said Alexander. He had already dismounted and now lifted Precious down from her horse. "Ain't no catchers riding faster than you, Miss Precious. We'll get your blanket out and you can rest a might."

After a half-hour lay-down, Precious joined the men as they sat on logs in a circle around the fire. The party had already eaten and Mathew handed her a tin cup of thin tea. She hesitated to drink it.

"You must eat and drink or you'll be too weak to ride," Mathew declared. "Even if you throw it up again, you must try."

Precious held the cup in her hands and took a sip. "Why did you come to fetch Alexander, Mr. Westlake?" She bit into a chunk of bread.

"Orders, ma'am."

"Why did you get such orders?"

"You are persistent, to be sure." Westlake grinned. "By aiding in the escape of slaves, General Brock believes he offers another reason for Americans to desire peace instead of war. And he wants Sergeant Alexander to lead a company of coloured militiamen."

"And why are you all fighting each other this time?" she asked, extending her hands to warm them over the growing flames.

"That's a question I'd like to know myself." Alexander leaned forward. "I mean, I know why I'll fight, but why are *you* fighting?"

"The Americans claim they are prevented from trade with France and complain that the British press their seaman into service," Westlake replied.

"Is it true?" Mathew asked.

"There's more than two sides to every story. Of course, French agitators are busy screaming in the newspapers — inciting passions or whatever else they can stir up over here."

"I fight for my King and country," Simpson announced with a flourish. "It's that simple." He poured himself a cup of tea and returned to his place of watch at edge of the alcove.

Parrish eyed him with a sneer before he spread out his blanket inside the circle of logs and lay back with his eyes closed.

Westlake continued, "The real question to ask is why have the Americans declared war." He threw another branch on the fire and sat back down. "As far as I can gather, the war hawks in Congress oppose an Indian buffer state between the Canadas and America. These same men would prefer the Canadas to become part of one vast United States. Do you see?" Westlake asked. "If they win this war, their victory will sweep away all such problems."

"But why do *you* fight?" Precious asked again.

"Miss Persistent again." Westlake glanced over at Alexander. "I endeavour to defend my home and hope to make a difference in doing so. Not very deep, is it?"

"All the ambition a man needs," Alexander concluded.

Westlake shrugged. "Time's up for the fire. Alex, shift those hot stones over next to Precious's blanket." Westlake kicked the logs of the campfire apart, as the others unrolled their blankets. He looked back to see Parrish already asleep. "I'll take the first watch — then Mathew, Alexander, and Parrish, so get yourselves some rest."

After a few days' travel, they again reached the outskirts of the Bauer farm. Westlake knew that Precious needed to rest properly, yet he hesitated at the track that led to the farmhouse. He imagined seeing Seffi's face and knew that he wanted her, but to stop here might put the entire Bauer family in danger. Then again, not to stop would risk a physical breakdown for Precious, and that might put the entire outcome of the mission in danger.

"Why are we waiting?" Simpson asked.

"I'm thinking, so shut up." A plan formed in Westlake's mind. "Let's go straight to that barn," he said, pointing the way. "Mr. Parrish, once you get there, unsaddle the horses immediately. Mathew can help you. Alexander, look after Precious, and Mr. Simpson, you are with me."

This time his reception at the Bauer front door began much better. Mr. Bauer invited Westlake inside. Wiping her hands on an apron, Katharina peered over his shoulder, no doubt looking for Parrish, until Westlake informed her that he was out in the barn, whereupon she rushed past him and headed through the open door. Moments later, Seffi appeared through the back door with a look of glee on her face. Speaking in German, Simpson notified everyone that he was very happy to be back.

Just seeing Seffi's face started Westlake's heart racing. He strained to concentrate on business while explaining the presence of three runaways instead of one and the delicate condition of Precious. Finally, he asked for the use of their barn for the night. By morning, he promised, they would be gone. The Bauers did not argue; as usual they would prove perfect hosts.

Although Westlake had made no mention of the river, late that evening, after he had eaten and slept, he descended into the hip-deep water for a thorough wash. Seffi came and laid a blanket there, as at their previous rendezvous. Without a word said between them, he knew all along that she would be waiting.

The night was a shade darker than the first time, but when she slipped her dress over her head, Westlake could still make out the beautiful lines of her body. She stepped into the cold water after him, and when he hugged her, the warmth of her skin made him sigh. He kissed her lightly on the mouth and she smiled, but neither of them spoke. He kissed her again, and they embraced as lovers would.

Westlake held the coarse soap in his hand and began to rub it slowly over her back and shoulders, then moved to her neck and finally her breasts. Seffi took the bar out of his hands and rubbed him all over, taking him in her hands. She then turned and threw the bar onto the small beach.

With a quick laugh, she held her nose and bobbed under the water. Westlake followed her. He felt clean for the first time in days and his skin smelled after the soap. Finally, he took her hand and led her out of the water toward the blanket. She began to speak, but he shook his head and put his finger gently upon her lips.

Westlake knew exactly what he wanted to do — and how he wanted to do it. Each time she tried to rush it, he resisted. Then she understood: she could have him but on his terms. They loved again and again and he sensed that, in his mind, she would be with him for the rest of his life.

Eventually, Westlake lay back, her head resting on his chest. A breeze cooled the air and he wrapped his blanket around both their bodies. He imagined waking up every day with the warmth of this woman next to him. He felt her every breath and realized this was where he wanted to be, beside her, forever. And then he knew, for more than one reason, he shouldn't have come.

"I've put your life in danger by coming back here. Dangerous men will follow us so I'm leaving Parrish behind with the extra horse, then he can catch up to us."

"I knew you'd come back … for sure." Seffi grinned. "We can protect ourselves fine, but Katharina will be thrilled with that news."

"No, you can't protect yourselves alone against these men. You must wear those hats, like when I first met you at the front door." He remembered the blond strands falling to her shoulder, and now he ran two fingers through her hair. "And dirty your faces with streaks of soot."

Seffi laughed, raised her head from his chest, and turned to face him. "You want me to look filthy?"

The moon drifted out from behind some scudding clouds. The light in her eyes grew bright and he wondered what the slave catchers might see in them, or want from them. In the moon's light, the shadows accented the curves of her cheeks and shoulders. She was beautiful, something of wild dreams, and Westlake heard the thumping of his heart.

"That's not enough," he said. "I want them to believe you're a killer." He kissed her lips as she slid on top of him.

She stretched her arms out to either side of his shoulders, then lifted her breasts off his chest and rocked forward so that they brushed against his mouth along with the rhythm of their movement. He had the sensation of floating … until she suddenly laughed.

"I feel your heart right through your chest. That means you can't resist me," she said, grinning.

"You're right, I can't resist — not even for the time of a single heartbeat." He gave her a light tap on the buttocks. "But that doesn't give you the right to be cheeky."

George Castor watched the beads of sweat roll down one side of the blacksmith's face. The man gave up information slowly. It sounded like a contrived story, but Castor also wondered now if he was telling the truth. The man appeared terrified enough, so why would he lie?

Fred Bennett swung a rope over a beam inside the workshop. On seeing the noose dangling at one end of the rope, the blacksmith's bowels loosened.

"Christ, you stink." Bennett slapped him hard across the face with the noose, and the man crumpled in a whimpering heap to the ground. "Oh God, that smells terrible." Bennett turned away, holding his nose.

"I've asked you not to speak like that of the Lord," Castor shouted in protest. "This fool's told us all he can. Let's get out of here. The faster we get to Pennsylvania, the better chance we have of catching up with them."

"He gave shelter to runaways." Bennett leaned forward, like an animal over its prey. "We should hang this dog."

"You really are stupid," Castor said. "We now know the first stop-off of every runaway nigger this side of Virginia and you want to kill him? Maybe we should burn this place down so we'll have *no* idea where to look." Castor gestured hard toward Bennett's horse, indicating for him to get mounted. "Understand?"

"Guess you're right … but hangin' 'im would be fun." Bennett laughed. "You want his boots maybe, Robinson?"

"That bastard Alexander's got my new boots, and those are the ones I came to get back," Robinson replied.

"But we can see your toes poking out." A man with cauliflower ears, named Fletcher, pointed to Robinson's foot.

Castor glanced down at the man's toes protruding through his old boot. "We're not here to steal — and we're leaving now." He waved his arm in a circle to the eight other men apart from Bennett, then pointed directly north.

Bennett gave the blacksmith a last kick to the ribs, angry at being shown up in front of the men. "If you've lied to us, I'm coming back to use this on you. Don't think I won't." He drooped the noose around the man's neck and chuckled again. The other trackers laughed with him.

"You're wasting time, Bennett. Saddle up," Castor ordered. "I want those slaves in hand soon. Let's ride." He gestured with this hand, pointing forward.

15

· · · · · ·

Two DAYS LATER, just inside the Pennsylvania border, Castor thought back to the blacksmith, so proud to be free. It didn't seem right that a nigger was free, and owning his own shop, but that was the law. Castor had been a catcher longer than he could remember, upholding the law, keeping order for society. And now he wondered if the world had gone mad, turned upside down.

He reckoned that the blacksmith must have told him the truth. In fact, he realized at the time the man was too scared to do anything but tell him what he wanted to know. At the southern end of a little town called Deer's Gap, just inside the Pennsylvania state border, he pulled back on the reins of his horse and studied the ground all around him. Tracking three riders from the plantation had been easy enough, but now there were at least six riders in front of him and maybe a seventh. If his slaves had joined up with other runaways, more slave money hung low for the picking.

From the foothills of the Appalachians, tracking them became like following a mob. The multiple hoof prints led him to the sweeping roadway that ended at the doorstep of the Bauer farmstead. The blacksmith had told the truth, but seeing that hangman's rope always provided a quick way of bringing it out.

As his crew trotted down the road, Castor surveyed the house and the barn. A small shed stood off to one side of the barn, and he supposed the outhouse lay out of sight around the rear of the home. At the woodpile close to the side of the house, he spotted a man drop his axe and run off through a side door.

Castor waved to Bennett, indicating with his fingers for four men to search around the back of the barn. If their runaway slaves were readying to bolt, the four catchers would have clear shots at them. He cocked the musket to fire. His heart beat faster, anticipating the end of the chase.

Riding his horse into the barn, he scanned the bales of hay one at a time. Not finding the slaves there, he returned to the front door of the main house. "Mr. Bauer," he shouted through the door. "I'm George Castor and I need to talk with you."

The door half opened and a large, rough-looking man with a mop of black hair and an unshaven chin appeared, but what Castor recognized first was the dangerous end of a musket.

"How can we help you, sir?" the man asked in an English accent.

"You don't sound German." Castor frowned. The way the man asked his question, he sounded more like a soldier. "Perhaps we're at the wrong place, but the sign said Bauer."

"That's not my sign." The Englishman grinned wide while scanning the men at Castor's back. Instead of displaying any nervousness, he seemed to be enjoying himself. Castor knew from experience that this kind of fellow would rather fight than talk.

"What's your name, sir? We're here searching for three runners — slaves escaping from the Caldwell place down south."

"They've been and gone." The Englishman jerked his head on hearing a sound somewhere behind him. "And you can warn your men at the back door that they'll be shot if they touch the latch again. Go on, give them a holler," the man urged. "Save their lives."

"Bennett, back away from that door now. You're about to get shot," Castor bellowed.

"That's a good fellow. My name's Parrish and I work for Mr. Bauer, doing the heavy lifting and keeping away the wild animals."

"Pleased to meet you, Mr. Parrish." Castor touched the tip of his hat. "You hiding my slaves here?"

Parrish shook his head no.

"They burnt down a barn, stole some horses, and tried to burn the master's home. On account of it, a young white boy hanged himself from a tree right in front. It's nearly destroyed his poor mother's sanity."

"And they stole my new boots," Robinson spit out.

Bennett and his four men had now ridden in behind Castor, and he glanced back to see a beautiful blond-haired girl being held up in the crook of Bennett's arm. She struggled to free herself from his saddle, but to no result. Castor frowned when he saw Bennett's hand on her bare breast. The girl must have fought him off because the top of her dress was torn.

There was a malevolence about Bennett that Castor knew he couldn't control. Whenever Bennett's right eye squinted, events got even worse, and right now his eye squinted plenty. The other men gawked at Seffi's beauty.

"Never liked masters myself, but sorry about the young man," Parrish said. "You've already inspected the barn and surrounding premises. They're not in here either. One man can dismount and come inside to check, but you'll not find them 'cause they've gone. By the way, you forgot the shed."

Castor grimaced. "Robinson, check the shed."

"What if we just shoot you and then look wherever we want," Bennett called out from behind his colleague.

Keeping his eyes on Castor, Parrish pushed the door open with his boot to reveal Farmer Bauer with two pistols and Katharina armed with a musket. A few of the men whistled at the sight of her. That made four bullets, and Castor figured Parrish would take out at least another two or three men before he died.

"That's right. Do your count, Mr. Castor. We'd take five or six of you to hell before you'd have your way with these women," Parrish said.

"Stand down." Castor turned his head to instruct the men ranged behind him. "And no funny business. I don't want myself getting shot." He dismounted, handed the reins of his horse to another rider, then walked slowly to the front door. "I'll take that look around inside, if you don't mind."

Parrish moved to one side. "Mr. Bauer, keep both pistols on his back, and escort Mr. Castor inside for a peek. Katharina, keep your musket trained on the man under the bowler hat." Parrish gestured toward Bennett.

Castor smelled bacon from the morning's breakfast and his stomach wrenched at the thought of food. He found a stack of dirty dishes, but no sign of runaway slaves. He took a long look at the young woman called Katharina and noticed her poor efforts to make herself appear unattractive. The sight of her reminded him that he couldn't remember the last time he had been with a woman.

He grinned at her, not because he wanted to do her harm, but because she was so wrong in her estimation of him. As a lawman his entire life, rape and plunder were not part of his character. The back bedrooms hid no one either and Castor turned to leave. He passed through the front doorway, careful not to brush against Parrish.

Robinson hauled up his horse in front. "Nothing in the shed, and I looked through the stables again to be sure. Nothing."

"So you've told the truth, Mr. Parrish. I thank you," Castor said.

"Honesty is the best policy, my mother always taught me. You and your men should be getting on your way. These triggers get slippery after a while," Parrish said. "And your friend can put the girl down now."

Castor watched a drop of sweat fall from the man's forehead and he had to agree that muskets sometimes did go off by accident. He quickened his pace and mounted up.

"Put her down," Castor ordered sharply.

Bennett tried to twist Seffi around so he could kiss her on the mouth, but she banged his nose sharply with her forehead and slid out of the saddle. She ran to stand behind Parrish.

"You bitch." Bennett rubbed his nose, his right eye narrowing again. "I'll be back *for you* when this is over. Count on it."

Castor tipped his hat to the ladies and gestured for his men to head on north. The Englishman, Parrish, had known from the start they would find nothing here. His game had been about stalling, and he'd succeeded. The house, the shed, the inspections of the outbuildings, was just a waste of time. Castor spurred his horse into a gallop. But, even with the delay, that dirty mound of breakfast dishes had told him his quarry was not too far ahead.

For the sake of speed, Westlake stayed on the same Indian path that they had taken when heading south. He understood the danger, but to keep their distance from the pursing catchers, the risk of meeting the same hostile Indians was necessary. He prayed they would have long moved on. Of course, the militia might still be searching for him as well. Yet, it was impossible for Precious to travel overland through rough bush, and he could hardly ask her to move faster when every morning she started off the day with a heaving stomach. He remembered throwing up with his hangover and shuddered at the prospect of the cycle repeating itself every morning.

Early one evening, just past a junction with a trail running east, Precious began to retch again. A late midday meal had obviously not sat well, though it was unusual for her to be sick this late in the day. Westlake had noticed a drop in temperature at night as they trooped north and approached Lake Erie. For the girl's health, he hoped weather conditions would not worsen.

They stopped off to the side of the path where some waist-high boulders allowed Westlake to dismount and sit himself down. The clearing here was some twenty paces square, with three tall maple trees in the centre, just behind the boulders. Sitting on any one of these rocks allowed him a clear view of their surroundings.

Simpson scouted ahead and Alexander watched out lest the catchers appeared to their rear while Mathew tried to make Precious comfortable. Westlake leaned back, scanning the sky, until he heard someone come crashing through the branches. Simpson galloped into view holding on tight to his hat. His hands were scratched from the underbrush and his face flushed with excitement.

"Indians ahead ... in warpaint ... must be twenty or thirty of them," he panted, looking down from his horse for Westlake's instructions.

"Did they see you?"

"I'm afraid so, sir."

"Ride straight back and fetch Alex."

Westlake reached for the carbine slung on the side of his horse and slid it out of its ring. When it was loaded, he placed it gingerly on top of the boulder. Then he snatched up his musket and twisted on the bayonet.

"Mathew, get Precious down behind that boulder. Is that musket loaded?"

Holding hands with Precious, Mathew slid down behind the rock. For the first time, Westlake noticed fear on both their faces.

"Fix the bayonet," Westlake urged. "This will get nasty."

"I can do it," Precious volunteered matter-of-factly. "I'm scared, but I can do this."

Alexander and Simpson galloped up, jumped down, and tied up their horses.

"No signs of catchers back there?" Westlake asked them.

"None that I could see," Alexander replied.

"Good. Simpson, secure all the horses tight to this tree right behind us. It's the animals they want. And fix your bayonets, both of you," Westlake ordered.

Simpson immediately reached for his bayonet, but his hand shook as he fumbled it on to the musket. An order to fix bayonets meant close fighting and no one wanted to engage in that with an Indian.

"Are you all right, Mr. Simpson?" Westlake inquired, putting his hand on the man's shoulder.

"I hope your reputation as a killer is justified." Simpson's expression was tense and his voice emerged in a strange quiver.

"Me?" Westlake grinned. "Just look at *him*. He'll kill them all for the both of us."

In the hands of Alexander, the musket looked puny compared to those of the other men. He snapped his bayonet into position with precision.

"They told me that you were once a nasty fighter. Are you prepared for this … Sergeant?" Westlake asked.

"Got these two pistols, the muskets, and that carbine. That makes seven shots between us. " Alexander grinned. "If we don't fire too soon and miss, we can take down seven of them. The other warriors will think twice. Indians fight the same as other folk; they don't like to die."

Alexander paused and took a step back. "But I'm better at fighting close in." He used his musket to spear the air at waist height, and Westlake saw from his stance that the big man had done this many times before.

"Did you hear that, Mr. Simpson? Don't fire unless the enemy is right on top of you," Westlake said.

"Of course, sir." Simpson's quick agreement was unusual, and Westlake wondered if he'd understood the order properly.

He considered Alexander's words. They could take down seven with accurate fire, but even if they were facing just twenty warriors, they were only five defenders. It would be unusual for the Indians to attack all at once, but if they so chose, Westlake knew that his small group would be overwhelmed in seconds. Then he glanced around and wondered how far back were the catchers.

The forest around them went quiet and he felt a chill arising from the early darkness. A crow fluttered into the clearing, landing on a stone at the perimeter. Westlake noticed Alexander frown before crouching behind a boulder. He knelt down beside him and again checked the pan on his musket.

"They won't, you know," Westlake remarked, still examining his musket. "They'll take some shots at us from the outside, then probe our position for weaknesses. But they won't all come at once."

Alexander laughed. "How did you know what I was thinking?"

"Because I was thinking exactly the same thing."

And then a musket banged and a ball whizzed overhead. Another crack and a ball smacked the rock beside Alexander. He raised his eyebrows just as another clipped the bark of the tree-trunk right in front of him. The attack had begun.

16

....

WESTLAKE PUT HIS RIGHT HAND over his heart and felt it thumping through his chest. He tried to judge his state of mind and stay calm. Terrified? he wondered. More like plain scared, but no feeling of panic. He thought back to other times when he had faced death and a type of quiet descended on him. His actions became more deliberate. And the killing just something that had to be done.

He stood on the right end of their little firing line, almost in the trees, with Alexander beside him. Behind the boulders situated in the middle, crouched Simpson. On their far left, Precious and Mathew also held their muskets at the ready. Both of them displayed a type of firmness that surprised him.

The light was fading fast so that within minutes they would be in total darkness. If Alexander died in this engagement, Westlake's mission would be a failure. His mind raced to think of an escape. He remembered having passed a trail leading east, only forty paces south of their current position.

"Alex," he whispered, "as soon as it's dark, I want Mathew and Precious to take that trail back there, the one heading east. Remember it?" Westlake made a motion with his hand, indicating south before east. "Then I want you to follow them. Simpson and I will give you a head start and then catch up."

Two muskets banged out and both balls creased the tree where Westlake stood. He dove to the ground, jarring his neck.

"Are you hurt?" Alexander asked.

"Only my pride." Westlake winced, rubbing the back of his neck.

"I can't run away from this fight," Alexander protested.

"No, but you can save Precious if you do as I say. She certainly can't stay here."

Alexander stared down at his boots, then looked Westlake in the eye and nodded knowingly. "It's not my first choice, but I agree."

Westlake crawled over on his belly to tell Mathew the plan. They had to stay on the eastbound trail until it swung north toward Lake Erie. Once they were clear of the Indians, the sooner they travelled north, the less chance they'd have of missing the lake altogether. If that happened, they'd have to cross the Niagara River — and perhaps even encounter the great falls. Westlake wanted no part of that.

A warrior fired not twenty yards in front of them, his face lit up by the discharge of his musket. Alexander fired back and heard someone groan. "Only twenty-nine left," he said. The forest went quiet.

"It's time. Mathew, quietly get your horses back to the junction. We'll keep up a steady fire here. Go," Westlake ordered. "Go."

"Thank you, sir," Mathew said. He shook Westlake's hand and gave a brief wave to Simpson.

In that exact second, a warrior charged out of the trees on their left, raising a tomahawk over his head. Precious was standing alone with the musket as Mathew turned away. Her musket rose and she squeezed the trigger. The warrior's feet kept coming, but his head jerked backward so that his legs lifted off the ground. She had pointed high, taking off part of the warrior's skull.

"Oh, God! What have I done!" she squealed. Precious held the smoking musket to her shoulder and stared back toward Mathew.

"Saved my life," he replied.

Alexander had crawled in beside them. Now he jumped up and gently took the musket from her hands. "I'm sorry but we've no time to lose, Precious," he whispered. "Look after this girl now, you hear?" he said turning to Mathew.

"They'll have to kill me first, sir."

"Good lad." He hugged Precious briefly with one arm, then gave Mathew a slap on the back.

"Thank you for everything, Mr. Westlake," Precious whispered, her voice cracking under the strain.

"That was a good shot, Precious." Westlake bowed his head. "Now go."

The smoke of discharged powder hung in the air, drifting aimlessly with the wind. An Indian fired straight in front of them and then another from the left, but the musket balls whizzed harmlessly overhead. They were merely probing to find reactions from their enemy, so Westlake returned to his tree and Alexander to his.

"Mr. Simpson, they've swung somewhat to our left, which suits our purpose. You may begin firing at will, if you please. Aim low."

Westlake pointed his musket toward the centre and fired into the darkness. Simpson banged away to his left and Alexander, after giving time for Simpson to reload, fired immediately after him. Westlake glanced over his shoulder but saw Mathew and Precious had been swallowed by the darkness.

Westlake heard no sound of his fugitives, and after a few minutes, he touched Alexander on the shoulder. "Remember, you must stay on the same trail. It has to curve north to Lake Erie at some point."

"I'd rather fight here with you, but I appreciate this," Alexander said. "You're a good man, Jonathan Westlake."

"No, sir. Just doing my duty, sir, no more."

Alexander untied one of the horses and crept quietly out the camp, heading south.

Within five minutes of him leaving, Westlake heard soft footsteps directly to their front. The moon had risen high in the night sky. When the swish of a bush caught his attention to the right, he glanced over at Simpson, who crouched so low he was likely to topple over.

"This was a bad idea, Mr. Westlake," Simpson gagged.

"Precious needed a head start," Westlake whispered.

The bush parted to reveal the silhouette of a warrior. Westlake jumped up, lifting Simpson under the arm, so they could fight back to back. "Prepare to use bayonet, Mr. Simpson."

The two men stood with their muskets pointing straight out in front of them. In his other hand, Westlake held a carbine.

The warrior charged foward, screaming, a tomahawk held above his head. The instant Westlake clearly saw the figure's outline, he discharged the carbine and dropped it. He then clutched his musket and steadied himself, ready to fight with its bayonet, as six more warriors cleared the bush at a run. Three of the assailants had muskets.

"Down." Westlake pulled Simpson to the ground, as the Indians let fire at the run. The muskets' spark and flame lighted their attackers for just an instant. A bullet brushed the hair on one side of his head. One Indian headed straight toward the horses. "Now stand up and fire in unison with me, Robert."

Westlake heard Simpson's musket blast, and with a glance over his shoulder, he saw a painted native collapse against Simpson face to face, the bullet having gone straight through the man's nose. Simpson froze and did not move his back from Westlake's. Westlake fired his musket and another native fell.

He heard the rumble of horse hooves in the distance as the three remaining warriors approached cautiously. Westlake lunged with his bayonet in a sweep to keep them at bay. Simpson remained steadfast at his back but didn't make any move to help.

The vibration of approaching hooves grew until out of the darkness a horse galloped hard through the clearing. From the saddle, Parrish swung the butt end of his musket, knocking senseless the Indian who was stealing Simpson's horse.

Parrish! Thank God for Parrish!

He galloped on and dove from his horse straight at the three warriors. All of them landed in a heap at Westlake's feet. Westlake stomped on one man's head before bayoneting him in the neck. Parrish took a slash to his arm from an Indian he was trying to strangle. Westlake stabbed the same man in the belly, and stared as the remaining warrior darted back into the bushes. Then it was quiet.

He scanned the ground directly in front of him, the bodies lying still. His guts churned and he slowed his breathing. From his knees, Parrish struggled to stand, his hand gripping his left bicep to slow the flow of blood. Westlake turned to Simpson and motioned with his head for him to offer assistance. But Simpson, who had not moved an inch after firing his musket, remained standing, stiff with fear.

Westlake shook his head and turned his back. He couldn't look the other man in the face and had to hide his disgust. Then he himself reached down to offer Parrish a shaking hand.

"The catchers are still a ways behind us, but they'll be coming, sir." Parrish nodded to the south. "I heard the shots here and figured you were in trouble. Those Indians will be back soon too, now they know how few we are."

"Leave the spare horse tied to the tree. We've got to hit that trail south before the catchers get there." Westlake was speaking fast. He glanced back to the trail. "We might get lucky and they'll think we're still here. By the way, Walter …"

Parrish turned to face his friend.

"… it is damn good to see you." Westlake smiled. "Another minute and …" Westlake gripped Parrish's shoulder. "Well, I guess there's no telling, is there."

"None too soon, sir." Parrish shook his head. "My mother always said, Better a minute early than a minute late." He laughed.

Castor hauled up his horse and peered through the night air. The musket fire had been quiet for a while. His slaves had to be just ahead — he could feel it.

Drifting clouds covered the moon, as if someone had dimmed a lantern to darken a room. He held up his hand for the others behind him to stop, but in the blackness they bumped into his horse until they could go no farther.

"Can you see up ahead there, Bennett?"

"I can't see my hand in front of my face, for Christ's sake. How the hell do you think I can see anything else?"

"I've asked you before not to talk like that," Castor said. "Did you hear … ?"

"I saw a horse," volunteered Fletcher.

The moon reappeared to show Fletcher's enormous ears. Castor stared past him, squinting to find the horse.

"See, by the tree, in the centre," Fletcher said.

"Where are the other horses?" Castor asked.

"Well, I don't suppose they'd all be standing up in plain sight. Did you —?" Fletcher tried to speak, but Bennett cut him off.

"Where there's one, there'll be more hiding. Let's go get our niggers." Bennett spurred his mount and Fletcher followed.

"Wait," ordered Castor, but it was too late as the other catchers pressed past him, too anxious to seize their prey. He shook his head and followed them toward the single horse tethered to a tree.

Within seconds of reaching the animal, the forest lit up with flashes of musket fire, illuminating painted faces. Castor jerked his gaze from one to the other as they shrieked all around him. *Indians!* They charged forward, brandishing tomahawks above their heads. Only a few feet away, a single warrior appeared, lifting his musket to fire.

Castor gasped as Fletcher twisted backward at the blast, gripping his chest. He rocked forward in his saddle, then fell off to one side, still holding the reins while his foot remained trapped in the stirrup. Castor threw his knife, catching the native full in the chest.

Another Indian snatched hold of the reins securing the spare horse and slashed at the knot. He then snatched Fletcher's reins and ran for the cover of the bushes, pulling both horses behind him. Fletcher's head bounced along the ground until he disappeared from Castor's sight.

"Ah, no!" Robinson called. "Fletcher!" He urged his horse after him, but Castor reached over and grabbed his arm.

"He's lost, man. Let him go," Castor hollered above the firing. "You'll only get yourself killed."

"We're in the crapper here and I don't see no niggers," Bennett screamed as he pointed his carbine and fired at the last spot where a musket shot had lit up a warrior's face.

The nine remaining men on horseback whirled around, looking for a way out. Bennett's brown mare bumped into Castor's thigh. Castor fired his carbine at a flame spotted in the dark, but his nervous horse reared back suddenly and the bullet carried high. Gun smoke floated in the air and stung the back of his throat.

"Back out, back south the way we came," Castor yelled. He yanked on his reins, jerking the head of his horse roughly, and then dug in his spurs. The animal bolted out of the pack, and he heard the others shouting behind him. He galloped along the path until the moon disappeared, and then he stopped for fear of losing the trail and crashing into a tree. Bumping and jostling, the others gathered around him.

"Son of a bitch, those runaways left that animal there to trap us. That's the only goddamn reason they'd leave behind a valuable horse," Bennett said.

"Next time we go charging in, let me decide when," Castor replied bitterly. "Beforehand, I wanted to ask if any of you had heard Indian screams like I did. Now we know for sure."

"So now what do we do?" Bennett asked.

"Head back south a few miles, where we'll make camp, and hope those damn Indians have had their fill of fighting for one night." Castor said. "We'll come back in the morning when we can see properly."

"But that's miles in the wrong direction," Bennett whined.

"You don't have much hair, but I assume you want to keep it," Castor replied.

He edged his horse around, as he squinted through the darkness. They rode until he found a suitable campsite, where they dismounted and tethered their animals. The men spread out on either side of the path and Castor posted a couple sentries to the north. Blankets were rolled out with saddles placed at the top end for headrests. Every man cleaned his musket and reloaded, expecting the warriors to return but praying they wouldn't.

Bennett tethered his horse next to Castor's. "So, where did our slaves get to?"

"I wish I knew. We'll do a circle in the morning. They can't fly so they must've gone somewhere... back to the Niagara River's my guess."

"Goddamn cheating niggers. If there ain't no bodies to fetch home, we got ourselves no pay," Bennett yelled. "Christ almighty, we're back in the same mess we was in with those first two."

Castor grabbed Bennett's vest and pulled his face close enough to smell the other man's foul breath. "I'll kill you if you raise your voice again." His anger of the night's debacle quivered in his own voice, and Bennett slumped warily. "And talking like that with the Lord's name isn't acceptable."

"Fine, fine. It's just that we can't let them go jumping in that river again," Bennett pleaded.

Castor let go of the vest, knowing he was the only man in this group that Bennett respected. "Maybe we head that way first and see if we pick up their trail. There's at least four or five of them together, and one of them must be real smart. That trick with the horse cost old Fletcher his life."

"And a few years off mine." Bennett started rubbing his forehead. "I'll take the first watch. Get yourself some sleep."

"In the morning, we'll wait a spell and then go real slow, on account of those Indians. I'm not interested in getting stung by another beehive."

"What about our runaways?" Bennett asked. "We gotta catch up with 'em."

"You won't catch nothing if you're dead. Ask Fletcher."

Once clear of the Indians, Westlake continued riding east. In the darkness it was difficult to travel fast, but they kept up a steady pace. At one point, Westlake asked Parrish how it went at the Bauer farm. Simpson leaned from his horse to listen in.

"Fine, sir." Parrish grinned. "I kept the wild animals at bay as you asked. There's one fellow with a bowler hat who laid his hands on Seffi, but she's fine now. Says he's going back for her after this thing's over."

"Mr. Bauer?"

"No better, sir. I don't know how long he'll live."

Westlake thought of Seffi and then of Mary, and finally of his guilt toward both of them. He wondered if it would ever go away. He slowed his weary horse and looked round to find Parrish still holding his arm. They had not caught up to Alexander, or to Precious and Mathew. He wondered how far they might have to travel to find them. Maybe his new friends had wandered off the path.

A fading moon reappeared as he rounded a bend and in its light he was startled to see Mathew tying his horse to a bush. Behind the bush, two small feet could be seen. Precious had gone to sleep lying on a blanket spread on the ground.

"Where's Alex?" Westlake asked as he dismounted.

"Said we should sleep while it's dark and the travelling is slow. He's scouting ahead."

"You did well in sneaking Precious away," Westlake said. "Good show."

Mathew grinned.

By the time Alexander returned, Westlake had bandaged Parrish's wounded arm. The knife had grazed his friend's forearm in a thin gash and Parrish joked that he'd had suffered worse cuts while shaving. The bleeding gradually came to a stop.

Simpson unsaddled the horses and laid out the blankets for their night's sleep. Alexander took the first watch, and Parrish the second. Simpson took over at dawn, the new day lighting a trail that had yet to swing north toward the lake.

"I'm starving," Parrish said with a yawn. "Who's for breakfast?"

"There's no time, and we can't risk fires," Westlake ordered. "The catchers should take a while, but once they pick up our trail they'll be coming hard."

"I've just the thing then," Parrish said. Out of his saddlebag, he pulled a cloth bundle that he unwrapped to reveal three loaves of bread. "Courtesy of Katharina." He held up a loaf and then put it under his nose before inhaling deeply.

Parrish broke off chunks and passed them to the outstretched hands of each hungry traveller. "Back at the Bauers', the man called Castor said how a young fellow hanged himself from a tree in front of the Caldwell place. It's nearly killed his mother."

"The punishment tree in front? Why did he do that?" Mathew asked, his eyes searching from Alexander to Precious, who just shook her head and shrugged.

"I really feel terrible about Percy," Alexander declared with a grin, then his face turned solemn. "That's the same tree they hung my son Hector's body from. Maybe that evil old bitch will hang herself as well."

"You'll never be free until you stop hating them. You taught me to forgive, but you can't do it," Precious said, echoing their earlier conversation.

"I'm free *now*," Alexander replied. "No master is telling me what to do." He flapped both his huge arms above his head, as if they were wings and the symbols of his freedom.

Westlake remembered that little English rancher striking back at the world in order to feel free. Was the Englishman really free or still trapped in his disgust for authority? Was anyone truly free? He wondered if he'd ever be free of his own guilty feelings. He washed down the last mouthful of bread with a swig from his canteen.

"Another one of the catchers said you stole his new boots." Parrish nodded toward Alexander's feet.

"I needed them more than he did. 'Sides, he already had his old boots."

"That makes you an arch-criminal," Westlake chided.

"An arch-criminal! Stolen boots!" Precious laughed. "Very funny, Mr. Westlake."

"When do we head up to Lake Erie?" interjected Parrish, who was not laughing. "This path seems to continue east."

"We have to avoid any militia along the Erie shoreline," Westlake explained, "but at the same time, we have to find ourselves a boat before we hit the Niagara River. I'm not playing 'devil dare' with those bloody falls."

"Then we'll have to steal one," Parrish said.

"What about in exchange for our horses?" Simpson asked, tearing another bite of his bread.

"One or the other, preferably a trade," Westlake replied. "But first we have to find the damn thing."

"Any idea where exactly we'll be when we do touch the shore?" Alexander asked.

"We've strayed a good way off course, so we're well to the east side of the town of Erie. And we can't risk going near a town with you three." Westlake shook his head, pointing to the path. "No, we'll stay on this track for a full day and then head north. That should put us on the lake somewhere south west of Buffalo."

"How's Precious feeling this morning?" Alexander asked.

"This morning's a good one; don't feel sick none at all." Precious smiled and tapped the cork back into her canteen. Throughout the entire trip, the girl had suffered her discomfort in silence.

"You've done well." Alexander nodded, chewing on his bread. "The catchers'll be coming. We should get moving."

"They're not going to give up, are they?" Precious asked Westlake.

He shook his head slowly, sorry to disappoint her.

"I didn't tell you last night, Alex, but we left a horse behind for the Indians, and for your friend George Castor." Parrish laughed.

Westlake grinned as he finished the tale. "While we snuck away, I could hear musket shots and screaming." He pointed at Alexander. "Seems the catchers thought we were still there with the horse. What they found, instead, was a hornets' nest of Indians keen on stealing that horse."

Once they started laughing, no one could stop. The tension had been too great for too long. Alexander doubled over, tears rolling down his face. Mathew hugged Precious tight as she giggled and clutched her belly. Westlake laughed until his cheeks hurt. Even Simpson, sullen since freezing in fear during the battle, once started, could not stop laughing.

"I wish I could've been there to see the surprise on Castor's face." Parrish chuckled.

"I'll kill him if I see him again. Both him and Bennett." All the laughter ceased after Alexander's comment. He spread his fingers, palms up, like he had Castor's neck in a grip. Then he pulled up his shirt from the bottom and turned to show a back disfigured with red scars. "Understand why?"

The hideous scarring reminded Westlake of Brock's words: *"Just get him and bring him back here. Sooner is better than later."*

"Let's saddle up." He glanced at the brightening sky. "I don't think we want to meet this fellow Castor and his friends any time soon. We've a ways to go to find a lake, and then a boat."

17

· · · · · ·

MAJOR GENERAL STEPHEN VAN RENSSELAER lay back on his cot with his hands behind his head and considered his chances of success. A blast of wind shook the tent and his numerous candles wavered, moving idle shadows about the walls. The rain kept a steady tap on the tent roof, yet it didn't distract him from his deliberations.

In the last weeks of September, Brigadier General Smyth had hiked into Buffalo with an additional seventeen hundred fighters. And even more troops were marching his way. Along the thirty-six-mile Niagara River, from Lake Erie to Lake Ontario, Stephen's force now exceeded six thousand soldiers, a number including at least four thousand regulars. And although Quartermaster Peter Porter still hated him, going so far as to spread rumours of cowardice and complicity with the enemy, supplies from Porter, Barton and Company continued trickling in.

An aide, rain dripping from the peak of his cap, pulled back the tent flap. "Colonel van Rensselaer's approaching, sir."

"Show him in directly."

Stephen closed his eyes and reviewed his plan of attack. *Almost ready now.* In a two-pronged thrust, Smyth's forces would assault Queenston first, to draw the British away from his main attack on Newark and Fort George. Everything, however, depended on the complete co-operation of Smyth.

"But Smyth, the pompous ass, won't even talk to me," the major general said to no one, staring up at the roof of his tent.

In any other army, there'd be a damn court martial for such behaviour. But in this, the new American army, men voted for their leaders. Stephen slammed a fist into the palm of his hand and cursed. At that exact moment a streak of lightning flashed, before cracking directly over-head. He jerked upright, staring at his fist, before he burst out laughing.

The weather had been poor for days, reminding him that only yes-terday two companies of the Second Regiment of Artillery had arrived, having slogged their four cannon through the rain. Their twenty-six-year-old commander, Colonel Winfield Scott, a Virginian by birth, stood six-foot five-inches tall and weighed all of two hundred and sixty pounds. Stephen wondered if the stories about his tough character were true.

Just then, Solomon van Rensselaer hustled into the tent, wiping his soaking brow with the back of his hand. "Cousin." He nodded.

From the edge of his cot, Stephen inquired, "What's your report on this fine October 8?" The sound of the rain increased to a cre-scendo. "Drink?" he shouted, gesturing to a white-clothed table where an opened bottle of red wine and several glasses stood waiting.

"Colonel Scott has approved a cutting-out expedition, right across from Black Rock," Solomon reported. "The ships *Caledonia* and *Detroit*, we presume carrying supplies from Fort Detroit, have just anchored under the guns of Fort Erie. At midnight, he plans to send a hundred men across the river in two longboats. He hopes thus to overpower what should be merely skeleton crews left behind."

Solomon shrugged and poured some wine. Gulping down a mouthful, he shivered. "We'll see soon enough if the man is any damn good," he continued. "Once on board, the men will cut the ship's cables and sail them back to our side under guns supervised by Scott himself. At least, that's the grand plan."

Sounds easy, thought Stephen, but can he do it in this horrible rain? The tapping sound on his tent roof grew even harder until sud-denly it disappeared. The major general poured himself a glass of wine and sipped. A sharp drop in the temperature raised his curiosity, and he poked his head out through the tent door. "Oh, bollocks!" he exclaimed. "Not this." The heavy rain had turned to sleet.

With his back to the shore, Lieutenant Colonel Winfield Scott of the Second Regiment of Artillery towered over all the other officers and men. Before addressing them, he wondered where his thoughts came from, because for some strange reason, his days in law school jumped into his head. The sleet slashed at his face and he turned away from the wind, wiping the melting snow from one eye and then brushing his eyebrows. In this weather, the mission could go horribly wrong, and a hundred men could easily lose their lives. But now they were committed, so he could show no trace of doubt. This wasn't a law-class debate. A cutting-out meant a fight to the death, of crushing one party over another.

"Thank you all for volunteering," he began, then cleared his throat. "Your enthusiasm is commendable. The task is simple, but I will not play down the danger." The wind gusted across the beach and he raised his voice to a shout. "Two boats, with fifty men in each, will row across to the *Caledonia* and the *Brig Adams*, renamed by the Brits *'Detroit'.*" He gestured over his shoulder with his thumb toward the water.

"Once there, you will board the ships, kill anyone who stands in your way, and axe the cables. Of course, tonight they don't know they're about to lose their ships to you men!" A vigorous cheer rose up as the excitement for battle gripped the assembled expedition.

"The sailors among you know your business. If you're not a sailor, your only purpose on this mission is to kill, and to protect our sailors. Any questions?"

Scott paused, praying no one would ask what their chances were. Many of these men would not return alive. They stared up at him with faces showing their anticipation and excitement; yet there was only silence. Each man no doubt had his own questions, but obviously they all preferred to get moving and leave the stomach jitters behind. He agreed.

"This'll be something to tell your grandchildren. Know that God is with you." Scott snapped to attention and saluted. "Good fortune to every one of you."

He pointed to his officers, who barked the orders to begin embarkation. A short way out into the lake, the vessels needed to traverse a high sandbank. Scott imagined that these same men would be forced to disembark into the freezing water to lighten the load for the boats to float across it.

Afterwards, they'd row into the main part of Lake Erie just before it flowed into the Niagara River. Then a three-hour hard pull in the dark, against the current and through driving sleet, would find them right next to their sleeping prey. He hoped that by then his expeditionary force would still be fit enough to fight.

They marched quietly off down to their boats, full of ambition and, no doubt, fear. Gaining possession of those ships could tip the balance of power on Lake Erie. Combined with the three ships under construction at Black Rock, these vessels, if captured, could change the course of the entire war.

Although he'd never met Isaac Brock, Scott smiled at the thought of Brock's chagrin on learning that two of his valuable ships had been stolen from right under his very nose. He inhaled the cold night air and peered directly into the sleet. "It's up to them now." And when he stared out beyond the shoreline of Lake Erie, the last contours of the boats' oars seemed to wave goodbye as they vanished into the blackness.

Atop his horse, Westlake pulled a blanket around him as the temperature dropped farther. He surveyed the scudding clouds and wondered when the weather might improve. In this incessant drizzle, they had ridden and walked for five days and now listened to the waves lapping against Lake Erie's southern shore.

His party of six travelled inside the treeline, well hidden from any coastal militia. For more than ten miles along the shore, he'd sighted no boats. As he rode toward Buffalo, enemy militia appeared in increasing number, and he feared discovery if they didn't find a vessel soon.

Precious continued heaving most mornings, and even after a night's sleep, she continued to look worn. She didn't once complain, but Westlake knew she was hungry. Their provisions eaten, he had to do something fast to improve their chances.

He glanced back at his small troop pressing its way through the woods. Darkness descended and the drizzle turned to a pelting rain. As they rounded a small bend in the trail, he turned to the shoreline and spotted a dozen longboats resting only a hundred yards away, hauled up at the edge of the beach.

A ride home stared him in the face, but his stomach clenched in dismay. At the midpoint between the forest and the waiting boats, at least two hundred militiamen stood at attention in three ranks with weapons shouldered. Until they marched away, he had no hope of reaching the boats.

Westlake held up a warning hand and edged back, deeper into forest cover. Though the light was dim, he saw that something big was happening here. He squinted through the rain and the ranks of militia to see blue-coated soldiers blanketing the shore behind them.

"Form up!" a voice bellowed. The men jostled for position.

The United States Army of the Center was on the move. "By the left, forward march!" At the shout of command, the entire assembled mass of men and arms began to march northwest, toward Buffalo.

In less than five minutes, they had left the beach almost deserted. A dozen militia remained to guard the boats. Most of the vessels were large enough to seat twenty-five men, except for two smaller longboats that might seat ten. Westlake set his eyes on one of the lesser vessels, wondering how he might steal it. A head-on assault wasn't appealing. They needed a diversion.

"Let me propose a fair trade to them, Mr. Westlake," Simpson whispered. "Our horses in exchange for a boat. What harm can come of it?"

"They'll kill you outright," Parrish replied.

"Rubbish. For what reason? I'll leave my musket and pouch here." Simpson handed his musket to Mathew and hung his pouch of cartridges from the young man's saddle.

"Parrish is right," Alexander said. "They'd just shoot you and get your horse for free."

"What exactly will you tell them?" Westlake asked, the hunger burning in their bellies foremost in his mind.

"That I have two friends coming along behind me who will trade their horses, along with mine, for a single small boat."

"It's a little daft," Parrish remarked, "but it might work."

"All they can say is no," Simpson replied. "But why would they do so, when offered such a generous bargain?"

"And if they say yes, then we arrive with the horses to make the exchange, then row down the shore, where we pick up our friends." Parrish nodded toward Alexander and his two companions.

Precious shook her head. "It's too dangerous Mr. Simpson." She shivered. "On the other hand, I don't know how else to get that boat."

"She's right," Westlake said. "This is a bad idea, but we've run out of food and time. If you insist, give it a try. But I hope you don't end up dead." Westlake offered his hand. "We'll watch out for any tricks from here."

Simpson shook hands with the others, and Precious even hugged him. He stood back, tugged down his blue waistcoat, and mounted his horse. After trotting a hundred yards along the forest edge, so as to not give away their position, Simpson broke out of cover onto the open sand and jumped off his horse. He proceeded to walk toward the small patrol with his hands in the air.

Westlake held his breath.

It seemed like an hour passed, but after only five minutes, just long enough for the patrol sergeant to disbelieve the story, he drove his musket butt into Simpson's midriff. As Simpson buckled over, the man lashed his forearm across the side of his head. Simpson collapsed to the beach in a heap.

Another man grabbed the horse's reins and, laughing, kicked Simpson in the ribs as he lay on the ground.

"Christ, I knew it was a dumb idea," Westlake declared bitterly. "He felt guilty about freezing up during that fight with the natives and now we have to bloody well rescue him. I've half a mind to just let him rot there."

"Then we'd still have to find ourselves a boat," Parrish observed.

Westlake had to agree.

The sergeant dragged Simpson to within thirty yards of the nearest longboat and forced him to his knees. Westlake figured they were content to wait for Simpson's friends to arrive, at which time they'd seize all their horses. *Dumb. Real dumb.* He should never have let Simpson do it.

As one man stood guard, with his musket trained on the back of Simpson's head, the rest of the militia hovered around the beach as if they were on leave. At least they seemed casual about the episode, doubtless assuming Simpson's friends would be equally as stupid as their captive.

Westlake shivered once again as the temperature dropped farther and the rain turned to sleet. Then he turned to Alexander. "I suppose you can already guess what we have to do. I'll act as the diversion."

"I hope you've all kept your firing pans dry," Alexander warned. "We're going to need them soon." He pointed to the hunting knife strapped to the side of Westlake's boot. "Mr. Parrish tells me that you're pretty accurate with that thing. At what distance would you not miss, even in the rain and the dark?"

Westlake drew the knife from its sheath and tossed it in the air above him. The thick blade was just over a foot long. Perfectly balanced with the handle, it tumbled twice through the sleet as it descended. The handle landed with a slap in the palm of his hand, already damp by the time he caught it.

The contest with Paxinos raced through his mind, already seeming like an age ago. "I can always blunder, but at twenty paces I haven't missed in a long time." Westlake shrugged. "Let's get this over with."

18

· · · · · ·

WESTLAKE EMERGED from the forest edge, gripping the reins of his horse and also his musket in his left hand. His right hand was empty and raised in the air, showing it held no weapon. He had strapped the knife to his upper back, so that its handle rode just below his neck.

Fifty yards to go and they hadn't yet spotted him. The guards loitered by kicking at the stones in front of the boats. Someone should have been watching, but in the dark and the sleet, even the sergeant had his head down.

Christ, I don't want to panic them into shooting Simpson. Just a little closer, a few more paces.

If they didn't see him soon, he'd be forced to call out. Westlake slipped on the sand, which reminded him to plant his feet firmly before he threw the knife. At forty yards, the sleet reverted to heavy rain and then, as good fortune would have it, the rain diminished to a fine drizzle. At thirty yards, someone put his head up, squinted, then slapped the sergeant's arm.

"Halt!"

A dozen men raised their muskets at Westlake, who took a few more steps before the sergeant yelled again.

"Stop right there or I'll order my men to fire."

Westlake stiffened but allowed his horse to walk a few steps. He took one more step until he judged himself about twenty-two paces from his target.

The soldier guarding Simpson lowered the muzzle of his musket to cover Simpson's back. The prisoner sat on the ground with his hands behind his head. He must have been half frozen because on seeing Westlake, he just nodded his head slowly, his face sullen.

"Take my horse and let my friend go," Westlake called out.

"Why don't we just shoot the pair of you and keep both the horses?" the sergeant replied.

"Because that wouldn't be wise, and my friend still in the forest would then have to shoot you," Westlake replied with all the confidence he could muster.

The sergeant peered around him to scan the forest. Westlake jerked slightly on the reins of his horse, and the animal stepped forward. Westlake himself took two steps more. *Twenty paces exactly.*

"I don't see no friend so maybe I'll take my chances. Present!" The sergeant paused, glancing round at his men with their muskets ready to fire. He turned slowly back to Westlake. "Put your musket on the ground, leave the horse, and both of you can walk away." When Westlake didn't move, he raised his hand.

The drizzle had stopped, and for a moment Westlake felt no wind on his face. The entire beach went quiet.

"You've played that trick already, and then I'd still need a boat," Westlake replied. He gave a last tug on the reins of his horse, and as the animal stepped in front of him, he reached behind his head. One swift motion of his arm launched the knife.

The sergeant dropped his hand. "Fire." Eleven triggers clicked. Most of the muskets erupted in flame, spitting lead toward Westlake.

The horse had taken its steps, and Westlake hit the ground behind it, jolting his chin on the sand. Not a single ball even came close to him, but the whinnying horse dropped its hindquarters to the ground. Westlake felt the earth suddenly rumble under the pounding hooves of other horses. He looked behind him to see Alexander, Parrish, and Mathew come galloping across the beach.

"Run, Simpson," Westlake hollered. "Run!"

The man guarding Simpson had fallen to his knees, eyes widening even as he died. He gripped the knife buried in his chest with one hand while still holding his musket in the other.

Cold and wet, Simpson struggled out of his stiffness to stand up. The other soldiers were frantically reloading. Twenty seconds for a trained soldier to load a musket — that was the time he had available to run. Simpson snatched the musket from the dying guard's hand and fired its charge into the belly of the next man closest to him. Then he quickly stumbled away, diving for the cover of Westlake's downed horse.

"Good show, Simpson — now let's go back at them." Westlake pulled the carbine from his horse's ring, thrusting it into Simpson's hands before rushing forward. The other horses pounded past him and Westlake jumped to one side and stared at the carnage that followed.

Alexander had a pistol and a musket in his hands. He drove his horse in a headlong charge into the midst of the patrol, knocking men to the ground like a bunch of wooden toy soldiers. They had taken too long to reload. Leaning from his saddle, he put the pistol to a man's head and fired. He slid down from his horse and with his musket blew a hole in another's chest. The man seemed to hop backward a step before slamming to the ground, already dead.

Parrish fired and then bayoneted a soldier in the neck. Someone in the troop had managed to reload as Westlake heard a single shot emerge from within their ranks. They were fewer now and after Simpson had fired the carbine, there was one less still.

Westlake saw the sergeant raise his musket behind Parrish, and he screamed a warning, "Sergeant!" just before firing his own musket.

The man glanced his way as Westlake's ball found its mark and the sergeant violently jerked back but did not go down. He raised his musket again, only this time aiming at Westlake. As he pulled the trigger, they were less than ten feet apart, a sure hit to Westlake's chest. The musket sounded. *Click* — a misfire! The rain had done its work. The sergeant grimaced and slumped down, before crumpling to the ground.

Westlake had held his breath and now exhaled in relief to still be alive. He stared around at the bodies strewn one on top of the other. Something strange squished under his boot. He peered down to find himself standing on a dead man's hand.

Once their sergeant fell, the four remaining militiamen threw down their weapons and lifted their hands in the air. It was over. The bloodstains on the chest of Westlake's shirt turned cold and his garment stuck to his skin. Alexander the Great stood beside him, sucking in deep breaths. The big man had killed two of the enemy himself, and his charge into their midst had been the catalyst to victory.

Parrish trained his musket on the four prisoners, yelling, "On your knees, hands behind your heads." He turned his head, searching. "Where's Mathew?"

Westlake scanned the beach, spotting Mathew lying face up on the ground. Alexander ran to lift and hold the boy's head clear of the massive pool of blood still gathering beneath his neck. That single shot fired had clearly caught him in the throat. The big man grabbed his hand and squeezed hard.

Mathew smiled and whispered, "Glory land, almost ..." as his life bled away. His head rolled slowly to one side, his strength and life finished.

"No. No." Alexander sank to his knees and hung his head. "I didn't see the shot. There was too many of them." He looked back into Mathew's face, closed the lad's eyes, and sighed. "He'll never reach glory land, now ... never see Luther ... never do nothing again."

"This is my fault, sir," Simpson said. "My foolish plan led to this."

"One way or another, we'd have had to fight them to get a boat," Westlake said, looking down at Mathew's body. "It's tragic but not your fault. It's just the war."

He raised his head and looked Simpson in the eyes. Westlake had never liked Simpson, considering him more of a millstone than anything else. Now, however, he deserved to be told the truth. "You fought well tonight, Mr. Simpson. Congratulations." Westlake wiped one bloody hand on his pants and offered it to Simpson.

"We have to go immediately, sir," Parrish urged. "Someone will have heard those shots."

"Alex, you'll have to tell Precious." Westlake gestured to Mathew's body.

"I know we don't have time to bury him, but just leaving him here don't seem right," Alexander remarked.

"How about we bury him out there." Westlake pointed to the water.

Alexander nodded his agreement. "I'll put 'im in the boat, then go get Precious."

But Precious was already running from the treeline, hands raised to her face. "Mathew! My God, Mathew, no."

Alexander hurried to meet her before she reached the body. He enveloped her in his huge arms, where she collapsed.

Westlake turned away to give further orders. "Strip our horses and pack the boat, if you please, Mr. Simpson. And I want all other long-boats pushed out into the lake, their oars dumped into our boat. We'll jettison them farther out."

"Sir." Simpson came to attention, saluted sharply, and ran off. Back to playing soldier. Westlake shook his head.

His horse, which had so far lain silent after being shot, gave a whinny. "Parrish, can you manage to tie up these four men without killing them?" He motioned toward the prisoners. "Then give Simpson a hand with the oars. I have to take care of my horse."

As Westlake began loading his musket, he glanced up to see Precious down on her knees, her head leaning against Alexander's leg. In the blustering wind, Westlake couldn't hear what was being said, but Precious sobbed before Alexander lifted her under the arms. The pair of them walked slowly over to the body.

Westlake glanced up at the sky and inhaled. "And we've still got a long pull ahead of us," he murmured to himself.

Only minutes later, the single boat pushed off into the black-ness. The oars had been too numerous to remove from each boat, so Simpson and Parrish had pushed the remaining vessels out into the lake, to float away with the current.

Westlake reckoned they were thirty yards from the shoreline when the pounding hooves at the eastern end of the beach made him turn his head.

"Pull harder! American cavalry," he choked out in a harsh whisper from the stern. "Pull for your lives!" The boat lifted with the current, straining for the safety of the lake's darkness.

Colonel Scott brushed his head on the top of the tent-flap door and squinted through the darkness at an incoming horseman. The drizzle had started again, but at least the sleet had not returned. He shivered, slapped his hands together, and gave them a vigorous rub. The black of Lake Erie gave no trace of his longboats starting the attack. Almost three hours gone, and he wondered when he'd hear the echo of gunshots.

A youthful aide came running up and halted beside him ready to take the reins from their visitor. The horse slowed from its gallop, then reared back to stop directly in front of Scott's tent. The messenger's shirt and hair were dripping wet. He jumped down from his saddle, shaking and out of breath.

"Sir." — the man splashed to attention and saluted — "the patrol guarding the longboats has been wiped out. Eight of twelve are dead, including Sergeant Hammond. One boat was stolen."

"Tonight of all nights." Scott motioned to the entrance. "Into my tent." He ducked his head back inside. "What else?"

"They shoved all the other boats out into the lake, sir. A few of them drifted closer to the shore, but they'd pinched most of the oars too."

"Do we know who did this?"

"The survivors say that at least a dozen whites and three escaped slaves rushed them on the beach. They called one of the white men 'sir'. He gave the orders and they would salute. It's unbelievable, but our men reckon he's an officer and the others regular army ... British Army."

"An officer of the British Army associating with slaves?"

"Story was that one of them runaways died in the fight, but I couldn't see no body left on the sand."

"Are they sure ... a genuine officer? And how do we know they were escaped slaves?" Scott again poked his head out through the tent flap, his mind constantly returning to the night's mission. Where were his own two longboats right now? And something unsettled him about this slave story.

"'Cause I have another report, sir."

"Make it quick, man." Scott signalled with his hand.

"Nine riders came on us after we'd untied our militiamen. They say they're catchers on the trail of escaped slaves from a plantation down south, and that one of them runners is a former soldier called Alexander." The man shrugged, as if the news meant little to him.

Scott searched his mind. There were many tales of slaves joining the British during the Independence War. He'd heard of a certain "Alexander the Great," but it was doubtful this was the same man. He wiped some drops of rain from his cheek.

"See, the thing is, sir, they followed me back here. Their leader, Mr. Castor, wants a boat provided to go after them."

"Bring him to me immediately." Scott waved the man ahead, then peeked outside, scanning for flashes of light amid the blackness of Lake Erie.

"Let me do all the talking," Castor ordered as he took off his dripping black hat and slapped it on his knee. When Bennett said nothing, Castor continued, "I didn't hear a 'yes.'" He clenched his fists and leaned forward.

"Fine, but one way or another we're going after them," Bennett replied, wiping moisture from the dripping brim of his bowler hat. "The boys want that reward money, and so do I. We've come too far ... and in this pissing storm." Bennett glanced up at the rain.

The escort preceding Castor halted his horse outside a large tent. A man appeared through the front opening, the biggest man that Castor had seen in his life. Castor dismounted and Bennett followed him. The big man simply motioned with his head while an aide held the flap open as he passed back though into the interior.

"Lieutenant Colonel Scott," the man introduced himself, holding out his hand. "What's your story?"

"George Castor, sir. Pleasure to make your acquaintance. This is my partner, Fred Bennett." The men took turns shaking hands. "We're chasing three criminal slaves who stole horses from the Caldwell plantation. That's after they set fire to the master's house and the main barn. One of them castrated the master's son and then the boy hanged himself."

A monstrous blast of wind rocked the tent and Castor crouched as if expecting the structure to collapse around him. A burst of hard rain struck the canvas, the staccato sound of the tempest making it difficult to hear anything else. One of the candles blew out, leaving the remaining one to cast only dim shadows. Castor's heart beat faster: it was as if he'd entered through the gates of hell.

Cupping a hand around his mouth, Scott shouted, "Your problems are not mine." He pointed outside with a big finger. "There's a goddamn war going on."

Castor winced at his words. "A blacksmith down south thinks that they are being helped by British soldiers, out of uniform."

"That's very interesting, and we will be on our guard. But they've vanished into the lake and there's not a whole lot I can do about it. I have larger concerns tonight." The wind died and the rain stopped as fast as it had started. Castor pondered what he should say next.

Fred Bennett stepped forward to look up at the officer. Before Castor could restrain him, he blurted, "Goddamn it, they murdered your men and stole your boats. At least give us a boat to go after the bastards."

Castor rolled his eyes, assuming all was now lost. He watched and waited for the explosion sure to come. But Scott did not oblige him. The big man, towering over Bennett, stared down into the shorter man's upturned face.

"I don't care about your slaves, and tonight I don't give a good goddamn about a few stolen boats." Though he was talking to Bennett, Castor felt the message was directed at himself. "The death of some of our men is a great tragedy, but do you know what would happen if I gave you a boat?"

"We'd have a chance to catch them," Bennett replied aggressively. His neck stretched forward like a determined bloodhound.

"No. You'd simply get lost in the dark out on Lake Erie. You'd never find them, and if you were lucky enough not to get captured by the British, most probably your boat would drift down the Niagara River — maybe go over the falls." Scott grinned.

Castor remembered the surging yellow and white power of Niagara Falls and with it the feeling of being drawn over. Colonel Scott was right. In a quiet voice, Castor asked, "What would you have us do then?" He reached out, grabbed Bennett by the sleeve, and tugged him back a few steps. Scott turned and headed for the door, where he peered out at the lake.

"Have your men stay with us. You'll be lodged in our tents, fed, and only have to wait a few days longer." Scott tilted his head to one side, listening. "Did you hear that?" He paused as a low boom, like thunder, echoed over the lake. "Then I'll send you across when the time is right." Again he asked, "Did you hear something? Listen."

"No, sir," Castor replied, glancing at Bennett, who merely shrugged.

"Hmm. You'll then be acting as part of a larger group. Cause as much trouble as you like to the British Army. What's good for the goose is good for the gander, huh."

"I don't understand, sir. You now say you'll help us?" Castor frowned.

"Brock wants to stir up trouble down here, so I'll return the favour. Go take your slaves back from the British, but remember, once those slaves set foot on Upper Canadian soil, they're free men. It's the law."

"Not *our* law," Bennett insisted.

Castor was confused.

"No, but you'll be breaking *their* law, so don't get caught," Scott said. "The U.S. Army will be with you, and all hell will be breaking loose. You should be safe ... Now, that was cannon fire." He pushed aside the tent flap and marched out into the rain.

Castor wondered how he would feel, breaking the law. The very idea made him uncomfortable. Doing God's work did not include going against the natural order or disobeying the law. What were they thinking over there, in Upper Canada? Still, these slaves had stolen horses and set fire to property, and that made them criminals who needed catching and punishing.

Castor followed Scott outside and Bennett trailed behind them. Booms and what sounded like echoes of thunder rushed across the lake. The rain had stopped, but the wind buffeted his face. Castor spotted regular flashes of light.

"You said only a few days' wait here?" Bennett wanted confirmation.

"They're engaged, that's for certain," Scott said. "Yes, no more than a few days' wait, that's exactly what I said." He rubbed his hands together, grinning. "Now we have to wait for the outcome. By God, I wish I was with them."

Castor stepped alongside Scott and peered up into his face. "Do you mind my asking, sir, what's going on?"

"Listen to that, a British shore battery. That means they're firing on their own ships. We've got them now!" Scott chuckled and gestured toward the light of cannon fire. "Well, Mr. Castor, it's like this: it seems as if General Brock stole one of my little boats tonight, so I'm stealing two of his bigger ones."

Within minutes of leaving the captured militiamen sitting on the beach, Alexander watched the shores of Lake Erie begin to fade from sight. His oar bumped against one of the floating longboats that Simpson and Parrish had pushed out into the lake. In the dark, they themselves appeared just one vessel among many.

Their longboat slid awkwardly across the lake's surface until the four rowers managed to establish a rhythm to their stroke. Alexander pulled hard and the current ran with them. By the time the captured militiamen pointed out to the cavalry which direction they had taken, the fugitives had disappeared into the enveloping blackness. A few shots fired off in anger, one lucky ball thudding the starboard side, but nothing more serious. Soon, even the white hulls of the empty boats had floated out of sight.

Recalling his conversations with Westlake, Alexander dreaded that somewhere ahead in the darkness, at the end of this lake, flowed the Niagara River and farther down that waterway waited its great falls. The image of Hector's broken corpse hanging from that tree jumped into his mind, and he quickly closed his eyes. Then he visualized Percy Caldwell hanging from the same tree. Alexander nodded to himself. *"How do you like it, Mr. Caldwell?"*

Strong winds buffeted the boat along in the same direction as the current. Instead of fighting any drift, he noticed that Westlake guided them by using the prevailing flow to gain speed while still slanting the boat toward the northern shore. Heaven was now within reach.

Their vessel flew across the water and Alexander stared back through the starless night. The shore bordering the United States had vanished behind them and the idea struck him that he could be finally free. It was possible, he grinned, as he thought of Luther's face again. *I'm rowing to see Luther.* His heart jumped. *Freedom.*

After checking again to convince himself that the shore was completely gone, Alexander sighed heavily. He'd now never get his chance to kill Castor or Bennett and a tinge of regret crept into his mind. Maybe Precious was right: he'd never be free of hating. He shook his head. *Keep pulling. You're pulling for freedom.*

"I'll believe it once I can touch the ground, dig my fingers into the earth," Alexander whispered to himself.

He continued rowing for what seemed a long time. Through the wind, the creak of the oars kept a steady rhythm. Rain came and went in huge sheets that dimpled the surface of the water all around the boat. The cold made no difference to him for he pulled with all his might and the sheer effort warmed his body. Finally, he called softly to their lookout, Precious, who sat watching diligently from the bow.

She turned her head toward the sound of Alexander's deep voice.

"It's time, Precious," Alexander told her. "Time we buried Mathew's body in the lake. I'm sorry."

The others stopped rowing and the boat slid sideways in the current.

"No." Precious put her hand on the arm of the corpse and patted it. "He stays with us until we reach glory land. That's what he wanted and that's what he gets. We owe him that much." She clutched the blanket tighter about her shoulders.

Alexander twisted around to face Westlake resting on his oar. The young ensign shrugged his shoulders and then nodded slowly in approval. Yes, the right way to see Mathew off, Alexander thought; they should give the boy a proper burial. The body would stay with him now until they landed in Upper Canada. Mathew would reach glory land after all.

Alexander guessed they had been on the water for at least three — maybe four — hours. Unused to strenuous rowing, his shoulders ached worse than after working a long day in the field. Out the corner of his eye he saw a flash. He jerked his head to see it light up the night and then vanish. He whirled round in his seat, hearing a succession of low booms.

"Did you see that?" he shouted over the wind.

"Did I see what?" Parrish asked.

"The flash, far ahead."

"There *was* some thunder," Simpson replied.

"I saw them flashes plain as day," Precious agreed. "Wasn't no thunder, either."

Everyone stopped rowing and turned in the direction of the sounds. The boat quickly began drifting sideways again.

"Pull," Westlake ordered. "Stroke hard."

They had travelled another thousand yards when the northern shore lit up under the clouds in a cacophony of cannon blasts. The sound reverberated across the water, shaking Alexander's body with the crash of each explosion. They were now almost under the guns at Fort Erie. Downstream, in those flashes of light, he spotted two ships drifting away from their moorings.

"Why would Fort Erie fire on British ships that were anchored under their own guns?" Simpson asked.

"They'd attack British ships only if they were being stolen." Westlake declared, at first unsure of his assessment. Then he shook his head in wonder. "We're watching a cutting-out, Mr. Simpson. The Americans are attempting to steal those vessels."

"Do we pursue them, sir?" Parrish looked to Westlake for an answer.

If their longboat turned away from the shore and headed toward the ships, Alexander feared he'd never see freedom again. At best, he'd be going back to slavery, and Mathew would have died for nothing. Again the cannon blasted, shaking their boat, and he noticed musket fire erupt on one of the ships. His stomach tightened and he tried to keep his expression calm so as not to show his apprehension to Precious. He stared at Westlake and Simpson as they studied the vessels ahead.

Simpson leaned forward, clearly eager to pursue, but for once the young man kept such thoughts to himself. *Good.*

Alexander was tempted to remind Westlake of his orders from Brock but decided to keep quiet. Besides, what could be achieved by one small group, escorting a pregnant woman? Even if they could catch up with the ships, a determined cutting-out crew would more than likely kill all of them.

Westlake peered into Alexander's face and seemed able to read his mind. "Keep rowing for the shore. My orders are to get Alexander and his 'present' to Upper Canada, and that's what we'll do. No sideshows tonight."

Alexander realized he'd been holding his breath and let it go. He took a last glance at the ships. One vessel had already set sail, but the other drifted aimlessly in the current. Then he took his eyes away from them to watch the British guns light up the northern shoreline.

The wharf of Fort Erie now loomed out of the darkness in front of them. Men waved weapons and torches, shouting obscenities at the escaping ships. Already excited when they spotted the longboat, they fired their muskets.

The balls whizzed overhead and Westlake shouted at them. "Don't fire, we're British!" The message either wasn't heard or wasn't believed because, in the flickering torchlight, the mob soon raised their muskets to fire again. The shore drew closer with every second. Alexander counted at least a dozen shooters. One of them would surely find its target.

"Down," Westlake yelled, and Alexander pulled Precious into the hull just as several balls creased the boat's side. Thirty paces from the wharf, and before the men could reload, Westlake called out again,

"We're British militia with a package for General Brock. I order you to lower those muskets immediately."

This time a single musket fired, the bullet chipping the rail above Alexander's head. At just six boat lengths from the shore, someone hollered, "Hold fire." The seconds drifted by, excitement suspended in the silence, then the longboat finally bumped against the great wharf, where two men lowered hooks to latch on to the side.

"Who the hell are you?" demanded an elderly fellow with matted hair clinging to his forehead. "Come on, out with it!" The angry men crowded around, muskets trained on the new arrivals.

From his time as a sergeant, Alexander remembered that it took a certain show of confidence to gain control of an unruly mob. Now he prayed that an exhausted Westlake could rise to the challenge of their predicament. If the jostling crowd, with muskets pointing at their boat, made *him* nervous, then Westlake must have felt some of the same fear.

Westlake jumped up on to the wharf and approached the old soldier who had spoken. Even from the boat, Alexander could smell the man's rank odour. Despite the cool night air, the man had sweat running down the side of his face. Westlake stepped close enough to peer into his eyes.

"We're British soldiers." His tone was calm and firm. "And you will lower those weapons immediately." The mob looked to one another for guidance. "I would hate to hang the first man here who fires."

The intensity of his words warned the old soldier that he had best do as ordered. He swung around to face the others and held up a hand. The men stepped back and the muskets were gradually lowered.

"Where is your commanding officer?" Westlake insisted. "We need lodgings." Guns continued booming from inside the fort.

"The fort's up back of us." A tall fellow on the edge of the crowd indicated with his torch. "But them runaways ain't sleeping near our men — not inside that fort, leastways."

Westlake pushed two of them out of his way, stepping forward to grab the man by the collar.

Before he risked being choked, the fellow sputtered, "I'm just try-ing to help you, mister. There's a secret slave house down the road where all the runners normally stay." The man paused and stared into the boat. "They'll be more welcome there … is that man dead?"

"The place is supposed to be secret, but everyone like you knows about it?" Westlake observed sarcastically.

"That's right — everyone but the catchers."

"The slave catchers actually come here?" Westlake asked, surprised.

"Where you been? Course they do. They go where they please, them catchers. No laws and no borders scare them." He pointed at Mathew's body. "You'll need to bury him."

Alexander needed no more convincing. He and Precious would definitely sleep inside the fort, with Westlake, Parrish, and Simpson as their guards, and God help anyone who tried to prevent it.

"You said you had something for General Brock." The old one who reeked stepped forward. "Well, you won't have to wait too long. After the loss of two of our ships" — he nodded toward the water — "you can bet someone's gone riding off to find him. He'll come galloping here like the blazes. You can count on it, fella."

As three guns crashed out in succession, the crowd all stared out at the lake. One ship was still sailing away while the other tilted oddly to one side, now grounded on what must have been a sandbank.

"Give us a hand, here," Simpson called from the boat.

From the bow, Alexander lifted Precious up into Westlake's two guiding hands. Then he carried Mathew's body over to where Westlake, Simpson, and Parrish struggled to hoist it on to the wharf. Men reached down with arms outstretched to pull up those still stand-ing in the boat.

Alexander climbed up on to the wharf by himself and took Precious by the hand. He guided her through the crowd to the end of the dock, where he knelt down and touched the earth. First he made small circles with his fingers, and then with both hands he jammed his fingers under the dirt. His heart pounded in his chest and his whole body quivered with happiness.

"We's free now, Precious. This is heaven." He gazed up through his tears into her smiling face.

"I knew you'd get us here." She stared around her. "Let's go find Luther."

Westlake smiled as he planted his boots firmly on Upper Canadian soil. *Home at last!* Perhaps the reception left much to be desired, but the disgrace resulting from the loss of two ships belonged to someone else. He'd brought Alexander the Great to safety as ordered. He offered his hand to Parrish and then to Simpson.

"We made it, gentlemen," he said. "Well done."

The sound of marching boots rose as a column of redcoats trooped down the path toward him. On the wharf, Mathew's body lay motionless, still waiting for attention. *Such a tragedy. All the boy's hope gone in an instant.*

Perhaps General Brock was already on his way. Otherwise, they would meet soon enough in Fort George. Suddenly Mary's face jumped into his mind, and his heart raced as he thought about his marriage to come. He would have to go and find her in Newark and have a talk. *About what? What would he say to her?*

Then, just as quick, he pictured Seffi's body. *Beautiful Seffi.* What was he to do? The problem of his marriage loomed closer now than before he had left. His stomach clenched at the thought, but he was too weary to think about it further.

"Parrish, and you men, help carry Mathew's body into the fort." He reached the end of the wharf to find Alexander on his knees with Precious rubbing his shoulder. Westlake slid a hand under the big man's arm, assisting him to his feet.

"Well, you actually got here," Westlake said.

"It's hard to believe." Precious stretched her arms exultantly overhead. "But I guess it's true." She grinned broadly.

Westlake smiled, making a bow, then made a grand sweeping gesture with his arm as if all of Upper Canada belonged to him. "Welcome to heaven, Miss Precious ... and you too, Sergeant Alexander. At least *we'll* have some good news for General Brock."

19

● ● ● ● ● ●

THE SUN HAD RISEN over Fort Erie by the time Westlake and his party were introduced to the officer in charge. When Westlake told him of Alexander's importance to Brock, he welcomed the entire party with civility. Precious retired to a private room. The men would sleep together but in spacious quarters apart from other soldiers, an inconvenience to someone but Westlake was too exhausted to worry about it.

His room had four bunks, a table and some chairs, a basin, and a fireplace. A soldier jostled into the room with extra firewood, then left the men to themselves. Westlake immediately heated some water in the great kettle that hung over the fire, suspended from two S hooks attached to a black crane.

He soaked his blistered palms in the water to ease the pain while he opened and closed his fist. The same soldier reappeared to announce that a late breakfast of porridge and tea was available in another building. The commanding officer was obviously trying to make a good impression.

Westlake arrived for his breakfast of porridge and collapsed into a chair at the table, almost falling asleep. He gulped down the food and sipped at his scalding tea, thinking only of sleep. By midmorning, he staggered to his bunk, flopped back on the coarse blanket, and closed his eyes. In seconds, still fully dressed, he sank into a deep sleep.

When he awoke, the sun's fading light barely lit the room. He must have slept a long time. The aroma of stew hovered in the air, reminding him of his growling stomach. He spied the source of the smell — a pot sitting on the table. From the look of unwashed plates, the others had already eaten and gone back to bed. Westlake did the same.

Early the following morning, he woke again and shivered from the damp. The fire had gone out, but a recently lit candle caught his attention. Exhaustion from the nighttime pull across the lake had left him drained of energy, and he closed his eyes again. His mind drifted back to the blacksmith and the race to Lake Erie. He'd been lucky in the chance occurrence of that fight between the Indians and the catchers.

A firm nudge on his shoulder shifted his body to one side. Barely conscious, he guessed that Parrish wanted his attention.

"Go away, Parrish. Let me sleep." Another shove reawakened all the aches in his stiff muscles. "Bugger off, Parrish. I won't tell you again!" As he squinted one eye open, he lashed out in a wave with the back of his hand. Someone grabbed it as he sat upright and stared.

"Well, that's a fine welcome I get." Major General Isaac Brock himself stood tall beside his bed.

"Sir! I'm sorry, sir. I thought ... it's a great pleasure to see you again, sir." Westlake forced his eyes wide open.

"No need for apologies, Mr. Westlake. Thought I'd have some fun with you." Brock glanced around at the other bunks. "After losing two of His Majesty's ships, we are in short supply of humour. It's been a particularly unfortunate time. You've injured your hand, I see."

"Not used to rowing, sir." Westlake slowly squeezed and then unclenched his fist, watching the blisters strain themselves. "Looks worse than it is. They're healing nicely."

Westlake stood up and straightened his clothing. "We've been on the run for such a long time, I've lost track of the date, sir. What day is it?"

"October 10, Saturday," Brock replied. "I rode from Fort George yesterday, when I heard news of the attack. Arrived well after sunset and surveyed what was visible in the dark." Brock moved to sit himself in a chair at the table. "I was happy to find you back safe and sound." He smiled. "Congratulations, by the way. Any trouble on your little trip?"

"Just the usual death and destruction, sir." Westlake chuckled, remembering Brock's orders for him to avoid trouble.

"There's a rumour going round that a small company of U.S. militia was almost wiped out on the American shore, just south of here. All their boats stolen too. Was that you?"

Westlake nodded, thinking back to the struggle. "There was no other way, sir. We were starving and needed a boat or we weren't going to make it at all. That battle cost Alexander's young friend his life."

"I'm very sorry. It must have been a close fight."

"Not at all, sir," Westlake replied with no emotion in his voice. "Most of them were dead within the first two minutes."

Brock shook his head, studying Westlake's face. "I received another letter from your mother. If I see you, I'm to say she sends her love and wishes for your safety and your return home soon."

Westlake rolled his eyes. If his mother ever learned what he did for Brock, she'd want to strangle them both. Then he thought of Maple Hill and imagined her waiting in their family's stone-built home. "It *is* wonderful to be back, sir."

"Sir!" Simpson sprung from his bed and hit the floor with a thud. He saluted, standing to attention in his underwear.

"At ease, Mr. Simpson. Get dressed," Brock said. "I see Parrish is the last of my agents to wake up."

Parrish opened his eyes with difficulty but knew well enough to keep quiet. Talking to officers had always caused him trouble.

Westlake walked over to Alexander's bed and shook him by the shoulder.

"Alex, an important visitor has come to see you."

The man groaned and rolled over like a great log. He looked as if he might drop off again so Westlake prodded him harder. Alexander frowned menacingly with his eyes still closed.

"General Brock himself has come to welcome you," Simpson explained, raising his voice. "For heaven's sake, wake up, man."

In his exhaustion, Alexander had sprawled on top of the blankets and, like Westlake, not bothered to undress. Now he climbed off the bed, still drowsy, and shook Brock's hand. "Pleased to meet you, sir." He rubbed his eyes. "I believe you know of my son, Luther?"

"Welcome to Upper Canada, Alexander. Your escort was adequate,

I see." Brock nodded toward Westlake. "Of course, I know of Luther ... a nice young man. While he works for us as a tinsmith, he's undergoing militia training with Richard Pierpoint."

"The boy makes a good impression wherever he goes, sir," Alexander said proudly. "Did you say Cap'n Dick is here?"

"Apparently, though I don't know him personally," Brock replied. A knock at the door interrupted them. "Enter," Brock called out.

A soldier carried to the table a tray piled high with pancakes.

"I took the liberty of ordering breakfast for all of us," Brock explained. "This little fort doesn't have many amenities, but it does possess a wonderful cook. I felt like enjoying a real Canadian breakfast — pancakes and maple syrup." He licked his lips in anticipation.

"Thank you, sir," Westlake replied. He glanced at his companions, who nodded vigorously and offered their own thanks.

"Captain Nelles will join us shortly," Brock added.

Westlake's appetite had now returned and he wolfed down several pancakes. The hot food finally banished the damp that had chilled him for a week. The soldier from yesterday burst into the room with additional kindling and within minutes the room warmed and brightened from the fire's glow. As he left the room again, Precious entered.

After being introduced by Alexander as his present, she sat herself down at the breakfast table.

Brock was visibly surprised. "Good gracious! So you're the package the Ranger mentioned?" he asked. "Welcome to Upper Canada."

"I thank you, sir. It's thrilling for me to be here and feel free ... and I have your fine escort to thank." Her smile signified her appreciation.

"That old Ranger recognized me when he came to visit the plantation," Alexander explained. "Gave me the location of the first conductor."

A former member of Butler's Rangers, now living across the border, had confused the message about Precious while visiting Fort George. Over time, the same man had helped numerous slaves escape by identifying the locations of the conductors on the underground railroad.

Westlake inquired about the prior night's events. He described seeing the ships drifting in the river until at least one vessel had set her sails. Surely they could be liberated?

"Last night we tried to rescue the *Detroit*, but the Americans fired the ship. A tragedy; and I'm afraid all is lost." Brock shrugged dejectedly, then shook his head. "Ah, here is Captain Nelles. Come and meet Sergeant Alexander and his 'package'."

A sombre Nelles entered the room and shook hands with everyone. "Well done, Ensign Westlake," he murmured.

Parrish stood up to offer him his chair.

"I should say rather well done all three of you, " he continued before sitting down to his breakfast. "We needed to hear some good news on this dreary day."

"Thank you, Captain," replied Westlake before turning back to Brock. "You were saying about the battle, sir?"

"We could have destroyed their naval base at Black Rock weeks ago but for the interference received from abroad. There was simply no need for this disaster." The loss was a direct consequence of orders from Governor General Prevost in Montreal: not to engage the enemy and to simply forbear. Brock then laid out the consequences of losing those ships. The balance of power on Lake Erie could easily shift, and if that should happen, the Americans could strike at will, anywhere on the lake.

"It's clear to me that the true interests of Upper Canada are better defined by the people who actually live here. All these counterproductive notions of armistice and appeasement have originated from outside the province. I'm afraid Upper Canadians must learn to stand up for themselves or risk losing their independence."

"Do you expect further attacks, sir?" Simpson inquired.

"At any hour." Brock glanced at Westlake.

"May I see my son, sir?" Alexander asked.

"Luther waits for you at Newark, a town beside Fort George." Brock leaned forward, his expression stern. "Alexander Johnson, the Coloured Company desperately needs a sergeant and I'm hoping that you're our man. I leave for the fort early tomorrow morning so you're welcome to accompany me." He wiped the edges of his mouth with a white napkin.

"The men call me by my first name, Sergeant Alexander, and for a chance to strike back at those bastards, I'd do anything you ask, sir. Excuse my language, Precious."

"Captain Nelles, draw a covered wagon and horses from the fort's commissary. It'll make travelling easier on Precious," Brock said as he stood.

Except for Precious, everyone around the table stood up, amid the sound of the chairs scraping on the wooden floor.

"May we squeeze in a day off, sir, before the fighting starts? Parrish and I" — Westlake hesitated, unsure how to plead his case — "we've been away a long time and I would like to go and see Mary."

Brock continued addressing Alexander, ignoring Westlake's request. "We've added another fourteen men to the Coloured Company, making it up to thirty-eight strong, but they need moulding into a unit. To my mind, you're just the man to do it. Westlake, Simpson, and Parrish — after their time off today — will stay with you while you complete your task." Brock slapped Alexander on the shoulder, nodded to the rest, and made his exit.

Attack at any hour … Battle … Westlake felt a slight twist in his stomach at the prospect. He'd never participated in a grand assault, either attacking or defending, only in skirmishes. How much time would he have to see Mary when his day off was spent in Fort Erie? If she were still in Newark, then tomorrow he'd at least be travelling in the right direction.

Castor pulled back on the reins and his horse came to halt. The ride from Buffalo to Lewiston had taken most of the day. Hidden from the Niagara River and out of sight from peering British eyes, he and his eight remaining catchers had trotted through a deluge of rain along mud-soaked roads and trails. They were just a small part of the thousands of soldiers marching to invade Upper Canada. Lieutenant Colonel Winfield Scott was making good on his promise of quick action.

Rumours of a Coloured Company training with the British Army had reached the American side of the river. Castor prayed that, if there were slaves among them, Alexander might very well be their sergeant as before. The prospect of catching a rewarding basket of runaways in a single swoop had his men cheering.

"Like snatching low-hanging fruit," one man remarked. "Three, maybe four, years' pay for just one job."

"Chance of a lifetime," laughed another.

"And remember, that big nigger Alex is double pay for all of us, either dead or alive." Robinson grinned. With his finger he made a slicing motion across his throat. "And I get back my new boots. Don't anyone forget that."

In charge of his little band, riding along in company with the army, Castor sat up straight in the saddle and puffed out his chest, imagining himself as a real officer. Unlike previous expeditions, where he and Bennett had hunted alone, he now felt the security of being part of something much bigger. And yet a certain apprehension gripped him as his hands fidgeted with the reins.

Bennett claimed there was safety in numbers, but in his heart, Castor knew differently. The men could think what they wanted, already imagining the reward money clinking in their hands. Sure, they'd blend in easily with hundreds of militia crossing the river, but what would be waiting on the other side? Not just a few pathetic runaways ready for the grabbing, but an entire British Army. His shoulders tensed when he realized he'd be engaging in battle against armed slaves.

Castor shivered in the wind, and under his coat he plucked at a sodden shirt. The grey skies made him think the rain would never end. Like everyone else, he hunched into a tight ball atop his horse, bending himself into the smallest target possible for the miserable weather.

The marchers suddenly halted and a messenger appeared with orders for Castor and Bennett to report to Colonel Scott at the front of the column. Castor glanced at Bennett and raised his eyebrows — Scott had clearly not forgotten them. Both men wheeled their horses off the road and followed the messenger until he held up his hand.

Through the slanting rain, Castor studied three officers ahead on horseback. Colonel Scott sat tall in the saddle and circled his anxious mount. His counterpart swayed slightly so that Castor guessed the man had been drinking. The third man, younger and more eager, waved his arms in protest at something, raising his voice toward Scott as their conversation progressed. "I'm sorry they stole your boats, but really this is too much, sir."

Scott pointed to Castor and, with a sharp jab of his thumb, ordered him forward. "Mr. Castor, Mr. Bennett, meet Lieutenant Colonel Fenwick and Captain Wool." The officers nodded, but did not offer to shake hands.

Scott turned back to the other officers. "Like I said, these two men, and seven others, are crossing the river with us. Consider them a type of militia or agents … though more precisely they're slave catchers. Just put them in a boat and then release them on the other side."

"With all due respect, sir," Captain Wool persisted, "you know it won't work quite like that."

"Captain Wool has agreed to take you … under protest." Scott gestured to the angry Wool.

"I have a battle to win," Wool said sharply, turning to Castor. "Men will be killed. You'll do exactly as I order or I'll shoot you myself — understand!"

Castor nodded silently.

"We're good at killing." Bennett grinned.

Before he could move away, Wool grabbed him by the collar and hauled him forward, their faces only inches apart, with Bennett hanging on to his saddle just to stay on his horse.

"Killing defenceless slaves is nothing like fighting against an army. You'll be lucky to survive through the day." Wool let go of Bennett's collar and shoved him upright.

"Bring up your men and assemble over yonder." Colonel Fenwick gestured to a meadow where hundreds of soldiers were already gathered. He suddenly jerked upright in his saddle, his slurred diction confirming Castor's suspicion.

"Yes, sir." Castor wheeled his horse away, not waiting for Bennett.

Darkness descended by the time his band finished setting up their tents. Castor felt sympathy for the soldiers packed into the field, just sitting there in the downpour with their musket pans tucked under their armpits to keep them dry. Several more hours passed before general grumbling started about the delay. A rumour filtered through the ranks: they were leaving at any minute so get ready ... the attack would take place at Queenston ... no, that story must be false, as the cliffs there were too damn high, a soldier complained.

Castor urged his troop to get some sleep and he attempted to do the same. He laid his head down on his saddle and dozed, but for how long he couldn't tell. A familiar nightmare racked his sleep, as it did on so many nights: yellow water and white foam sucking him down under the current, where he saw again Hector's bruised and bloated face. He jerked upright on his blanket.

"What a cursed thing to be thinking now," Castor grumbled to the roof of his tent. He laid his head down again, but the image of Hector's battered corpse churning in the river stayed in his mind. "This has to stop," he finally yelled at the imaginary corpse. His eyes flashed open in the darkness as the dream ended. "Christ, now I'm talking to a dead slave." Castor cut his eyes across the tent to hear Bennett still snoring. "Forgive me Lord, for taking your name in vain, but I beg you to strike these demons from my mind. The man's dead. I didn't kill him, so just let him stay dead." He rose from his blanket and peered out through the tent flap.

The army sat in that same field all night, until the sky began to lighten. The anticipated order to embark never came. At one point, two drunks staggered by Castor's tent claiming that someone had lost all the oars to the boats. The battle would be delayed for at least another day. He sat down, resting his back against the saddle, and let his head droop on to his chest. There, he finally drifted off to sleep.

Two dozen red-coated dragoons surrounded Brock's party as they set off at a slow trot along the banks of the Niagara River. With Precious under canvas and Parrish driving the two horses, Sergeant Alexander rode closest to the wagon, and Brock to the other side of him. The sergeant had never before ridden a horse in such impressive company and he glanced over his shoulder to observe Westlake and the others following at the back of the wagon.

Issued by the Fort Erie stores, the party's dark riding cloaks flapped in the stiff north breeze. Whether it was his new cloak or the effect of simply being free again, the sergeant's chest swelled: once again Alexander the Great. He looked around him, trying to suppress a grin for fear of appearing foolish.

The morning light of October 11 descended in a cool drizzle. He wondered how much Luther had changed, and if freedom allowed him to grin all day long. Every time he thought of his son's smile, his heart rose in anticipation. He chuckled, peering upward to feel the rain strike his face. *Freedom.*

The river gushed along to Alexander's right while row upon row of fruit trees grew in the fields on his left. Even in the rain, black workers continued to pick apples, filling their baskets to the brim. He remembered working the fields recently alongside Mathew and then thought back to yesterday morning's quiet burial. At a sad affair for a young fellow who didn't deserve his fate, Westlake had said a few words about remembering the boy's wonderful spirit.

The party travelled for some time before proceeding past a row of apple trees that butted the very edge of the road. While lifting his three-quarters-filled basket, a fruit picker turned to stare at the passing company and carelessly spilled his apples on the ground. In no particular hurry, the man then gathered the fruit back into his basket.

Alexander scanned the surrounding trees for an overseer with his whip but saw none. He turned to Brock. "Those apple pickers, sir, they slaves or they free men? Where's the bossman?"

"The residents of Niagara are very proud that theirs was the first township in the whole British Empire to phase out slavery. The owners can keep the slaves they possess for a limited number of years, but no new slave ownership is sanctioned." Brock gestured to the nearby river. "An African escaping across that border becomes a free man. In any event, there's no bossman here like you are used to down south."

"I appreciate you sending those boys to help me and mine escape. I'll do you proud, sir — that's when and if the enemy tries to cross."

"They will come, Sergeant, you can count on it. I only wish we could attack first instead," Brock said. "Hit them now where they're weakest."

"Why don't you, sir? Them fellas at Fort Erie were itchin' for a fight."

"If only it were possible … there's eight million Americans against less than five hundred thousand of us here in the Canadas." Brock shook his head. "The longer we give them time to organize, the worse it'll be for us. But my orders are to forbear and do nothing to anger the enemy." Brock pointed at the river, to where a large island came to a tip. "We have now passed Grand Island."

The drizzle thickened throughout the day and Alexander often had to shake the water from the brim of his hat. He swung his horse out of line to better peer into the river where the water picked up speed and boiled through a series of rapids. Promptly the drizzle turned to a hard rain, with the sound of thunder in the background. The current raged and the entire river churned white and yellow.

Someone shouted behind him, and Alexander turned his head. Brock sat stationary in his saddle with his hands cupped around his mouth. "Behold the spectacle of Niagara Falls," he hollered and pointed ahead.

"Oh my God!" Alexander exclaimed.

He had ridden on top of a huge rock directly beside the falls and stared straight down into the rush of roaring foam. While the dragoons stayed mounted, the rest of the party easily ascended on foot up to the same rock, where its surface was flat as a table.

"The catchers said my boys went over it, sir. How far down does it go?" Alexander asked.

"About a hundred and fifty feet on our side and a good hundred feet on theirs." Brock motioned to the American bank of the river. "Notice the rocks jutting out at the bottom over there, whereas here, although it's a longer fall, there's a much softer landing — no rocks below."

Alexander peered straight down into the churning water at the bottom of the falls and then over to the American side. "If my boy Hector dropped over there, he died instantly when he hit bottom," he observed. A sharp pain jabbed him in the stomach and his eyes filled with tears. He sobbed, thankful for the rain and the river's mist so no one could see the tears streaming down his face. The son he'd loved had died right here. *Right here.* He shook his head on remembering Hector's broken body hanging from Caldwell's tree. Rage welled up inside him. He clenched his fists and his whole body tensed.

Then he remembered Luther's face when they said their goodbyes, full of excitement and anticipation. The boy could barely stand still long enough to shake hands properly. Alexander could feel that final touch of his hand even now.

"Stay with Hector," his own last words had been. "You do what your brother tells you to do or I'll cuff you good when we next meet." He closed his eyes and saw Hector smile. As the older brother, it must have been his idea to jump in the river, and Luther obediently followed him.

"Look at that drop," Alexander exclaimed, but the others had already drifted back to their horses and left him alone with his thoughts. After one deep sigh and a last glance at the gushing falls, he turned away.

Alexander rode farther down river, along the gorge cut out by the receding falls. On both sides, a steep cliff edged the surging current. He spurred his horse and soon caught up with the main party.

"Where are they going to cross, sir?" he asked Brock. "There's cliffs all along, hereabouts."

"One option is to try their luck here at Queenston. Look over to your left." Brock gestured with an inclination of his head. "It's that little village at the bottom of the hill. But my guess is that it's much easier for them to attack closer to Fort George or, perhaps, closer to Fort Erie."

Alexander scanned the town and counted all of twenty-five rooftops that showed themselves. He looked up at the heights, where a long-barrel cannon poked out between the trees — an obvious site for a battery covering the approaches from the river. Anything floating across the waterway would be an easy target for cannon fire blasted down from above.

He swung round to see Brock gazing up at the same piece of artillery. While they were staring up at Queenston's Heights, their horses had carried them down the road to a wide gap in the trees growing along the riverbank. Alexander surveyed the American side from his new position and pulled back on the reins.

"I think you should take a gander, sir. Are there usually that many big boats in the river?"

"My goodness, what have we here?" Brock concurred.

On the other side of the river, far down to their left, floated more than a half-dozen American bateaux large enough to hold at the least thirty soldiers each.

The dragoons, the wagon, plus Westlake and Simpson came up and joined Brock in staring across the river. Alexander heard the pounding of horses as six other riders galloped along the road, their hooves throwing up clumps of mud. Black capes waved in the breeze behind two of the arrivals.

Alexander turned back to study the river. "Why would they try to attack at a cliff face?" he wondered out loud.

"My thoughts exactly," Brock said.

The approaching riders hauled up alongside. A caped officer wheeled his horse around close to Brock. "Apparently, they tried to cross last night, sir, but we're told the fools lost their oars. It sounds almost too good to be true."

Disbelief grew on Brock's face, even as he grimaced at the news. "And good afternoon, Captain Williams. Do you want me to believe that a few missing oars ended the American invasion of Upper Canada?"

Williams shrugged, then nodded yes.

"How do you know this?"

The other caped officer had meanwhile dismounted and stood

pointing down river toward the bateaux. "Captain Williams is telling the God's truth of it, sir. Six of those idiots tried to desert last night in the dark, by swimming across the river. The current drowned four of them, but somehow two managed to flail their way across this morning. All their oars were apparently in one boat, and that boat disappeared. And good afternoon to you too, sir." Captain Dennis smiled.

"Then we've indeed been lucky, for now, though I've a hard time believing this to be their main invasion force. And where are the rest of their boats?" Brock took out a telescope and scanned the American side. "I can see men still coming and going, Captain Dennis. Any recent news from our friends in Fort George?"

Dennis shook his head. "No, sir."

Brock snapped the telescope shut, and Alexander realized that the general had made a decision.

"Captain Nelles, escort the wagon and Alexander here to his son in Newark," Brock ordered sharply. "Ensign Simpson will rejoin the 41st forthwith."

Brock wheeled his horse to face Westlake. "Mr. Westlake, stay with Alexander until you get orders to do otherwise. I'm activating all available militia units once I arrive at Fort George. Gentlemen, I bid you goodbye." Brock touched his hat in salute and spurred his horse to a gallop.

The dragoons closed in behind him, and Alexander guessed that his own opportunity to fight might not be too long in coming.

20

· · · · · ·

LUTHER OPENED THE FRONT DOOR into a large whitewashed room, and let Richard Pierpoint enter ahead of him. Punched out of a shiny oval sheet of metal above the doorframe, read the words GOOD TINSMITHING. The acrid scent of molten tin assailed Luther's nose as he hurried around the front counter to make the proper introductions.

"Mr. Good, this is my friend, Cap'n Dick of the Coloured Company militia. He's a real soldier and you said I could show him where I work."

The master tinsmith squinted up from the hearth in the centre of the room. He had just pulled out a soldering iron, and now replaced it gently amid the red coals. He wiped his hands on a white towel, but Luther noticed he left no trace of dirt on it. Somehow Mr. Good always managed to remain clean.

Luther scanned the interior of the workshop to be sure that everything remained how he had left it. From the windows, through a blanket of cloud, the sun cast its dim light on the benches. The countertops and floors were scrubbed as clean as a kitchen, while the work implements hung neatly from steel hooks overhead.

"This is my bench, Cap'n Dick." Luther paused beside a workbench and snapped to attention as if he was back in the militia.

The tinsmith strode briskly around the front counter where a tall candle burned and offered his hand to Pierpoint. "Albert Good. Pleased to meet you, sir."

Pierpoint shook his hand, studied Luther's bench, and then looked up to the light. "Fine shop, sir. You have a lot of windows."

At first, Good frowned. "Ah, yes, we have." He gestured to the two big windows on either side of the room. "A tinsmith must have excellent light when soldering and so the windows … and also the candles." He indicated several candles, their light wavering over the benches.

"I *see*." Pierpoint chuckled. "Well, I hope this young man is a decent help to you, sir, and not a hindrance. He's an honest lad and could make someone a fine apprentice, given the chance."

"A hindrance? I may own this shop, but I'm under no illusions, Cap'n Dick. This boy knows more about tinsmithing than any other man I know. Truth is, I'm learning all I can from him before he rushes off to get himself killed."

Standing by his bench, Luther grinned widely at the compliment. He looked down at his feet as he proudly explained the source of his skills.

One spring day, more than five years ago, a German immigrant had arrived in a covered wagon at the Caldwell plantation. His wagon contained all the tools and raw materials necessary for a tinsmith. Master Caldwell promised the tinsmith Luther's labour and an order for fifty dollars' worth of tin goods if he'd train the boy in the trade. The German agreed and so Luther's training began. Eventually, he was even allowed to accompany the tinmaster on his working visits to adjacent farms.

The man taught him all the latest secrets from Germany. Twice a year for the next five years, the tinsmith returned to the plantation and Luther would work alongside him for six weeks at a time, travelling again to Caldwell's neighbours. Each time the German departed, Luther continued working, however, honing his skills as he made cookie cutters, kettles, lanterns, and the like, products that Master Caldwell then sold to his neighbours. At the end of his final visit, the German pronounced Luther a journeyman tinsmith in his own right.

"Master Good has given me my own tools." Luther held up in turn a chisel, an awl, snips, and compass. "They're mine forever."

"I don't ask him to call me master." Good shook his head. "I pay him too — it's not much, but I pay him. His lodgings are spacious at the back, and he's no slave here. Just look at the quality of his work."

"How did you make that?" Pierpoint asked.

Luther held up a circular lantern, each side of which was punched with holes.

"On the guillotine, there. I cut these tin sheets down to the size of the lantern. The big sheets come from England."

"Cornwall, more precisely," Good added.

"I punch the oval holes with my tools." Luther grinned, showing off patterned circles in one finished sheet. "Then I curve the sheet round on this bender." He pointed to a machine where three steel rollers were laid one on top of the other. "Once each sheet is properly curved, I just solder the lantern together with this soldering iron and some lead. Two circles of flat tin need to be cut out to make the top and bottom. I solder them on later, but that's the easy part. And look at my handle, fits right around your fingers."

Luther picked up a spare handle and wrapped Pierpoint's fingers around it.

"He hasn't yet told you what's special about his lanterns," Good continued. "They don't blow out in the wind."

As if on call, the wind hammered at the front door, lifting and slamming down the rooftop shingles of Good Tinsmithing. Luther glanced at the ceiling, waiting for another gust, but nothing came.

Pierpoint appeared puzzled and he scratched the side of his head. "That's impossible. How can any candle stay lit in the wind?"

"I swear it. I didn't believe it myself until he constructed one," Good said. "Luther, stick a candle into that one and show the Cap'n what I mean."

Luther reached up to a shelf and lifted down an already finished lantern. He placed it on his bench and pulled open a small door in one side. Then he inserted a candle in the centre, where a little cup held it firmly in place.

"I didn't tell you how I make the door with this hinge," Luther said.

Pierpoint held up his hand. "It's okay, just light the candle."

Luther eased a flaming candle off the countertop to light the candle inside the lantern and closed the little door. Through the oval holes arranged in concentric circles, the candle's glow lit up the entire bench.

"Now blow on it hard," Good instructed.

Pierpoint blew at the holes that were level with the candle's flame, then reeled back in amazement.

"Maybe you didn't blow hard enough." Luther laughed.

Pierpoint blew again, but still the candle barely flickered. Good stepped forward and ran his finger around one of the circle patterns punched into the lantern's side.

"Rub your finger over these holes," he suggested.

When Pierpoint had finished rubbing, Good continued, "As best I can figure, the ridge around the rim of the oval seems to deflect any wind away."

Luther picked up the lantern by the looped handle on top and swung it around fast at the end of his arm. "No wind can blow it out," he declared. "That German fella knew a lot. He showed me, and then I showed Master Good," Luther said proudly.

A knock at the door drew their attention away from the lantern. This time Luther knew it wasn't caused by the wind.

Westlake dismounted in the steady drizzle, watching the cedar shingles flap on the roof, while Captain Nelles rapped on the white door underneath a sign that read GOOD TINSMITHING. Alexander stood waiting in the rain, several paces behind the captain. Nelles knocked hard again, and it almost appeared that the occupants did not wish to be disturbed.

"Perhaps, with this wind, they couldn't hear you, sir," Westlake said.

"I can see light through the window and there's smoke coming from the chimney," Parrish yelled. He'd halted the wagon at the far edge of the building.

Nelles knocked a third time and shrugged.

When Luther finally opened the door, he couldn't see his father waiting outside. "Master Good, there's a captain here to see you," he announced over his shoulder.

"No, Luther, there's someone here for *you*," Nelles replied, then stepped aside to reveal Alexander standing in the rain.

Luther put his hands to his head. "Father!" he said in a whisper, just before he bounded forward.

"Luther!" Alexander cried. "I never thought I'd see you again." The two men embraced, their knees buckling under them, sinking them to the ground.

"Luther?" Precious called out, but Parrish had stopped the wagon too distant from the door for Luther to hear her. Westlake ran to help her step down from the perch as the rain continued tapping on his shoulder. Precious raised her head to witness the two men on their knees, hugging silently.

Luther finally looked up at the sound of her voice. "Precious!" He stood up, raising Alexander with him, then went and kissed Precious full on the mouth. "*I prayed!* I prayed it was possible." He laughed and hugged her too.

Now the three former slaves all embraced together, arms thrown over one another's shoulders.

"Hallelujah, hallelujah, *hallelujah*." Alexander's voice rose with each word uttered and he tilted his face back up to peer into the falling rain before closing his eyes tight. "Thank you, Lord, God Almighty, for this gracious day. My son in my arms again, I never … oh my." He cried. "I never … it's just that …" His shoulders heaved and he sobbed deeply. "Oh, my …"

Luther kept tight hold of his father's hand while squeezing Precious close to him with his other arm. The rain fell harder, but no one seemed to care. Luther glanced down and noticed the slight bulge in her stomach.

"Yes," said Precious as she looked away. "I'm sorry."

"That's no matter," Luther replied quietly. "The baby's yours, and that makes it … ours." He beamed.

"This is my girl…" Luther announced proudly to everyone. "Yes, sir." He glanced back toward Good and Pierpoint, who were still wedged into the doorway, happy to witness the reunion. "Yes, sir, this is my girl, and we are free *together*." He finally let go of his father's hand and embraced Precious with both arms.

Westlake smiled. Luther's spirit revealed itself exactly as Alexander had described, but the young fellow now enjoyed an independence that Westlake was sure his father had never seen. Freedom had grown on Luther until he had matured into a young man in his own right. With his girl beside him, Westlake thought, such happiness was a wonder to see. Then the idea struck him. *His own girl. Time to get moving.*

"Captain Nelles, sir. May I know the whereabouts of Miss Collins?"

"At the other end of this road, and two streets over, you'll find a small log cabin with a green door. It's the house in town that stands closest to the fort." Nelles indicated the direction with his thumb. "Mr. Parrish, you will accompany Mr. Westlake and remain present at all times. That's an order."

"Sir." Parrish saluted.

"After I sort out this lot, I'll be along shortly. On your best behaviour Mr. Westlake, you can go visit her." Nelles confirmed permission with a dismissive wave of his hand.

Alexander ran across and shook hands with Westlake and Parrish. "Before you leave, I want you to meet my son, Luther," Alexander called out to him and motioned for the young man to hurry. "These fellas helped Precious and me get here. Without them, well … I don't want to think what might have happened."

"Thank you all." Luther shook each man's hand in turn.

"Our great pleasure to be of some assistance." Westlake glanced at Alexander. "Unfortunately our attempts were not without a failure."

"Oh, I'm ashamed," Alexander said. "In all my excitement, I forgot to tell you some bad news."

"I already guessed that Hector died back at the falls," Luther murmured.

"You're right, but I'll tell you more about your brother later. In our battle to get here, your friend Mathew was killed." Alexander put his hand on his son's shoulder. "I'm sorry."

Westlake watched the ultimate joy of being reunited with his girl and his father drain from Luther's face.

"Mathew never hurt anyone." The young man shrugged in protest and closed both his eyes.

"I'm sorry for your friend," Westlake said. "He fought on the beach with the rest of us. It happened so fast."

"You did your best, Mr. Westlake," Precious said. "And I for one am surely glad the three of you marched to fetch us. Without you, we wouldn't be here now. Simple as that."

"Alex did the impossible ... escaping the plantation ... scattering their horses. Brock's railroad most happily did the rest." Westlake tipped his hat to Precious. "Goodbye to all of you. I'm sure we'll see you soon." He gave a final wave and remounted his horse. "Captain Nelles, sir." He saluted.

Parrish untied his horse, which had trailed the wagon, and mounted up.

"Until the next time." Westlake spurred his horse and his heart gave a jump because he was already thinking about Mary.

The green door sat dead centre in the front of a log cabin that stood back thirty paces from the road. The walls of the building were constructed from dark beams varying from a foot and a half to two feet square at each end. There were no windows so the cabin must have been one of the original Newark dwellings, and Westlake hoped for Mary's sake that its builders had decided to provide the luxury of a wooden floor.

Behind the closed door, Westlake imagined Mary sitting by the fire or eating dinner. Whatever occupied her, his moment of truth was fast approaching and he knew it. His mouth had gone dry.

"Parrish, give me a minute alone. It's stopped raining." Parrish began to protest, but Westlake cut him off. "I heard your orders, but the captain said he wouldn't be along just yet," Westlake pleaded.

"I'll stand guard here, sir. But the second I see Captain Nelles, I'm coming through that door. Make no bones about it, I'm not aiming for the lockup again."

"You're a good man, thank you."

"I'm a bleedin' idiot for disobeying orders." Parrish shook his head. "Mother always told me I was bloody daft."

Westlake knocked.

He didn't have to wait long. A small woman with ivory-pale skin, straight black hair, and dark eyes opened the door. She stood still at first, until a broad smile suddenly lit up her face. She wasn't beautiful, in fact her face was rather plain, but those intense black eyes drew him in until he could see nothing but the girl he loved.

"I'm back," Westlake said with a grin.

"Of course you are, silly. Come and kiss me." She held out her arms and he stepped into her embrace. He offered a gentle kiss, but it was not a Seffi kiss. At the thought, he let her go and stared at the ground. *Do not think of Seffi now.*

"Good afternoon, Mr. Parrish. Mission accomplished?"

"Good afternoon, Miss Collins," Parrish replied and touched his hat. "Well, yes, at least we're back."

"Thank you for returning him in one piece. Come in out of the weather, if you please."

"My pleasure, ma'am, but I'll wait out here for a spell, if you don't mind."

"Suit yourself."

Mary's arm slid under Westlake's elbow and she guided him forward through the open door before closing it. The interior of the cabin was a single room that showed the same rough-cut logs as the exterior. A curtain strung across the rear offered limited privacy for the sleeping quarters. At least the floor was made of wood and not bare earth covered with straw.

Immediately, Westlake noticed the warmth coming from a fireplace large enough to heat a cabin of twice the size. Too long in the fresh air, his collar suddenly seemed a little tight, and he even began to perspire. He unbuttoned his coat and laid it on the back of a chair before strolling over to the fire and stretching out his hands. Several candles placed around the room provided the only additional light to the fireplace.

"Mary, there's something I need to tell you." When he turned, she was directly behind him.

"Not yet." She put two fingers to his lips, reached for both his hands, and brought them to her face. Her lips pressed on the back of each before she placed his palms on either side of her cheeks.

"I've worried so much that you might never come back. The nightmares I've had …" She shook her head. "I can't tell you how happy I am to have you here with me. Kiss me like you did the last time … before you went away." She reached up and slipped her hands over his shoulders.

Her moist lips touched the side of his mouth and then moved on to his lips, a passionate gesture, warm and loving. Anything missing in that kiss came from him rather than in her. But it was easier for him to continue the kissing than to start the dreaded conversation. He embraced her close to his body and imagined making love to her … before turning away.

Westlake snatched up the iron poker and prodded the logs burning in the fire. It wavered and sparked as the wind outside bore down on it through the chimney. The temperature dropped with the end of day, but the reawakening embers worked to warm him in the little cabin. Or perhaps he just imagined it so.

"Have you been warm enough in here? I noticed your cough has gone."

"It's only got cold recently, and some men of the Coloured Company brought me all this chopped wood on the orders of Captain Nelles."

"How about your bed? Comfortable enough?"

"Do you want to try it?" Mary laughed.

"Don't tempt me." Westlake grinned. "Captain Nelles himself will be along soon."

Mary looked away and shrugged. "I don't sleep that much anyway. I prefer to stay busy. Last week, I picked apples on the outskirts of town with some other women. Look." She gestured to a darkened corner, where a basket of McIntosh apples sat full to the brim. "Want one? They're crisp as a winter's day."

Mary grabbed an apple and tossed it underhand to Westlake, but the throw was wide to his right. He flashed out a hand and like a cat, snatched the apple in mid-air, before immediately taking a bite. "Mmm … they *are* crisp."

She stared in disbelief at the speed of his reaction. "That hand was faster than a bullet," she said.

He was still laughing but proud of his deftness. "It's all the fresh air I've been getting."

"What is it you need to tell me?"

Westlake stopped laughing, taking another bite of his apple to buy himself time. He had rehearsed it all in his mind before arriving at this house, but now that he stood in front of Mary, he couldn't think. Resolved to honour his promise of marriage, he nevertheless hesitated.

Where to begin? "I don't deserve to marry you" or do I just tell her about Seffi and let her decide?

"When I go off on these secret trips for General Brock, I meet all kinds of people — some very good and some bad."

"Who did you meet this time, good or bad?" Mary warmed her hands over the fire.

Westlake remembered the boy militiaman on the Lake Erie shore, his eagerness and how he had died so easily. "Probably good — but that's not the point of my story. Just listen for a minute."

"Why are you telling me all this?"

"Will you listen, please? I meet men, and women too, and it's usually in situations of tremendous stress." He paused and waited for her to acknowledge her understanding of his words, but she stayed utterly silent and still. His heart was pounding. He took a deep breath and urged out the words, "And I find myself under the same strain."

Don't make an excuse. Just tell the damn story.

"We visited a farm during this last trip, a poor place run by an ill farmer who had no sons, only daughters." At least here she nodded a response.

A knock at the door and a cough interrupted his monologue.

"Sir, I have to come in." Parrish opened the door and backed his way inside, but he continued facing the closed door.

"It's all right Parrish, there is nothing untoward happening here. Turn around man … you look foolish," Westlake said.

"Captain Nelles approaches on horseback, sir." Parrish finally turned to him.

"I suppose we should greet him. My story must wait, Mary." Westlake hugged her small frame close, feeling almost relieved that the time for words had ended. "Parrish." He nodded to the door.

Nelles was dismounting even as Parrish opened the door. The wind blew hard and Westlake felt the damp immediately.

"Saddle up, gentlemen. I found quarters two and half miles toward Queenston for the pair of you." Nelles held the reins of his horse and when Mary stepped through the doorway, he tipped his hat. "Look for the brick building with a white picket fence on the riverside of the road. There's a room in the back that's quite comfortable, and the owner is expecting you."

"May I inquire why so far away, sir?" Westlake asked.

Nelles held up his fingers and counted off. "Firstly, it's a discreet distance from Miss Collins. Secondly, the general does not want his secret agents mingling by day with the town folk of Newark nor the garrison of Fort George. Thirdly, with the influx of troops, there's no other lodgings available."

"And I suppose we are to start on our way now, sir." The wind gusted and Westlake gripped his hat.

"Tomorrow evening, the general would have you as his guest for dinner at Government House. Miss Collins will be present, also." Nelles turned to Mary, catching her eye, and touched his hat, again. "You'll be meeting Miss Collins at dinner, Mr. Westlake."

Mary smiled and half curtseyed.

"And I'm sorry about you, Parrish, but this is for officers and female guests only," Nelles concluded.

Parrish shrugged, appearing pleased enough to be out of the company of officers. He untied the reins of his horse and pulled himself up into the saddle.

Westlake reached out with both arms and gave Mary a final

embrace while the wind whipped around her cabin. They huddled together for just a moment before he said goodbye.

"Until tomorrow Mr. Westlake," she called after him into the wind "I too have a story, though a short one, then you can tell me yours at dinner."

"I'm looking forward to it," Westlake lied.

21
······

In the predawn hours of Monday, October 12, 1812, Lieutenant Colonel Solomon van Rensselaer rolled over in his bed from one shoulder to the other. His recent bout of the ague had receded, but the aborted attack on Queenston had sapped his strength. While he needed rest, his mind couldn't stop churning. He closed his eyes and saw the hopeless looks of frustration among his soldiers waiting in the downpour. The invasion of Upper Canada cancelled due to lost oars — preposterous — embarrassing.

Suddenly, the image of his wife's face came to mind. He recalled reading her letter just before the recent fiasco. What a joy it had been to learn her thoughts and touch her words with his fingertips. He'd put her letter to his nose and then to his lips. Why had she not written sooner? Love could not be that fleeting; surely he was not already forgotten? But he had the proof of her love in his hands, and he had replied to her immediately.

> *My dearest Arriet,*
> *The happiness I experienced seeing your handwriting for the first time since leaving home is beyond any power of mine to express.*
> *My enterprise this night will shorten our separation, if I survive I will soon be with you, how pleasing the Idea and how Happy will be that moment.*

Some enterprise. What a spectacular failure. As the troops marched back to their camp, the militia had threatened to go home if they weren't allowed to fight immediately. They shouted, "Cowards," because of the delay. "Cowards!" The insult directed at him and his cousin Stephen.

Even officers of the regular army, who knew better, who rightly knew the men needed a rest, pressed for another attempt at invasion. Perhaps they were correct, the longer they waited, the more illness spread through the camp. The missing oars had eventually been found and the boats were ready now with the army close at hand. Thank God the damn rain had finally stopped. Why not give it another try?

The wind lashed around the tent till the walls tugged at their guy ropes. He shifted to lie flat on his back, and his mind changed tack again. Any fool on the British side could see his thirteen transports moored at the water's edge, eliminating all chance of surprise. Peering eyes couldn't miss spotting the thousands of soldiers ready to embark.

Yet they would also soon observe these same men marching away from the shore. The enemy would never guess that they would try anew in the exact same spot two days later.

"I wonder what Arriet is doing this very second?" he asked out loud. "It's not just our militia that wants to go home." He thought of her body … the comfort of its warmth. He sighed heavily.

In the semidarkness, Solomon sat up in bed, eyes wide open. *Invasion it is!* His mind raced with plans for the attack. Stephen, the officers, and of course, the militia will all be happy to get this war started. We can do it, and yesterday's attempt will then be like a practice, a mere drill — nothing wasted.

Tonight we'll reassemble, and by this time Tuesday morning I'll be in Upper Canada. "Praise to God I've made up my mind about this."

Solomon flopped back on his bed, the weight of a decision lifted off his chest. He pursed his lips and whistled like a kettle blowing steam. The pillow felt softer and he pulled the coarse top blanket up under his chin. For a moment, he studied the wavering shadows on the tent's ceiling, once again seeing the dark Canadian shore of the river as viewed from the American side. In his mind's eye, British muskets flashed along the hillside, echoing down the Niagara Gorge. The current swirled by … and the water carried him away. In an instant, he slept.

A cold day dawned, its sky packed with black racing clouds. Luther fully expected it to rain soon on the Coloured Company, as they mustered inside the closed gates of Fort George. Along with thirty-seven other militiamen, he wore two leather belts that crossed his chest diagonally, holding a cartridge pouch on his right hip and a bayonet on his left. Cynics might complain that these leather belts were no uniform for a proper soldier, but to the men of the Coloured Company it set them apart from civilians — elevated them to be recognizably part of the army community. Lieutenant Cooper told them that the twin belts comprised their company uniform — and that after all was the point. No sooner did he slip the belts over his head and pick up his musket, than he felt special. Luther grinned. He looked soldier-like and he would now prove to his father that he was a good one.

When he wasn't soldiering, Richard Pierpoint always dressed like a gentleman. He slid the belts over his threadbare green uniform and nestled the cartridge pouch into place. Luther glanced toward one side as his older friend snapped to attention. Someone hollered an order behind him, and the massive wooden gates creaked open.

"At the ordinary, march," a deep voice growled. The Coloured Company stamped off in synchronized motion. Mounted on his horse by the open gate, Lieutenant Cooper observed with his usual expression of disgust while Sergeant Alexander the Great barked out the order.

Their new sergeant terrified the company through his size, his voice, and the rumours of his ferocious exploits during the Revolutionary War. A few old Rangers and their descendants within the company had embellished these stories so that Alexander seemed an almost supernatural being: twisting off an enemy's head with his bare hands; shot through a dozen times but still kept fighting, the wounds hindering him no more than mosquito bites; and finally, breaking the bonds of his captors only to strangle them with their own chains of imprisonment. Impossible but true, the storyteller would insist in a tone of sincerity.

Luther viewed his father differently, however. Alexander seemed to stand straighter now than when they had lived on the plantation. Dressed in his leather belts, as soon as he gripped the musket his expression changed to one of intense menace. But he remained his father and Luther smiled, glancing at him as he marched past.

"Soldier, keep your eyes to the front," the sergeant bellowed into Luther's ear. Luther tensed his shoulders. This was not the same father he'd known when growing up. He wished Hector marched beside him. His brother would understand both his pride and his fear.

"Why does a British soldier always keep his eyes to the front?" The sergeant marched alongside his company. "Because he is marching as part of a grand machine. And each part of that machine has to concentrate only on the single task at hand. That is what makes the trained British soldier superior — as you are now superior. You will concentrate, therefore, on the single task at hand."

Was his father talking to him or to the entire company? Luther dared not look again. If Alexander thought him superior, then it meant he was. From Fort George to Butler's Field, he never took his eyes off the man in front. Cooper had drilled them to perfection, and now Alexander slammed that superiority in their faces. The machine marched as one man, and Luther figured that not only he but also every man in the company knew they were flawless. His chest swelled with pride, but he tried to keep a serious face.

They marched past a troop of the 41st Foot standing at ease and a soldier shouted out an obscenity. Mad Dog was mouthing off again. Alexander turned sharply from the front line of his company and glared at him. Immediate silence followed. Lieutenant Cooper stopped to say something to the officer in charge, but Luther couldn't hear his words.

On reaching Butler's Field in good order, Sergeant Alexander ordered the Coloured Company to stand easy. Cooper's horse trotted in behind them. A damp stump became Luther's chair as he watched his father talking with the lieutenant. The windswept field smelled fresh in the morning air, and Luther inhaled the aroma deeply.

Finished with Cooper, his father wandered among the militiamen and then stopped near Luther's stump. "There's been a problem with the prime-and-load drill … just for some of you," Alexander announced.

Luther winced. He belonged to the "some of you" group.

"We're going to practise this drill today, but you will not have a problem."

Petrified to do otherwise, every man listened intently to the sergeant's words. They pressed in closer around the stump, and Pierpoint jogged Luther's arm, nodding briefly in the sergeant's direction.

"Lieutenant Cooper won't let me shoot you if you blunder, but that's what the enemy will do," Alexander continued as if conveying a simple matter of fact. "Instead, he has allowed me to cuff on the side of the head any man who fails to concentrate — you see, that's the only way you will make a mistake, if you fail to concentrate." The big man held the flat of one thick hand in the air while turning to stare each soldier in the eye. Luther had felt the weight of that hand before.

"Focus solely on each manoeuvre. Don't think about shooting the enemy, or about him shooting you. Don't think about what the man next to you is doing. Don't think about firing in unison. Think only about executing your single task at hand. Simple." Sergeant Alexander ended with the sharp clap of his hands, and Luther sprang up from the stump while Pierpoint and the others jumped back a step.

"Coloured Company, fall in!" the sergeant ordered. The company scrambled to form two lines, every soldier standing elbow to elbow.

"Prepare to load," Alexander bellowed. "Handle cartridge!"

Luther withdrew a paper cartridge and peeked along the line to see that everyone else had his musket aligned across his chest. As soon as he looked, his head jerked from a slap to one side of it. For a second, the entire field tilted and then righted itself. The sergeant stood directly behind him.

"Focus now! Prime!"

Luther bit off the end and poured a little powder into his firing pan before snapping shut the frizzen. He didn't look anywhere or think about anything other than his immediate task. He swung the musket vertical to softly rest on its butt.

"Cast about!"

The surplus powder he poured down the musket's barrel, followed by the ball and its paper tube. Luther listened for the next order and realized he had the hang of things now. *Concentrate.*

"Draw ramrod!

"Ram down cartridge!"

He slid his ramrod down the barrel. On the order to return ramrod, and shoulder arms, he heard thirty-eight muskets smacking thirty-eight shoulders in unison. It was easy. *Don't think about anything but the individual motions, your motions, just like making a lantern.* Total absorption in the task at hand.

Sergeant Alexander marched over to where Lieutenant Cooper sat astride his horse.

"Sir, Coloured Company ready to fire, sir!"

The company fired. And did it again and again, all day, until three rounds a minute became the standard. Alexander had done it. Even Luther found it simple. He enjoyed hearing his musket scrape and click in unison with the others.

"You've done well, Sergeant," Cooper said to Alexander.

"You did all the work, sir. They were already drilled past anything I've ever seen. Now they believe in themselves. That's all I did."

"Still, today there's a sharp difference." Cooper nodded and smiled.

Sergeant Alexander spun around to face the company and stamped to attention. "I'm proud of each of you," he called out. "Don't concern yourselves with what other regiments think. And don't fret either over what the enemy thinks. Your only worry is what *I* think. And *I* think you are superior and that you're ready for battle." The sergeant allowed himself a smile, but the company obediently kept their eyes front.

Luther's heart soared … finally a soldier. The enemy was in for a stormy reception.

Westlake's ride from his single-room beside the Niagara Gorge to Government House took thirty minutes along the muddied road. He dismounted and spent the next half-hour brushing his pants clean. By the time he strolled into the dining room, the chill from the wind had worn off and his stomach grumbled for food.

Everyone in the room held a glass of wine and seemed to be talking at once, creating more noise than a dozen muskets firing simultaneously. The skirmish on the beach flashed into his mind. He felt safer there. Here, officers in scarlet tunics and gold epaulettes bowed to gloved ladies in low-cut dresses. The candles shimmered along the wall, and the fireplace to his left burst with new light just seconds after he opened the door. The entire scene before him mirrored the large painting of a dinner party that hung on one wall.

In anticipation of autumn, and before setting off on his mission, Westlake had asked Captain Nelles to send to Maple Hill for his trunk. Now, he shifted stance in his finer clothes and gave a tug at his collar. More than a year had passed since he'd been required to dress formally, and then only for attending church services in York. Even a clean shirt became a luxury out on the trail, he'd learned.

For Seffi … that was the last time he'd worn a clean shirt. He envisioned her face, the beauty of her smile and those liquid blue eyes. Eventually his thoughts drifted to Mary and to the speech he had prepared for her. He swallowed hard and forced his attention back to the crowded room.

Before him stretched a long table draped in white linen and covered with silver plates, waiting for the guests to be seated. A chandelier flickered above the midpoint of the table, where a servant stood on an upholstered chair, reaching to light two of the candles that had lost their flame. Out of the gathering, a red-coated soldier wearing white gloves approached him, jiggling a silver tray laden with full glasses.

"Thank you," Westlake said, taking a glass of red wine and gulping down the entire contents at once, only to exchange his empty glass with a full one from the waiter's tray. He hated feeling confined and hoped the wine might ease his tension in the crowded room. Instead, it burned his throat on the way down and within a few minutes his head was spinning. *Enough of the wine.*

Westlake looked from face to face, hoping to recognize someone familiar. The crowd parted briefly and he spotted Mary, smiling in the centre of a small circle of men. He stepped toward her, listening hard to hear her words.

"The kitchen was packed with warriors ready to strike. He said in a low voice like this, 'I am friend of Tecumseh and Paxinos. Leave now and you will live.' You should have seen how he didn't flinch an inch under the Indian's tomahawk. Of course, the Indians backed down and I lived to tell the tale." Mary beamed and the officers surrounding her all laughed.

"There he is." She pointed out Westlake to them as he edged into the circle.

"Ah, Mr. Westlake, her hero." A big man stepped forward and quickly held out his hand. "Captain Henry Vigoreux at your service, sir. Is it true? Did you simply stare down the savages?"

"It wasn't exactly like that, sir." Westlake swallowed another mouthful of wine. "Miss Collins kindly gives more credit than is due. They were terrified of Tecumseh, so there was no need to be worried."

"Good show, young fellow. That's what I like in a man, casual courage in the face of adversity," the captain said.

"A disciplined man will push off the reckless enemy every time," a stern voice added.

As Westlake had edged toward Mary, he had not noticed the officer standing behind him. He turned to see a stout man of some fifty years with wavy grey hair and a countenance such that he appeared overly dour.

"Sir?" Westlake inquired.

"I said, Discipline and training will defeat the enemy in every instance. Count on it," the man said.

"Have we met, sir? I'm sorry," Westlake asked. Gulping the last of his wine had made him somewhat light-headed, but he sensed a guarded unease creeping into their circle.

"Mr. Westlake, forgive me. Let me introduce Major General Sheaffe," Vigoreux said.

Sheaffe stared Westlake in the eyes, expecting a retort, then he extended his hand as if it was a chore.

"I'm sure you're correct, sir," Westlake said, taking the general's hand. "But if the enemy is equally disciplined, is not a certain boldness also required?" The crowd around him went silent.

Sheaffe's face immediately flushed red. He took a sip from his glass, his chest heaving in a deep breath. Westlake knew the challenge he'd offered would not be taken lightly. He felt all the room's eyes concentrating on him in the silence.

"I see our fur trader has arrived."

Westlake turned away from Sheaffe to see a gleam in the eye of the smiling General Brock. The big man had strolled right into the centre of their circle, and in his dress uniform, he projected the authority of someone naturally in charge. A waiter approached and whispered in his ear.

"It seems dinner is ready — so I'm just in time." Brock grinned at Westlake. "Let's eat, shall we. I'm half starved."

Brock took Westlake by the elbow and offered an arm to Mary. On the way to his place at the head of the table, he warned quietly, "Never drink on an empty stomach." He gestured to Westlake's depleted wineglass. "You may say things that you'll regret later."

"I'm sorry, sir," Westlake replied. "He just rubbed me the wrong way. I'm not even sure I know why."

"I only know that lesson because I've done it myself. Sit with me, here." Brock motioned to seats near the table's head and stood behind the end chair. "The general is sitting at the other end, so that should keep you out of trouble. I'm sure you've already heard he has a habit of rubbing people the wrong way." Brock laughed.

Westlake directed Mary to the seat on Brock's immediate right and claimed the chair beside her for himself. Directly across from Mary stood Captain Vigoreux.

"Ah, Mr. Simpson, I wondered where you were," Brock said.

Ensign Robert Simpson hurried to the chair beside Vigoreux and nodded to each of the guests around him. Brock scanned the assembly, who all stood, waiting for his instructions.

"Let's all be seated and enjoy our dinner together," he said.

The waiters filled each guest's glass with wine, then a clergyman sitting halfway down the table recited the grace. Brock next proposed a toast to the King. Westlake raised the glass to his lips but remained careful not to drink. The murmur in the room gradually rose to its former volume.

Waiters scurried in carrying great trays of steaming plates. The aroma from a lavish dinner of roast beef, baked potatoes, and boiled vegetables wafted up in front of Westlake's nose. He asked a waiter for a glass of water. The clang of cutlery reached a pitch as the tableful of guests began to eat. The beef fell apart in his mouth and he groaned with sheer pleasure at the taste. He had not enjoyed so fine a dinner since his visit to the Bauer farm a month earlier. Again, Seffi's face came to mind, but vanished just as quickly when Simpson began to speak.

"I heard rumours that the bluecoats lost their oars, sir. Quite funny really, everyone is laughing at them." Simpson let out a dramatic guffaw and tapped his fork. "Do you expect the Americans to try again soon, sir?"

The man was at it again, and Westlake winced. Did Simpson never learn?

The room grew noticeably quiet as those at Brock's end of the table leaned toward him, straining their ears. The waiters, cradling carafes of wine, stood back behind the guests so as not to interfere with their line of sight to Brock.

"Only a fool laughs at an enemy who is intent on killing him," Brock said. "I doubt they'll misplace their oars a second time."

Simpson's grin quickly disappeared. He gulped more wine and cleared his throat. "What about their invasion, sir?"

"No one can say for sure." Brock gave a small shrug. "It could be anytime — next week or even tomorrow." He bit down on a forkful of beef.

Westlake peered down the table to where a plump woman in a pale blue evening dress with ruffled shoulders, stuffed her face as if she was loading a cannon's mouth. Far too many people jammed into one room for Westlake's liking. He sliced a potato with his fork and watched as the steam lifted away.

"And how many soldiers do they have, sir?" Mary asked, almost in a whisper.

"Good question, Miss Collins," said Captain Vigoreux. "We are wondering the same thing." He leaned forward, stooping down to look directly into her face. "However, our best guess is seven thousand at a minimum, of which well over a third or more are regulars. The balance is the New York militia, a second-rate lot and no real worry to us."

Mary questioningly looked to Brock, who smiled.

"I wouldn't say *no* worry. The bigger question, to my mind, Miss Collins, is how many men can or will cross that river," Brock said. He placed his last remaining forkful of beef in his mouth and chewed.

"And on our side, sir? How many do we have to oppose whatever number does manage to cross?" Westlake asked.

"We have half their number of regulars and a quarter in terms of militia, which includes our Indians." Brock raised his glass to Chief John Norton, who sat mid-table across from the clergyman. The chief acknowledged him with a nod and leaned back as a waiter cleared away his empty plate.

"But here I take sides with General Sheaffe," Brock continued. "Our soldiers are better disciplined, and even our militia are better trained and equipped — partly thanks to our victory at Detroit." He gave a broad smile.

"Hear, hear!" A rumble rose as a number of officers drummed their fingers on the table and shouted. "Good show." A toast was proposed to the Detroit victory and everyone joined in.

"And in this weather, their soldiers sleep in tents at best, or under the open sky," Sheaffe called out from the far end of the table, "while most of ours are billeted in more permanent quarters. The longer they wait, the more illness will spread."

Another round of "Hear, hear!" spontaneously erupted, until the room drifted into a welcome silence.

"What are you thinking," Mary whispered in Westlake's ear. "You look far away — lost in your thoughts."

"I'm thinking how pleased my mother will be to meet you." He smiled. "She gets very lonely all by herself at Maple Hill."

Up and down the table, the guests leaned one way or the other while waiters gathered up empty dishes and delivered the dessert. On Westlake's plate, the apple filling oozed from under a golden brown crust, the aroma reminding him again of Maple Hill. His mother often cooked apple pie, and he wondered what she was doing at this very minute. He decided to write a letter to her later that night.

Dessert had scarcely begun when a mud-splattered officer charged into the room heading to where General Sheaffe sat enjoying his pie. Panting in an attempt to recover his breath, the man bent over and gripped a corner of the table. The general scanned him up and down, frowning both at the interruption and the man's filthy appearance in the dining room. Sheaffe wiped the corners of his mouth with a white napkin and calmly stood up. The intruder uttered a few inaudible words and Sheaffe took him by the elbow, escorting him out the same door he had entered. A low murmur instantly drifted around the table.

Westlake glanced over at Brock, who raised his eyebrows and smiled. No cause for alarm yet. Brock leaned over to speak quietly with Captain Vigoreux.

"Miss Collins." Westlake finally took a sip of his wine and turned his head. "I have to talk with you, privately."

"What is it, Mr. Westlake?"

"Perhaps we could stroll over to that picture." A gold-framed portrait of King George III stared down at them, and Westlake gestured to the side table and two chairs sitting beneath it. He stood up and pulled Mary's seat toward him, allowing her to rise.

Sheaffe hastened back into the room, brushing away several strands of grey hair that had fallen over his forehead. He glanced at his slice of uneaten pie and grimaced while the mud-stained officer trailed behind. Sheaffe made directly for Brock, who pushed back from the table and stood to meet him face to face.

"I'm truly sorry, sir, but this fellow is most insistent," Sheaffe explained. "Seems some extra militia have jammed in on the American side at Lewiston. Damn fool thinks we are to be invaded any second, at Queenston."

"Let's keep our voices down." Brock motioned him away from the table, where Westlake stood watching with Mary. "Why would they attack at a cliff when there are so many other better places to cross?" Brock asked. "If they are planning to attack — and I emphasize *if* — this may very well be just a feint."

Westlake leaned against the wall, holding Mary by his side. He tried not to move an inch lest he be noticed and sent away. Captain Vigoreux stood up too and was soon joined by Lieutenant Colonel McDonnell and Captain Nelles.

"I travelled across the river under a flag of truce, sir," the dishevelled officer continued. "Regardless, they shot at us as my men rowed and then held me off at gunpoint. That's when I spotted the boats concealed under brush all along the shore."

McDonnell interjected, "They've had boats there for weeks, and haven't they already tried this surprise once?"

"You can't see them from our side, sir, but they've added more. And hundreds of soldiers are streaming in as well," the man said.

"Calm down, man, that's enough," Brock replied. "Come with me to my office. There is no need to alarm the ladies."

As they moved away, Sheaffe announced quietly to the others, "Man's near hysterical. The Americans won't cross tonight, in this wind. They'd be mad to even try."

"Stranger things have been attempted, but I agree." McDonnell had brought his wine with him and now took a long drink. "And why would they attack at Queenston for a second time? It makes no sense."

"I, for one, am going to finish my pie," Sheaffe concluded. "And then I think a good stiff port is in the offing after all this kerfuffle."

Sheaffe and McDonnell returned to their seats, while Nelles left the room with Captain Vigoreux. Westlake nudged Mary's elbow and she sat down with him under the King's portrait. The continuing buzz of conversation in the room made it difficult for him to think, but he wanted to begin his story.

"Remember, I have a story to tell also, Mr. Westlake." Mary looked down at the floor. "A confession really."

"You do?"

"But go ahead with your tale." She leant forward, her face beaming again. "I bet I can guess what it is."

"You can?" Westlake said in surprise. This was really too much. His stomach grew into a knot as his mouth went dry. She could not have guessed. It surely wasn't possible.

"You've picked a date, haven't you?" She smiled in anticipation. "You are a rascal, Mr. Westlake."

"A date?" Westlake frowned. "A date for what?" he asked in frustration.

"Our wedding, of course," she sighed, her brightness lost the instant she saw his frown.

Westlake glanced up. Brock had re-entered the room and a general stir ensued as ladies and even officers shifted in their seats. Gone was his jovial mood, his pleasant demeanour replaced by solemnity. The entire table fell quiet and everyone turned their heads toward him as he hovered at the table's end. Even the plump woman, who now stuffed her mouth with the clergyman's pie, stopped shovelling for a moment, leaving her spoon in mid-air.

Westlake had seen this expression on Brock's face before, serious yet with a studied appearance of calm. With the guests all staring, Westlake knew that Brock had something important to say. "We should go back to our seats," Westlake said. He quickly led Mary back to the table and slid the chair in underneath her. The general twice tapped hard on the table with his fingers as if bringing a meeting to order.

Every officer in the room rose up as one, with a loud scraping of chairs.

"I'm sure you have all noticed the comings and goings of our enthusiastic major." Brock gestured to the back of the room, where the muddy officer gulped some warm tea. "He has spared no effort in bringing us news of recent enemy activity opposite Queenston. We thank him and, while there is no need to be alarmed — war is not something to panic over — I must order the militia and all our regular forces to stand ready for immediate action."

The rotund lady, balancing some pie on her spoon, blurted out, "So the enemy will attack us tonight?" Absentmindedly, she transferred the spoon into her mouth.

"Ma'am, there is no need for concern. No one can say when they might attack, or if they will attack at all. However, I can you assure you and everyone present that our men are ready to do their duty, and any enemy invading the shores of Upper Canada will receive a rude welcome."

"Hear! Hear!" The officers pounded the table, rattling cutlery against plates. The lady in the blue dress squealed at the commotion.

"We *are* ready, sir," Simpson shouted loudly, although he was only standing six feet away from Brock. Westlake found himself standing with the rest. His heart was racing and he felt the need do something immediately. He reached for his wine, following the example of the others.

Brock lifted his own glass and smiled as every officer around the table prepared to raise a toast with him. He waited, gauging the moment. "To victory!" he bellowed.

"To victory!" the officers shouted in response, just as the wind hammered the walls and the candles flickered.

Brock continued, "To the King and Upper Canada!"

The officers repeated his words in unison with a cheer.

"Now, perhaps we should curtail our festivities and make this an early night," Brock concluded. "We may need all our wits about us in the early morn."

A further scraping of chairs ensued as the men helped the ladies to their feet and everyone began jostling toward the door. One officer gulped down the rest of his wine before rushing out. Armed with silver trays, the waiters approached to clear the table of empty plates and glasses.

Brock touched Westlake on the arm. "Excuse me, Miss Collins, but I need a word with your fiancé."

Mary nodded with a reluctant smile.

Brock walked across to stand under the King's portrait and turned to Westlake. Captain Nelles joined them with his glass in hand. "I'm promoting you to lieutenant, Mr. Westlake — as well as Mr. Simpson. While it's a little early for a lieutenancy, your work at Fort's Mackinac and Detroit was exemplary, and rescuing Sergeant Alexander has done the army a valuable service. My congratulations." Brock offered his hand. "You've come a long way."

Westlake could not help grinning. This is what he'd fought for more than anything: respect. "Thank you, sir. This is an unexpected honour, indeed." He'd write letters forthwith to his friends and especially to his mother — she'd know what this meant. How would Alexander and Parrish react? And Mary, she would be happy for him. His mind raced with thoughts, thrilled with the knowledge that Brock was proud of him.

Westlake glanced back at the rest of the room and wanted to shout out his delight. His angular face held an exaggerated grin, like a man who'd won a great prize. He suddenly realized he was still vigorously shaking Brock's hand. Nelles offered his own congratulations, so Westlake let go of Brock's hand only to begin shaking again.

"Captain Nelles already has the paperwork prepared, but now I would like you to leave forthwith to find Sergeant Alexander and tell him to have his Coloured Company ready before sun up. And also find Lieutenant Cooper of the 2nd West Lincoln regiment — he's their commanding officer. You'll like him, I'm sure."

"And Miss Collins, sir?" Westlake hoped Brock would at least let him walk her home, nearby.

"Captain Nelles will be her escort; it's not far. After you've done your duties, get yourself to bed. You may be called upon sooner than you think. Congratulations, again." Brock shook hands with him a last time before he beckoned to Macdonell and Sheaffe. The three men went off to engage in discussion, while Westlake and Nelles walked back to the dining table.

"I'll get her home safe," Nelles promised. "You can count on it."

Westlake returned to his chair. "Mary, I have received orders from General Brock to leave this instant. Captain Nelles will escort you home. And," he added, grinning, "I've just been promoted to lieutenant."

"I suppose congratulations are in order," she replied flatly. "But what was it you wished to tell me?" There was a tension in her voice and Westlake knew that she was disappointed in his early departure.

"I'm sorry. I'm afraid it will have to wait." He stood again, relieved that there was no time to discuss the events at the Bauer farm. Mary rose from her chair too, and he gave her a hug and then a kiss on the lips. "Goodbye." He looked in her eyes and felt a pang of guilt. He embraced her again, but she barely moved.

22
......

WESTLAKE STARED OUT though a small window into the blackness and listened to the night's wind twisting around the house. He'd managed to sleep several hours before the storm disturbed his slumber. The rain lashed the rooftop, accompanied by a distant boom of thunder. He thought of the previous evening's meeting with Sergeant Alexander and Lieutenant Cooper, both men more than eager to prove the readiness of the Coloured Company. By the time he had reached his own quarters, lightning flashed and the rain fell in bucketfuls. Happily, he climbed into bed.

He slept with dreams of gunfire, Indians, and a beach, the separate images merging together. When roused awake, at first he wasn't sure what he was hearing ... thunder and more thunder? The far-off sound repeated itself again and again until Westlake lurched around, inclining his ear toward the window.

"Parrish, did you hear that? Wake up."

"Did you call me?" Parrish yawned. "What?"

"Cannon fire, man!" Westlake yelled. "Did you hear it?"

"No, sir. Are you sure you wasn't dreaming?"

Faint but continuous echoes of booming cannon ricocheted down the Niagara Gorge toward their quarters.

"That's it ... I'm riding over to warn General Brock." Westlake's hand was already thrashing about under the cot for his boots. After fumbling the buttons on his jacket, he raced for the stables like a man possessed. Behind him Parrish appeared at the back door still clad in his nightshirt.

"What if it's just a storm?" Parrish asked. "If you just give me a chance, I'll saddle a horse for you properly, sir."

"There's no time," Westlake yelled over his shoulder. "Saddle two horses and wait for my return."

With the force of the wind, the unwieldy barn door flew from his grasp and crashed against the stable's front wall. Inside the building, the horses whinnied and stepped nervously in their stalls. Westlake ran stall to stall, searching for the black mare he'd noticed when putting his own horse away for the night. She looked back at him with calm eyes and he patted her nose.

"We're going to go for a ride to see General Brock, you and I. No time for a saddle, okay?" Westlake opened the gate. He placed a bridle around her nose and the bit over her tongue and, pulling the reins over her head, leaped up on to the horse's back. With the heels of his boots, he gently urged the mare out of the stable, into the bone-chilling wind and the damp night air.

He had ridden the drenched trail from Government House only hours before, so he knew his way, but in the blackness of night, the potholed road grew treacherous. The rain diminished, but the muffled boom of cannons reached his ears again and again. Somewhere along the river, the invasion had already started. Another thirty minutes passed before Westlake and his mount reached Government House.

The two sentries sheltering under the narrow veranda roof jumped to their feet on spotting his black horse. He watched them squinting through the drizzle, wondering who might approach at this time of night. Not wearing a hat, he wiped his dripping forehead with the back of one arm.

"Stand and identify yourself," one of the sentries commanded.

"Lieutenant Jonathan Westlake with an important message for General Brock."

"Are you aware of the time, sir?"

Westlake dismounted and tied his horse to a post. He ran up the veranda steps only to be confronted by a pair of bayonets.

"The invasion of Upper Canada has begun upriver, gentlemen. I'm here to inform the general."

The sentries glanced at each other, then stood aside.

Westlake charged on through the front door and bounded up the stairs, heading for what he assumed was Brock's bedroom. He knocked on the first door and opened it. Brock rolled restlessly in his bed. With an encouraging nudge to the shoulder he turned over, opening and closing his eyes quickly.

"Sir, I'm very sorry to disturb you, but from my quarters two miles south, I've heard continuous cannon fire." Westlake panted. "It can only mean the invasion has begun."

Brock rubbed an eye wearily. "Wouldn't our sentries have heard it, Jonathan?" he groaned and stretched.

"The wind is blowing so hard I barely heard it myself, sir. The sound is continuous, so it's not thunder."

Brock was now awake and sitting up. "Very well. Order my horse saddled. Tell them I'll take Alfred today."

"Sir."

"I can hardly believe the Americans would cross near Queenston, only to sit at the bottom of a cliff."

Lieutenant Colonel Solomon van Rensselaer inched his horse forward through a throng of soldiers crowding the embarkation points. Just south of Lewiston, U.S. regular army and militiamen jammed together at the foot of a ravine. From here, men portaged boats and equipment around the great falls located even farther south. The buffeting wind threw one man off balance, pushing him backward into Solomon's horse.

"We could have used a few of Mr. Porter's new vessels for the crossing, sir. The regulars meant for the second wave have already crowded the first compliment of militia out of the boats." Captain Wool cupped a hand around his mouth, shouting to make himself heard above the wind. "Do you want me to order the regulars to disembark?"

"I wouldn't use Porter's boats even it meant I had to swim across. These thirteen vessels will do us fine. Leave the men be where they are," Solomon ordered. "Push off now, before the enemy realizes what we're about."

He swung back to face those waiting on shore. Even in this moment of excitement, he noticed the smell of fresh water racing past him. From his saddle, he yelled to the massed militia waiting on the slope, "You men will go with the second crossing. The boats will be back in a flash to take you over. You'll each get your chance to invade Upper Canada. Something to tell your grandchildren about!"

A great cheer went up, and he waved his hat as he dismounted. The thirteen boats, carrying more than three hundred men, pushed off and Solomon leapt into the last one. At four o'clock on the moonless morning of October 13, 1812, he and his fellow Americans were finally invading Upper Canada.

Only a few yards off the American shore, he had to grip the rail to steady himself as the swirling current tugged his boat sideways. The oarsmen rowed even harder to keep them from drifting downstream. For at least five hundred yards they had to struggle against the flow to reach a Canadian beach of shale and stone. Solomon could see Wool's boat ahead, fishtailing in the surge of water.

When his own boat was across midstream, the British shore exploded with musket fire, the bullets peppering all around him. Solomon heard a man scream. "Pull harder," another yelled, fear echoing in his voice. "Row, you lousy dogs," one oarsmen urged the others.

The British fired again, lighting up their position against a looming wall of rocks and dark brush. Exactly like in his dream, Solomon saw the enemy perched on a hillside crest fifty feet above the water, firing straight down into his boats. *Jesus wept, we're like sitting ducks. So much for my surprise.* Someone in his boat yelled desperately, "Come on, pull faster! We'll all be dead soon at the rate you lot row."

The boat lifted on the renewed strength of the oars, and Solomon relaxed until another vicious blast of fire lit up the crest above. They were so close to the Canadian shore now that he could see the intense concentration on the enemy's faces in the volley's light. A ball plucked at his sleeve as, all around him, the surface of the water popped with musket balls. Suddenly a distinctive boom crashed out above and he instinctively ducked his head, along with everyone else in the boat. *Cannon fire.*

He glanced up to see the men from Wool's loaded boat already disembarking on the shore in front of him.

"Just a few more yards," he urged. "We can do it." For the third time in as many minutes, he reached for his hat as it flew from his head in a gust of wind. He was too late and watched it go. Muskets blasted somewhere above him and a few men in the boat screamed from their sudden wounds.

The boat crept ever closer to the shore. As it slid in over the stones, the soldiers leapt over the sides and Solomon jumped with them. He turned back to give some final orders and noticed a man lying dead between the seats. Others too wounded to move lay on the bottom of the hull.

"Take our dead and wounded back across," he ordered the rowers, "then bring the others fast as you can." The water's edge boiled with musket balls and a few smacked against the boat's stern.

He turned and began to run, but the crest above him lit up in a sheet of flame. A ball ripped through his right thigh and he fell to the ground. Lying there in agony, he realized he had to reach shelter soon or die. He hauled himself up, ready to run, when a ball from a second volley caught him in the same thigh. His leg burned as if on fire, while he crawled toward the protection of the riverbank. A soldier jumped out of cover to drag him to safety.

Solomon pulled back his pant leg to see that his heel and calf had also been clipped by the volley. Less than an hour before, in the calm of his tent, he had joyfully tied a blue scarf around his neck to keep out the damp. Now, in a sweat, he retied the same scarf around his bleeding thigh to slow the blood. He swore. How long could he command if the bleeding persisted, he wondered.

Across the water, a cannon fired from above the right side of the American ravine, lighting up the shore where the New York militia had come down to embark. Finally, his bluecoats were answering British cannon with artillery of their own. A cheer went up from the soldiers around him.

The British returned fire, only this time their cannon balls cut gory swaths through the men crowded into the ravine. The cannon blasted again and, in the light, Solomon witnessed the carnage and heard the moans. Men and horses scrambled for cover, choosing to be anywhere away from the incoming boats. He watched an officer attempting to wave them forward again with his sword as soon as the boats touched the shore.

Solomon called out for Wool, who had been advancing up the beach, but no reply was forthcoming. On the water, a second wave of boats pushed out from the American side but immediately drifted away downstream. Then he watched in horror as those same vessels put back for the comparative safety of the Lewiston docks.

Sheltering under the overhang, Solomon ordered his men to rest. His leg continued to bleed and he knew that, for this day at least, his fighting was over. The element of surprise had been lost, but if more men crossed the river, he sensed the day could still be won. Again, more boats pushed off from the American shore, and the men around him hollered their encouragement across the water.

"You can do it," a man shouted right beside him.

The river flashed in the reflection of bright light and then just as quickly returned to darkness. Solomon couldn't tell if it was due to artillery or lightning until the cannon balls meant to destroy the boats in midriver crashed into the water, throwing up a giant plume that soaked the rowers in a freezing spray. That is, until one ball unfortunately hit dead centre. The boat carrying twenty men exploded into woodchips and slivers. One second there was a boat, packed and rowing determinedly for the shore, and in the next second it was gone — and so were its crew — vanished but for debris of wood and body parts.

Solomon turned his head away and winced. "Get me that damn Captain Wool," he ordered the man next to him. "And give me your greatcoat." As soon as the man ran off on his errand, Solomon wrapped the coat around himself, concealing the blood that dripped from his wounds.

Captain Wool hobbled toward him along the beach, staying close to the protective wall of the riverbank. The musketry from above the shoreline had diminished, but fighting could be heard just north of their position. Wool slid down gingerly beside him.

"Your report, Captain Wool?" Solomon demanded.

"On seeing our numbers, they retreated from the beach. I have about two hundred and twenty-five of the Thirteenth Infantry still with me. We pushed them north a ways at first, toward the village," Wool winced and shifted from one buttock to the other. "But they regrouped and pushed us back to where we started."

"You wounded, Captain?"

"Seems I've been shot in the rear end, sir." Wool actually grinned. "More the hip area, to be quite honest. Burns like the devil." Wool rubbed his hip and considered the cliff above them. "Been severe casualties on both sides, sir. I'm afraid we've lost a number of officers."

"We have to get off this beach and seize the heights," Solomon said. "Their artillery is knocking the stuffing out of us. The day is lost if we can't do so. You understand?"

"It's finding a way up that's the problem, sir. There's no sign of this fisherman's trail or the fisherman to guide us, but we're told there's a path somewhere." Wool leaned out from the bank and surveyed the terrain above them. "There has to be a way up, otherwise all these good fellows will be slaughtered for nothing."

Solomon sighed and paused to admire the man sitting before him, full of energy and commitment to his men. Small-framed for a warrior, Wool made up for his lack of bulk with brains and determination. His neck and head looked too small for the rest of his body. "How old are you, Captain?"

"That's a strange question, sir, if you don't mind my saying," Wool replied. "I'm twenty-three."

"I meant no offence. I've lost so much blood that I can't even stand." Solomon closed his eyes for a moment, feeling dizzy. "You're a good man, Captain. I'm shot full of holes … you're the senior officer in charge now." Solomon flung away the greatcoat to show the wounds in his thigh. "You can do this. Just find a way up, and shoot any man who won't go with you."

"I'm sorry for your wounds, sir. Nasty work, this, but we'll find a way. You have my word," Wool replied.

Along the six-and-half-mile road to Queenston, Alfred splashed his way hard through the puddles, kicking up a spray of mud. The high-bred horse had been a gift from a departing governor and now carried the "Saviour of Upper Canada" into battle. Brock didn't feel much like a hero with mud splattering over his crimson coat and white pants. Only a week since his forty-third birthday, General Isaac Brock rode against a determined wind in his face.

He reached just past the halfway point of his journey and glanced over his shoulder. Westlake should have roused the entire fort by now. On the young lieutenant's confirmation the invasion had begun, the Niagara Light Dragoons would be riding to alert the militia for a march on Queenston. "I still can't believe it," he said out loud. "Must be a damn feint."

Booms echoed down the gorge and light flashed regularly above Queenston. It was a tremendous feint if this wasn't the real thing. Like a thunderstorm that never paused, unceasing lightning followed the extravagant cannon fire. He wondered how his friends Captains Dennis and Williams were faring when thirty York militiamen came marching by, heading double time toward Queenston.

Brock rode Alfred over to the side of the road but did not stop. Instead, he slowed to a trot, took off his hat, and waved it. "Push on, brave York Volunteers."

A great cheer went up as he passed them. He smiled and shook his fist in the air. Lousy weather, poor food, and separated from their families, yet these volunteers marched along with enthusiasm, in defence of their homes. The York Volunteer Militia had been with him at Detroit and now here they were marching to battle on the banks of the Niagara River. Their enthusiasm fuelled him on.

The blast of cannon grew louder as he rode into Voorman's Point battery. Brock stopped, as much to give Alfred a breather as himself. Strangely, the eighteen-pound carronade sited on the riverbank suddenly rested silent. Its crew stood still, staring downstream at the American boats floundering in the river.

"Why don't you fire that gun?" Brock called out to the lieutenant.

"Sir!" The lieutenant snapped to attention. "We didn't see you come up, sir. The enemy is too distant, the balls all fell short, so we stopped."

Brock peered upstream to see the boats slipping sideways in the current, but well out of range. "It can't be helped." Brock shrugged and spurred Alfred on.

He'd been in the saddle for a full hour, riding at a steady trot, when the landscape around Queenston began to lighten. Dawn arrived with the barest glimmer and the scudding rain clouds guaranteed that the coming day would remain dull. Brock guessed it to be about six-thirty in the morning. He gripped the reins tighter as the smells and sounds of battle enveloped him. Puffs of gunpowder drifted on the wind from the unceasing crack of musket fire and cannon blasts.

A half-dozen wounded soldiers of the 5th Lincoln militia lay to his right, sheltering in a damp gully beside the road. In the ditch with them, sprawled more than twice their number of captured bluecoats, all groaning from their battle wounds. This was the bloody periphery of the battleground.

"Where's Captain Dennis?" Brock called from his horse.

"Good to have you with us, sir." A man saluted but couldn't stand. He merely raised a shaking hand to point. "Just follow the road toward the fighting. Not far ..."

"Thank you." Brock touched his hat.

After two minutes of hard riding, the sound of musket fire increased and a ball zipped past his ear and then another smacked into a nearby tree. He soon passed Hamilton Cove, where he waved a greeting to some members of his old regiment, the 49th. In front of him, the shoreline snaked its way south, and along both sides of the road he could see the backs of at least forty redcoats. The men of the 2nd York Regiment maintained a withering fire aimed at an unseen enemy farther along the beach.

To his right in the little village of Queenston, an explosion shook the ground and Alfred veered slightly to the left. Brock squinted hard but saw no smoke above the village. Moments later, he found Captain Dennis conferring with two officers behind a stone wall that ran perpendicular to the road and into the town.

"Enemy cannon fire has hit something in town," Brock remarked loudly.

"Sir." All three officers saluted as Brock dismounted.

"They've knocked out our nine-pounder, sir," explained Dennis. "And good morning to you, sir." He smiled.

"Good morning, gentlemen. Is this the real thing, Captain?" Brock shook each man's hand in turn.

"We've been going at it for over two hours, sir. If they're just joking, it's one hell of a feint," Dennis replied.

Brock surveyed the American shore, then glanced up the heights behind him to study the redan battery.

"I'll get a better view from up there," he decided. "Can you hold?"

"As long as the buggers don't get behind me, we should be fine. Boats crossing the river have slowed to a trickle, and I've still got over four hundred good men here." Dennis grinned and looked up at the grey skies. "Yes, sir, we should be fine. Lovely day for battle."

Brock put one foot in the stirrup and swung his other leg over the saddle. He saluted the three officers and gave Alfred a touch of heel. The horse followed the wall for a stretch, then pressed some distance up the embankment to the redan, where an eighteen-pounder let fly, blasting out fire and ball together. Brock's body shook with the vibration and the horse under him reared back. The smoke from the cannon caught in his throat and he spit out its bitter taste.

From the water, he was more than half way up Queenston Heights. The dawn's light had spread sufficiently so that when Brock observed the panorama of the Niagara Gorge, he had to take a calming breath. He squinted again, unsure that his eyes were seeing true.

Across the river, on the open ground leading into the ravine, thousands of men jostled for position waiting to embark the boats. This was no feint; the enemy was invading Upper Canada here at Queenston. They were either fools for attacking at a cliff face or brilliant for selecting the one spot where he had placed the fewest defenders.

Located at the redan, he looked up to see Captain Williams and the 49th Light Company staring down at him from the crest above. Brock waved his hand and Williams clambered down to join him.

"Good morning, sir." Williams saluted.

"Morning." Brock returned his old friend's salute. "So this is their much awaited invasion."

"Yes, sir. Your orders?"

Brock smiled. Ever-efficient Williams. "Send two couriers on horseback: one to Chippewa and the other to Fort George. I want all the reinforcements they can afford to send us. Tell General Sheaffe to marshal the militia, the 41st, and the 49th, and march them here immediately."

"Yes, sir." Williams saluted again. "Bloody boats in the river, sir." Williams pointed sharply to one side.

Brock looked back toward the river to see four longboats packed with soldiers making for Hamilton Cove on the Canadian side — and well behind the position of Captain Dennis. If they landed successfully, Dennis and his men would be trapped between two opposing forces. Exactly what Dennis had predicted could lead to disaster. If the worst should happen and Dennis be forced to surrender, the Americans could land their entire army at will … anywhere along the river … and the battle for Upper Canada would be lost for sure.

"Captain Williams, you can see where Dennis is fighting for his life." Brock paused to let Williams survey the massive flash of musket fire pouring from the four hundred redcoats along shore. "He's has to stop those boats from landing. You have to take your Light Company down there to support him," Brock ordered.

"My great pleasure, sir. However, it does mean the crest up behind us will be left undefended." Williams hesitated, staring up at his former position.

Brock understood the man's fear. Losing that crest above the cannon could also mean catastrophe. "The battle is lost for certain if Dennis surrenders." He shook his head, the decision already made. "It's a chance we have to take. Go now."

Within seconds of a bugler sounding his signal, Captain Williams and his Light Company charged their way toward the battle below. And the crest above General Isaac Brock lay undefended.

23
......

"I PROTEST, SIR," Castor pleaded. "You promised we could cross, but the regulars have crowded the militia away from the boats." All he wanted was a single boat with at least nine seats for him and his men, but the embarkation point had grown into a quagmire. The ravine near the water's edge lay soaked in six inches of mud and no one seemed to be in charge. At the howling sound of screaming Indians on the other side, the New York militia now hesitated to cross.

"Hold your tongue or I'll it have cut out. The bowler hat stays here." Lieutenant Colonel Winfield Scott pointed sharply at Bennett. "You, on the other hand, march with me."

Castor shrugged at Bennett and took up his position beside Scott while two aide-de-camps followed closely behind. After a hundred paces on a worn path up the slope, Castor's thighs began to ache as Scott raced ahead of him, hauling his big frame along at a steady pace. At the sound of two enormous bangs, the ground shook like an earthquake and then it shook again. Castor stared as Scott put both his big hands out to the side, to steady himself.

"Where are we going, sir?" Castor puffed.

"To get me across the river. And when I go, you can go too."

"Can we take a rest, sir?" Castor gabbed at a bush and used it to pull himself forward.

"No. And once we get there, shut up. You're there as evidence of militia willing to cross, not for your advice."

"Where exactly is there, sir?"

"We're almost —"

Boom! Another mighty crash deafened Castor, forcing him to jump back. His entire body rigid, he covered his ears too late to save the pain. Equally taken aback, Scott stood wide-eyed, hands pressed to his ears. He said something, but Castor just shook his head and pointed to his own ringing ears. Then he remembered the last time and the second blast, so he kept his ears covered just as the ground trembled. He glanced up at a sky full of gun smoke.

Scott waved him on, even as an aide urged him forward by tugging at one elbow. They passed through some breastworks, and the puzzled look on Castor's face must have prompted the aide to speak.

"Fort Gray, sir," the man explained. "Just a breastwork involving a few men and two-eighteen-pounders. Not much really, but those two beasts can do wicked destruction." He grinned, raising his eyebrows. "The cannons were floated down the lake when the British gave up blocking the waterways during the armistice." He shook his head and shrugged.

Their small group entered the breastworks through an opening at the rear. A few steps down to the left, Scott approached two officers whose spotless uniforms looked as if they had dressed for a dinner party rather than a war. Standing in conversation, he pointed a finger back at Castor. The two spotless officers looked immediately in his direction.

"Who are those two men?" Castor asked the aide.

"You must be joking. That's Major General Stephen van Rensselaer and his personal advisor, Major John Lovett."

Van Rensselaer stepped closer to the gun crew and held up his hand to silence Scott. He appeared to give them new instructions for sighting their gun because immediate adjustments were made. Once pounded home, the charge was ready and an artilleryman then lit the fuse. The officers quickly stood back and covered their ears. Castor did the same and soon the vibration from the shot shook the ground again, pulsing through his chest.

For the first time since entering the fort, Castor stared downward and across the river. What a sight! Musket fire, its flash and smoke, blanketed the hills around Queenston. By the time the noise echoed down the gorge, a single musket shot sounded like a strong clapping of hands. And on this morning, with dawn spreading its dull light, the sound of the panorama in front of him was like that of an audience that wouldn't stop applauding.

The officers surrounding the gun suddenly raised their arms in the air and began cheering. The general even slapped Major Lovett on the back. The readjustment to the gun's sights had worked its magic; something shattered in Queenston.

Colonel Scott lumbered over to where Castor scanned the far shore. From the guns, Major Lovett shouted to him. "Mr. Scott!" Lovett pointed to the second gun.

Castor covered his ears just before the cannon's next blast. "What's the verdict, sir?" he asked the colonel. The aides closed around him.

"An oarsman has reported that Van Rensselaer's cousin Solomon is wounded," Scott replied. "He's set for evacuation and I'm taking charge over there."

"What about my men, sir?" Castor asked anxiously.

"With the gory casualties crossing back over the river, our militia is getting somewhat reluctant to join the action. You're to accompany me and set the example. Perhaps that'll give 'em a little backbone once they see others commit themselves."

"Set an example, sir?" Castor puffed out his chest, elated at the thought. "Backbone, you say?" he added. "I can do that." The reward money hung within reach. *Those slaves won't know what hit them.* He could barely maintain his composure. Even Bennett would have to smile.

Lieutenant Colonel John Fenwick, U.S. Light Artillery, stood swaying behind the cover of a sturdy maple. He leaned his hand on the trunk as he began peeing to one side. After rebuttoning his pants, he turned and crouched behind the same tree, but not before taking a swig from his silver flask. He then tucked the whiskey inside his blue jacket and took a peek out across the river.

Since arriving at the foot of the ravine in the early hours, he'd watched continuous cannon fire from Queenston rip through the packed columns of soldiers waiting alongside him. Dead and wounded lay scattered in the mud. Those among the wounded who could, cried and stretched out their hands for attention. The carnage had been almost too much to bear, and he'd ordered everyone to run for cover. The troops put to flight like a flock of geese and suddenly the ravine lay empty.

Now the enemy cannons had gone quiet and Fenwick guessed that American artillery up the hill had knocked the Queenston cannon out of action. He stuck his head out from behind the tree for another look. Nothing but drifting smoke forming a haze over the river, but above the village of Queenston the sky was clear … the big guns finally silent. He shivered. *Christ, it's damp.* Time for one last swig of courage.

"Embark," Fenwick bellowed, once refortified from his flask.

A few soldiers peered out from around the tree trunks, cautious at first. No one wanted to die needlessly and he couldn't blame them. He strode out into plain sight, and shouted above the wind.

"Board the boats, now" — he waved his sword toward the water — "before they start up with that damn cannon again."

The men quickened their pace, their boots making sucking sounds in the water and mud. They stepped lively into the boats, soon filling all four vessels. Their oars were out and rowing before some men had even sat down. Fenwick remained standing in the bow of the first boat.

"Are we heading to join Colonel Van Rensselaer, sir?" asked a concerned voice from behind him.

"Goodness, no. I'm not climbing that goddamn cliff. We'd be cut to pieces over there." The current was already pulling them downstream and away from Solomon's position. Under the pounding wind, the boats soon picked up speed. Fenwick pointed to a nearby cove. "There — pull for that beach. Much easier on all of us."

Fenwick's boat had begun in the lead, but with the current tugging them in the opposite direction, he was now at the tail end of the twisting four-vessel convoy. To begin with, the odd musket ball either whizzed overhead or smacked the boat's side. By the time he passed midstream, a constant thud peppered the hull. The oarsmen sensed the danger and rowed with renewed vigour.

Something zipped through the air and his shoulder jerked. He glanced down to where a ball had pierced his new greatcoat. The worst part of it was that he couldn't take a sip from his flask without the entire crew knowing he was scared out of his wits. Another ball bit through his coat at his right elbow.

Fenwick watched the boats zigzagging in front of him as they approached the landing. He saw the lead boat pulling hard and then … it was gone. Oars and splinters flew. Body parts splashed into the water beside him. Blood spattered his cheek. A cannon ball had smashed right through the boat's middle, killing or wounding all twenty of its passengers.

Fenwick forced himself to take a breath. Unconsciously, he reached inside his coat for the silver flask, then gulped down several mouthfuls. The spirits burning the back of his throat, he shook himself alert. Musket balls clipped the hull again and then at his side. He realized he had been standing the entire way and now plonked down on a seat.

An oarsman behind him screamed, and Fenwick turned to see the man had no jaw, his face torn in half and staring at him with shocked eyes. The two vessels in front collided with the shore. As the soldiers jumped for safety, they were thrown off their feet by a murderous volley of musket fire. No one was left standing.

Fenwick's own boat scraped the shore's edge as the stones in front of him tapped with musket balls. He, too, leapt for the safety of the beach, further shots plucking at his greatcoat. A ball slapped the side of his face and his head snapped backward. The pain seared into his brain. *My eye! My God, I can't see out of my right eye.*

He didn't realize that he was lying flat out on the beach until a face loomed over him. The officer began saying something, but Fenwick couldn't hear him. Then a hand gripped his own and tugged him to his feet.

"We have to get you out of here, sir," the officer shouted. "This attack is done for."

"Yes, of course," Fenwick managed in a low voice that didn't sound like his own. "Bad choice. Sorry." He was helped into the waiting boat, gripping the arms of two muscled oarsmen.

"Bad choice, sir?" the officer probed.

"The landing. Bad choice for a landing. My fault. Sorry." Sure that he was going to pass out, Fenwick's face burned as if a match flamed under his cheek.

"Not your fault, sir. Would've been even worse over at that wall of a cliff," the officer reckoned. "That's all of us, push off."

"The only ones left, are we?"

"I can't tell from all the smoke, sir. I suppose so." At the bow, the officer stood on his toes and squinted through the haze. "Dead, wounded, or captured seems the order of the day for our efforts. Push off, damn you," he ordered.

Fenwick watched the officer scan the beach for their soldiers. Two empty boats drifted aimlessly, bumping the shoreline. A man pulled an oar out of its ring, crouched low, and pushed their craft off the stony beach."

"Hands away from those oars. In the air, where we can see them." A dozen British redcoats emerged out of the gun smoke, aiming muskets at the departing boat.

"Oh dear, captured. Seems to be the fate of the whole enterprise." Fenwick reached inside his jacket. "Want a drink?"

"We've found a way up, sir … off this rat-infested beach. Someone has come to help us." The tall lieutenant, a confident, well-proportioned man with an intelligent face, beamed as he stood in front of Captain Wool. A bullet then tore through the officer's sleeve, and he instinctively crouched.

"Who is the fellow? Can we trust him?"

"Won't give me his name, sir. Says he's a fisherman, but he doesn't look like any fisherman I've seen. Still, what choice do we have?"

A full volley blasted from above, twitching the stones around them. Wool stared at his officer, surprised that neither of them had been hit.

"None at all. If we stay here, we'll be slaughtered." Wool glanced up the cliff and wondered if he could make it. Musket balls had grazed both his hips. Even the slightest twist and a blazing pain shot up his spine.

"I'll leave a troop to provide covering fire, sir." The lieutenant gestured down the beach. "The rest of us can go up straight away. Let me give you a hand, sir."

"This will either be one hell of a surprise to the British," Wool grunted as he stood, "or it means a musket ball for each of us. Take the lead with your fisherman."

"He'll be the first to die if it's a trick, sir."

The path, concealed by overhanging tree branches and low-growing brush, was in places little more than a rut on the steep hillside. Captain Wool winced with every step on the trek up the cliff face, as bolts of pain ripped through his body. He crawled upward through a fog of gunpowder that seared the back of his throat. The men around him appeared to waver as if drunk.

Three-quarters of the way uphill, Wool called a halt. The soldiers nearest him nodded, grateful for a pause. Rivers of sweat streamed down his back despite the cool morning air. His hands stung from a dozen cuts and his heart thumped as if ready to fly out of his chest. After almost three hours of fighting, he could go no farther without a rest, so he sat down and looked out over the Niagara River Gorge.

Clouds of grey and black smoke blew in the wind, and for a moment concealed the American side of the river. He squinted to see Fenwick standing upright in his boat, mid-stream in the river. Then he watched in horror as another boatload of men was blasted apart. They had floated downriver, close to the Canadian shore. Yet, in a single instant, they were gone. He had now seen enough; the terrible sight spurred him on.

"Up everyone, up!" Wool whispered. He peered up the hill but could see nothing other than grey skies. If the British were waiting there, they were still well hidden. He gripped his sword, using it to help him stand. An oozing dampness made him glance down at his shoes. Blood. Both hips had continued bleeding on the way up the path. There was nothing else to do but press on.

As the men struggled upward alongside of him, he whispered to one, "You there, man, what's your name?"

"King, sir. Sergeant Nathaniel King." The man came to a slanting kind of attention and saluted.

"Fine. I want you and this fellow…"

"Private John Green, sir." Green too saluted.

"What's in your packs?"

"Ammunition, sir."

"Give them to this man here and then get yourselves on either side of me. Help me up this damn cliff."

"Gladly, sir," both men said in unison. They tore off their packs, only too willing for someone else to take the burden.

"This is Private Oliver Ambler, sir. He won't mind carrying our packs so we can help you along, sir. Will you, Oli?" King grinned as he threw Ambler his pack, and placed a supporting hand under Wool's right arm.

Green did likewise and supported Wool's other arm. Grunting with every step, Ambler could barely progress up the hill. Wool grunted too and thought he might faint from the pain. He glanced over to the American side of the river, praying the other officers and their men would cross regardless of the terror.

Wool finally reached the very top of the incline. *Where were the British?* He surveyed the large plateau but saw only the bluecoats proceeding ahead of him. Even their fisherman guide, whom he had yet to meet, had vanished. The men trailing Wool poured over the ridge and flopped down on the tall grass all around him.

A rest — Wool just needed a rest. With a moan, he laid back and watched the rain clouds. Blood seeped between his toes as he wriggled them inside his boots. He grimaced in pain until becoming aware of the lieutenant's face staring down at him.

"Are you all right, sir? I've scouted the crest and you're not going to believe where we are."

"Help me up." Wool reached out with both hands. Leaning back to balance his weight, the lieutenant rocked Wool to his feet. The captain took a step forward and groaned.

"Can you walk, sir?"

"I'm fine, Lieutenant, just awfully sore after that trek up the damn cliff. Show me what you've found that's so important."

They had reached the very heights of Queenston. Wool scanned the panorama around him and found he could see for miles. Even the spray thrown up from the great Niagara Falls was visible from this height.

As Wool struggled toward the edge of the plateau, he could see clear across to where American troops, huddled together, waited to embark at the ravine. Very few vessels were docked near the shore, and only a few boats in midstream rowed for the Canadian side. He desperately needed more troops. His stomach tightened, and he took a step back, at the thought of being left here alone to die on Queenston Heights.

Closer to the edge, exactly at the rim, the lieutenant slowed his pace and crouched down. Wool followed his example and the officer pointed down from their perch to where a small group of enemy artillerymen was currently loading a cannon. The lieutenant's eyes widened as he turned and stared into Wool's face.

Wool motioned him away from the rim. He strained to rise out of his crouch, groaned, and sat down again. The earth shook as the cannon below them fired, and a cloud of smoke drifted upward.

"Is that who I think it is, sir?" the lieutenant asked.

"I don't know what he looks like, but that damn cannon could be ours if we're smart about it." Wool winced again. "Do you realize, Lieutenant, if we can seize that gun, we'll win the day? We'll turn their own artillery on them. Rest time is over — marshal the men for an immediate attack."

"Sir." The lieutenant stood and saluted. "We'll give 'em a taste of their own hot medicine."

The lieutenant was good to his word and within a few minutes the men, tired and grumbling, were assembled just back from the edge of the crest, concealed only by a curtain of old oaks.

"You are going to fire one volley and then rush them. Fix bayonets," Wool ordered. Concerned faces stared back at him on the order to fix bayonets. Few men ever longed for hand-to-hand combat. "Don't any of you worry — they'll run when they see our numbers. You have my word; not a man of you will be lost." Wool offered his hand to his subordinate. "God be with you, Lieutenant."

"We'll give them more than they bargained for this day," the man replied. "On that, sir, you have *my* word."

24

······

"You've increased the charge?" Brock asked.

"And the mortar is carrying farther, sir — as expected."

"Let's get another round in, gentlemen," Brock ordered. He peered across the river to see the enemy scattering like ants newly disturbed. They clambered down to the foot of the Lewiston ravine and then spread out along the shore, hiding behind trees and then running again. The earth trembled as the mortar fired, the vibrations shaking his legs. His horse whinnied and stepped around.

Black smoke hung in the air, obscuring his view until the wind pushed it away. Another boatload of bluecoats landed at the base of the Queenston cliff, while a longboat trailing close behind still struggled against the current. The Americans were coming, perhaps now only in a trickle, but they were still coming.

Captain Dennis must have ordered another volley because a sheet of flame erupted along the British line, sending musket balls ripping through the new invaders. A bluecoat swung one leg over a boat's side, jerked in midair, and then twisted back to collapse into the bottom of the hull. A second man took his first steps on the stones of the beach, dropped his musket, and fell, clutching his shoulder. Two soldiers hauled him up under the arms and ran with the rest of the boat's compliment for cover.

Dennis's line was holding, but just barely. Williams and the 49th marched into view to assist, and Brock heard himself say out loud, "That's better. Now prepare to engage." His express riders with orders for reinforcements would be halfway to Chippewa and Fort George by now. *Just hold for a few hours, and all will be well.*

A jarring volley of muskets crashed out behind him. The cannon

266

clinked from the striking balls, and the ground all around him thudded. His artillerymen spun around and gazed at him in confusion. Brock stared up at the crest and for a few seconds refused to believe what his eyes were seeing.

There, in the dim morning light, he saw the dull steel of bayonets and the grinning half-crazed faces behind them. Every man wore a blue coat — *regulars*. They'd know their business. His chest tightened. *Think.*

He heard someone shout out the order. "Charge!" He had only one thought.

"Spike the gun," he bellowed.

Around him a handful of artillerymen stood frozen in fear.

"Now!"

A man woke from his daze, grabbed the pick, and jammed it into the touchhole, snapping it off. Brock glanced behind him to hear the Americans holler as they charged. He had only seconds remaining to disable the cannon. Another man lifted a sledgehammer, pounding the broken end of the pick flat into the touchhole. That done they stared at him for a further order.

"Now run!" Brock ordered.

The men scrambled down the steep hillside in front of him. The last to leave the redan, Brock snatched Alfred's reins as the bluecoats came charging not twenty paces behind him. A musket cracked out and a ball spit past his ear. There was no time to mount. He ran and staggered, tugging on the reins to urge his horse on. A ragged cheer went up, and glancing back, he caught sight of the Americans — laughing, with their muskets raised in the air.

"Huzzah! Huzzah! Huzzah!"

Brock peered back a second time to see if they followed him, but they were too wise, too well trained, and instead held firm at the redan. He gritted his teeth and cursed when he saw American regimental colours unfurled in the wind on his heights. Alfred stumbled, bumped against him, and sent him flying in the air. He landed on both knees in damp grass, using the reins to help regain his balance.

In minutes, Brock reached the base of the hill and led his horse to safety behind the perimeter wall. His stomach in knots, he mounted Alfred and raced to the north end of the town until he encountered some men of the 49th Light Infantry. He also spotted the flank companies of the 5th Lincoln and the 2nd York and shouted loudly, "Follow me boys." The men fell in behind him at a run.

When he finally dismounted back behind the garden wall, his knuckles gripping the reins were white with anger — anger at not defending the heights and anger at losing the redan battery. *This cannot stand.* Whoever controlled those heights would win the battle.

Macdonell, with Westlake trailing, galloped over to the cover of the wall where Williams, puffing along on foot, soon joined them.

"How many are up there, sir?" Macdonell asked.

"They must have found a way up the bloody cliff behind us. Dammit!" Brock punched the air with his fist. "I'm really not sure how many ... at least a good fifty." He shrugged and shook his head. "There wasn't time to count." He handed Alfred's reins to Westlake.

"We should establish their number, sir," Macdonell said.

"I could reconnoitre the crest for you, sir," Westlake said.

Brock stared up the hill, his face set in fury and the beat of his heart pounding in his ears. *How did this happen ... happen to him?* He took a deep breath and made his decision. They couldn't wait. If the Americans consolidated their position, they might not be dislodged and the day would be lost.

He remembered his oncoming reinforcements. Perhaps he should delay. But, then again, it wouldn't be long before mortar shells from the crest would start blasting the hell out of Dennis below and then leave the entire shoreline wide open to invasion. The risk of delay was too great. He'd lost the heights and his responsibility was to get them back. The only option was an immediate frontal attack.

Captain Nelles and Parrish galloped in, their horses rearing to a stop beside Westlake. They looked to Brock for direction.

"You will stay here with the horses and guard our rear, Mr. Westlake," Brock commanded.

Westlake made to protest, but before he could speak, Brock cut him short.

"That's an order and I have no time to discuss it." Brock put his hands on to the top of the wall and with a jump pulled himself up. "Good to see you, Captain Nelles." He stood legs apart and stared around at the upturned faces. "Are you ready for some morning exercise, men?" Brock shouted and turned to glance back up the hill.

A cheer erupted.

"The enemy have taken our battery and we're taking it back. Now!" he declared with a smile. Another cheer arose and men pumped their muskets in the air. Their enthusiasm pleased him. His heart thumped with excitement and he relaxed his clenched fists. "Let's get at them."

When Brock jumped down on the far side of the wall, fifty other determined men followed him up and over it. *This is going to be hot work.* He drew his sword and started up the hillside before taking a single glance back. He pointed the weapon once at Westlake and nodded sternly to emphasize the order to stay put. Once over the wall, the other officers scrambled after him as he began running toward the enemy.

Just get the damn battery back and be done with it.

Westlake clenched his teeth and watched the general's back ascend the hill.

On the other side of the wall, Nelles took a few quick steps up the incline, then turned around sharply. With a furrowed brow and his thin face set like stone, he was a man ready for battle. "This is not your type of fighting, Westlake. And remember his promise to your mother. I have a letter from him here for you." Nelles tapped his breast pocket twice.

"I'll be waiting here, sir," Westlake lied with sincerity.

Nelles turned and began jogging up the hillside.

"Two minutes, Parrish. I'll give them just a two-minute head start." Westlake tied the first pair of reins around a tree. "Here, help me." He handed another pair of reins to Parrish and finished tying the others.

"There's not a chance I'm missing this," Westlake said. "Can you jog up that hill?"

"How long have we been hiking, sir ... nine months ... but you'll be disobeying orders," Parrish replied. "And if the enemy steal these horses, we'll be deep in it." He patted Alfred's nose.

Westlake had loaded his musket and put a hand on the wall. "You don't have to do this. I'll understand."

"My orders come right from the general, sir. Protect Jonathan Westlake. Said so himself, he did."

"Very well then, up and at 'em." Westlake leapt on to the wall and then slid down to the other side. From there he jogged straight up the hill.

Within minutes he arrived in the midst of the fifty soldiers already clambering upward. He spotted Brock, right at the front, with the other officers slightly behind him. Suddenly an explosion of musket fire brought him to a standstill. Brock jerked his hand in the air as if he'd just been hit.

His men cheered, assuming that the Americans had fired too soon. They renewed their charge, believing the enemy line would break easily as they reloaded, but instead another round of sparks spit from the brush in front of the redan, their balls whizzing by seconds after the first volley. When the enemy showed themselves, they were obviously too numerous to overrun.

An enemy soldier stepped from the underbrush, and a single shot rang out. Westlake stared in stunned disbelief as Brock reached for his chest. The general sank slowly until he lay on his back. Westlake ran forward to hear a young man kneeling beside Brock ask him, "Are you much hurt, sir?"

Officers ran toward the general. Seconds later, the ground around them rippled under the impact of musket balls. Brock slowly reached for his chest again, but it was to be his last movement. His chest went still. The general was dead.

One by one the officers and men scrambled in to stand gawking at his body.

"I can't believe it," the young man cried. He stood motionless, staring down.

"We can't stay here," an officer ordered. "Dear God! What a waste of a great man." He moaned.

Westlake stared down, sick to his stomach, feeling worse than if he'd lost his own father. He knelt beside the body and lifted Brock's hand. Above him another volley spit lead, and then the cannon finally fired. The hillside shook and a soldier fell back, landing across the dead general. Westlake eased him off.

"He should never have led," sobbed another. "Stood out like a sore thumb, I'll bet."

"Get off this damn hill," Nelles shouted. "Take his body down to the wall — where you should still be," Nelles ordered sharply to Westlake. Musket balls thudded into the surrounding trees. Nelles spun around and fell. A musket ball had shot right through his arm and knocked him over.

Westlake reached under Nelles's back to lift him up and Parrish ran to assist. Nelles staggered, clutching his injured arm.

"Can you manage, sir?" Westlake asked.

Nelles grimaced and nodded, his breathing coming in short, unnatural breathes.

"Stay with him, Parrish," Westlake ordered.

"Fine, I'm sure I'll be fine," Nelles said as he blundered down the hill with Parrish supporting his other side.

Westlake and four others strained to lift Brock's body and descend. Each man supported a limb and Westlake cradled the dead general's head. He heard the crack of musket fire and balls slapping the ground around him. Something plucked at his sleeve and his arm stiffened. He glanced down to feel blood trickling from his left bicep while his skin burned like a scald.

Every step of the way down, Westlake peered into Brock's face, expecting him to open his eyes. *How could he be dead? How could such a large life end so quickly?* He stared at where the ball had pierced the general's jacket. A small hole in the centre of his chest marked where the ball had struck his heart.

Westlake's shock and sadness slowly turned to anger. *Nothing would ever be the same again. How could they face the enemy without their leader?* The world as he knew it was gone. Dead. His jaw tightened and his shoulders stiffened with rage. By the time they reached the small stone house in Queenston, Westlake craved revenge.

A wounded soldier limped out through the door trailing two men with bandaged heads. Parrish followed the corpse in, his hand still supporting Nelles's underarm. As Westlake backed toward a large kitchen table in the centre of the room, he lifted the dead general's head so that the others could raise the rest of the body up. Gently they laid it on the table.

Flopping down into a chair with a wince, Nelles let his head rock backward. Parrish ripped up a strip of rag and wrapped it tight around the officer's arm. Westlake stood, watching helplessly, as Nelles's face flushed different shades of red to finally end in a pale grey

"He needs a doctor," Parrish announced. "Thinks that ball must have broke his arm."

A nurse appeared with another length of cloth and tied it around Westlake's arm. "Lucky, you are." She glanced at the body on the table. "We've a doctor here, but he's busy." Her eyes filled with tears. "I've not met the man personally, but surely that is our general."

"Thank you for bandaging my arm, ma'am," Westlake said quietly, "but please get your doctor directly. This wounded man is General Brock's aide and the body on the table is indeed the general himself."

"My God. I'll see what I can do." She wiped the corner of her eye, put a hand to her mouth, and fled the room.

Westlake glanced at the grim-faced Nelles as he opened his eyes. "Both of us wounded in the same arm, sir." He held up his bandaged arm for Nelles to see and then nodded. "You'll be good soon enough."

Nelles inclined his head forward as if about to faint. He brushed Westlake's hand. "Get to General Sheaffe … tell him what happened here." Nelles gestured to Brock's corpse. "Go, now, for he must be told. An army doesn't run without a firm hand in charge."

Westlake hesitated, glancing at Parrish.

"I'll be fine here, Mr. Westlake. This is your type of mission. Take Alfred," Nelles said. "Parrish can go with you, but be careful along the road. Without the battery to repel them, the enemy could be landing anywhere."

"Colonel Macdonell is organizing another attack, sir. I'd like to be part of it if possible," Westlake said. "If I leave now, I'll miss — "

"That will take him some time yet to organize. If you're back before they charge up that goddamn hill, you can go and kill yourself alongside him. You have my word, but get to General Sheaffe first."

"Then I'll be back in no time, sir. You'll see." Westlake touched Nelles's right shoulder.

Nelles nodded his agreement and waved his hand to encourage him to get moving. "We're losing, Westlake, and that can't happen. We have to win ... if only for him." Nelles turned his white face toward the body. "... if only for him." He leaned his head back and fainted.

25
......

LUTHER WOKE EARLY on the dull morning of October 13. As soon as his eyes opened, he remembered once again that he wasn't a slave. In the immediate days after his ride over the falls, he was never quite sure when he woke that he wasn't dreaming, but as the weeks slipped by he slowly became accustomed to his newly found freedom. Even now, every day started with his eyes opening warily until his entire face broke into a grin.

The previous week, all regular and militia units were ordered uniformed and armed before first light and "not to be dismissed till broad daylight and distant objects seen." That meant someone had to see across the river to assure himself that the Americans weren't coming.

Luther strapped on his cross-belts. He straightened his shoulders and pulled down his shirt to firm up the belts. Alone, he snapped to attention with a musket at his side. He grinned again. A real soldier.

The Coloured Company would form up outside Fort George to do a few drills, then he'd return to building lanterns at Good Tinsmithing. Everywhere he walked, men carried his lamps and he smiled with so much pride his cheeks hurt. Finally, Alexander asked him to stop saying, "There's another one of mine," so he'd just point, mouth the words to himself, and laugh.

From the back bedrooms at the tinsmith shop, he heard a rider gallop by, announcing, "Enemy in sight! Form up at the fort. Civilians inside, off the road. Enemy in sight!" Luther poked his head outside through the side door to see the dawn's early shadows. As best he could see, there were no civilians on the street. The town, in fact, looked strangely deserted.

Dressed and belted, Alexander burst through the curtain separating their beds. "Outside, Luther, let's go."

Precious came in from the adjoining room and took his elbow from behind. "Don't do anything foolish. You have more to live for now." She patted her swollen belly and whispered. "I love you, Luther."

"I won't let them take us back." Luther held out his arms and she stepped into his embrace. Her lips were warm and she kissed him as if this was the last time they might ever hold each other. Her stomach gently pushed against him and when he looked in her eyes, he kissed her again on the cheek.

"C'mon, Luther. Now!" Alexander lumbered past him, musket in hand. "Precious, you stay inside."

"That's for you too, Father. Don't be stupid. Just come home to me; that's your main job today," Precious said.

Luther stepped off the porch and hurried around to the front of the workshop. Already, soldiers on horseback galloped through the streets, while a woman ran past, a child jiggling under her arm. Now, everywhere he looked people were in a hurry. *Today might not be just another day like others.* His grin faded even as the first rays of sunshine were finding the ground.

By the time Luther caught up with Alexander, they were almost at Fort George. The first of the Coloured Company to arrive, Richard Pierpoint waited there patiently, dressed in his faded Ranger uniform. Luther shook his hand to wish him a good morning, then jumped in surprise when a cannon fired from a nearby bastion. A few natives gathered close by hooted at the sudden sound of the blast.

More of the Coloured Company raced up to stand at attention beside Pierpoint and himself. The wind gusted with such force that their ranks fought to maintain a straight line. Luther caught sight of a blue pennant flying above a bastion, the signal for general assembly, and redcoats came pouring through the gates to form up with their various regiments.

Not far from the Coloured Company, dozens of natives assembled in a circle hollering sounds he didn't understand. Black and red warpaint stained their faces and their incessant screams sent his stomach quaking until he remembered they were fighting on his side. As soon as Chief John Norton arrived, the entire circle lit off toward

Queenston, without waiting for any further instruction from the military.

The 41st Regiment formed up beside the Coloured Company, including the same men who had shouted obscenities in Butler's Field. However, on this morning, when every man fought a twitch in his stomach, old grudges mattered for nothing and Luther felt a common bond with these same white soldiers. Mad Dog nodded to him as they dressed their files, and he sensed the man thought the same way.

The wind delivered a powerful blast and the front line of the 41st wavered like a flag before straightening out again. Each man stared right ahead, ready for the command to move out. Just what Alexander had taught him: focus on the task immediately at hand. In their red coats and white cross-belts, the 41st already looked like a fighting machine even before their sergeant bawled his commands above the wind.

"Fall in. Atteeeention! Shoulder arms! We have a seven-mile march to Queenston, where the enemy has invaded the heights." Luther heard some nervous chuckling in the lines. "We will do so at the quick." The laughing ended.

"Form four deep!"

"To the right, face."

"At the quick, march!"

The 41st jolted into motion, heading toward Queenston, and Luther heard Lieutenant Cooper call out to Alexander. The sky brightened and Cooper's normal expression of disgust seemed tighter and more pronounced on this morning. His father came to attention and saluted Cooper. Their conversation finished, he marched sharply to his position in front of the men. Luther's heart raced in anticipation of combat.

The sergeant delivered the same orders as had been given the 41st and the Coloured Company turned into the wind, and starting by the left foot, lurched toward Queenston Heights. Dressed in civilian blue shirts, brown coats and grey pants, the leather cross-belts singled these black men out as soldiers. The fort's cannon shook the ground in a single blast as if to say goodbye, and Luther marched off to battle with thirty-seven others who looked just like him. What began as an apprehensive twitch in his stomach had grown into a gripping knot.

Alfred had not galloped far before the American wounded and dying jammed River Road as they flooded in from Hamilton Cove. Westlake veered his mount into a ditch and the horse stepped lightly around the throng of bodies. With fixed bayonets, a few soldiers of the 49th Regiment of Foot guarded these unarmed prisoners.

Led by a boy no more than twelve years old, a horse-drawn wagon tipped over on the sloping roadside, tumbling four wounded men out the back. Westlake grimaced at the sound of the moans. One of the men had a bloody hole in one hand, while his other hand was a shredded mess. The boy alone had no hope of lifting the wounded into the dilapidated cart.

Westlake glanced at Parrish. Even with the urgency of his message, he felt an obligation to help. They dismounted and together heaved the cart upright again.

"Be more careful where you lead the horse," Westlake admonished the lad, angry at the delay. "The wagon follows the damn horse, and you'll end up in the ditch again if you're not careful."

Parrish lifted and rolled each man gently back into the cart. The last one, lying face down in the gulley, had a particularly huge belly. Parrish rolled him over. "No need to bother, sir. He's dead."

"Leave him be for now. Let's be on our way."

Westlake put one foot in the stirrup and swung his other leg over Alfred. With the touch of a knee, the horse pulled itself up on to the main roadway. Once clear of the traffic, Westlake set off at a gallop again. They passed Vrooman's Battery and Brown's Point, where the solitary guns had gone silent, their detachments having raced off to defend Queenston.

With the wind in his ears, and the echoes of war fading behind him, Westlake found it odd that this day could sound and look just like any other. He noticed the trees were fast turning to their crimson autumn colours; winter snows were not too far behind. At least the fighting would stop for a few months.

To his left, an apple orchard still laden with fruit reminded him sharply of home. Maple Hill would be scrambling to bring in the harvest, but his mother would manage somehow. He smiled as he imagined her directing everyone on the farm with specific marching orders. She could be tough when called for ... but how would she take the news of Brock's death?

He took a deep breath, knowing in his heart that there was more to Brock's relationship with Elizabeth Westlake than just a mere friendly acquaintance. Brock had been king of the whole province, so why shouldn't he have been attracted to its most beautiful woman — even if she was married?

And why shouldn't his mother also have sought some companionship. With his father away for such lengthy periods and rarely taking the time to write, his parents had no doubt grown apart. His father had been gone more than a year now, his face beginning to fade from memory. Westlake wondered if his parents still even loved each other and guessed his mother asked herself the same question.

He closed his eyes for a few seconds, recalling his concern several months ago at leaving his mother alone there with Brock. *Had they become lovers?* He thought of Seffi, the warmth of her skin against his own.

A single rider approached wearing a blood-red sash and a green scarf that fluttered in the wind. Indians from the Six Nations, led by Chief John Norton, were heading to Queenston. Westlake pulled back on the reins and Alfred reared to a halt. The natives soon covered both sides of the road, overflowing into the apple orchard.

Norton brought his horse alongside Alfred. "Morning to ye, Mr. Westlake," the chief said with a smile. "The battle you seek is that way, my good fella." He indicated the direction with a nod.

Westlake still felt it strange that any Indian chief would speak with a strong Scottish accent. He remembered that Norton's mother was a Scot, so her son had attended school in Scotland. Other Indians gathered around their horses.

"I need you to ride with me a little," declared Westlake, wheeling

Alfred away. Norton followed and once they were out of hearing distance, Westlake told him the news of Brock's death.

"Are you sure?" Norton blurted in dismay.

Westlake frowned.

"Aye, of course, it must be true, but this is just so hard to believe. It will shake everyone terribly."

"It's better you tell them now," Westlake gestured to the warriors, "than they should find out in the middle of a battle."

Norton nodded in agreement, still appearing as if he had just been punched him in the gut. "Aye ... you are right. This news will not help us win today."

"I'm off to find General Sheaffe." Westlake reached over to shake Norton's hand, then spurred Alfred on.

"Parrish." Westlake pointed to Fort George and trotted through the natives as they parted to allow a path on the road.

Within a few minutes, Westlake found River Road crowded again. He edged Alfred to one side while the 41st regiment marched by.

"Good grief, Parrish, are we ever going to reach Newark?" The echoes of cannon fire reverberated down the gorge, only this time pounding from the direction of Fort George.

A hundred yards behind the 41st marched the Coloured Company in perfect order, Sergeant Alexander leading from the front. Lieutenant Cooper, on horseback, rode quickly toward the new arrivals.

"Mr. Westlake, where are you going ... on the general's horse too?"

"I carry a special message from Captain Nelles for General Sheaffe, sir. General Brock, I fear, is dead," Westlake announced.

For a moment, Cooper simply stared at him. "You're sure of your information, young man?"

"There's no doubt, sir. When you reach Queenston, everyone will be talking about it, so it's best that these men hear it from you."

"Mr. Westlake," Sergeant Alexander called over with a smile on his face. "Good morning for a fight." The sergeant didn't stop but marched on with the Coloured Company trailing behind.

"I'll let them all know when we stop for a rest." Cooper saluted and turned his horse.

"We'll join you straight away, sir," Westlake hollered after him.

While River Road was again clear, Westlake galloped Alfred right to the gates of Fort George. Parrish caught up and halted beside him. Three sentries ran forward with fixed bayonets trained on the visitors.

"Stand and identify yourself."

"A message from Captain Nelles for Major General Sheaffe."

A gate soon creaked open and the two men were escorted to a small headquarters building where four light dragoons stood, reins in hand, ready to deliver messages. There was no need to summon Sheaffe, for he was on his way out the front door in full uniform.

"General Sheaffe, sir." Westlake saluted. "A message from Captain Nelles. Regretfully, General Brock is dead."

At first Sheaffe didn't react and Westlake wondered if the man heard him correctly. His aide, an officer Westlake had met at dinner only the night before, stepped forward and asked, "Did you actually see the body? To confirm he's dead?"

"Unfortunately, sir, I did. The general's body presently lies in a stone house on the edge of Queenston village." Westlake added. "I'm very sorry to deliver such terrible news."

Like an earthquake, the ground shook under cannon fire and grey smoke rose above a bastion nearby. Fort George's cannon had erupted to life. The aide turned to Sheaffe, whose blood had drained from his face. Suddenly, metal balls pounded into the fort, an answering volley shot from Fort Niagara directly across the river. One ball ripped through a section of palisade, leaving a gaping hole and showering the ground with slivers of wood. The officer ignored the shelling. "Orders have already gone to all units operating here, sir. I suggest we repair to Queenston forthwith."

"Do you know how he died, young fellow?" Sheaffe asked in whisper.

"The enemy overran the redan battery on Queenston Heights, sir. To take it back, General Brock led a frontal attack up the hill. He fell with a ball through the chest. I'm sorry." Westlake looked at the ground, feeling ill.

A stable hand rushed up with Sheaffe's horse and offered him the reins, but the general ignored the lad.

"I need to sit down." Sheaffe turned to the other officer. "We've made our deployments and we'll collect our forces on arrival. There will be no charges made up any hills. Come on to the heights from behind, after we are deployed in proper battle order, and then we'll thrash them." The aide opened the door to his office and the two men stepped back inside, leaving Westlake and Parrish standing there alone.

The cannons roared back into life.

A ball whizzed overhead and passed the fort, heading for the town. Another missile bounced across the drill square and smashed into a storage shed. Westlake gazed on as the shed burst into flame. *The Americans using heated shot!* His fears were confirmed as another red-hot ball bounced and then rolled, scorching the grass before it came to a halt, still smouldering.

Three militiamen stampeded by like crazed cattle. One man exclaimed, "A ball just struck the magazine roof. If it burns through, it'll blow the whole fort."

Parrish yelled, "Cowards!" at their backs before Westlake grabbed him by the arm and raced toward the magazine structure situated in the middle of the fort. On its roof, the lone figure of Captain Vigoreux tugged at a copper shingle in an attempt to dislodge the smoking ball. *Christ, this could go bad!* Westlake pictured himself and the entire fort blowing up.

He hollered up to the captain, "Water?"

"At the back, by the ladder," Vigoreux shouted down. "Damn good to see you again."

Westlake darted around to find the barrel where a bucket lay beside it. He dipped the bucket into the barrel and ran back to hand it to Parrish before climbing halfway up the ladder. Parrish stood directly behind him. "Quick, man, hand it up," Westlake ordered.

Vigoreux crouched at the edge of the roof where Westlake handed up the bucket. After a dozen bucketfuls, the three men subdued the smouldering cannon ball. It shrank as it cooled and eventually

Vigoreux extracted the ball from the shingles with a rag wrapped around both hands.

"They're lobbing in heated shells from the roof of the Castle, the swines." Vigoreux nodded toward Fort Niagara. "But they've missed as much inside the fort as they've hit. The town hasn't been so lucky."

"The town?" Westlake asked.

"Sure. The dumb bastards have been overshooting us all morning. The courthouse is already burnt to the ground." Vigoreux wiped sweat from his brow. "Apparently the jail is still on fire."

"Any other buildings, sir?" Westlake demanded, the tension rising in his dry throat.

"I can't say for certain, but odds say yes." Vigoreux tapped his foot at the point where smoke rose out of the charred roof. "They've been using some howitzer bombs, as well."

From his place still on the ladder, Westlake frowned toward Parrish as his mind imagined Mary trapped in her shattered log cabin. "If the magazine is safe, we should be on our way, sir," Westlake said. He climbed part way down the ladder and then jumped, rolling away as he hit the ground.

"No telling what might have happened if you hadn't been here to help me," Vigoreux called after him. "I owe you two men my thanks."

Parrish nodded and gave the captain a salute. Westlake followed with his own less formal salute even as he turned to run. "Blast the hell out of that Castle, sir," he yelled, and didn't wait for an answer.

He unhitched Alfred from the post outside headquarters, then galloped him hard for the front gates. The sentry barely had them open before Westlake shot through as fast as Alfred could carry him. Leaning into the wind, he glanced over his shoulder to see Parrish following on his own horse some distance behind.

The smouldering town of Newark rose before him within minutes. As he passed through the main street, a bucket brigade ran by with water to douse the courthouse. He turned off at the alley where the first house stood and gasped. Great fingers of flame shot from the roof of Mary's cabin. The entire structure blazed and must have been burning for some time. Despite the strong wind, a pall of black smoke hung over the little house.

Westlake leapt down from his horse and dashed to the entrance. He yanked open the green door and flames burst through it, throwing him back. Two thick beams had collapsed from the bomb's explosion and blocked the door from the inside. Once the fire had started, anyone inside was trapped. Westlake quickly glanced up at the roof, where it appeared that the cabin might have been hit twice. Again, he approached the open front door, shielding his face with his hands as he peered through the flames. For a moment, he saw the barest outline of a figure lying on the floor.

"Mary," he yelled, "is that you?"

He ran all around the cabin, frantically searching for another way in, but found no other door, no other way inside … not even a window to smash his way through.

"Mary!" He raised his arms in the air, shaking helplessly at the spectacle. "Mary!" he cried again, then tugged at his hair in despair.

He heard no reply, only the fierce crackle of burning wood and the rushing of flames. Black smoke billowed out between the cracks in the roof to further deaden an already grey sky. The wind encouraged the blaze with every fresh gust, the burning embers on the roof glowing brighter.

Parrish dismounted and stood gaping at the spectacle and then at Westlake. "What can I do?"

"Help me move those beams." Westlake pointed beyond to the door frame.

"But they're on fire, sir."

"The grass." Westlake wiped his buckskin sleeves on the sodden grass and ran back to the door where flames lifted up from the floor. Hands tucked inside his soaking sleeves, he pushed against the beams with his forearms. But they wouldn't budge. They were obviously jammed tight and needed more weight to shift them.

"Stand aside, sir," Parrish said.

Parrish kicked at a beam with the bottom of his sodden boot. It moved a few inches. He'd soaked his right shoulder and now propelled it full force against the blockage. Both beams fell away instantly and Westlake seized Parrish by his left arm, preventing him from flying head first through the exposed door. As Parrish spun around, Westlake slapped at his smoking shoulder to dislodge some small embers.

The interior of the cabin was an inferno.

"I have to try." Westlake took a deep breath as Parrish grabbed his arm and held on tight.

"It's madness, sir. You won't make three steps before you'll burst into flame. Please, don't even attempt it."

"She's my fiancé, for God's sake." Westlake felt his hope fading. "I'm going in." He readied to launch himself headlong through the flames.

And then the roof collapsed.

A great swoosh followed that sent sparks, embers, and smoke shooting into the air. Westlake instinctively jumped back, jerking up one arm to cover his eyes. Seconds later, a side wall tumbled inwards, dragged down by the crumbling roof. Westlake dashed around the cabin again, to find a way inside, but a wall of crackling flame confronted him and he knew that Mary was gone. Hands over his face, he sank to his knees and began to shake.

He felt Parrish's hand on his back. "There's no hope, sir. You did your best."

"I'm going to puke." Westlake heaved, but there was nothing in his stomach to toss.

"Try to get up, sir." Parrish lifted him with his hands under both arms. "I know it's hard, sir, but we should leave this place."

Westlake wiped his sleeve across both cheeks, blackening his face. He pounded his leg in frustration. "I'm sorry for this, Mary." He stared up again at the flames, feeling helpless. "I never told her. I should have … but I never told her about Seffi. Such a coward." He wiped his face again, feeling the tears on the back of his hand. He couldn't remember the last time he'd cried.

"What would that have accomplished for the poor girl, sir? Besides, there was nothing to tell. You didn't stand a bleedin' chance against Seffi."

Westlake swung round, punching Parrish in the face so hard that the man fell backward on to the ground and laid there. "Don't say another word," Westlake ordered, pointing a finger. "I know exactly what I bloody well did … and Mary gave me no excuse for it."

Parrish stared up at him. Again, Westlake's stomach churned and heaved. This time his friend was less sympathetic.

"No man alive could resist Seffi's beauty and still call himself a man. And you're no saint, Jonathan Westlake, no better or worse than the rest of us." He rubbed at his jaw where the punch had reddened it. "And never, ever, strike me again, *sir*."

A series of cannon blasts from Fort George shook the air, and Fort Niagara replied in kind. A ball seared overhead and Westlake followed its path to where it struck a maple tree. He watched the same tree begin to smoulder just as another ball, arching too high, bounced on the ground close to him, plowing up the grass with a hiss of molten steel on dew. This was surely the worst day of his life.

Parrish lay still on the ground, and Westlake offered a hand to help him up. "I'm sorry, Walter. I don't know what came over me. Just stupid anger, I suppose." Parrish stood up and Westlake put his other hand on the man's shoulder. "Forgive me, friend, and let's never talk of this again."

"It's forgotten, sir." Parrish nodded. "We should go."

Westlake cast a last glance back at the inferno that was once the small cabin. The drizzle began again. "Goodbye, Mary. Know that I loved you," he murmured quietly to himself. He sucked in a long breath as the raindrops hissed in the flames. Then the thought of Mary burning alive overwhelmed his senses and shook him to his knees. "Oh, Mary, how did this happen?" He put his head in his hands and bowed his face down to the ground. Brock was dead. Mary gone. Her face came to mind and how it lit up a room. Twice in the same day, his world had died. He clenched his fists, pounded the grass, and his face flushed red in sudden anger.

Westlake slowly lifted up his head. "Let's ride," he growled. He rose, leapt into the saddle, and danced Alfred round until the animal faced south. "We've a battle to fight in Queenston. The enemy has won enough for today." Brock's horse reared up on its hind legs as Westlake gripped the reins tighter. Then both rider and horse charged toward battle, bloodshed, and desire for killing.

26

· · · · · ·

To THE SOUND of slapping musket balls, George Castor swung his leg over the longboat's side to crunch upon the stones of Upper Canada. He ran for the protection of the cliff's face, focusing on the backs of Lieutenant Colonel Winfield Scott and his men ahead of him. Scott had been the first to leap over the boat's side and hit the beach running. Already, he was heading off the landing area toward the path that led to the summit of Queenston Heights.

Castor had thought to thank Scott for keeping his promise. Now he wasn't so sure he was done any special favours and decided to keep his thanks to himself. Despite the wind blowing along the river, the stench of burnt gunpowder hung thick along the water's edge to score the back of his throat. Fred Bennett jumped out of the boat before it pushed off into the swirling current of the Niagara River. Bennett scampered up beside him, his hands clawing as if to make himself part of the rock face. The remaining seven men trailed in fast behind before throwing themselves up against the cliff.

"Well, now what do we do?" Bennett exclaimed in terror. "The whole goddamn place is sizzling with musket fire." His bowler hat had twisted sideways on his head, but he just left it where it sat.

"Shut up and do as I tell you," Castor ordered. "And straighten your bowler. You look ridiculous."

Bennett reached for his hat. "It's got a goddamn hole in it!" he howled, eyes wide open. The men closest to him leaned forward to inspect the damage. He shoved a finger through the bullet hole before placing it on his head and pulling it down by the rim. Musket fire crashed out from somewhere down the shoreline, sending balls whizzing close to his belly.

"We can't stay here," Castor decided. "Our best bet is to follow them up that path." He motioned to the backs of Scott's soldiers. "From the top we'll get a better view where to go."

"Them niggers could be anywhere," Bennett shouted. "We can't just go waltzing around with this shit flying."

"There will be no waltzing anywhere. We'll hit the nearest town — this Queenston place most likely — but first we have to get off this beach." Castor leaned out slightly from the cliffside to speak to the men.

"I'm following the army up the cliff so I can take a look around. At least those redcoats can't fire down on us when we're up there. Let's go."

The men murmured in agreement and stayed close behind as Castor darted toward the path. He climbed hard for five minutes before his calves and thighs began to burn, but the incessant musketry forced him to press on, enduring the fire in his legs. Bennett cursed with every excruciating stride, taking the Lord's name in vain at will. The musket balls zipped into the grass around him, convincing Castor that he'd be dead at any second. He continued climbing persistently while the men behind him whined.

Three-quarters of the way to the top, Castor finally allowed himself to pause for a rest amid a few steeply angled trees. The hail of bullets had ended and he peered through the branches toward the river's east side, wishing he'd never crossed over. American cannons boomed somewhere in front of him so that he could see the passing arc of the balls pummelling Queenston. Perhaps that wasn't such a good place to begin their search. He sighed, rubbing his throbbing legs, then recommenced the arduous climb.

When he finally crested the heights, crawling a ways to further make sure the edge of the cliff was well behind him, he hung his head and rested on his hands and knees. "I made it," he congratulated himself. Then he stood up and helped Bennett to his feet.

"Would you look at that!" Castor gasped. The Niagara Gorge, with its river, spread out before him for several miles. At first he thought he'd climbed higher than the clouds but then realized that the gorge cradled gun smoke from the continuing battle. There was more smoke to come. Flames burst and disappeared as fast as lightning — musket and cannon fire momentarily lighting up both banks of the river.

Castor turned away to face the plateau beyond. On his right, and down a steep embankment, lay the rooftops of Queenston village. Like ants, redcoats were crawling away from it on their bellies at the very bottom of the hill. To his left and front, the farms and forests of Niagara gently sloped into the distance, but the most pleasing sight was that of bluecoats by the hundreds packing the neighbourhood around him. Castor inhaled a deep breath. With all these soldiers providing safety, he could plan his next move. As they reached the plateau, his exhausted men gripped their muskets for support before falling to their knees in a circle around him.

Colonel Scott stood a few paces away massaging his thighs. The big man had felt the strain of the hike up the cliff and now ached like everyone else. Castor grinned. *Nice to know he's human like the rest of us.* An officer approached Scott, snapped to attention and saluted.

"The second attack was vicious, sir. Over a hundred of the bastards charged us and we thought we'd lost the crest, so we spiked the eighteen-pounder." The man looked away as if ashamed.

"But there's over four hundred of you!" Scott exclaimed.

"We stuck a pole up a bees' nest, sir! Brock is wounded or dead, and the redcoats continued attacking in the face of murderous fire. We shredded their line, but they just kept coming." The man's face brightened as another thought came to him. "They lost a good many officers — including the one leading the rest. They're near lunatics, the lot of them."

"Drill out your damn spike. I want that gun firing again."

"Sir." The officer saluted and rushed off, just as several other officers appeared for words with Scott.

Castor's little troop finally stood, leaning on their muskets. They'd missed a bloody encounter, and that suited him fine, but he sensed that the tough questioning would soon start among his men. A man named Endicott, with flaming red hair, couldn't hold his tongue any longer.

"So where's dem niggers got to? I been riding hard, shot at, and

climbing cliffs and I ain't seen no runaways yet," Endicott complained.
"I want no part of this fight of theirs. I just want my money for dem
slaves."

"He's right," Bennett added. "Let's get the niggers and get out."

Castor gazed south, wondering where his fugitive slaves might
have run. "They had to cross in those boats well before they came up
as far as this gorge." He gestured back toward the river. "So I figure we
head south a ways — to Lake Erie — and we'll run right into them.
Let's get going." He happened to glance up just as he and his men
were picking up their packs. At that moment, through the trees, he
spotted a pack of Indians with painted faces.

"Warpaint, oh shit!" he shouted. "Everyone, down!" He grabbed
Bennett by the shoulder and pushed him to the ground.

A volley of musket fire erupted from the forest directly beside
them. He'd dropped down flat, while the screams of the Indians grew
closer. Scott bellowed orders to the bluecoats to form three ranks,
then suddenly someone was lifting Castor by the collar.

"Looks like you're working with us today," Scott declared. "Form
your men here, right where you're standing."

"I'm not right for this," Endicott said, combing a hand through
his red hair.

"Sergeant," Scott called out.

A little man with sailor biceps bulging under his bluecoat ran to the
colonel and snapped to attention. "Sergeant King at your service, sir."

Scott drew his sword and poked it into Endicott — just a touch so
it hurt. "Kill this man immediately if he tries to run. You two" — he
pointed with the sword — "assist the good sergeant here with the rest
of our new militia friends. Kill any man that breaks our line and tries
to run."

"Fix bayonets," King ordered.

Green and Ambler did as ordered, firmly pointing their weapons
at the slave catchers.

Castor's mouth dropped open in dismay, and Scott turned away to
face his own three ranks who had formed up in an instant. He raised

his sword again and pointed it to the trees where the Indians were busy reloading.

"Front rank, make ready," Scott ordered. "Present. Fire!"

"That means you lot too," King prompted the catchers.

Castor's group stared at the little man and then cut their eyes back to Castor. He shrugged his shoulders. "Well, fire like the man said!" All his men raised their muskets and this time fired just as Scott gave the order for the second rank to fire.

"Here they come," Scott bellowed. "Third rank, fire!

"And again." The sergeant nudged the petrified Endicott with the butt end of his musket. Hordes of Indians were screaming right in front of them but now started edging to the left.

"There could be thousands of the buggers." Endicott's musket was visibly shaking. "Their faces, my God! Hankering after my blood," he shouted the unfairness of it all at Castor.

The sergeant cuffed him on the side of the head with the palm of his hand. "I never said you could speak, you worthless sack of shit. Concentrate on loading your damn musket."

Endicott glared back at him, astonished. He was a free man, entitled to come and go as he pleased.

"Just give me an excuse," warned the sergeant, the point of his bayonet pinching Endicott's ribs.

Castor began to reload and gestured to his men to do the same. The first rank fired again and Castor felt the pressure to keep up. He rammed the ball home but in his hurry fumbled the ramrod on the underside of his musket and, just before he was ready, the second rank fired. He scanned his men. Even Bennett was panicking in his effort to make ready. Castor's men raised their weapons.

He heard Scott shouting, "Third rank." This time there was a pause. "Fire!" The slave catchers fired along with them.

"Make ready, but you will not fire," Scott said.

The little sergeant marched up in front of Castor. "Your men did well — one round to every three of the regulars. That's about what can be expected of useless militia. Make ready and hold fast."

Bennett stared at him, puzzled.

"That means load your goddamn musket and wait," the sergeant explained in disgust.

Castor searched with his eyes between the trees for Indians, but instead of attacking directly forward, they continued to circle away from the cliff toward the open end of the plateau. Their screams bothered him most, bloodcurdling screams that made it impossible to think. He gripped his weapon so hard his fingers hurt.

He managed to reload his musket and stand at the ready. His men's faces betrayed their terror as they stared at Scott and then looked to the sergeant for orders. Scott squinted as he peered at something moving in the distance. Drifting clouds of gunpowder obscured his vision. Castor followed Scott's eyes and there, marching steadily, an extended line of redcoats trudged along a road skirting a line of trees.

"I can't stand for this, Castor," Endicott whispered.

"You can leave anytime," Castor replied, nodding toward the native warriors. Endicott twisted and turned, searching for a safe way out.

Bennett laughed. "You fool, those Indians want that red hair of yours."

Endicott put a hand to his head and the other men laughed, relieved that they were still alive.

"But — " Endicott was frantic.

"But nothin'," Bennett said. He nodded to the forest. "Those savages will be back and our best bet is to stay right here with that little bastard of a sergeant — and the fellows who can fire three times as fast."

The men nodded silently, and Castor gained time to think, at least until the next attack.

In a shallow ditch adjacent to the main road, Lieutenant Cooper slowed his sweating horse from a gallop to trot alongside Sergeant Alexander. The road ahead had been crawling with redcoats of the 41st and now the soldiers were marching off sharply into a designated field, their sergeants leading the way. Alexander watched their sections melt into the long grass, many of the men unwilling to flop down on to the wet ground. But they had marched and occasionally run seven miles in three hours, and everyone needed a rest.

Cooper raised his voice: "We're going to stop just ahead, by the farm. We'll wait for further orders in that field, there,"

"Yes, sir," the sergeant replied. "Do you have any idea where we are? How close to the battle? I can hear shooting ahead." As if to confirm his observation, cannon roared into life, jerking everyone's attention toward Queenston.

"I'm told the fight is up on Queenston Heights, so we're maybe a mile away," Cooper replied. "That's Durham's farmhouse." Smoke from the kitchen fire curled out of a chimney into the grey sky.

"The men are hungry, sir. It'll soon be noon and we've had no breakfast." This wasn't entirely true because on the way out of Fort George, just past Newark, Luther had stolen an apple for each man from an orchard. Nevertheless, Alexander's stomach grumbled.

"I'll see what I can scare up at the farm. What's growing in that field?" Cooper pointed.

Alexander stepped off the road, over the ditch, and into the field. He bent down. "Potatoes, sir." He raised his eyebrows and grinned. "Potatoes to eat."

"Gather 'em up and I'll have them boiled for you," Cooper replied.

The sergeant turned back to his men and shouted, "The column will wheel right, on me."

In minutes, the Coloured Company had dug up three potatoes per man. Pierpoint had already spread a blanket and all the potatoes were piled in the centre. He gathered the four corners in hand, tied a knot, and then handed the bundle to Alexander, who in turn lifted it up to Cooper.

"Be back in no time." Cooper slung the bulging blanket over his saddle and trotted off to the farmhouse.

Alexander found a convenient stump in the field and sat down, watching a company of the 41st arrive, exhausted from their morning march. The air shook again with cannon fire, and he wondered why there seemed to be no hurry. Cooper returned from the farmhouse to report that the potatoes were cooking as he spoke, and Alexander decided to ask him about the lack of urgency.

"General Sheaffe is in charge now and will do everything by the book. So we're waiting for reinforcements from Chippewa." The cannons blasted again and Cooper's horse nervously stepped sideways. "By charging up a hill into enemy fire, apparently General Brock got himself killed."

"That can't be." Alexander frowned. "No, not him."

"I'm afraid so."

Alexander returned to his stump, staring at the ground. The general had seemed larger than life only days before. Without Brock's rescue plan, Precious and he would now be facing the lash or worse. "My God, what a waste," he said out loud.

"Aren't you nervous about the battle — even a little?" Luther interrupted his thoughts. "Those cannons sound mighty big."

"General Brock's dead and I can't believe it," Alexander replied. "And yes, it feels strange marching toward them Southerners when all we's been trying to do is get away from them. Same feeling in the Revolutionary War — weird."

"I'm nervous," Luther confessed. "Truth be told, I'm scared."

"I want my chance to kill those bastards for what they did to Hector. Now they've gone and killed the general." Alexander felt his rage building inside him again. "I hate them and everything they stand for."

"What about Precious and forgiveness and being free of them thoughts? Anyways, that's what she's been telling me. And it does make you feel better when you forgive."

"I was free the second I threw that lantern through old man Caldwell's window." Alexander spit. "I'm happy Percy hanged his self. That old bitch got what was coming to her. On the same tree as Hector."

"You don't sound free of them. I can be a soldier with drilling and all, but I don't know about the killing part."

Alexander glanced at his son from the corner of his eye. He was nervous too but not about the coming battle. His nerves were more about Luther and what might happen to him; that made his guts churn. Between the two of them, Hector had always been the fighter and Luther the soft and smart one.

The gale-force winds suddenly gave way to a light breeze and Alexander peered skyward. The clouds, once heavy and grey, now thinned and a ray of sunshine shone through on to the field. He watched his only son tilt back his head to feel its warmth. If he lost this boy, he'd have to go on killing Southerners forever, and even that might not be enough.

"You'll do as I tell you to do," Alexander growled. "When I tell you to fire, you fire. But when we charge them, you stay behind me. Let me do the killing for both of us, understand?"

"I can fight like Hector," Luther protested, as if reading his mind. "I just meant that I don't need to kill nobody to feel free."

"Forget this talk about freedom. This is war, and you'll do as I say or I'll leave you behind." Alexander rose off his stump and stared Luther in the face. "Go ahead, say it. Right now!"

"Yes … yes, I'll do what you say, but I still get to fight."

Alexander scanned the heights as the cannons boomed. "I guess I am a little nervous." And then, in a louder tone, he announced, "But I wish we could just get started. It's the waiting that kills me."

"Then you have your wish." Lieutenant Cooper had ridden quietly in behind him and, with the cannons, Alexander had not heard him approach.

"We advance through the fields to York Road." Cooper pointed. "You will form up in fours in front of the 41st."

"Coloured Company, in fours," Alexander called out to his men. He turned his head to Cooper. "What about our breakfast of potatoes, sir?"

At that moment, Captain Dennis rode up beside Cooper. To Alexander, the man's countenance revealed nothing of the optimistic fellow he'd seen joking with Brock only days before. This officer, his shirt and pants covered in dried blood, looked like he'd seen a ghost. His face was set in grim resolution: a man you would not want to meet in a fight. Accompanying him were a few soldiers on horseback, a troop on foot, and another officer. Cooper greeted them all and seemed to forget about Alexander until Dennis gestured that the sergeant was waiting.

"Sergeant Alexander, we have six hundred and fifty soldiers ready to attack. Are you suggesting that all of us wait while the members of Coloured Company eat their precious potatoes?"

"No, sir," Alexander replied. "Just didn't want all that cooking to go to waste." He sighed, relieved he'd eaten the stolen apple. Then, turning away from the lieutenant, to make sure the men were formed up in an orderly column, Alexander shouted, "Company will advance at the ordinary. March."

Cooper rode alongside Alexander as he marched. At one point, the lead soldiers broke down a fence so the men trailing could proceed freely. They reached the York Road but did not stop, as Cooper waved them on, farther from the river and the guns, until the entire column that stretched ahead of Alexander turned left again. He asked who the soldiers were that they had passed in the field.

"The 49th," Cooper said. "Brock's old regiment, plus the York Volunteer militia. And if you look back carefully you'll see my outfit in the old faded red jackets. The Lincoln militia," he added, proudly.

A Niagara Light Dragoon galloped toward Alexander on a huge black mare, and then reared back on the reins, sliding to a halt in the mud. He slapped Cooper on the shoulder, like a brother, and Cooper punched the man in the arm. Alexander leaned his head forward so he could hear what they were saying.

"Everything going by the book, James, except today the old man's reading the book backward." The two officers laughed. "The order of battle has been reversed. Your company was supposed to be on the other end. They're all going to stand aside while you troop through to take up the left flank as we approach the heights. Awful mess, if you ask me." The officers both laughed again. "Anyway, make sure your

group stays smart like; the whole bloody army will be watching you."
The dragoon jerked his horse sharply and galloped back along the
same road he came.

"I know you heard all that, Sergeant, so you know what we have to
do," Cooper said. "Look smart, eyes front and stay in step. No wavering column — just march as if we were performing a drill."

Alexander hesitated to speak.

"Can our Coloured Company do it, Sergeant?"

"I need a moment with them, sir, alone."

"Very well." Cooper trotted ahead and stopped where the 41st continued to empty off the road.

Alexander hurried back to the Coloured Company. "Listen to
me carefully." He held up a fist. "Today we're given a great honour.
All those soldiers you see are moving off the road for us. We must
turn around and march past many of Lieutenant Cooper's friends."
Without looking back, Alexander gestured over his shoulder with
his thumb. "I want to show him that we appreciate his faith in us.
Each man has to concentrate on his step, stay in perfect line, stare
straight ahead, 'cause there ain't nothing in them fields you need to see
anyway. We're not just another militia company, now are we? We're
special. You *know* we're special. We're the Coloured Company and we
are going to show these soldiers we're as good as any others here. Am
I right?"

"Yes, Sergeant," the company answered in single cheer.

"Now put on your killer faces. We're marching into battle and I
want you to scare the hell out of these white boys." Sergeant Alexander
grinned. "Atteeention!" The Coloured Company stood ramrod-
straight, muskets at their sides, eyes front.

Alexander spun around on his heel. "Coloured Company, at the
ordinary, march! Change direction to the left. Right shoulder forward!"

In one swift, coordinated movement, like the cogs in a watches'
wheel, the company began its march. The 41st had just moved off
the road when Lieutenant Cooper's horse, a few steps in front of his
sergeant, passed its tail end. The sergeant stepped ahead sharply, his

expression stern and prepared for killing. He knew the men behind him would not let him down. They had drilled too long and hard to fail now.

As they continued past the 41st, Alexander heard a strange murmur run through its ranks, a sound he'd not heard before. For a second, his eyes slid toward the field, where the two soldiers named Mad Dog and Trash stood, showing two thumbs-up. When the company had passed completely, the drummer of the 41st fell in right behind them as if he too belonged to the Coloured Company. Now they marched to a drumbeat and the sergeant felt an extra edge to his step. They passed the York militia next and the murmur grew louder until they were right in front of the Lincoln's, among Cooper's old militia friends, where that murmur broke into an enthusiastic cheer. A few men started to clap and the rest joined in. Alexander felt a proud tear start to form and bit his lip to hold it back. By the time the Coloured Company reached Brock's old regiment, the 49th was already cheering and clapping.

"Good show, Lieutenant," a man said.

"Spot on today," another shouted.

"Well done, sir," a fellow officer congratulated. "Well done, indeed. A frightening lot if I ever saw one. Exactly what soldiers should look like."

When they had finally passed everyone, Sergeant Alexander called his men to a halt. He turned to see the 41st following along the road behind them. Still farther back, the 49st and the other militia had started clambering up the bank and on to the road, their black boots covered in muck. They had been cheering while standing in a ditch full of mud and water.

Lieutenant Cooper turned his horse and rode slowly back to join his sergeant. Alexander felt a hand on his shoulder and peered up.

"You *are* Alexander the Great for more than one reason, and I thank you for that," Cooper said.

"You trained 'em, sir. You can thank yourself and every one of them." Alexander motioned to the Coloured Company. "They're the ones who suffered through those extra drills."

"You're right. Of course, you're right." Cooper swung his horse around and called out. "I'd like to say thank you to each and every man here. You made me proud back there, and you should think proudly of yourselves. Thank you again. We've only a short way to go now."

Sergeant Alexander and the Coloured Company marched on south to the Portage Road, where they turned right. They had proceeded in a great semi circle around the heights, well back from the guns, and were now approaching the heights from the northwest.

A cannon fired from across the river, and an instant later Alexander heard the ball sizzle far overhead. Out of the trees ahead a few Indians emerged with distinctive red and black stripes painted on their faces. He figured they were within yards of the cliff. He raised his arm to a few of the warriors and immediately they screamed and hooted in response. If their demeanour intended to frighten someone half to death, he reckoned they were succeeding. For the first time today, he was scared.

27

· · · · · ·

WESTLAKE AND PARRISH galloped hard toward Queenston, the cannon blasts growing louder with every step. Well on the outskirts of town, the sustained crack of musket fire filled the air with pockets of smoke that drifted grey against the crimson colours of autumn. Wounded soldiers from both armies crawled to safety, clogging the road where no one seemed to distinguish between friend and foe. Some reached up to beg for help from Westlake and Parrish. The fight had gone out of these men, and they were now free of the battle raging less than a mile away.

The Durham farmhouse rose up ahead of Westlake, but at this point Parrish's exhausted horse slowed down and then stopped altogether. The ride had proved too much for it and the horse wouldn't budge an inch further.

"Cripes, would you imagine? Damn this horse!" Parrish muttered as he dismounted. "Go on, then. I'll walk him in."

Westlake pushed on while Parrish nursed his weary mount. Around the farmhouse, men scrambled in and out of the front door. As he stood outside, he heard moaning and then a scream. A man in a red-stained white apron came bursting through, carrying a bucket of amputated limbs sloshing in blood. Westlake turned his face away.

"Excuse me, sir, is Captain Nelles here?" Westlake asked, directing the question to the back of the orderly's head.

"Brock's man. Second floor, back bedroom." The man turned his head slightly. "Good fellow — doesn't complain. Dreadful about the General."

Westlake took the stairs two at a time and hurried to the rear, not looking into the rooms full of wounded on either side. The entire second floor stank of blood, sweat, laudanum and some other chemical Westlake couldn't name. He reached the last doorway and peered in to see Nelles sitting on the edge of the cot, his arm in a sling and two narrow boards tied tight to his left forearm. Poking just his head around the door frame, Westlake gave him a nod and a half-smile.

"Not much bloody good like this, am I?" Nelles grimaced. "Painful as hell, but the butcher of Queenston says it'll heal nicely."

"I'm happy for you sir." Westlake felt his whole body deflate, dreading the news he was about to deliver. "I've some very bad news, I'm afraid."

"Not more? This day gets worse by the minute."

"Mary's dead."

"What? No!" Nelles face immediately turned the colour of his sheets, the intensity of his reaction surprising Westlake. "Oh ... by the love of God, no." The captain looked like he was about to cry. "How did it happen?"

"Heated shot or maybe a couple mortar bombs from Fort Niagara, sir. Difficult to guess ... but direct hits. Let's hope the first impact killed her outright." Westlake shook his head, imagining Mary struggling to shift the beams that blocked the cabin's only door. He clenched his fists, feeling the anger rise in him again. "Otherwise, she burned alive."

Nelles tried to stand up, but light-headed and off balance, he tilted to one side. Westlake rushed to grab his arm.

"I'm okay ... just a little woozy. That is horrendous news. Poor Mary, such a beautiful person. She didn't deserve that ... you don't look too well yourself, Westlake. Sure you're all right?"

Westlake lied by nodding yes. A whole lifetime ahead of her ... gone. And he couldn't tell Nelles that he felt racked with guilt for not having told his future bride the truth. The sickness in his stomach returning, he gave a slight heave.

"I should tell you that the general asked me to keep an eye on Mary while you were absent." Nelles looked away and staggered to a window. "I dropped in several times to visit and the truth is I came to care for her, and I think her feelings were the same for me." Nelles turned to face Westlake.

He back stared at Nelles, unsure what to say. Already angry, and now a touch of jealousy crept up his spine. However, if Mary had found kindness in another man for the short time left in her life, how could he resent her for it? What right had he to judge? He imagined Mary in Nelles's arms, perhaps leading to a kiss. The thought made his muscles tense, but if she experienced happiness, even briefly, from a good man like Nelles, then it didn't matter. This must have been her story of confession she wished to tell him.

"I'm sorry, Jonathan, but that's the truth of it. Probably just loneliness, but when that young woman smiled, it was — "

"Like the sun?" Westlake interjected. "I understand, sir. Please, don't be sorry. Such a disaster. I'm happy she found a good friend such as yourself. Unfortunately, when this day is over … perhaps you and I together … well, we both have to live through the day first, don't we?"

"Thank you, Jonathan. Knowing you understand means a lot to me. Blame it on this bloody war. Relationships can get a little crazy. Let's get out of here." Nelles gestured to the door and then glanced back at the bed. "Some other poor bastard can die in that cot."

Out in the passageway, the moans of the wounded combined with the general stench to fill Westlake with dread. Suddenly he remembered the reason why he had come here.

"Macdonell's second charge, sir — I suppose I'm too late?"

"Come with me."

The first bedroom at the top of the stairs had its door closed, which was never a good sign. Often it meant the doctor could do no more for the patient and had given up. Nelles tapped on the door and turned the handle. On the bed lay Lieutenant Colonel John Macdonell, his eyes closed and his face noticeably flushed. The last time Westlake had encountered him the man brimmed with confidence that General Brock could roll up the entire east side of the Niagara. Now the colonel lay half dead.

"Are you awake, sir?" Nelles whispered.

Macdonell sucked in a deep breath and opened his eyes. "I'm dying, Nelles. Too many holes in all the wrong places." He smiled even as he grimaced in pain. To Westlake, he looked like any ordinary man, with his red jacket gone and his hair all askew. How could this happen? Thoughts of Brock and Mary flashed again through his mind.

"I have a visitor to see you, sir. Lieutenant Westlake is here." Nelles took Westlake's arm and guided him close to the bed.

"Sorry I missed your charge, sir," Westlake apologized softly.

"Bloody failure anyway." Macdonell suddenly gripped Westlake's arm. "They *can't* control the heights. Whoever owns the heights will win this day, and all of Upper Canada."

"I'm going to pitch in with the Coloured Company," Westlake said.

"Aye, Brock's not-so-secret mission." Macdonell's hand slid farther down Westlake's arm to grip his fingers. He took another deep breath, his voice now just above a whisper. "The general had great faith in you — said how you reminded him of himself at your age. Be bold, young Westlake; it's the only way the Canadas will survive."

Macdonell's gaunt face flushed a deeper red. His eyes closed and the strong hand grew weak as it fell away from Westlake's fingers. He'd drifted off to sleep.

"Why did he lead a charge up that hill?"

"Duty. To avenge his general's death," Nelles replied.

"It's one thing to be bold but …"

"Any other course of action would have seemed to him dishonourable. He was trapped by his own sense of honour," Nelles explained flatly. He winced suddenly and used his right hand to support the sling.

"But, sir, up the same hill?" Westlake shook his head.

"You think he felt free to walk away? Not a chance," Nelles said. "He *had* to make that charge."

"Then a foolish sense of honour will be the cause of his own death." Westlake took a last long look at a great man who had once appeared so vital, and then he strode away.

Nelles inched his way down the stairs with Westlake supporting him under his good arm. When they reached the bottom, he found Parrish just outside the door, holding the reins of both horses. Relieved to be outside again, Westlake took another couple steps just to breathe in some fresh air. He turned back to the farmhouse and found himself face to face with Nelles.

"Sheaffe's organizing a counterattack to kick the Americans off the heights," Nelles said. "He's going in from behind. You'll find the Coloured Company deployed on one of the flanks. *Keep your head down*," Nelles recited a favourite saying that he remembered from Detroit.

He reached into his red jacket and from inside his left breast pocket a white envelope appeared. "I was given a letter last night by the good general. It's for you, but read it later. No need to rush … not now." The captain flopped down on the veranda's top step and rested his back against the post. "I'll be along shortly."

Westlake saluted, put the letter inside his buckskin jacket, and then took the reins from Parrish. The wind had died to a light breeze and the sun came out. For a moment, Westlake tilted his face to enjoy its warmth.

"The weather's turning, sir," he called out to Nelles, still peering up at the rolling clouds. "Perhaps so will our fortunes." He smiled and mounted his horse, happy to be on his way again.

Westlake spurred Alfred across a well-trampled field on the way to York Road. He crossed over the avenue and swung around the back of the heights, continuing through muddy boot prints until he hit Portage Road, where he turned south. The sound of cannon and musket fire followed him all the way. And so did Parrish.

They trotted into a copse of trees where four Indians with faces painted red and black jumped out and grabbed hold of their reins. Westlake began to explain who he was when a man wearing a red bandana shouted something and the natives withdrew. Amid the trees Chief Norton laughed and crowed, "Be more careful, laddie!"

"Coloured Company?"

Gesturing for them to stay low, Norton indicated straight ahead. Westlake dismounted and handed his reins to Parrish. "Stay here."

"My orders are to stay with you at all times, sir."

"General Brock is dead, so you are now relieved of those orders."

"Are you sure, sir?" Parrish asked intently.

"Of course, I'm sure. I need to look ahead and there is no point for both of us showing ourselves to the enemy." He jogged for thirty paces into the copse before halting behind a tree. There before him the Coloured Company stood alert trying to locate the enemy.

Westlake clambered up on to a shoulder-high boulder and peered through the trees. Far ahead, the enemy jostled to organize themselves into ranks, obviously expecting an attack at any minute. He spotted a group of officers conferring behind the lines. Westlake beckoned to Parrish as he slid down off the rock.

Parrish secured both horses to a tree, then jogged along as Westlake moved in beside Luther and Pierpoint.

Lieutenant Cooper stood up in the stirrups to scan ahead of him and then, seeing Westlake, dismounted.

"Ah! Good to see you Mr. Westlake, Parrish." Cooper continued in a loud whisper, "The enemy is a hundred yards ahead, ranged on the other side of those trees. Sergeant Alexander, make ready and prepare to advance on the general signal, but make sure you wait for it."

Mid-afternoon, and in the open-air breezes on Queenston Heights, Lieutenant Colonel Winfield Scott gripped a handwritten note tightly on each side lest it blow away. He handed it to one officer and gestured for the man to pass it around the circle of six other officers so that each could read it in turn. The note flapped in the air as they leaned forward expectantly, anxious to know the news from the American side of the river.

A cannon fired from the village below, and Scott studied the Lewiston embarkation point. Men began running for cover before the ball smashed harmlessly into a tree. He wished to silence that piece of artillery, but instead he could only shake his head. Anyone foolish enough to venture off these heights would fall victim to Indian scalping knives, so he let the enemy gun continue its dirty work.

Signed by General Stephen van Rensselaer himself, the contents of the note registered on the officers' faces. No further reinforcements were coming to the rescue, no more ammunition, and no entrenching tools. It seemed the boatmen were refusing to cross the river, disobeying direct orders. And even if the boatmen would venture out again, the American militia was standing fast. No amount of threats could make them join the fight.

"Goddamn screaming Indians are scaring the shit out of everyone," an officer declared as a loud boom signalled another cannon blast from Queenston. "And their artillery's back in business — bastards."

"Van Rensselaer's a simple militia general," remarked another. "He's no stomach for this. No wonder they won't cross."

"Be careful what you say, sir," Scott chided.

"Well he's not here with us, sir, is he?"

"Twenty-three hundred militia on that side and only seven hundred on this bank — what kind of organization is that?" asked the officer clutching the note. "Those are good men, who were more than ready to cross this morning. Give any man long enough to think about dying and eventually he'll decide to live."

"What do we do, gentlemen? I say we stay and fight." Scott peered down the incline toward columns of redcoats snaking along the road. Again the cannons sounded below, followed by blasts from the American side.

"They're coming at us with every man they've got, sir. I doubt we can maintain an orderly retreat under fire if we're forced to climb down there." The officer gestured beyond to the cliff face. "If we're going at all, we should go now."

An officer handed the note back to Scott. "The general left it up to you, sir. I say we fight. Too many good men have already given their lives for these heights. Solomon's shot to hell and Wool's ass has extra holes in it. We *have* to fight."

Although some nodded reluctantly, Scott was content they were in agreement. He scanned the trees to his left, where a few shots rang out. Indians. "So fight it is. The men performed well against the Indian attack," he said, trying to throw a positive light on the situation.

"With all due respect, sir," another officer interrupted. "Injuns are one thing, but trained British regs are another. We'll soon see if our men stand."

And Scott knew he was right. The British would keep coming, determined to break his line. Only withering fire could hold them. With his back to a cliff, it was either stop them or face a massacre.

The officers had turned as a group to study the movements of the British farther down the hill. For a brief instant the sun appeared and threw into stark contrast the redcoats against the autumn trees. Scott tore the note into small pieces and let the wind carry it away, and with it his own personal chance for escape.

With a loaded musket resting across his knees, Sergeant Nathaniel King sat on a small log, unconsciously picking at its bark. Privates Green and Ambler relaxed on either side of him, waiting. That's what you did in the army, King thought, hurried off to fight and then hung around doing nothing.

He stared at the slave catchers wondering what kind of men they were? Free to come and go as they pleased, but now trapped with him and the U.S. Army of the Center. Not one of them had a family, at least none that they would talk to him about. But, when he thought about it, how could you build a family if you were always on some far-away trail chasing runaways? These miserable men lived hand to mouth, just like the slaves they chased. Yet while the slaves ran for a future, the catchers pursued them only to pursue again on another day.

The red-haired man, Endicott, approached him and he knew it could only be about one thing.

"How's about you just look the other way and let me go."

"How's about I shove this bayonet up your arse right now, you goddamn coward." King ran a finger along the tip of his bayonet.

"This isn't my fight," Endicott complained. "And, if truth be told, it's not yours either." He slid his eyes away from King to his two companions.

"Don't tell me what's my fight," Ambler replied. "I want payback for what they called my mother."

"They fell over laughing at us," Green added.

"And took potshots across the river. Pissheads'll get what's coming to them, and soon," King said.

"I can pay!" Endicott whispered.

"Shut your gob," Green said.

King cut his eyes away to his buddy Green and then back to Endicott. "How much? It would cost my stripes or worse if I get caught letting you run."

From his pocket, Endicott produced a couple gold coins. Rubbing them together between two fingers, his eyes grew wide as his face broke into a smile. They were right there for the taking. King swallowed. He knew that he'd smiled too quickly, showing his hand, and now he looked away toward the copse that fringed the plateau.

One hundred yards away between the trees, Indians crept along, stopped, and ran again to keep hidden. They were back in numbers, brandishing tomahawks, war clubs, and muskets. They were already pressing closer and King tensed at the sight. He snatched the coins from Endicott's grubby fingers. "Go! You'd run anyways, you coward, but don't blame me if you get yourself scalped."

King jumped up together with Green and Ambler. "Keep an eye on those Indians. I need to report them." But before he could leave, some other catchers approached. They had seen Endicott frantically gathering up his pack.

"Don't you think you should say goodbye? Remember, you forfeit your share the minute you walk out of here."

"Castor, I've ridden a long ways with you, bin shot at by Indians – twice now – had our boat peppered by redcoats, and climbed this here mountain, but I've paid my bribe money. Nothing can stop me from leaving this death trap," Endicott replied. "And if the rest of you had any brains, you'd come with me. This is a *war* you're in!"

The other catchers had meanwhile gathered around.

"What money, you puke?" King snarled. "Go on, git, before some officer comes and I have to shoot you." He took a step toward the red-haired catcher and, after giving him a light poke with his bayonet, gestured with his head toward the copse. "Go on." King turned back to check on the Indians' position.

"My God, what's this?" King pointed to the woods. "In those trees closest to us — look to the left of the Indians and tell me that my eyes aren't playing tricks. In leather cross-belts and with muskets."

"It's too dark in those woods for me to see properly," Castor replied. "But something's moving."

King came right up beside the man and pointed to where he wanted his eyes to follow. "Right there."

Castor opened his eyes wide, staring first at the copse, then at his men, and finally back to the trees. "Niggers, boatloads of them."

Bennett rushed up beside Castor, bumping against his shoulder to get a better view. "Boatloads, you say?" Bennett squinted desperately toward the copse. "I can't see too well in this light."

"What are they doing in cross-belts and carrying muskets?" Castor wondered aloud.

"They have muskets?" Bennett spit out. "Here we go again! Damn cheatin' niggers!"

Castor glanced skyward at the slow-moving grey clouds. Except for the odd patch of sun, the mid-October light was dulling fast. If the British were coming, it had to happen soon. All he had to do now was wait, no need to chase them down. They'd come right to him.

"I reckon I count thirty-eight of those leather belts," Sergeant King announced. "I gotta report this to the colonel. Shoot anyone else who tries to quit us," he ordered Green and Ambler before scurrying off.

Ambler raised his musket to Castor.

"Put that away, you toad.' He slapped away the tip of Ambler's weapon and continued scanning the trees. "Must be four years' wages there for every man jack of us. I can finally escape this business and start a place of my own," he promised himself. He thought back to that girl in the farmhouse and how she had sneered at him. No more looks of disgust for George Castor. People just didn't understand. He was finished now … done his time working for society.

"All these slaves have come to fight us," Castor said to the other catchers. "Time to take them home."

"You're both crazy. Look at them; they're standing in line now," Endicott whined. "They're not slaves no more. Those muskets make it even worse! I'm outta here, right now!" He shot an angry glance Green. "I paid." He stuck a finger in the other man's face and kept going.

Green shrugged toward Ambler as Endicott picked up his pack and musket and ran for the cliff behind them.

"More for the rest of us," Bennett snarled.

Castor fixed his attention on the slaves, counting again. His eyes ran to the edge of the pack, where a big man stood defiantly, slightly in front of the rest. "It's our boy, Alex!" He grinned, pounding a fist into his other hand.

"Where?" Bennett asked excitedly.

"Right at the end of their line, there." Castor grabbed Bennett's arm and pointed. "My God, it's a miracle!" He ran forward a few steps. "There's Luther too, right behind Alex. They're worth a fortune."

"D'you see that horse-thieving Mathew?" Bennett asked. "I suppose the girl might just fall out of a tree into my lap." He laughed. "No matter, we'll find them. The others'll talk." Bennett stroked the knife in his belt and grinned.

A troop of bluecoats ran in beside the slave catchers and formed up in three ranks, staring ahead, muskets ready at the shoulder. Sergeant King rushed in, but before he could speak Castor had something he needed to say to his companions.

"There's eight of us now. That's four and a half niggers per man, and Alex and Luther will be counting extra. Careful trying to catch them, 'cause they got their own muskets — "

"No nigger can shoot straight that I ever know about," Bennett interjected, yanking his knife from its sheath and waving it menacingly in the air. "Try and take one of 'em alive so they can tell us the where-abouts of that wench, Precious. She's worth a bundle to Mrs. Caldwell." He made an imaginary round belly with the swoop of his hand.

"I firmly believe that God sent them right to us for what crimes they done to poor Percy and his folks … stealing horses, setting fires, and all," Castor declared. "That's the only reason for our good for-tune. Remember that … a loving God is with each one of you to do his work."

And, as if God controlled the timing especially to help Castor, a bugle sounded on the heights, a cannon blast split the air, and out of the copse marched the company of slaves. On the side nearest the cliff, the gang of painted Indians hooted and screamed, but on the other end of the line marched more redcoats than Castor could count. Having stayed below the treeline until the bugle sounded, they emerged in two perfect ranks with their muskets at the shoulder. He looked to Bennett and shrugged.

"That's the 41st," Sergeant King explained. "You catchers, form up at the end of this line. You're going to face the runaways while our boys face the regulars — 'bout all you fellas is good for. And this time try to keep up."

That suited Castor fine. He felt a tug on his sleeve and looked around to find Bennett beside him.

"Redcoats don't worry me none," Bennett said. "White folk don't ever march to save niggers."

"Here they come," Castor cheered in a wide grin, as if he could not believe his good fortune. God was finally smiling on him.

28
••••••

WESTLAKE TRIED TO BREATHE DEEP. The waiting had twisted his stomach into a knot and he belched. His head ached and his palms sweated. He and Parrish were positioned at the end of the Coloured Company's line, standing closest to the 41st Regiment. *Please, can we start.*

Lieutenant Simpson rushed in to take his place at the left of the regulars' line. He tugged down on his clean red jacket and stood sharply to attention, eyes front. Westlake immediately wondered if Simpson would freeze up again when the shooting started.

"Mr. Westlake, Parrish." He nodded toward them. "I've been racing around all afternoon on other duties but didn't want to miss my first real engagement. How do I look?"

Westlake had himself fairly well under control, but now to suffer Simpson just before the battle commenced was asking too much. Was he to be saddled with this fellow throughout the entire day, perhaps his entire life?

"How do you look, Robert? Why should I give a shit how you look? You look lovely — I'm sure the birds will notice." Westlake glanced skyward.

"An arsehole if you asks me, sir," Parrish whispered the words out the side of his mouth.

"An officer has to set a good example to his men," Simpson persisted. "Especially a newly commissioned lieutenant. By the way, where is your uniform, sir?"

"Our men and the enemy are crapping themselves, like you were before arriving late. No one gives a fart what you look like. Now shut up and make sure your sword will come out of its bloody scabbard so you can fight." Westlake turned to glare at Simpson. "And just so you know, I don't own a uniform on direct orders from General Brock himself."

312

Simpson looked down and jiggled his sword to assure himself it would draw. "All that may change now. You may have to become a proper soldier soon," Simpson declared with some satisfaction. "No more sneaking around in the backwoods for the likes of you and Parrish."

"Don't ever open your mouth again about what we do," Westlake stated flatly. "Men can die many ways on the battlefield, Mr. Simpson. You shouldn't offer me any temptation today."

"I say, sir." Simpson's eyes glared back. "Steady on!"

Westlake felt better for releasing some anger on Simpson, but he secretly knew the man was right. If Nelles couldn't find him a mission, as before, it was off to join the York Volunteers, a uniform, and the confines of the York garrison drill square.

He suddenly thought of his mother back at home all by herself. Mary would have been the solution to that problem. Mary. Just the thought of her and the anger welled up inside him. Anger at her death. Anger at himself for not telling her the truth. She'd given him no cause to cheat. He gripped his musket so tight that his fingers hurt. Anger at the world because the face he saw when he closed his eyes was always the one face he shouldn't see. Seffi Bauer's. The more he tried to forget her, the more his thoughts returned to her. The anger raged inside him, and then the bugle sounded, a cannon fired, Indians screamed nearby, and Jonathan Westlake knew that his battle for Queenston Heights had begun.

"Coloured Company will advance at the ordinary, march!" Lieutenant Cooper yelled from his horse.

Westlake heard the same orders being shouted to the 41st. He peered in their direction, farther along where the redcoats and militia now advanced in line. Two companies of Brock's old regiment along with the Lincoln militia had begun marching straight down the centre of the heights. Someone in the 49th shouted, "Avenge the general." And a cheer went up. Then the companies together screamed, "Avenge the general." A drummer kept up a steady beat. The soldiers marched to its rhythm. An American six-pounder crashed out, the ball smashing through two men in the advancing ranks. A sergeant in the 49th shouted, "Close up the lines, quickly now."

Even as they marched, Alexander the Great glanced around at Westlake, giving that reckless smile, the same one he'd seen when they were stealing the boat. The madness seized Westlake too. He relaxed a hand from his musket, touched the tomahawk and knife secured in his belt, and then, just to make sure, he felt for the knife slung on his back between his shoulder blades.

Every man in the two advancing lines knew that the Americans were going to fire; it was just a question of time. The lines had to absorb that fire, and then they would get their chance to return the favour. At a hundred yards from the enemy, Sergeant Alexander extended his neck forward, trying to make out something in the distance. He gestured back to Parrish and waved him forward.

"You met the catchers at the Bauer farm. Are my eyes playing tricks or is that the buggers at the end of the enemy line?" Alexander asked.

Parrish ran up beside the sergeant and stared ahead as they marched. At ninety yards, he stopped, nodded his head, and hustled up to Alexander again. "That's them, no doubt about it."

They were ascending a slight incline that made the catchers appear larger than in real life. The American six-pounder blasted again, and Westlake instinctively tensed his shoulders.

Alexander turned back to face Luther but kept up his steady pace. "Those men at the end are definitely not militia. They're the same bastards that whipped me and hung Hector's body from the tree. *I'm going to kill every one of them today.*"

Luther gave no reaction that Westlake could see. Parrish rejoined the line alongside him. "See that man with the bowler hat and stupid moustache, second from the end." He pointed with his musket. "That's the same whoreson that grabbed Seffi. Name's Bennett. Says he's going back for her when this is all over ... so he says."

Westlake studied the man for a moment. Hatred. He didn't know what else to feel other than the rage inside him readying itself to explode. "That's the thing though, Parrish. *All* those catchers know where the Bauer farm is. Killing Bennett only opens the door for another of them." Westlake shook his head. "I'm with Alexander.

Every single one of them has to die, or Katharina and Seffi will never be safe."

"Suits me fine, sir. Even God can't help them if you and Alexander both feel that way."

"God's not here to help anyone today," Westlake said.

A terrible shriek caught Westlake's attention. Near the cliff's edge, two warriors dragged a screaming man along by his thick red hair.

"That's a catcher they've got," Parrish said, "and you know what those Indians will do to him. Best thing he could do for himself right now is just die."

"One less for me to kill," Westlake muttered. "How many of those swine did you say there were?"

"I counted ten at the farm, but only eight over there. Redhead makes nine, so let's hope one already died in their fight with the Indians."

The red-haired man held his pack and wouldn't let go of it, the Indians jostling to drag him into the copse and the man kicking to fight his way free. One warrior lost his grip, and the captive swung his pack hard to break free of the second Indian. He began to run back toward the catchers and had taken three clean steps when a war club caught him in the back of the head. He collapsed in a heap and the Indians wasted no time dragging him farther. One tore his pack away as another pulled back his greasy hair while sliding a knife underneath. The warrior howled a cry of victory and held the red-haired scalp in the air.

Westlake could see blood dripping from its underside before he turned away. "Eight to go," he announced flatly.

Lieutenant Cooper suddenly called a halt. "Coloured Company, you will fire, load as you march, and then fire again. After which, you will charge the enemy with bayonets." Cooper turned his horse and rode up to the edge of the line.

"Make ready!

"Present!" Cooper scanned his troops closely to see that every man had his musket raised.

"Front rank, fire!

"Rear rank, fire!"

The muskets spit a line of flame and balls, but from his position, Westlake saw no effect on the enemy. He wondered for a second why the army even bothered trying to fire with such inaccurate weapons. His own recoiling musket had rammed against his shoulder the second after he pulled the trigger.

Then the enemy fired.

They were sixty yards away, but shooting slightly downhill, making it more difficult not to aim a little high, as was common. The balls whizzed overhead, and miraculously no one in the Coloured Company yelled from a wound. To Westlake's right, someone in the 41st cried out. Trash dropped to his knees, holding his arm, but the lines moved relentlessly past him.

Westlake gave his shoulder a rub and began to reload on the order. From what he could see, every man in the enemy's line was frantically trying to do the same.

"Advance!"

He watched Cooper's lips move but heard little, the explosions of musket fire all around him having deafened his ears. Slowly a normal resonance returned to the sound of ramrods scraping down the barrels. The enemy fired again, only this time he felt something pluck at his coat. When he looked down, two holes appeared near the coat's rim between his legs. The balls had passed clean through. *"A little higher and ... "* He grimaced and shook his head.

The Coloured Company was only twenty paces from the enemy when Lieutenant Cooper called a halt. The mixture of former slaves and Butler's Rangers — thirty-eight of them — raised their weapons on his command to present. With addition of Westlake and Parrish, their two lines each presented a front of twenty men across. Westlake could see the wide-eyed expressions on the catchers' faces.

The enemy fired yet again and another man from the 41st dropped like a stone at the end of their line nearest to Westlake. Mad Dog had received a shot to his shoulder and now writhed on the ground. Westlake took another deep breath and glanced at Parrish.

"Fix bayonets," the lieutenant shouted.

Again, Westlake heard the scraping of steel as he twisted his own bayonet to lock on the end of his musket. Odd that before the battle he had been all nerves, and now that he was in it, even with hatred raging inside him, he felt totally calm. No longer sweating in fear, his breathing was unconsciously deeper. He grinned to himself, figuring a path to get himself close to the man in the bowler hat.

"Present."

"Front rank, fire!"

"Rear rank, fire!"

"Forward, march! Port arms!"

"At the quick, march! Charge bayonets!"

This time Westlake had jammed the musket's butt well into his throbbing shoulder before squeezing the trigger. He'd aimed at the slave catcher closest to him, but the ball must have missed because the man showed no ill effect. Then Westlake ran with the rest of the Coloured Company. "Kill!" he screamed. "Kill!"

The bluecoats stepped forward and their line expanded, overlapping and blocking most of the catchers for the first clash. Immediately in front of Westlake stood a young man his own age. He knew exactly how this fellow would die. The enemy raised his weapon, the bayonet ready to impale Westlake as he ran forward. Three strides away, Westlake tossed his musket like a spear and drew his tomahawk. The fellow parried the musket to one side with his own, grinning, thinking he'd won. But before he could swing his musket back to the front, Westlake's tomahawk sliced across his throat. He pushed the dying man aside like brushing away a tall reed, then ran at his next rival.

Luther heard Lieutenant Cooper bark the order for the rear rank to fire. He pointed and pulled the trigger at precisely the same time as the other eighteen men in his line. A catcher fell in the middle of their gang. *Did I kill the man or did someone else fire that shot?* He knelt down and instinctively began to reload as the rear rank prepared to fire seconds later. His stomached churned at the thought he might have actually killed another human being.

The battlefield between himself and the catchers choked with drifting grey smoke before Cooper hollered the order to charge bayonets. Both the catchers and the bluecoats could have left the field for all he knew. Vanished behind the smoke. He prayed they had. When he tried to spit, he found his mouth had gone dry.

The men around him yelled obscenities as the front rank charged. Luther stood up and darted forward through the cloud of smoke, hoping no one would be there. He'd longed for soldiering, but now that he had his chance, he trembled nearly witless. His comrades cried for revenge, full of anger and hate, but Luther felt neither of those emotions. His craving had been just to prove himself to Hector and his father. He hated no one. Soldiering was for others, not him.

As he ran through the smoke, the catchers suddenly appeared. His father turned to make sure he was close by and simply nodded once. They were now fifteen paces from the enemy. Seconds later, Sergeant Alexander knocked aside an enemy bayonet and stabbed the catcher so hard the weapon would not come free. Another catcher jabbed at the sergeant from the side but missed. The man lunged again, sure to run Alexander through the ribs.

"Father!" Luther cried. He pulled his musket's trigger and watched the catcher stagger back with a ramrod sticking out of his chest. In his panic to reload, he'd never retrieved the thing from the barrel.

Alexander finally wrenched his musket loose of the dead man's chest and jerked around to face him. His father's jaw dropped and Luther glanced over his shoulder. A sword deflected away from his face, its point meant for him. Simpson fenced with the bluecoated officer, but the sword had shaved Luther's ear and blood dripped from its lobe. If Simpson had acted just a half-second later, the back of Luther's neck would have been slashed through as easy as an apple.

Westlake pushed between himself and Alexander. As the enemy edged backward, Luther felt the pressure ease. A cannon blasted only yards away, forcing friend and enemy alike to instinctively crouch down.

"Don't let the bastards escape," Westlake hollered.

After drawing his tomahawk, Westlake had hit the enemy line on the dead run. The bluecoat reacted as expected, and it was easy to slap away the bayonet and then slice through the man's neck. The blood spurted on to Westlake's face and jacket as he charged toward the next man. Someone hollered, "Oliver!" and the bluecoat in front of him glanced away to his left for a heartbeat. The man cried, "Green" as Westlake battered down on his head with the axe. Green gaped and rammed his bayonet at Westlake's stomach. Westlake hooked it with the tomahawk as it scraped his belly and then stabbed up with his knife, under Green's chin. Three ranks of bluecoats pressed forward and he found himself fighting two men simultaneously until Parrish and the rest of the 41st arrived at his back. He pressed the enemy line to give way.

Hook, thrust, slash, he fought shifting to his left, toward the slave catchers. An officer lying on the ground and appearing to be dead reared up and jabbed his thigh. Westlake stomped on the man's throat and then clubbed his head. "Bugger." He slid the knife into its sheath, jammed the axe through his belt, and snatched up the dead man's musket. His thigh seemed on fire, but there was no time to stop.

He pushed past Luther, through to the catchers, where he simply bashed the first man in the head, killing him outright with the butt end of the musket. The catchers began falling back, preparing to run. The stench of fear, blood, and sweat filled his nostrils. The suppressed anger of the former slaves, tore into the bluecoats as well as the catchers, like a bear ripping into flesh.

"Don't let the bastards escape," Westlake hollered. He glimpsed the catcher called Bennett, backing slowly away, and imagined Seffi at this man's mercy. Immediately, his mind jumped to Mary trapped in the burning cabin … and what was left of his self-control vanished. His thigh burning, he ran limping directly for Bennett.

Another catcher stood in his way. Again, Westlake lunged with the musket, the man taking the bayonet in the chest. Westlake, face blackened and bloodied, smiled like a madman. *Killing is easy.* As he ran, drawing the large knife from behind his back with his right hand, he found Alexander running beside him.

"Castor's mine — on the left. You kill Bennett," Alexander screamed, before emitting a frenzied howl. His eyes bulged and he grinned with teeth clenched, as if inhabited by some kind of devil. His enemies had turned, running for the cliff.

"My pleasure," Westlake replied with solemn malevolence. "Bennett, you coward," he yelled after him.

Bennett and Castor swung round with their muskets and fired together. The blast shot wide of Westlake. Alexander moaned, tumbled to the ground and cursed.

Westlake ran right at Bennett as the catcher jabbed with his musket. Westlake hacked down with the tomahawk, then slashed the knife to one side of Bennett's neck.

Bennett dropped to his knees and gripped his throat, the blood pumping out between his fingers. He peered up at Westlake, his eyes wide in disbelief. "Why you fighting for niggers?" he gasped.

Westlake let him get the words out. He glanced up to see Castor near the cliff's edge, frantically trying to re load his musket, which meant he had no more than twenty seconds before the man could fire. "Remember Seffi Bauer, who you were planning to rape?"

Bennett's eyes glazed over and he made no reply, the entire front of his shirt soaked in blood.

"She sends you her regards." Westlake knocked off the bowler hat with the knife and grabbed the man's last remaining tuft of hair.

"Stop!" a voice yelled. "That's not who you are." Parrish had been behind Westlake from the beginning of the encounter and now he held his hands in the air. "Don't scalp him. What would the general say?"

Westlake's breathing came in short, staccato gasps. His face and hands dripped with blood. He glanced down at Bennett's bald head and looked up again at Parrish. Then he slid the knife across Bennett's throat.

"Now, would you deal with *him*?" Parrish pointed to Castor.

"Stop loading or I'll kill you where you stand," Westlake shouted as a roar went up from the 41st. The enemy had broken and the bluecoats ran for their lives. Some men dashed for the sloping hillside, but, when Indians appeared, they changed direction like a herd of cattle and headed for the cliff.

"Take him with your knife. It's only twenty-five paces," Alexander moaned.

Westlake reached back and let fly with the knife. Castor lurched to one side, dropped his musket, and slumped to his knees, the knife sticking in the right side of his chest. Bluecoats scrambled by to jump over the cliff's edge before the Indians could capture them. None stopped to look at Castor.

Westlake slid his hands under Alexander's armpits and helped him stumble the twenty-five paces to where Castor kneeled on the ground.

Alexander turned to Westlake as they walked. "You said you were only good up to twenty paces with that knife," he groaned.

"I was showing off just now." Westlake smiled. "You need a doctor."

"Kill him, and then find my boy. My belly's long past doctoring."

Westlake reached Castor and looked down at him, recalling the scars on Alexander's back. The catcher mumbled a prayer. His face had changed colour from sheet-white to red within seconds.

Alexander breathed heavily as he collapsed to his knees, clutching his belly, so that he was almost face to face with the dying Castor. "Why did you come here?" he demanded in a whisper.

Castor peered up at Westlake and then turned to Alexander. "I uphold the law," he choked out the words. "I had to come. Young Percy got what he deserved, but you belong to the Caldwells, you stole horses, and set fire. God will reward me for doing his work."

"You hung my boy's body on a tree!" Alexander cried. He reached out for Westlake's hand to help him get up, the blood oozing from his stomach.

Westlake reached down and yanked his knife out of Castor's chest. "You won't be needing this."

Castor gave a loud gasp and stared up at Westlake, marshalling his strength. He struggled with one last effort to stand. "Let me go to my God," he said, holding his bleeding chest.

"That's only fair," Alexander growled, hatred driving him on. "Go get your reward." He grabbed the wounded catcher by the lapels and edged him a few feet back toward the cliff's edge. Castor clutched at Alexander's arms, but the big man shook off his grip with one hard thrust. Castor flew through the air and vanished in an instant.

Westlake grabbed hold of Alexander's collar just before the man took the plunge himself. "Christ! You were willing to go over just to see him dead! You wouldn't have seen Luther again."

"I hate that man and everything he stands for." Alexander slumped down on the grass.

Westlake leaned out over the cliff to see Castor's broken body on the rocks far below. "When you speak about Mr. Castor, you're now talking in the past tense." He looked around for Parrish. "You had better go find Luther."

29

......

TEARS STREAMED DOWN Luther's cheek as he cradled his father's large head in his hands. Alexander still lay close to the cliff where he'd shoved Castor to his death. Every few minutes, another bluecoat would emerge from the trees to begin the long climb down to the river. The fighting over, and the battle won, no one paid these stragglers any serious attention.

Westlake stood back to allow Luther and Alexander space of their own. He peered down at the rocky beach below to where a half-dozen twisted bodies of the enemy laid motionless. These American soldiers had leapt to their deaths rather than face a scalping knife. Now, retreating bluecoats jostled for position near the shore, but no boats came to their rescue.

The odd Indian still hooted or a musket cracked, but otherwise the sounds of battle had ended. Staring back at Luther, Westlake tried to imagine what recovering a father would be like, only to lose him two days later. And Precious, too, would have to be told.

"Why didn't you wait for the rest of us?" Luther cried.

"They would have got away," Alexander whispered, and he reached for his son's hand.

"So. Look what you've done to yourself." Luther wiped tears from his cheek. "What do I tell Precious?"

"I'm sorry, I am truly sorry ... but now you're both free of those men. You can build a life here in glory land." Alexander managed a half-smile.

The Coloured Company, led by Pierpoint, gathered around their fallen sergeant. Lieutenant Cooper rode up and dismounted, but didn't say a word. A few redcoats drifted in to get a closer look at Alexander the Great.

"Precious and me were free already 'cause we don't *hate* them any more," Luther cried out in frustration. "That's what you taught us — but seems you didn't believe your own lesson. This is what comes of it." He put his head on Alexander's chest and sobbed. The big man put a gentle hand over his son's face. Slowly the hand lost its strength and then fell away.

Alexander the Great was dead, and Luther wept.

The rest of the company milled around with heads bowed, unsure what to do. Minutes later, Lieutenant Cooper instructed Pierpoint to haul up a nearby cart. "Carry his body back to the road. Carefully. He's one of our own." Once the body lay in the cart, Cooper escorted it down the hill.

Parrish approached after assisting with the cart, hair dishevelled and his hands badly cut. "Is there anything I can do?" His face splashed with blood, he had the look of a man on the brink of exhaustion.

"I don't think so." Westlake stared after the rolling cart. Luther walked alongside his father, one arm stretched out to rest on the body.

"Alexander always wanted to be free. Now he is," Parrish said as he stood watching.

"Dead men aren't free, Walter. They're just dead. Freedom's only for the living."

Parrish shrugged and looked up at the darkening sky.

"We're finished here," Westlake continued. "Are you cut?"

"It's the other guys' blood, sir. But those are my thoughts exactly. About being finished here, I mean. I counted seven dead catchers back there. That leaves two missing. One of them is the guy with holes in his boots — Robinson."

"Not two," Westlake said. "Only one is unaccounted for. Castor went over the cliff. You might say he lost his grip."

"A good one, sir." Parrish laughed. "A good one for us to end on. I've found a little path leading down." Parrish stared out over the river. "I'm running now, you know."

"I know," Westlake said with a twinge of sadness creeping into his voice.

"Since I'm free of my orders to protect you, sir, — like you said yourself — I'm going after Robinson and I'm not coming back. He knows where the farm is and I can't take that chance."

"I'm happy for you, Parrish. Katharina has found a good man." Westlake slapped him on the back.

"I've learned a lot on my travels with you, Jonathan. We've had some wild times, so we have, you and me."

"Don't get sentimental on me, Parrish. Go kill that last bastard, and be careful for God's sake. Someone has to protect that farm."

"You could come with me, sir? Seffi needs you and that farm is half the size of England."

"My place is at Maple Hill, and until this war is finished...." Westlake shrugged and left the words unspoken. "Someone more worthy will come along, you'll see. Now be off before a real officer spots you."

"Thank you, Jonathan. Remember to forgive yourself for ... well, you know my thoughts already. I'll say hello to Seffi for you anyways. Maybe we'll all come north for a visit one day." Parrish flashed a smile. "I'm finally going to sleep in one of those big beds like you have at Maple Hill."

Westlake grinned and reached out to grab Parrish's shoulder while shaking his hand. "And, Walter, keep your head down."

Parrish nodded, gave a casual salute, and sauntered over to the cliff's edge. He took one step down the hidden path, turned and pumped his musket in the air, then he was gone.

Lieutenant Westlake sat on a dry rock atop Queenston Heights. Although only late afternoon, the sun was hidden and a chill had descended. The smoke had cleared, and he finally had a chance to view the plateau in its autumn glory. Ringed with trees, the heights themselves were relatively barren. A few men still lay on the ground, the dying and wounded together.

Through the silence floated a familiar voice.

"Lieutenant Westlake, I should have known I'd find you at the summit." Captain Nelles gestured with a sword held in his good arm.

"Wonderful to see you've got your bearings again, sir." Westlake stood up and returned the salute, though the pressure on his leg made him wince. He sat down again and inspected his wound. The bayonet had torn the buckskin and creased the outside of his thigh. The gash stung and in places it still bled.

"Let's have a proper look at that," Nelles said. "I'll help you to the Durham place where I know the doctor rather well." He grinned and held up his broken arm.

"I'd rather not, sir. A cold dip in the lake would do just as well — probably help my arm too."

"Suit yourself. Where's Parrish?"

"Dead, sir. Went over the side while fighting their militia. Deserves a bloody medal, that man does."

"Did you actually see him die or did he just run?"

"Could you survive that fall, sir?" Westlake limped over to the edge of the cliff and gestured down to the rocks below. "No, you can take it from his lieutenant that he died in battle on behalf of his King and country."

Nelles didn't bother to look down into the gorge but instead stared Westlake in the eye. "It's a shame to lose a good man. Parrish does deserve a medal. Simpson is being recommended, I thought you should know. Whereas you … well, as General Brock always said, you don't exist." Nelles finished with a chuckle. "Not much glory in being an agent, is there?"

"I'm just happy to be alive, sir. I sort of lost myself in the fighting this time … it's strange really." Westlake held out his hand and it began to quiver. "I need a rest, sir. I'm going home — back to Maple Hill. Tell them that my friends the Iroquois carried me off."

"The Indians did well today. Colonel Scott's surrendering even as we speak. The Iroquois nearly scalped him, waving his little white flag or not." Nelles began to laugh. "Scared the hell out him, they did."

Westlake chuckled at the thought of the big colonel waving a tiny flag at an Iroquois warrior.

"He held out his white cravat like this" — Nelles laughed harder as he imitated Scott's motions — "and thought he would be safe. You should have seen the look on his face when some knife-wielding warrior grabbed him by the hair!" Nelles was almost doubled over. "And General Sheaffe, the pompous ass, stamped his foot and threatened to resign his commission if the Indians didn't desist from scalping prisoners this instant! Someone" — Nelles could now barely speak for laughing — "someone from the ranks yelled, 'Scalp him quick.' So Sheaffe finally drew his sword but couldn't find the heckler. Oh God, Jonathan. I only wish you'd been there."

Westlake gradually stopped laughing. "So Scott has surrendered?"

Nelles got his own laughter under control. "The sad part ... the really sad part is that Sheaffe is offering another truce. Can you imagine?" Nelles swung his good arm around in disgust.

"After all this effort," Westlake said. "If Brock were still with us, nothing would have stopped him from rolling up the entire Niagara region. Nothing and no one, not even Prevost. This battle should never have happened. Prevost might as well have killed the general himself."

"Be very careful to whom you say that. In fact, don't ever say it again. The general knew the chance he was taking."

"But why did he have to lead that attack himself?" Westlake pleaded for the answer that everyone was seeking.

Nelles sighed and eased himself down on to the same rock. He winced, adjusting the splint on his arm. "We'll never know for sure, but I knew him as well as any man." He peered up at the sky. "I think he was embarrassed at losing the heights, at the mistake he made in allowing William's Light Company to vacate the high ground. Though how the Americans found their way up that cliff in the nick of time is a mystery.

"For him, regaining the heights became a question of honour. Same bloody thing for Macdonell." Nelles shook his head. "It's almost as if the pair of them had no choice. Damn shame. A great man gone in the flash of a musket," he murmured wistfully. "He was my friend." Nelles turned his head away.

"But we stopped them." Westlake pointed to the ground in front of their feet. "Right here, we stopped them cold. Maybe they'll erect a plaque or something." Westlake surveyed the heights. "The men did well, same for the Coloured Company. Not a man of them ran or flinched, you know. Two volleys, and they charged like demons."

"The Coloureds did that?" Nelles scratched his unshaven chin and yawned. "Damn good show. The general figured they'd fight. Well, we have our victory."

"Let's go, sir. I've spent enough time today on these bloody heights. And we have one last duty to perform." Westlake reached down and grabbed up a fallen musket, before straightening to look at Nelles. "Would you help me bury Mary's remains?"

"It would be my great honour, Lieutenant Westlake."

With a musket for support, Westlake limped across the plateau, one thigh still burning and his left arm stinging. In front of him, a long line of wearied redcoats dragged their feet downhill, moving slow and ponderous like a funeral procession. Westlake inhaled and then blew out in a whistle. For him it was time to go home to York, time to go home to the stone house on Maple Hill, and there to find his bearings.

Perhaps if he told Nelles of his adventures in Pennsylvania, it might not actually free him from guilt, but he hoped it might bring some closure. He reached the edge of the battlefield and stared back at the bodies strewn on the ground. Some redcoats still wandered about searching for comrades, staring down at agonized faces.

Victory at the battle of Queenston Heights. Westlake didn't feel like he'd won a bloody thing.

EPILOGUE

HENRY, LORD BATHURST, stared through the parlour window of 10 Downing Street. A persistent silver rain washed the streets, carrying away the daily business of London. His mind wandered as he imagined the battle after reading the file of papers he held in one hand. Drizzle, cannons blasts, the charge up a steep hill into the murderous flash of fire. He shook his head at the madness of it all.

A voice from behind startled him. "What do you have for me, Lord Bathurst?"

"Afternoon, Prime Minister. Sorry to disturb your meeting, but I have news from Upper Canada."

"You don't look too pleased. Out with it." Lord Liverpool gestured with a hand for Bathurst to be quick.

"It's this fellow General Brock, sir. He's got himself killed near Niagara Falls. A certain General Sheaffe assumed command and secured the final victory."

"The Americans attacked us?" The prime minister viewed him warily.

"Across the river, sir, at place called Queenston Heights. Brock remained as ordered — strictly on the defensive."

"Good show!" the prime minister enthused. "Now, Brock —" He paused. "Didn't we just give him a knighthood? Sir Isaac Brock, I recall." Liverpool walked toward the fireplace with hands outstretched as the rain beat furiously against the window. "It's bloody damp in this room. I'll never actually live here."

"Same fellow, yes. Stupendous victory." Lord Bathurst lowered his eyes, disappointed at the prime minister's reaction to Brock's death. "But I fear a greater loss."

"You don't think this Sheaffe can replace him?" Liverpool rubbed his hands together briskly over the fire. "Where's that damned footman?"

"It's only a fool who thinks Sheaffe or Prevost could have engineered those victories at Michilimackinac and Detroit. Brock seized an area larger than France and did it all after we ordered him to use *defensive measures only.*'" Bathurst beckoned impatiently to the servant entering the room with two glasses on a tray.

"Did you know he employed an all-coloured company on the heights? Fought beside the 41st apparently … performed damn well, I hear." Bathurst grinned as his long fingers claimed a glass after the prime minister had taken the first. His quarrel with Liverpool about slavery never seemed to end. "Must drive the Americans crazy, forced to fight their own slaves." He took a sip from his glass, and then grimaced once more at the thought of Brock's death.

"Don't start on that slavery business again. We've other priorities. Next they'll demand their own officers." Liverpool held up two fingers to the footman, indicating an order for more port. Then he clinked his glass on the side of Bathurst's. "To victory at Queenston Heights."

"To Queenston Heights, sir." Bathurst allowed the mouthful of port to roll down his throat. Just one question mattered now, but he'd only stake his reputation if prodded. The prime minister opened his mouth and, knowing the question, Bathurst already had his answer.

"Can our man in Quebec … ?" Liverpool frowned.

"Prevost, sir, Governor-in-Chief Prevost."

"Of course, Prevost. Can he manage the war without Sir Isaac?"

Bathurst turned to the fire, relishing its warmth on his face. He chose his words carefully before replying, "So long as we maintain a policy of doing nothing apart from defensive measures, then Prevost can certainly handle things. In fact, the man embraces our strategy enthusiastically."

"Good show, Henry. You're a brilliant secretary of war."

"That's kind of you, sir." Bathurst bowed his head modestly.

"The full cabinet waits next door to hear your latest report on

Wellington." The prime minister raised his glass once more but noticed it was empty. "Where's that damn servant got to?" He peered past Bathurst, shrugged, and proposed the toast regardless. "To Sir Isaac Brock."

"I didn't know the man personally, but I wish I had." Bathurst raised his glass, a trace of sadness in his voice. "To Sir Isaac Brock."

HISTORICAL NOTE

Go to the landing spot along the Niagara River where so many escaped slaves made it to "glory land." See the Magazine building in Fort George where a heated shot nearly blew everyone up. Visit Old Fort Niagara in New York State and touch the stones of the Castle inside the fort. Wonder at the climb of American troops scaling the cliff face of Queenston Heights, under the leadership of John Wool and Winfield Scott. Follow in the footsteps of Sir Isaac Brock, as he charges up Queenston Heights to meet his death. Smell the river air in early morning beside the Niagara Gorge and gaze at the great falls in wonder. History is not some long ago idea that cannot be understood. It rests beside you, waiting for you to feel it.

In 1793, the tiny legislature of Newark, on the Niagara River, was the first in the entire British Empire to pass an act that would lead to the abolition of slavery. Since there were not enough votes to end it outright, in what was to become typical Canadian style, slavery was to be phased out over a period of time. What's important for our story is that no new slaves were allowed inside Upper Canada from 1793 onward. This meant that if a slave could reach Upper Canada by boating or swimming across Lake Erie or the Niagara River, he was automatically a free man.

While it's hard to imagine now, just as hard as it is to imagine Canadians and Americans once killing each other, slave catchers actually crossed the international border at will to grab runaways and take them back to their Southern owners. They would appeal to the authorities to help them because the slave had committed some crime in the course of their escape — often stealing a horse. There are documented cases of rioting by the local Canadian population to prevent a slave's handover by the local police to the catchers. Finally, the legislature came to consider slavery a greater crime than horse thieving and so ended any extradition on those grounds.

The slave escapes described in *Brock's Railroad*, while fictional, are all very plausible. Yet I have found no documented evidence of any runaway surviving a trip over Niagara Falls or that members of the British Army ever helped them to escape. Those are the fictional elements in my tale. I should add, however, that Luther's lanterns that do not blow out in the wind can be found in the tinsmith's shop at Black Creek Pioneer Village, York University, in Toronto.

My Coloured Company is a fictional fighting unit. However, before you are disappointed, there was a real company of African-American men that fought at the battle of Queenston Heights. Its name was Captain Runchey's Company of Coloured Men. Not much is known about this company other than its thirty-six to thirty-eight members were a mix of ex-Butler Rangers and ex-slaves. The Rangers had fought on the British side in the American War of Independence and had granted freedom to any slave who joined them. Unfortunately, if revolutionary forces then captured any ex-slaves, they were returned to their previous owner, and that gave me the idea for Alexander.

We know that the Runchey's Coloured Company fired one or two volleys and charged alongside the 41st Regiment, at which time the Americans were forced to retreat under the command of Lieutenant Colonel Winfield Scott [later to conquer Mexico]. Nowhere have I read of any desertions from this historical Coloured Company before or during the fighting. On October 13, under extraordinary circumstances during the battle, the entire company performed as well or better than other fighting units.

All African Americans in *Brock's Railroad* are fictional except Richard Pierpoint, often called "Captain Dick." He actually petitioned British authorities to form an all-black company several months before one was finally approved in August 1812. Today, the only reminder of the Coloured Company's charge is a small plaque next to Brock's monument on Queenston Heights. A pilgrimage to this plaque, where ex-slaves fought for their newly won freedom, should be part of Ontario's school curriculum, especially for everyone of African heritage.

The underground railroad reached its peak in the 1840s and 1850s. I took the liberty of positing how it might have looked in the beginning during the period around 1812. In fact, no one is sure when or where the name "underground railroad" came from. There is a story that a slave catcher wondered out loud how the slaves were managing to disappear so quickly. In frustration, he's reported to have said, "They must be getting on an underground railroad."

Whenever slaves planned their escape, naturally they could not speak openly about where they were going, so they developed language codes. Their code word for Canada was "glory land" or "heaven." And Dr. Martin Luther King Jr. mentioned this fact during his Massey lecture address in November 1967.

Chief John Norton of the Six Nations Iroquois had a Cherokee father and a Scottish mother. He was raised in Scottish schools, and after careers as a soldier and fur trader, he drifted into a life as an interpreter for the Indian department, where he ingratiated himself with the Six Nations reserve on the Grand River. While the natives performed well at Queenston Heights under Norton's leadership, their larger contribution was in scaring the hell out of those two-thirds of the New York militia who refused to cross the river and join in the conflict. Who in their right mind would be happy to cross the river into the waiting arms of a horde of screaming natives?

That same October, Brock was still miffed about the fact that only sixty warriors from the Six Nations had assisted him at the fall of Detroit. It seems to me that he was so concerned about winning the war that he never really understood the natives' precarious position. And they were right to be wary, considering the way they were treated after the war. Of the five hundred natives who had initially showed themselves willing to fight, the number had been reduced to about three hundred screaming warriors by the morning of October 13.

It is important to note that not all natives on American territory shared Tecumseh's vision or agreed to fight with the British. Fewer than two thousand sided with the Americans, although I can find no evidence that they actually fought in 1812. They were interested mainly in survival and in protection of their lands. It is to Tecumseh's and Brock's credit that most of the natives in the Detroit area chose to fight with the British, and this aided greatly in the fall of Detroit.

While a good deal is written about Brock's old regiment, the 49th, comparatively not much is reported on the 41st, who earned more battle honours than any other British regiment during the war. They came to Canada in 1799, and although scheduled to rotate back to England, they were forced to stay as American threats escalated. Indeed, they represented 80 percent of the British regular forces defending Upper Canada at the war's outbreak.

Most of the American military mentioned are real characters, with the exception of King, Green, and Ambler, who are purely fictitious. Imagine the president of the United States today sending men into combat with only a few bullets each. It's unthinkable, yet that is exactly what Madison did to the Army of the Center. And then he allowed the inexperienced Stephen van Rensselaer to run the show. Even his cousin Solomon knew that Stephen shouldn't have been in charge. It's sad that the Republicans, who declared the war, needed a Federalist to fail along the Niagara and that this would cost so many young men their lives.

Or how about Peter Porter selling supplies from Porter, Barton and Company to himself as quartermaster for New York? Do you think he might not have had a conflict of interest in being a congressional proponent of the war? It is little wonder the Van Rensselaers squabbled with the man. I think this led to not using Porter's extra boats on the morning of the attack. And the lack of boats delayed the militia crossing, which gave the howling natives time to frighten them into inaction. It should be noted that even with all the delays and poor organization, seven hundred New York State militia did manage to cross into the maelstrom of fire.

Stephen claimed he attacked at Queenston because he needed

winter quarters for his troops. But why launch the attack at a cliff face? Sure, there were fewer British troops there, but it was madness from the outset to attack an area that was near impossible to secure. Drive along the American side of the Niagara River, above or below Niagara Falls, and examine the Canadian shore. It rapidly becomes clear that if there is one place you would not mount an attack it is at Queenston Heights. And remember, your invasion plan includes no way of ascending the cliff because at the time the fisherman's path was not yet known.

To John Wool's everlasting credit, he led the U.S. Army of the Center off that shore, scaled the heights, and won the first half of the battle. American colours once flew on Queenston Heights! He cannot be blamed for a lack of a follow-up plan after winning his battle. Today, you can climb those heights yourself and feel the strain involved. Try doing it carrying the weight of a musket as if your life depended on it. You will start to understand how those Americans invaders felt during the cold morning hours of October 13, 1812.

As much as the Americans bungled the invasion of Canada, the British government did almost everything they could to help them win the day. Put yourself in Brock's position. By late August, he has the momentum gained by victories at Mackinac Island and Detroit, but Prevost undermined him by signing a truce *that included the waterways*. It was as if Prevost gave the Americans a gift of transporting cannons from Oswego. I would love to have been in the room when Brock met Sheaffe for the first time after the latter negotiated the truce. My guess is that Brock would have to be restrained from strangling the man.

Of course, Westlake, Parrish, Nelles, the conductors, and the three women are all fictional characters, as well as the slaves, the catchers, and their masters. All others on the British side are historical except for individual members of the 41st, Simpson, Mad Dog, and Trash. While the Van Rensselaers contended with Porter and the politicians in Washington, Brock argued with Prevost and the politicians in

London. Certainly a theme for both sides in the early days of the war was the lack of cooperation between the commanders on the ground and their political masters.

Frustration for Brock must have been the order of the day, knowing that the enemy just across the river had little ammunition and a rapidly deteriorating morale. With brilliant victories behind him, he surely believed rolling up the Niagara River against a poorly armed opposition was a mere matter of marching — as Jefferson once said about the conquering of Canada. And if conquering Niagara was easy, then why not a follow-up knockout blow by attacking Dearborn at Albany.

Alas, Prevost vigorously followed his orders from London: do nothing that might antagonize the people that had declared war. He thus instructed Brock, and that gave the Americans time to organize for a war they were initially unprepared to prosecute. The problem for Brock and Upper Canada was that, to survive as an independent entity, the invasion had to be stopped almost before it got started.

Meanwhile, the main interest of Great Britain was to defeat Napoleon, and for that Wellington needed tons of grain and beef from New England over the course of the war. No wonder New Englanders wanted no in part of the conflict. No wonder London wanted peace maintained with the United States.

The War of 1812 has been described in many ways. To the British whose generals ran the war in Upper and Lower Canada, the war was simply a sideshow to the war against Napoleon, and little more than a distraction. To the Americans, depending on which American one talks to, it was a continuation of their war for independence. On the other hand, for the native population, the war was about gaining a buffer state and trying to keep the peace with side that might win — an impossible task when seen in hindsight.

For those in the Canadas and the Maritime provinces, the war took on different meanings depending upon when its significance was assessed. In the beginning, the fur trade mattered a great deal. The voyageurs and Metis played their part in the early victories, securing their livelihoods for at least a few more years until European styles of fashion changed.

However, the war quickly came to be seen as a fight for a different kind of society, one based upon a British form of government versus a republican one. In my view, the War of 1812 was Canada's war of independence. Pierre Berton sums up the difference between the two countries as peace, order, and good government versus life, liberty, and the pursuit of happiness.

In writing *Brock's Railroad*, I relied on numerous sources for historical research, including Brock's personal letters. However, I would urge everyone to read *A Very Brilliant Affair* by Robert Malcomson, who captures the battle of Queenston Heights with a sense of fear and excitement not found in many works on the war. A more recent study on Brock himself can be found in Lieutenant-General Jonathon Riley's book, *A Matter of Honour*. I highly recommend it.

I need to provide one final note — on Brock's horse, Alfred. He was given to Brock by departing Governor-in-Chief Sir James Craig. Although there is a monument to Alfred at the bottom of the heights, no historical documentation exists that confirms Alfred made it to Upper Canada. However, why would Brock leave such a prize animal in Lower Canada? It seems more likely that he would have the horse with him, so it could be put to some use. Although historians will scoff at the idea, I followed Pierre Berton's book *The Invasion of Canada* and have Alfred present at the battle for Queenston Heights.

Westlake is on his way home for a much needed rest. However, our friends the Americans are intent on capturing York, now called Toronto, so I suppose Westlake will have to fight again.